Pinner dragged me outside for a smoke.

We stood by a barrel someone filled with kindling and set ablaze. He dragged a long inhale and then blew it out with passion. "You need to cool off."

"Shock's an asshole."

"I *said*, you need to cool off."

Damn it. "I know."

"Didn't know red hair was your kryptonite. Always pegged you for an equal opportunity kind of guy."

"Listen to you talk. Mr. Brunette to blonde."

"That's enough." Pinner's scowl deepened. He had one of those unfortunate faces that was ugly most of the time. But when he frowned, he was downright hideous.

"Well, I think you know that you should know better," I started.

"As should you." The warning note in his voice was unmistakable.

"My kryptonite is whores," I stated proudly.

"No, it ain't."

I crushed my cigarette under my boot and squinted at him. "Of course it is. My mother was a whore. Anyone who mistreats 'em gets on my bad side."

"Is that what this is? You sure?"

"Yeah. That's all this is." It should be, right?

"You're lying. Maybe even lying to yourself. You met your type. And it's 'damsel in distress.' "

He was so wrong. "Oh, now *that's* bullshit." My sainted, unsaintly mother was no damsel in distress. She was a proud whore who managed to make a promising career out of prostitution. Even her brief interlude of motherhood hadn't affected her life plan of making a bundle of scratch by taking dick and then retiring early. I'd learned a lot from her wisdom. Foremost was that women were prettiest when happy. Even prettier when they glowed with pride.

Fragile women never turned my crank as much as strong ones did. I enjoyed seeing that gleam of spirit shining from them nearly as much as I loved watching them cum.

"Bullshit or not, son, that woman is trouble."

"No shit." One of the biggest rules of the club was, "Do not covet your brother's shit."

Misfit Ink
5257 Buckystown Pike, #215
Frederick, MD 21704
MisfitInkBooks.com

Ordering Information:
For details, contact theAuthor@CaliaWilde.com.

Disclaimer:
This book is a work of fiction. Any references to historical events, real people, or real locales are used fictitiously. Other names, characters, places, and incidents are the product of the author's imagination, and any resemblance to actual events or locales or persons, living or dead, is entirely coincidental.

The following is an indication and acknowledgement of potential content that may be upsetting or triggering, but is clearly not exhaustive:

Vulgar language, abuse (physical, sexual, emotional, verbal), rape, sexual assault, excessive or gratuitous violence, kidnapping (forceful deprivation of/ disregard for personal autonomy), death or dying, and blood.

Blue-Eyed Jacks is a work of fiction that does contain emotionally disturbing content. While there is ultimately a happy ever after for the main characters, they and other characters are depicted as living through painful experiences. Please be aware of your own tolerance for the triggering content mentioned as well as use your best judgement about reading when your own emotional reserves are low. Sometimes it is the little things that can tip the balance into dark spaces.

Table of Contents

BLUE-EYED JACKS

A Skilletsville Destroyers MC Romance Novel

by

Calia Wilde

Misfit Ink Books

Maryland, USA

CHAPTER 1

A Bar Outside Sturgis, South Dakota, August 14, 2022—Jackson

What would happen when the conqueror became a king? Would he grow fat and lazy, relying on old methods to maintain his position, or would he dare risk failing by using a fresh approach to consolidate power? It was easy to see where my 'boss,' Nonno, fit on that spectrum.

The National President of the Destroyers MC sat on a specially carved wooden chair. It rested on a dais of hastily cobbled plywood spray-painted black with automotive primer that was so fresh it seeped into the porous surface. The grain of the cover veneer got more visible with each second.

Around him, the tableau was farcical. An easy spectacle, rampant with strippers, hookers, booze, loud music, and bikers like me paying homage to their new leader.

I was present as a witness and an accomplice. As the lord-baron of my very own fiefdom, I participated in the spectacle with my center of power strategically placed off to one side with my crew. Including me, our group totaled six. I should've brought more. Pittsburgh's president brought twelve, for fuck's sake. Then again, he always had a thing for numbers between ten and twenty.

"Jackson, have you seen the—" Sprout's words were cut short by the approach of Hanger—which was the shortened version of "Hang Her High"—the road name of Chicago's Sergeant at Arms. He had biceps four times bigger than my VP's. Despite the bulk, Hanger could reach almost as far as Sprout, my club's secretary, an officer position more honorary than effectible.

"Hang," I acknowledged him.

"Boss wants to see you."

Fuck. When he said *Boss*, he didn't just mean his boss. Boss was, in relative terms, *the* boss. Where Chicago leaned, we all fell over ourselves to tilt further down the path. Nonno may be king in name, but Hang's boss was *the* boss.

"What the *fuck* did we do now?" Sprout's mouth was going to get us in trouble. Well, more trouble, one of these days.

But hell, trouble was my middle name. I tested the murky deep. "I'm right here. Does he need glasses?" I motioned to the table. If that motherfucker wanted to pull rank on me, he'd have to force my hand. With Nonno now firmly entrenched as the national president, Big G and I were on the same tier, mostly.

"Get your ass up. Bring two guys, not him." Hanger indicated Sprout and walked away. I resisted the urge to flip him off.

An urge Sprout had no problem with. "Fucker." He twisted up a double bird and let it rest for a few seconds before wisely hiding them under the table again.

I turned to my VP with a question, not a request. "Wolf?" As in, "what is your take on this, Wolf?"

"Divide and conquer?" he suggested as Big G's strategy.

"Not on my watch."

Wolf swore quietly under his breath, then muttered, "Tits is better at this shit than I am."

His wife, goddammit, admittedly was light years better at this political crap than either of us. But I'd look like some sort of pansy installing her in an all-male club's officer role. "She's good at flashing those double-D's." I wasn't trying to piss him off. It just came out of my piehole that way.

His jaw dipped sideways, proving he was either trying to swallow my sarcasm, or trying not to laugh. It could go either way.

"Bear, Skinner." I picked my two, leaving Wolf with Grizzle and Sprout. Griz was a right bastard, and Sprout was fast. Blended with Wolf's tactical sense, he was well protected. Bear was enough muscle to fuck with Hang. And Skinner? Well. If Big G wanted to talk about money, he was the right guy for it.

It also made me look "weak" taking a scrawny man like Skinner as one of my bodyguards. And that was the point. I was subtly insulting Big G by not bringing Griz. Moreover, it could be read as I trusted Big G not to fuck with me, therefore brought the B-Team, which wasn't insulting at all.

Power was a funny thing. It was as alluring as beachfront property with warm breezes all year long. But it came equipped with land mines and was subject to flooding at any time. Therefore, as pretty as it was, I'd kept to the shadows as much as I could afford.

Big G sat near the center of the room and nearest to the catwalk where Nonno paraded his best strippers. Hookers jumped out of their seats and into laps to make room for me and mine.

"G." I reached out for a slap of the hand. When he didn't lift a finger, I diverted the action to a smack on the shoulder, proving I could touch him whenever I wanted. No one was immune. I settled into the chair a pretty little thing had just hopped off of. She had an ass like a peach. Sue me, it distracted me for a moment.

"I see you still have an eye for the ladies."

"Plural." I gave up trying to twist my head like an owl and faced Giovanni Accardo. Big G. One of three men in Chicago who had more say on world affairs than most foreign leaders. "Been a bit. What was it, bumfuck West Virginia?" He'd popped down to help our sister club and scope out expansion properties. That was working out well.

"We had those redneck cops shaking in their boots." G smiled at the memory.

"Fucking great moonshine. I'll send you some."

"Walt already did."

Fuck. I plastered a smile on. He called him Walt, not his road name—Disney. If he was that tight with the chapter on my southern border, I was screwed. "Then I'll get you some primo weed. Sprout's holding."

"What did you do to piss Nonno off?"

He wasn't one for extended small talk. Luckily, I had a quick and honest answer. "I let Wolf marry his niece."

G's head snapped sharply left to the table where Wolf sat. "Niece? That chick with the—" He held his hands out in front of his massive chest and got the size about right.

"Yup."

"Huh. Poor guy. You don't buy the cow just cuz it's got big udders." He leaned in and lowered his voice. "It isn't just that, though, is it?"

Damn it. I couldn't lie to him. Such a thing would bite me in the ass. I'd been protesting a rate hike in our monthly dues. "Skilletsville isn't exactly a hotbed for intrigue these days. I pay my shit on time, fully. Nonno's got nothing to bitch about." And that was the truth. Just because we were pulling in more scratch legally than illegally shouldn't be an issue. The bigger issue was the vacuum between Nonno and our club, which had no buffer. We needed a Regional President to bitch at, instead of going directly to the fucking top. That was bound to get old soon.

G's smile cracked just a hair wider. "He's upping your payments, isn't he?"

I nodded. Inflation sucked balls.

"Can you afford them?"

I glared at him. "Affording isn't the question. It's a matter of *fairness*. We pay what everyone *else* pays, not more. You'd do the same."

He leaned back in the chair, pondering the situation. Hopefully, he was trying to see it from my point of view. Just because my membership had three millionaires on paper, and one skyrocketing multi-millionaire, it didn't mean the chapter had to eat Nonno's shit. G wasn't a poor man. He had almost as much, maybe even more than Sprout. All of it skimmed from wallowing in the cesspools of Chicago's crime money. The trouble was that Sprout's money was all legit. Filed on tax forms, making headlines, and every son of a bitch from here to Timbukfuckingtu wanted a piece of it, especially the new national president for the Destroyers MC.

"How many did you bring on this trip?"

He was asking about my men, members, and liabilities. "Half," I begrudgingly replied. Besides Wolf, Sprout, Griz, Skinner, and Bear; Baldy and Sketch rode with our enclave. We had three RVs, two of them pimped to the fucking nines, and three old ladies with us. The rest of the crew—Trout, Poke, Cutty, Coop, Rocket, Big Joe, and Hickey were back in Pennsylvania making money to replace the scratch flowing out on this stupid trip. But it was one we had to make. If I wanted any shot at being a regional president, attendance was mandatory. Failure to appear would be seen as treason. I'd lose not only my chance but possibly my life.

Big G finished musing. "That was a mistake."

No shit. "Got businesses to run." Too fucking many, but that wasn't my fault.

G set his hand on the table slowly, warning me he was controlling his temper, but only barely. "You'll pay the extra this month for that."

"And next month?"

G shrugged. It was too early to breathe a sigh of relief. Next month would be a whole new set of shit. Movement to my left had Bear shifting his bulk to shield me from whoever was approaching.

G's man stepped forward, too. Interesting. We were all brothers here, but like any fucked up family, we hated each other more than anything else. In my small window of blindness, I searched G's face for clues about who it could be.

His eyes squinted in displeasure, and his usual scowl deepened. He saved me from having to look by saying, "Did you bring me a present, Shock?"

Ah. The biggest asshole in the room. Considering I was present, that parsed things closely. I shifted in my chair to see what had caught G's interest.

She was a little thing. If I had to guess, given the location, company, and Shock's proclivities, she was barely seventeen. Sweet little C-cups and freckles she tried to hide with goop. But the heat and closed barroom melted that shit, and those little brown specks stood out against her pallor. Besides liking them young and freckled, Shock liked 'em scared. She fit the bill nicely.

"Meet my wife." He shoved the girl forward.

Lying asshole. "Which one is that? Number twelve? Or are you still searching for a *twelve-year-old*?" I should've kept quiet until I was on my feet.

Bear went down, and the girl went somewhere screaming and scrambling under his feet.

Shock barreled through the pile and knocked me, my chair, and the table in front of G to a broken mess on the floor.

Beer, whiskey, and blood flowed. Shock landed on top of me. His fist broke through my block and clipped my jaw.

That was just fine with me. I pummeled his head with jabs and elbows. I locked his brace leg with mine and kicked his balance point loose. The bulk of him squashed me, but I was already moving, pulling, shifting, and twisting. Once I was on top where I belonged, I locked him in place with an arm bar and wrenched it hard.

With the momentum of the move, I slipped a hand free and locked it around his head. My whole body worked to pin him in a choking headlock, and if I was lucky enough, one twist and all my troubles would be over.

Except for a murder-one charge. But that never stopped me from trying to make it happen—especially with Shock.

"Enough!"

Nonno's enforcer, G's enforcer, hell, my *own* enforcer jumped on the pile trying to peel me off that fat fuck. It took them and Shock's man to tear me off—which meant Shock was free to fire a cheap-shot fist into my gut.

I wheezed out air I couldn't afford to lose. My stomach spasmed as nature tried to fix the lack of it in all the wrong ways. Stars broke out at the corners of my eyes and my knees felt like Jello. But I'd be damned if this was the end. I locked my right leg and sucked in air and blood between my teeth with a hiss. "Cheating fucker!"

Fresh energy surged through me. I broke Bear's hold and was only tethered by Hang.

Nonno's man stood between us, but I couldn't see him…only the rage I'd held onto for sixteen years and Shock's ugly face. "I'm gonna *kill* you." That was a vow. And it wasn't the first time I'd thought about it. But it was possibly the first time I'd ever said it out loud.

"You'd like to try. Where's my wife?"

"Which fucking one?" I spat back. Even amped on adrenaline, and still trapped in a tunnel of red hate, I managed to guard my mouth, or at least not think about the words.

"You know goddamned well which one. The *legitimate* one. Kate. Where the fuck did you hide her?"

The girl at my feet gasped. I was certain her name wasn't Kate.

She squeaked out a plaintive, "You're already married?"

Oh my God. What a fucking soap opera. "Yeah, sweet tits, he's got a real wife." Shit. I almost outed myself. I hastily tacked on, "Or *had*, but her body ain't shown up yet."

"You lying motherfucker. She better not be dead!" Shock roared and broke through the line of men between us, trampling on his little piece of ass in the process.

But I was ready for him this time. Using a dirty trick my father taught me, I twisted to the side and used his own momentum to smash his face into the stage behind me.

"Enough." Nonno waded into the melee, brandishing a shiny new baseball bat. I stuck both hands up in the air.

"That dick jumped me twice, and I'm the one standing!" I *owned* my victory, with witnesses and fucking everything.

Shock tried to get up but got tangled in his woman. He hauled his hand back to clobber her, and Bear caught my eye with a sharp shake of the head. The blow landed, and I felt every ounce of that pain. My men knew why, and both Bear and Skinner flanked me just in case I'd get stupid and try to save the bitch. But I'd learned that lesson *years* ago.

"He stole my wife." Shock repeated to anyone who'd listen.

The girl blubbered in the background, and I couldn't tune her out. The sobs grew louder in my mind. She was so young and... *dumb* to let someone like Shock break her that way. Foolish to take up with a biker off his leash like so many were during this event. And too much like my own damn mother for me to forget that from whore to lady, you don't win by treating them poorly.

I should've kept my mouth shut. *I really should've.*

"No one *stole* your wife. She fled your dumb ass because you treated her like shit."

Shock got his feet under him and pointed, singling me out from the crowd. "And how would *you* know that?" To everyone else, he pled his case. "He knows that because he helped her leave. He betrayed the brotherhood!"

No, just you, *asshole.*

CHAPTER 2

A Destroyers MC Clubhouse, Skilletsville, Pennsylvania, June 18, 2005—Kate

Today was the day I'd been waiting for since my father sold me to pay off his cocaine habit. Melodramatic? Yes. Illegal? Absolutely. It was so far-fetched, no one believed me. Except for the ones who'd orchestrated it, which meant they enforced their secrets hard. I was only seventeen and branded as a slut for "marrying" the president of the local one-percenter motorcycle club. Even months later, the whispers would start wherever I'd go in Pittsburgh.

"I hear she rode a train. Every member of that club has had a piece of her."

"How could she sink so low? She came from money, you know?"

"He's twice her age."

"Her father is a lawyer; you'd think she'd be smarter than that."

"I bet she's one of those girls who likes getting abused."

But I wasn't in Pittsburgh anymore. We were halfway across the state of Pennsylvania, where no one knew me, no one would whisper about me, and where, if I was lucky, I might find someone brave enough to stand up against Keith "Shock" Weaver, my *legal* husband who I hated down to the screaming depths of my soul.

Daddy saw to the paperwork himself. He signed my life away, then snorted a line of coke off the marriage certificate. My "husband" joined him. Then consummated the marriage in my bedroom under my music-themed decor and a plethora of boy band posters. Their smiling faces laughed at me and my pain. When Shock's men packed up my room, they tore those faces down and rolled them into tubes of a reality I'd never know again.

I burned all of them. *Bye. Bye. Bye.*

The van lurched through a gated wall. *No one said there'd be gates.* My heart rate picked up.

The prospect assigned to the van to watch me noticed me taking note of the surroundings. "Skilletsville is so cheap they stuck their club in a junkyard. But don't worry, the building has two floors, and the top floor is *all* bedrooms."

A lump of bile crawled up my throat. My insides churned with panic. I wasn't going to get away tonight; I'd arrived at a deeper level of Hell.

"Girls through the back, Toro wants them checked first." Shock's VP, BamBam, pulled women from the other van and shoved them toward the end of the building. There was a small access door propped open. A dumpster sat behind it, overflowing and squalid. It matched the tableau of stacked rusty cars and dirt. The piles were so high in spots I couldn't see the pine trees surrounding the compound.

The prospect dragged me out of the van. "Come on, Kate. Shock'll get mad at me if you're not ready."

I'd never be ready, not for any of this.

"Whoa. Where ya going?" BamBam grabbed my arm and snapped his fingers at the prospect. "Get your ass in the front, Shock's got errands for ya."

His grip was much tighter than the prospect's had been.

"You, kitchen is to the right as you walk in. Don't go upstairs."

Oh, thank God. I followed his directions and hovered in the entrance to a modest industrial kitchen to note if the back door would remain open. But BamBam slammed it shut with a bang. And the distinct rattle of chains being looped through the handle crushed my hopes.

"What are you doing standing there? Get upstairs with the others." A blonde woman, dressed in scanty red satin and black fishnet stood at the bottom of the stairs. In her right hand was a joint, held like a cigarette. Her elbow propped against her hip, artfully angled to resemble an old movie harlot.

Her skin was almost as pale as her hair. It contrasted with her bright red lips that matched her outfit. She had smoky kohl eyeliner, smudged grunge style. Despite the obvious wear, was Playboy model pretty.

"I was told the kitchen."

Please don't make me go upstairs.

A barely five-foot-tall woman pushed me aside as she barreled out of the kitchen. "Jewel, get your ass upstairs and stop harassing the guests."

"She ain't no guest." Jewel, the blonde, eyed my clothes with contempt. Every item of my clothing except for the "property of" vest on my back was borrowed from someone in the club's arsenal of hookers. I tried my damnedest not to think about where the hand-me-down thong used to reside because it was either that or go commando. Never go commando around bikers. It's like waving raw meat in front of a grizzly.

That was why I'd layered on a pair of booty shorts over the thong and under the black leather micro mini school girl skirt.

On top, I'd layered more clothing over a red lace Demi-bra. A muted gray Henley no one claimed, a ripped lace body suit, and a slouchy tank top with the slogan "Lifestyles of the Tattooed and Famous" written on it in glittery gold script. It clashed with the muted vibe I desired, and if pressed, I'd ditch it or turn it inside out once I got free. Ditching it was secondary. If I was going to wander the streets of Skilletsville after dark, summer or not, I'd need warmth. Only the vest would go. And with it, every tainted memory of the Destroyers Motorcycle Club.

I was *not* property.

But first, I also needed to get free of this place. I made myself as small as possible against the wall.

"Are you an old lady?" A little girl, maybe seven or eight, pulled on my left hand and played with the ring there.

To a normal seventeen-year-old, that question would sound ridiculous. But three painful months changed my entire vocabulary. I knew she meant "significant other" or "wife" by that question. *Technically*, that included me, as much as I didn't want to admit it. I glanced at the girl's mother, who regarded the girl's question with interest. "I'm Shock's." That killed me to admit. I wasn't his. I belonged to myself. Or would as soon as I could get free.

The mother's face changed from guarded to defiant. "Hear *that*, Jewel? She's the Pittsburg's President's ol' lady!" My defender, all five feet of her, looked like an older clone of the little girl still holding my hand. Both had curly black hair, deeply tanned skin, and gorgeously wide, dark-brown eyes with thick eyelashes. The mother, I guessed, also hated Jewel. It proved true in the scowl she sent the woman and the sharpness of her voice.

"Whatever, I'll fuck *him* first. I hope you don't mind." Jewel singsonged that last sentence and then retreated upstairs.

"Bitch," the mom muttered.

"Bitch," the little girl mimicked.

"Poppy, don't. We don't swear."

"But you just did."

Poppy's mother noticed me against the wall and used an introduction as an excuse not to answer. "I'm Hilea Hikialani-Albert, Pinner's wife. You should call me Lea or Lady High, I guess. This is my girl Poppy. Kitchen?" Her outstretched arm invited me inside.

"Are you messing with Jewel again?" A middle-aged woman with brown hair, hazel eyes, sun-tanned skin, and a streak of gray emanating from one temple noticed me next to Lea. "Hey, 'name's Regina, but everybody calls me 'Ma' or just Gina." She held out a sudsy hand. I took it and marveled at the sensation. It had been four months since anyone dared to greet me before they greeted my jailor/husband or his crew, and even longer since any woman looked at me with anything other than pity or scorn. I swallowed and finished the handshake before I made an impression.

"Kate." I refused to go by any last name, or any nickname given to me by the asshole men or women who enabled them.

"Nice to meet you. Lemme see that ring."

Ma, or Gina, snapped her fingers. Whoever she was, she seemed to run this room. I opted for compliance rather than fighting because she'd been equitable to me so far.

"Looks fake."

"It probably is," I answered. Shock Weaver wouldn't give me anything of value. Not even clothes. So, I had to assume this was a highly gaudy piece of horseshit. I'd know as soon as I found a pawnshop.

"Cheap bastard," she muttered under her breath. Then she plastered a smile on her face. "You didn't hear that."

"He is."

"Why are you with him?" Lea asked.

I debated how to respond.

Gina dipped her head at Poppy, reminding me there were small ears in the room. I tried to smile but couldn't. "Let's just say I didn't have a say in it."

"That's cow poop." Out of the mouths of babes…

"Poppy!"

"I didn't swear, Mama. You say poop, and that other word I'm not supposed to say. And Daddy says—"

"No, no-no-no-no no… you do *not* repeat your daddy's words."

While they hashed out semantics, Gina studied me. "You on the pill?"

I shook my head. "I have an implant, and it's good for another year and a half."

Gina nodded. "I'm a nurse; let me know if you need anything else on the down low. Within reason, that is." She glanced at the door opposite the back hall. Constant noise came from that direction, but it had increased significantly.

A young biker popped his head in. "Ma? Have you seen—" he saw me and pointed. "Shock wants to introduce you to the club."

Oh, God. My hands trembled. I barely survived the first "meet the club" experience. I glanced at the back hall and the bolted door.

"Ma?" The boy-man asked.

"Give her a minute; she's in the bathroom."

"She ain't," he pointed out.

Regina stepped between us. "She is. I'll send her out in *one* minute. You have my word on that, now go pass that along, and while you're out there, check on my son, will ya? Make sure he knows I *told* you to check on him. That should keep him out of trouble for another ten minutes."

"Okay, Ma, but one minute only." He shut the door behind him and the noise reduced.

"I'm going to ask once; give me a straight answer. Did that bastard husband of yours hurt you?"

I nodded.

"How bad?"

Tears blurred my vision. There were many ways I could answer, but the worst event stood out. I'd never stuttered in my life, but the word didn't want to come out cleanly. "T-t-train."

"Oh shit. We don't do that here. Chin up." She wiped my eyes and swept my unruly hair away from my face. "You blotch when you cry. I bet you bruise easy, too, don't 'cha?"

I pulled the long sleeve on my right arm up. The black-blue-and-yellow marks where Shock deliberately hurt me hadn't faded, and the injury was over a week old. "Ten days ago he tried to break my arm."

Her jaw went to the side as she tried to contain her anger. She tugged down the sleeve and held my chin. "I can't guarantee anything, but I'll try. Lea, swear Poppy to secrecy. Not even her dad gets this. Poppy?"

The girl nodded. Her eyes were a little too wise for her years.

"Now. Don't make a liar out of me. Go out there, play by the rules, and I'll see what I can do from here."

There was nothing she could do. The hierarchy was simple. Men made the rules, enforced the rules, and dealt out punishment if you forgot or fought back. I smoothed my expression and braced for the worst as I exited through the door to the main room.

The building was one of those metal barns, but the inside had been altered to suit the club's needs. It had a second level, side rooms or offices, and a large bar at one end of the open section. Metal poles held up the roof framing, and mis-matched furniture littered the space, creating little groupings of use. There was a pool "room" with a dart "room" mirroring it, and between them, round wire spools laid flat to be used as tables for beer drinking. Couches ran along the side where the hookers already paired off with men.

I walked through the crowd to the middle where Shock sat in one of the few overstuffed recliners. Next to him sat a grizzled man with the name "Toro" embroidered above a president patch on his vest. They were deep in discussion. A small barrel sat between the chairs. On it was a bottle of Jack

Daniels and two shot glasses, along with a plastic cup of beer. Shock had a matching cup in his hand. I halted just outside of arm's reach and waited.

As I did, I noticed Toro's bodyguard. All clubs had one officer with the sole job of protecting the president. They gave that person the rank of Sergeant at Arms. Skilletsville's answer to BamBam wasn't ugly. In fact, he was one of the better-looking men in the room. I dipped my eyes so no one would catch me looking. His name patch read, "Jackson." I wondered how he got such a normal-sounding nickname.

Shock interrupted my thoughts. "About fucking time you showed up. Toro, this is my wife. Ain't she the palest bitch you've ever seen? Babe, lift your shirt and show him your pink tits."

I couldn't. The lace body suit would have to be unsnapped, and I'd be damned if I did that here. Instead, I tugged as much fabric away from my shoulder to show exactly zero of my boob and only a bit of my shoulder. It was enough to also display the hickeys that asshole marked me up with this morning.

"I said tits, *bitch*."

"Shock, are you hearing of any action on your west side? The Legion are giving our boys south of here some shit."

"Fuck those bastards."

I wasn't trying to listen, but wondered if he meant the Destroyers' allies or enemies. With Shock, it went both ways.

Toro leaned in to talk shop. I stood, shaking with fear, and trying to keep as silent and as still as possible so Shock would forget I existed.

No such luck. He motioned to his feet and pointed a finger at the floor. His not-so-subtle signal I needed to park my ass on top of one of his boots and fawn over him like a slave.

I sat but did no fawning. And I avoided touching him, opting for leaning against the chair instead.

He kicked me in the thigh, then planted his boot between my crisscrossed legs, dragging me closer and pinching me between the chair and the floor each time he leaned forward to make a point with Toro. I tried to edge my leg out from under the chair to avoid the worst of the pain.

The cold concrete floor was sticky and filthy. It smelled like stale beer, and the air held the distinctively pungent odor of weed. I had eaten little, was wearing too many clothes for the closeness of the party and the weight of Shock's warm leg against me, and a sickly sweat broke out over my skin. More than my extremities trembled as I fought the urge to puke. It would serve Shock right to vomit on his shoes.

Maybe then I'd have just one night of peace?

CHAPTER 3

Jackson

Shock's current flavor of the month looked like she was going to pass out. Her pale skin flushed an unhealthy pink. Her hands blotched white and deeper pink as she braced them in clenched fists against the floor, as if she was holding the world in place by sheer will alone. Her strawberry gold hair cascaded over her face with glinting rose-colored strands that twisted into tight spirals, but overall, it flew every direction.

I knew women of every shape, size, color, and creed. I hadn't seen her face, but could fill in the blanks. She'd have blue eyes, I was almost certain. Maybe, if she was one of the rare types of Irish-Celtic strains influenced by unique genetics, they'd be clear green. She had freckles, golden to brown. They dotted her skin in tiny little flecks of color. As a whole, she wouldn't hold a candle to someone like Pinner's Polynesian beauty queen, Hilea. But in her form, she was still perfection in a misty isle fairy-touched way.

And she was scared to death or in withdrawal. There was no mistaking the tremors rocking her entire body. She was going to puke. It was only a matter of time. In my active monitoring of the room, I noted that. All while I listened in on Shock and Toro's conversation, keeping another ear on the tenor of the room. I was new to my role of Sergeant at Arms, and responsible for the kicking of anyone's ass who threatened my president. I intended not to screw this up. Therefore, I was hyper-vigilant tonight.

Which was a natural fit for me. I'd learned early to fight dirty and hard, while keeping one eye open for the next threat. While I wasn't a monster in size, I made up for it in sheer will and attention to detail. I knew pain, knew how to wield it decisively and quickly. And I didn't let stupid shit distract me.

So why the fuck did it matter if some whacked-out chick puked on Shock's shoes?

It shouldn't.

Was I bored? This meet was club only. Tonight's potential threats were cat fights amongst the hookers and the usual drunken assholes who bumped chests. Even my counter part, BamBam, wasn't much of an opponent. He'd relinquished his .44 at the gate. Without it, he was a mass of beer fat with a short reach.

A wrecking ball, sure, but slow. I'd have him on the ground with his throat cut and bleeding out life in five seconds flat. He'd be dead in thirty. And by that point, I'd have stabbed him at least fifteen more times. He had no fucking clue how to defend Shock. Could I be tuned in to the wrong shit because there was no other threat?

But of course, there *were* other threats. There always were. Despite wearing the same patch, drinking the same booze, and fucking the same whores, my brothers were always a threat. Some of them were not worth the urine to piss on them with. Shock being the main one.

Despite pushing forty, he had definition. Big, sure. Most bikers packed on pounds as they got older. But he also was goddamned ruthless. I measured his potential for violence as he talked shop. In my determination, he had no soul. Nothing stopping him from drilling me between the eyes, brother or not. And unlike his SoA, he kept his gun. Only a fool would tangle with that combination of ugly mean and armed.

Again, why the fuck did this girl matter so damned much?

She didn't. In the grand machine of crime, she was cog grease. A statistic. Someone who shouldn't factor.

But Shock thought enough of her to make her one of his pet projects.

I caught Sprout's attention. He was Jolly's kid. The club let him hang around out of respect for his fallen father. Jolly had been a legend and one of the deciding factors when I chose this quiet little town west of Harrisburg as my home club. He'd left us too soon, leaving behind a wife and Sprout. Murdered by the fucking cops. Which made vengeance nearly impossible. To make up that lack, we all raised the kid. Wrong? Sure. But Sprout was useful. He was barely fourteen and already doing more than most prospects ever did—without one peep of complaint.

"Sup?" He grinned like an idiot. It made his ears stick out. I often wondered if that was on purpose.

I slipped him my phone. "Give this to your Ma."

He pocketed it. "And?'

"And nothing. Just tell her I gave it to you." His ma was a smart woman. She'd figure it out.

"Sure thing." He hovered.

"What the fuck you waiting for?"

He grinned. "I'll get you a beer first."

Goddamned kid. Too fucking helpful. He ran across the room, picking up two cups and filling each to the brim. He brought them back cautiously and handed one to the president first, then to me. "Here."

Then he took off toward the kitchen.

"What? None for me?" Shock laughed, but under his friendly tone was a hint of accusation.

I handed my beer off, moving close so I wouldn't spill it. The girl looked up at that moment.

Snared. Like a rabbit in a trap.

Her eyes were the gray-green of dense early morning fog hanging over a lake. Or the glistening pale scales of a juicy fresh-water bass. I forgot about the cup in my hand and when Shock grabbed it too hard, the foam sloshed over the edge, coating my fingers and breaking the spell. I smiled at him. "I'll get one for myself later."

His eyes narrowed and dipped down to the girl. A cruel grin twisted on his lips. "I'm sure you will. But this one's *mine*." He locked his stare on my face, daring me to argue, laying his verbal bait, and waiting to see if I was dumb enough to bite.

"Not a problem. We got plenty to go around." I raised my eyebrow, acknowledging his game and begging for a reaction.

He slammed the beer, belched, and then turned his anger toward the girl. *I'd fucked up.*

"Didn't I tell you to show your tits?"

Sweat dotted her forehead, and she was unusually pale.

I stepped back, snagged a trash can, and slid it closer, just in case. It bumped against her shoulder as she struggled to get to her knees. The smell of it must have triggered something because she spun, grabbed it with both hands, and practically donned it as a hat as she wretched into it.

"Fucking Christ!" Shock jumped to his feet. Toro leaned back, but his eyes moved to me. In them, I read the question. "How did you know?" I sent him a wink and waited until the spit and bile sputtered to a halt.

But Shock didn't give her any quarter. Almost as soon as she wiped her mouth on her sleeve, he was on top of her.

"Fucking bitch." His fist hit her head. "No fucking sense whatsoever." Another blow fell, this one to her back.

The trashcan spun from her grip, and I caught it before it could topple over. A prospect was nearby, so I slid it in his direction to take care of. I whistled to get the attention of another to bring a towel and began issuing orders. "Get Ma." I handed the towel to Shock, who wiped off his vest and pants before dropping it to the floor.

He hadn't even gotten sprayed.

I picked up the towel and passed it to his woman. Then, I stepped between them to run interference. "You okay, man?"

He glared up at me. "What the fuck you think? She puked on me!"

She hadn't.

I snapped my fingers and pointed at the closest whore. "Jewel, take him upstairs, make sure he's cleaned off and comfortable."

She grinned too widely. "Sure thing, sugar." She oooed and awed over Shock's predicament. As she led him to the main stairs, I caught Pinner's glare. I shook my head at him. He'd been stepping out on his wife with Jewel for a while. But since he was still married, and Jewel was one of our stable, he had no claim. And he knew it.

That cost me precious seconds.

Toro stood up and directed the party's attention away from the girl on the floor. BamBam wasn't as easily fooled, though. He stood over the girl, staring at me like I'd orchestrated the whole thing.

He was giving me too much credit. "What the fuck are you staring at?"

His fists clenched.

As much as I'd love to lay him out, there wasn't time to waste. The longer things lingered in this limbo of fucking bullshit, the harder it would engrave into memories. "Don't you have a president to protect?"

He frowned. The debate about staying or going upstairs was evident in his hesitation.

"Cookie, show him where Jewel's room is. If the door's closed, make him comfortable outside." Cookie was a sweet little brunette with a penchant for sucking dick. BamBam would be happy while he waited. Meanwhile, I had a lot to do in a very short amount of time if I was going to keep the two clubs at peace with each other, but also figure out what the fuck was wrong with Shock's chick.

Ma helped the girl up. I quickly laid out the problem. "She got sick. Figure out why and fast."

"Should I call Toolbox?" He was her doctor "friend" she'd introduced to the club. We all had to pretend they were just friends for Sprout's sake, since he had no idea his mom was finally getting some after years of mourning.

"Do it. Make sure he knows it's urgent."

She hesitated. "You're playing with fire. Stop."

Pinner had the ill timing to slap me on the back to announce his presence. "Get her in the back. Tell my wife to keep Poppy away in case she's contagious."

"She seemed fine earlier," Ma noted.

"I'm fine," the girl mumbled, which was a damn lie. She was still pale and shaking. Her cheek was red and swollen where Shock clipped her. A trickle of blood trailed along her hairline. I ached to touch her, inspect the damage, and…

Pinner squeezed my shoulder. "Son, let's not make fools of ourselves."

I huffed out a laugh. "You're one to talk." I slid him a side eye that wandered pointedly to the ceiling.

"That makes me eminently qualified to dish out wisdom. Let's get a drink."

I could do that. I could play along with the lie that none of this mattered, that we were all just good friends here and not assholes of the first order. Smile and laugh despite wanting to spill blood and entrails over the dirty concrete floor.

We slammed two shots. Between them, I bullshitted and joked. Same as always.

When it came to shot number three, my joking mood turned snakily bitter. It didn't go unnoticed.

Pinner dragged me outside for a smoke.

We stood by a barrel someone filled with kindling and set ablaze. He dragged a long inhale and then blew it out with passion. "You need to cool off."

"Shock's an asshole."

"I *said*, you need to cool off."

Damn it. "I know."

"Didn't know red hair was your kryptonite. Always pegged you for an equal opportunity kind of guy."

"Listen to you talk. Mr. Brunette to blonde."

"That's enough." Pinner's scowl deepened. He had one of those unfortunate faces that was ugly most of the time. But when he frowned, he was downright hideous.

"Well, I think you know that you should know better," I started.

"As should you." The warning note in his voice was unmistakable.

"My kryptonite is whores," I stated proudly.

"No, it ain't."

I crushed my cigarette under my boot and squinted at him. "Of course it is. My mother was a whore. Anyone who mistreats 'em gets on my bad side."

"Is that what this is? You sure?"

"Yeah. That's all this is." It should be, right?

"You're lying. Maybe even lying to yourself. You met your type. And it's 'damsel in distress.'"

He was so wrong. "Oh, now *that's* bullshit." My sainted, unsaintly mother was no damsel in distress. She was a proud whore who managed to make a promising career out of prostitution. Even her brief interlude of motherhood hadn't affected her life plan of making a bundle of scratch by taking dick and then retiring early. I'd learned a lot from her wisdom. Foremost was that women were prettiest when happy. Even prettier when they glowed with pride.

Fragile women never turned my crank as much as strong ones did. I enjoyed seeing that gleam of spirit shining from them nearly as much as I loved watching them cum.

"Bullshit or not, son, that woman is trouble."

"No shit." One of the biggest rules of the club was, "Do not covet your brother's shit."

"Why did you slip Sprout your phone?"

He'd noticed that? I supposed someone would. I'd been in the center of the room. All eyes were on the two presidents, or should have been if you gave a rat's ass about power.

"He wanted to call his girlfriend," I lied.

Pinner sighed. "That is a rotten lie. That boy has access to no fewer than six hookers who'd gladly pop his cherry. He doesn't need a girlfriend, let alone have one. Stop blowing smoke up my ass. Why?"

I scanned the party dregs that landed outside the club's main building. I even searched the shadows between the rows of cars piled up around us. "To give to Ma."

His grunt was something between acknowledgment and disagreement.

Toro joined us. "Are you hijacking my Sergeant, Pinner?"

Pinner laughed. "Naw, just catching air. I'm going to go in and see if my lady needs me to take her and Poppy home. That okay with you, boss?"

"You might want to stay home with them, and a word of advice, *don't* offer anyone else a ride, got it?"

Pinner's eyes shifted to mine. "Understood."

Toro waited until Pinner shambled to the back door by the kitchen. He unwound the chain some numbnuts wrapped around it.

"We gotta go inside."

"Yup." I didn't move.

"You are an ambitious man. I saw that in you the day you arrived on our doorstep with your dad's blessing. One of these days, you're going to replace me. So, I'm giving you advice. Don't get derailed now. Not over some gash."

His word choice needed work. That single moment of fog-green fantasy was enough to tell me a sordid tale. She wasn't a junkie, whoever she was. Those eyes were clear, not feverish or hazed out in a funk of drugged stupor. And she certainly wasn't gash. Every molecule of my body screamed that this woman was defiant to the core, but Shock was breaking her.

And when he succeeded, the world would lose an angel.

But unlike most men, I knew angels weren't the sweet passive things that strummed harps and made sickly music to lull men into bondage.

Angels were demons with a righteous call to avenge the wrongs of evil. And they were damn sexy doing it.

Pinner was right in his own twisted way. I did have a type.

CHAPTER 4

Pittsburgh, Pennsylvania, February 23, 2006—Kate

Six months before this horrible week, Gina held a phone in front of my face. "Memorize this number." I barely had time to before Shock packed up the entire crew, and we lit out of Skilletsville just after midnight. Life was kicking my ass, and my eighteenth birthday was the lowest point of them all.

Shock thought it would be "fun" to take me out in the cold and snow barely dressed with my ass hanging out of a borrowed miniskirt and a coat that truly didn't deserve the title.

As I shivered in the ladies' room, coughing so hard I couldn't breathe, a total stranger called 9-1-1. In the mayhem of police and firefighters, Shock abandoned me. Only BamBam stuck around. I was on a stretcher getting oxygen between bouts of coughing blood when he slipped one of them a fifty to "talk" to me. They parked the stretcher behind the vehicle and disappeared.

I honestly thought I was going to die on my birthday.

He poked a blade against my neck, under my ear, and leaned in to say, "You squeal, you die. We'll be watching." The last I saw of him was the ugly skull on the back of his jacket.

* * *

A Week Later

"Who should we call for your discharge?" The nurse busied herself winding the mask and plastic tubes that saved my life.

My silence drew her attention.

"Parents?" Her eyes dipped to my ring. "Husband?" As she said the word, she pointed to the bruises on my arm and followed up with, "Someone else? Someone you feel safe with?" She checked the door for any visitors, but there were none. No one came to the hospital. I could've died, and no one cared. But they were watching.

"Can you show me how to dial out?" I didn't trust her. I didn't trust anyone. I couldn't.

She explained the phone system. "Who should we expect?"

Honestly? I didn't know. And it would be better if no one here knew. "No one."

Her face tightened. "I can give you a help-line. Would you call it?"

"Is it local?"

She smiled and nodded.

"No."

"They *can* help you."

No service was untainted between my father's and my husband's influences. "No."

Her lips pursed into a knot. "Fine. The doctor will be in later this afternoon with your discharge paperwork and prescriptions."

That didn't give me much time. It was at least three hours from Skilletsville to Pittsburgh. I needed everything in place before I was discharged. I tapped out the numbers.

It rang long enough that I doubted anyone would pick up.

"It's your dime. Talk." The man who answered had a rich voice despite the sarcastic greeting. It wasn't Gina. But I had to assume it was someone she knew who could help.

"This is Kate. I'm at Mercy Hospital in Pittsburgh. I'll be discharged some time today. I need—"

He interrupted me, "Hang on. I'll look up that part."

What? We didn't have time for this. Someone could walk in at any second. "I'm getting discharged. They're probably going to call my father, and he'll call Shock, and I don't—"

"Sure, we can deliver. It'll cost extra. Address?"

Was this code? I didn't have money. But this was my only chance. "Are you talking to someone else?"

"No."

Oh. "Is there someone with you?"

"Yup. That's why we charge extra."

He wasn't making a lot of sense. "Gina gave me this number."

"Yeah, figured as much. I can swing by the dealership and have it to you in about three hours."

My insides sang with hope. "Is this Jackson?" I'd seen him hand a boy his phone. And it was the same phone Gina showed me later.

He scoffed. "Listen, do you want the part or not?"

If *part* meant freedom, absolutely. "Yes."

"Cool. What's your card number?"

"I don't have any money." The lack of any was one way Shock controlled me.

"Okay, let me repeat it." He rattled off a string of numbers. "Expiration date?"

I hoped he was still pretending to be conversing with a customer. But in case he needed information on timing, I said, "As soon as possible?"

"Thanks. I'll run it and get on the road. Hey, Pinner, I'm heading west, do you want me to drop off those tires for you while I'm out?" The latter half was slightly muffled, as if he'd covered the microphone.

There was a murmured answer in the background.

"No shit. It's going to take me all fucking day."

I tried to be patient, but this conversation didn't guarantee he would help. For all I knew, the numbers had gotten crossed, and I was listening to a completely different conversation.

"Yeah, fuck ya later, dick." There was a rustle and more noise in the background. It sounded like hammering and loud rock music. "I'm out, assholes, parts delivery."

Then the noise decreased dramatically. I heard the squeak of a heavy door and the beeping of a vehicle door alert. "Okay, babe, Kate, is it?"

"Yes."

"I'm in the work truck. They'll tag the mileage, so here's what to expect. I can be outside the hospital in three hours, but I'll be in a bright fucking yellow tow truck. And that's no fucking good. We need to meet somewhere that this bitch isn't going to stand out. How about a gas station or coffee shop?"

"I don't have clothes." Or a ride, or money, or anything.

There was a pause. "No shit?" His voice was filled with innuendo and intrigue.

"Jackson?"

"That's the name, don't use it where ears can hear, got it. Call me Bill for now."

He didn't have to tell me twice. "Bill. I don't even know if they saved what I came in wearing."

"Mercy Hospital. Fuck that's by the river. I'll have to make a couple of stops. Are you calling from a hospital phone?"

"Yes."

"*Double fuck*. After you hang up here, call a couple random numbers. At least one business, got it? Keep them on the line as long as you can. I need you to stall for four."

"Hours?"

"Kate, do you want help or not?"

My life depended on it. "Yes."

"Stall. And make a trail of numbers so this isn't the only one. I'm ditching this phone as soon as I can."

"Thank you."

"Thank me when we're as far as fucking possible from where you are now. Until then, keep your shit tight. Understand? I don't do fucking crying or hysterics, got it?"

"Got it." I would not be that woman. I managed this far. I could do a few more hours. Or days, or months, or for-fucking ever if necessary. As long as I was free.

"No fucking clothes. Sheee-it. That's a man's wet d—" He hung up, still talking.

Three hours and forty minutes later, there was a soft knock at the door. I clutched my blanket, worried someone had found me.

Jackson stuck his head in. I hadn't paid much attention that night, but he was handsome. Devilish arched eyebrows, little smile lines forming along the outside of his blue eyes, and a well-kept beard. His hair was light brown, short, and a bit messy, but trimmed cleanly around the sides and back. He wore a dark gray wool coat and a brown scarf. Under it, he had a polo shirt and gray khakis. He didn't look like any biker I'd ever met. And he was carrying a large shopping bag with the local discount store logo plastered on the sides. He was everything a contemporary white knight should be.

Then he opened his mouth. "You look like shit."

"Gee, thanks. I almost died." A slight cough came out, and I held my ribs where I'd pulled several muscles that still ached. Just sitting up and swinging my legs over the edge of the bed winded me.

He set the bag down on the bed. "I guessed a size small on most of it but added medium in the mix." His gaze was glued on my bare legs. There were fresh bruises and scrapes on my knees and finger-shaped bruises on my thighs that had turned an ugly green.

"Underwear?" I wheezed. This wouldn't work if I couldn't breathe. I dug into the bag of medicine on the night stand, pulled out the inhaler, and took a long puff.

He pulled out a red lace boy short style and set it on my lap.

I glared at him while taking the second puff.

"You said no clothes."

I let out the air and coughed once. "I suppose the bra matches?" It hurt to bend over to pull the undies on.

The corner of his mouth went up. "No bra." His eyes dipped to my chest. "I didn't remember the size. But I'd guess at least a thirty-four C?"

"Thirty-two." But he got the cup size right.

His mouth formed a little "oh." And his eyes hadn't moved from my tits. "Pink nipples?"

If I wasn't dependent on him, I'd kill him. "You will *never* know."

That snarky reply took his attention off my tits. His grin got bigger, and he bit his bottom lip. "Okay. Do you need help getting dressed?"

"No." I climbed to my feet, holding onto the metal frame in case I got dizzy again.

"Are you sure?" His eyes trailed down my legs.

I snatched the bag of clothes and glared at him. But maybe he needed a reminder of what I'd been through. "Do you have a gun?"

He nodded. "In the truck."

"Too bad. I'd ask you for it right now, because, if another biker ever touches me again, I'll shoot 'em." With that, I turned my leg so he could see the horrific blotchy green bruises on the inside of my thighs near my crotch. I didn't give a shit if he could see the new underwear he'd bought or my pubes or anything. I needed him to get it through his head that he was not here to flirt with me. "That is courtesy of my fucking husband. Understand?"

The smile fell into an angry line. "Yeah. Hurry. I bribed the nurse on duty."

Shit. I left the door to the bathroom slightly open so I could listen for trouble. "Do you think she'll remember you?"

"She'll remember. That's why I didn't give her a real name."

I tugged a sweater over my head to cover my nipple points that graced the simple white t-shirt he'd bought. "She didn't get suspicious? Ask for ID?"

"Bribed, Kate. Of course she's suspicious. Let's go. The hall is clear."

The snow boots he brought were a size too big. But they'd have to work.

"Come on." He tugged my hand with a squeeze. But then stopped me from moving. "Wait." He twisted the wedding ring on my left hand. It pinched the skin under it.

"Ow."

He dropped my hand. "Take it off. Leave it on the nightstand. Nothing from that world comes with, got it?"

"It's stuck."

"Spit on it. Hurry." He kept an eye on the hallway.

I did. The ring slipped off with a little force. I set it right on the discharge paperwork I wasn't going to take with me. I stuffed the medicine bag into the now almost empty shopping bag. "Ready."

My heart rate picked up as he took my hand again. "Here." He dug out a black knit cap. "Put it on and tuck all your hair into it while we're in the elevator. When we get off, go left. Straight to the doors. I'll go right."

In the elevator, he pressed keys into my hand. "Black SUV, Ford. New York plates." He described the location as I pocketed the keys and pulled the cap over my head.

He pulled off the gray coat and wrapped it around me. Then he took the shopping bag, and the doors opened. He went right, and I turned to the doors on the left.

Five minutes later, I found the fucking vehicle. There were seven black SUVs in that section alone. I was coughing hard and needed my inhaler. I started the car and turned on the heater. The driver's door opened, and I screamed. It wasn't loud, but triggered a harder coughing fit.

Jackson looked completely different. Somehow, he'd changed into an ugly Steelers jacket with a bright yellow scarf and hat.

"Move over."

I bruised my leg climbing over the console. He dug under the seat and pulled out a Pennsylvania plate. "There it is."

He was gone for only a moment to swap out the plate on the back of the car. Then we were on the move. He took the interstate north. I took it in stride, knowing if we were followed, going north wouldn't lead them directly back to Jackson.

Hours later, we were heading east on 80. Once we passed Milton, I got worried. "We're not going to Skilletsville?"

"Fuck no."

Oh.

He fiddled with the radio. "What kind of music do you listen to?"

Anything but pop. But those words didn't come out. Instead, I said, "I don't. I hate music."

"I beg your pardon?"

It was too long of a story to explain. "Can we please just be quiet?"

His scowl deepened. Then he said, "No. I either need music or conversation when I drive. Pick one."

Both were land mines.

He tossed out ideas. "Here's a topic. Favorite football team."

"I don't have one."

He glanced at me. "Not even the Steelers?"

Especially not them. Shock loved the team. "Shock bets on every game. When they lose, he beats me."

"Beat. Past tense. Favorite food?"

I didn't think. "Chocolate."

"Chocolate isn't a food."

"Yes, it is." I froze. Would he think I'm arguing with him?

"Chocolate cake is a food. Chocolate ice cream is a food. Chocolate is a flavor."

I put it as neutrally as I could. "It's my favorite."

"You mean to tell me you'd eat chocolate-flavored shit?"

Yuck. "No."

"See? *Not* your favorite in all things. Which chocolate foods are your favorite?"

"You're a jerk." I crossed my arms and regretted it because it reminded me I wasn't wearing a bra.

He tilted his head toward me to confide, "I'm a correct jerk. What foods?"

"You're making me hungry."

"That can be fixed." He flicked on the blinker to take the exit.

"Wait, we can't stop." Panic seized me. "What if someone sees us?" What if there were cameras that could be hacked? What if someone followed us?

"Relax."

He sounded so sure of himself. What I wouldn't give for that kind of confidence.

"Should I continue calling you Bill?"

"Hell no. James. Call me that."

"Why do they call you Jackson?"

"Jack's son." He said it as two distinct words.

"Your father's name was Jack?"

He nodded. "John, Jack. Same difference. The club all called him One-Eyed Jack."

"Did he lose an eye?" Sometimes, biker nicknames were on the nose.

"Ha, no. He got that from always winking at the ladies." Jackson's grin was devious. His wink was even more devilish.

"Ah." The apple certainly didn't fall far from the tree.

He turned into a small-town diner parking lot. When he parked, he spent a moment studying me. "Ah, what?"

I smiled at my thoughts. "It's hereditary."

"What is?" He crossed his arms over the steering wheel.

"Flirting."

"Hell, babe, that's like calling water wet." He got out and circled the car to open my door. He even offered a hand so I wouldn't slip on the ice as I got out.

And he didn't let go as we walked into the restaurant. I told myself it wasn't because he was a gentleman, but because he needed to control me. Then chided myself for thinking the worst.

Inside, it wasn't much of a restaurant. Barely a dozen tables and a tired teen manning the counter. He set down his phone and grabbed two dirty menus as we took a table near the back. "Here." He shoved them at us.

Jackson slid them to the side. "We'll take two hot chocolates. Could you bring them while we figure out what we want?"

Once the kid disappeared into the back, I hissed, "Why'd you do that?" Ordering my food was something Shock would do.

"You like chocolate."

"I can order my own food." And why two?

"It's like that, got it." He rifled through his wallet and laid forty dollars on the table before tucking the billfold back into his coat.

We waged a silent war with our gazes. The server set down two mugs, which broke the spell. He noted the menus still stacked at the edge of the table. "I'll give you a few more minutes." Then he retreated.

Jackson spoke, "I'm not him."

The kid was still in listening range. I waited until he picked up his phone before replying, keeping my voice quiet without whispering. "I don't know that. I don't know anything about you."

"Now's your chance. My favorite football team is the Eagles. And I don't bet more than fifty bucks, ever. I don't bet on things to win. I work to win. *That* I take very seriously. But if I can't control it, there's no point in giving a shit, understand me?"

I ran his words through my head carefully, searching for traps. "Control? Me?"

"Oh, *hell* no. Women can't be controlled. That's why I'm single. Eventually, I'd piss 'em off and they'd kill me. And I like living too much for that shit." He stretched out, draping his arm over the chair next to him. His demeanor was easy, but an edge of danger hung around him. Maybe my perception was conditioned to see black leather and equate it with danger. He had come to my rescue when I called, drove hours not only to get me, but move me somewhere far away from where we were. And all without any promise of payment. He didn't deserve my judgment.

"I'm sorry."

"Drink your cocoa. Let's see what's good, shall we?" He picked up the menu and began to search the list.

I hesitated to tug my menu closer.

"Kate?"

I searched his face for a clue on how to proceed. He tipped his head to the table where the menu sat. "Pick anything you want. I'm buying." He tapped the forty on the table.

My hand trembled as I picked up the coated paper. The offerings were simple. Burgers, soups, sandwiches. Even breakfast all day. But if I was going to get healthier, I needed a balanced meal. I picked the soup of the day and the chef's salad.

Jackson ordered a burger with extra fries. As we ate, he slipped fries from his plate and dropped them next to my salad. After the first five, I began snitching them from the platter in front of him. The second time I did it, he smiled. But never in any of it complained or corrected me.

By the time I'd finished my soup and pushed around some of the wilted lettuce, I was stuffed and tenuously happy. It had been so long that I'd forgotten how it was supposed to feel.

"Any thoughts about where your dream vacation is?" Jackson had kept a running commentary during dinner, shifting topics around and dropping tidbits of information about him, but never divulging much about his life as a biker.

"Warm. I don't care where. Just warm." A couple of patrons arrived with a gust of winter air. It seeped under the sweater I wore and made me shiver.

"You don't look like a warm-weather girl."

"Normally, I'm not. I love autumn and the smell of burning leaves. But I also *hate* being cold."

Jackson glanced at the door. The day had disappeared, and with the twilight, snow began to fall. "We should find a hotel."

My fork clattered against the plate.

He wiped his face with a napkin, ran his fingers down his mustache, and twisted the beard at his chin into a point. "You trusted Gina, and through proxy, me. I take that seriously." His gaze bored into mine.

"Why?"

"Trust is the *rarest* gift."

I got snared in his sincerity. The simplicity and monumental importance of it shimmered in the air. If I could reach out and wrap my hand around it, I'd never be scared again. But words and concepts were intangible things. Spoken and forgotten. Lost in the blink of an eye.

"Did you want another hot chocolate?" The server's words snapped me out of the fantasy I'd fallen into.

"I'm good."

Jackson added another twenty to the pile. "Can you box up some of that cake to go?" He pointed at the counter. I hadn't noticed the desserts in the glass case. But he had. A fancy chocolate ganache with cherries and cream held court in the center, between pieces of pie and assorted cupcakes.

"I should've never told you I liked chocolate." I had a feeling he'd stuff me with sweets until I hated the flavor.

His eyes dipped to my chest.

I checked for spilled food. There was none. Nor was there much for him to see. The sweater was doing an excellent job of coverage. "What are you staring at?"

Busted, he smiled and looked away. "What is your second favorite flavor?"

"Strawberries."

"That is a food."

"It's a flavor," I argued.

He laughed. I'd made him laugh. Moreover, I'd contradicted him and didn't pay a price for it. It gave me hope there wasn't one. But time would prove me wrong. Dead wrong.

CHAPTER 5

Danville, Pennsylvania—Jackson

The motel room was about as typical as you can get. Two full-size beds, a shared nightstand in the middle, a TV with porn twenty-four-seven if you could afford it, and an anemic coffee machine that spat out one cup at a time. Kate stiffened when I led her in, but relaxed a little at seeing the two beds.

I got busy, first tossing all but one of the pillows on the bed near the window. "That one's yours."

"I don't need all these pillows."

"Make a pillow fort with them." I had calls to make and not a huge time-frame to make them in. In my haste to get to Pittsburgh, I couldn't find my most recent burner phone. And I didn't have time to waste with the salesperson at the discount store to discuss features and options and that shit. I'd pushed speed limits as much as I dared with one of the club's "Sheila's." That was code for a car with no registration or license plates, and nondescript enough to blend in. We swapped out stolen plates from various cars we collected in our repossession and junk business, and the two plates I nabbed didn't match the vehicle.

That's why it got backed into the parking space—and for good measure, I made sure all of our shit was out of it before getting inside. If I had to, I'd hot-wire a car.

Kate was a lot of trouble for a girl with almost zero reason to be in the sights of the MC. Then again, she was also feisty. During the meal and the ride I caught glimmers of the girl she'd been before Shock got his ugly mitts on her. And each time I saw that fire, I liked what I saw. Someday, she'd get that back. And it was my job to make sure she was safe enough to get there.

Which meant I had a plan. But first, I needed an alibi.

"I seriously don't need these." She tossed two back on my bed.

"You're team no-touch then."

"What?"

Christ, me and my big mouth. "Mom, a hooker if you wanna know, had a theory about some of the girls. They either sleep with a shit-ton of pillows, making a fort no one can trespass in, or they sleep with nothing around them so they're aware if something or someone wants to fuck with them."

Her mouth fell open. "I—Your mom was a hooker?"

"Dad's favorite. And when I came along, his only. For a while." Until the law split them apart.

There were things she wanted to say but was too nice to say them. The way her face blotched red at her cheeks and the quick close of her mouth told me so.

"I was about thirteen when Dad knocked over a liquor store. Third strike and all that shit. Mom went back to hooking for a while. But working for herself, not my dad. That is how I know most of this shit. I couldn't tell you how many women I drove across the state, or the number of Johns I beat up, all before age twenty when I prospected at Dad's club. But I rolled over to Skilletsville because I didn't want to walk in his shadow. Is that enough for you? Or do you need to know more?" My verbal vomit ended sourly, like most puke sessions.

"She's not a hooker anymore?"

"Nope. Married a dentist. Lives in suburbia with a fat 401k and an Etsy shop that pays the bills until he retires."

Her face paled then.

"What did I say wrong?"

"There's life after this."

It wasn't a question. It was a statement. One she obviously dreaded. "Yeah, Kate. There's life after. For most." Why the fuck did I tack that on? She didn't need to know the facts. I should be telling her about rainbows and kittens and that ilk, not the three-times rate of suicide, or the two-fifths recidivism, or the lifetime problems with PTSD. Not to mention the poverty and loss of self-identity.

Christ. And it was worse for her because she not only had partner abuse but the whole damn rotten Pittsburgh chapter's abuse. That was evident when they showed up to party. Not a goddamned one of them looked out for her, and they should have. She was the kind of woman who tugged at a man's instinct to protect and procreate.

Whoo-boy, I was in this mess fucking deep.

"The life you have now, and from now on, is yours. Pillow fort, starfish, whatever you want."

She stared at the carpet for a few more minutes. Rumination complete, she grabbed one of the pillows back.

"Gotta make a call, close your ears, and stay quiet." I dialed one of the VPs of a feeder chapter of ours. It was a gamble, but Disney hadn't let me down yet. "Yo, Diz. I gotta problem."

I listened to him bitch for a minute. The man always had something sarcastic or snide to say. If it put him in a good mood to complain, I'd let him. Finally, he asked what was up.

"So… I went on this run earlier. Stopped at a bar on the way back and uh, met this chick. Forty-four D's man."

His laugher and crude comments were almost exactly as I imagined it.

"Anyways, I still got the truck and shit, so could you call up Pinner and tell him you needed me to do a run for you? Or tell them I went fishing with you or something."

I held my breath. But he was like, "Anything for you, man. What she look like?" I waxed on about the redhead I'd picked up. In my retelling, she looked nothing like Kate. As I described the imaginary woman, Kate held her hands in front of her, trying to picture what forty-four D would even look like. She was a bit off, so I moved her hands in place as I joked around. "Hey, Diz? She's getting cold, man. I gotta go warm her up. 'Smell ya later."

I hung up and confirmed the line was dead before addressing Kate. "Alibi complete. They won't miss me until tomorrow night, maybe even Saturday morning."

"Forty-four Ds, huh?"

"Don't knock it. Mom's still got the rack for the sack. Yet…I kind of like 'em a bit…" My eyes lingered on the t-shirt she wore. She'd ditched the sweater when we got to the hotel. Her tits were the kind that sloped like a ski ramp. The tips poked at the thin fabric.

Her hands flew to her chest and covered them.

"Sorry, babe. Caught staring. It'll happen again."

"You're so…"

"Full of it?"

"That." Her cheeks colored. But her eyes sparkled.

There it was. That spark. *Damn.* "Okay, here's what to expect. Tomorrow we'll head southeast. Cross over into 'Jersey. I'm going to get you to Trenton. There's at least seven shelters there. We'll call around until we find one that can take you. You should be safe since you'll be out of state and technically in Demon's territory. Well, safer. Don't mess with any Demons, got it?"

"I don't intend on it. After the shelter, what happens?"

"Anything you want. My job ends at getting you in the pick-up van. They don't give out addresses, and I won't know where you are or anything."

"But what if something goes wrong? What if I need—"

This is where things would get complicated. She'd already attached to me. "I go back to being the same shitty asshole I've always been. And you forget about me."

Her mouth opened to argue.

"No, Kate. I'm dead, just as dead to you as Shock. More so. He'll kill me. Don't call."

And I was officially an asshole. The crinkle between her eyebrows gave her thoughts away, even if she didn't say them.

"Sleep. Tomorrow is going to be a lot for you. Did you take your medicine?"

I noticed her slip a pill earlier. I sincerely hoped those were from the hospital, not something Shock got her hooked on. *Maybe I should ask?*

Or maybe I should just *not* give a fuck. It would be a lot easier to cover my tracks if I did. Shock would know she had help. And if that nurse talked, fingers would point. All it would take was a little jog of memory, and he'd remember how I stood between him and Kate at the junkyard. Another jog, a few calls, and Disney's alibi would fall flat. He'd tell whoever asked that I was with a chick.

Maybe I should've taken the alibi a little further from the truth?

It would be a long ass day for me, too.

But if Kate got the help she needed and never came back, life would be fine. Eventually, Shock would forget about her. Move on to a new girl. And then I'd be in the clear.

I only needed time. And a teleportation device to be as far away from Kate as possible.

But if wishes were landmines, there'd be body parts flying everywhere.

"I'll take it now."

The defeat in her voice killed me. I pulled out a deck of cards and shuffled. Solitaire was no fun with a marked deck, so I dealt out two hands. "You play Gin?"

"Gin Rummy?" She settled on the end of the bed, crisscross applesauce. Her bare knees mocked me.

"Yup. I'd offer spades, but you probably didn't learn with the best spades players on the planet so…" Even not trying to hustle her, I slipped back into the habit.

"I know hearts. Same thing."

Our eyes met. In the dim lamplight, I couldn't see any color at all. Only light gray. But she was smiling. If only on the inside, it was enough to light up her face. Her cheekbones disappeared under rounded cheeks, and her lips were… off limits. "That's a metaphor for us, you know? I'm spades, you're hearts."

"The Jack of Death, huh?"

"And the Queen of Hearts." *Shit*. Why did I say something so sappy? "Did you know they call the Jacks knaves?" I cut the deck and offered her a pick to see who had the lowest card. That player would go first.

"You're a knave, alright." She pulled a two.

I flipped over my card, a Jack. I hadn't even looked at the marks. That boded well.

"I try." Just like I tried not to pay any attention to the backs of her cards. But she made it damn easy for me to see the scratched corners. And because she made it easy, I made it easier for her to win. She'd been dealt too many shit hands in her life so far.

After four games, we called it quits. I won one just to make it seem fair, but she was catching on. "Do you always carry a marked deck?"

I threw my hand down. "What gave it away?"

She sifted through the discard pile and pulled the queen I'd practically gift-wrapped for her. The one she ignored. "You had the run."

"I did."

She leaned forward. "I see you."

"No, you don't."

Her eyebrow flicked upward, daring me to lie again. But I wasn't lying. Not about this. "You *think* you see me. But what you got is only what I'm willing to show. There's a lot more under the surface you'll never get. And that's a good thing."

"You talk about your parents like you love them."

And she hadn't said a peep about either parent. "I do. Even though my dad is no longer in this mortal coil, he was a hell of a man. Did anything and everything he could to teach me all the bad shit he knew. And also the good shit. Ma? She did the same. I couldn't ask for better parents. They were honest with me. That, my little Kate, is much better than lying your ass off and giving kids foolish dreams."

I held her eyes and saw my words sink in to her brain. What she didn't know was that I dug around after her appearance at our clubhouse. I knew all about her junkie-lawyer dad's involvement. I also dug up dirt on her absentee mother. The one who got a nice divorce settlement and took off to Vegas without the kid. She married a fourth or fifth-tier mobster down there. And her life was shit. He ran a restaurant that was on the skids, and she was batshit crazy, talking to her twin peek-a-poo dogs like they were children. She treated those damn dogs better than Kate. It sucked balls.

Her gaze dropped. "I'm tired."

I'd be, too, with that shithole family. She moved to her bed to rearrange the pillows but kept flipping around, not quite comfortable. I tugged the extra pillow from under my head and stood over her fortress of down. "Put this one against your chest. Hold it tight."

She moved around and got it in position. I tucked one of the strays against her back. "That pillow?" I pointed at the one she strangled. "That's me."

Her glare spit fire.

I smiled. She'd make it. No matter what life threw at her. She'd make it.

CHAPTER 6

Trenton, New Jersey, July 15, 2008—Kate

The same gray sedan I'd spotted yesterday was back. Different plates this time, but the scratch on the front bumper was an exact match. "Cara, may I borrow your phone?"

"Are you calling the cops?" She'd noticed my unease.

"And tell them what? I'm being followed?"

"Yeah, that's how it works."

Not if there was someone on the payroll. Not if a biker gang was out of their territory, stalking you. I'd been privy to enough of Shock's inner workings to know how he operated. And I'd learned just enough from Jackson to spot cars by their distinctive marks, not their plates. He'd proven to me that the plates could be altered, registrations forged.

Cara and I were working our shifts at the local thrift store. I was on the floor, returning stock and sorting out constantly ransacked displays, while she worked the register. Her ex, an alcoholic, was in jail for at least two years. That meant she could take public-facing jobs easier. My role had an escape route out the back, or the ability to hide in the back rooms behind any number of ex-felons or rehabilitating addicts ranging from the scrawny to linebacker size.

"You didn't see who was in it, did you?"

"Sorry." She pointed at the cash register. It faced the store, not the windows. A mistake, if you ask me. So what if someone stole from Goodwill? They obviously needed it more than we did. Having the register face-front instead gave the workers the advantage of seeing who walked in. One some of us desperately needed. "Are you going to call them?" She held out her phone.

"Yeah. I'll take it in the back."

She'd find out on the next bill that I lied. But hopefully, by then, I'd be long gone. I'd make it up to her somehow.

My hands were shaking as I dialed the business number for the junkyard. I memorized the number after spotting a pattern of surveillance. Call it instinct or an overactive imagination, but it started right after I filed for divorce. The very next day, my spine itched right between my shoulder blades. And it wasn't from bedbugs or lice, which ran rampant through shelters.

Why did I let that stupid counselor talk me into filing?

Right, I was supposed to be moving on. *Healing.* Giving up the past.

That stupidity made me a target. Shock wasn't going to give me up. He was the Rick-Roll of biker assholedom. And if I ever wanted to be truly free, someone needed to put a bullet between his eyes. Too bad I couldn't afford a gun. I'd do it myself.

Yeah, I'd reached the anger stage of grief. That was a hell of a lot better than the other ones. At least I was doing something. And even though I knew better, I dialed anyway.

"Junk in the Trunk," the bored voice on the other end sounded young. Probably a prospect.

I affected a breathy, singsong tone. "Hi." I waited.

"Hey baby. What can I do for you or *to* you?"

"Oh, sweetheart, you sound *so* helpful." I licked my lips, even though he couldn't see it; maybe he'd "hear" it. "I need..." I trailed off, waiting for him to take the bait.

"And I've got anything you want." His high-pitched voice lowered.

Donning my very best Marilyn Monroe kitten voice, I breathily said, "I *want...* Jackson."

"Oh, fuck. Jack! One of your bitches is on the phone. Hang on. He's in the shop."

Problem solved. I'd managed to fool the gatekeeper. That was good, right?

"Babe, I'm at work. Can't it wait?"

"Are you alone?" I dropped the breathy act and went straight to business.

"Uh, yeah. Like that. Talk my ear off and get my dick hard, babe."

"I think you know who this is, but if not, it's the Queen of Hearts. I'm being followed. I know I wasn't supposed to call you, but this is my friend's phone, not traceable, not connected. I need help getting away."

"Fuck. Hang on." The phone crackled as he moved from where he was to a place we could talk freely. A door snicked shut, and he spoke again. "I'm in the john. They're going to think I'm whacking off in here. What's going on, who's following you?"

"I'd guess Shock or one of his people. I filed for divorce. The next day, I got a bad feeling. All this week I've been seeing the same gray sedan parked outside work, at the bus stop I wait at outside the shelter, and outside the grocery store when we went in the shelter van."

"Have you told anyone?"

"Everyone who needs to know. The shelter staff have awareness. They traded out vehicles with another location. We're escorted to work now."

"We?"

"Cara and I work at the same place. It's a precaution because we're often together. They might target her."

"It sounds like they got it covered."

I had to impress on him how serious this was. "They don't. They're used to normal people not…"

"Kate, I know what you mean. I'm one of them, remember?"

"Absolutely, that's why I need you."

"You don't need me," he protested.

Which was where he was wrong. "I need someone who can outsmart Shock. I know you're that guy."

He exhaled a little too loudly. "Remember the nurse?"

Oh shit. "Yeah."

"She washed up along the Ohio River a week after you disappeared."

I let out the breath I was holding. Unfortunately, I'd expected retribution. "Did he target you?"

Jackson made a noise. "He tried. Fucking Disney came through, covered my shit, and then some. Lied his ass off to a patched member. I owe him big-time."

"Good."

"Naw, not good. I can't help you. He's probably watching me."

Shit. I must have said it out loud.

"Kate," his voice was soft.

"What do I do?"

His silence stretched out. "I'd say run. You got any cash?"

"Four hundred saved."

"Jesus. That and a fucking dime would get you to exactly mother-fucking nowhere. Wait. That's what you need. Mother-fucking nowhere. Step one, do you know anyone with a car?"

"A few people."

"Any men you trust, big guys. The kind you don't mess with?"

"One." George would say yes. He was the linebacker-sized stocker here. He'd once been a football player in high school. College came, and his scholarship wasn't enough to help him escape his urban plight, and he started down the path of drug abuse. He was about five years clean and sober, and coaching middle school kids in the local Rec league. He was a teddy bear of a human, but like most bears, you didn't want to be on their bad side.

"Okay. Can you hold out a week?"

"I can try."

"You can. You're smart, brave, a fucking hurricane in little human form. You got this. Next Tuesday morning, get up and on the road as early as you can. I want you to get your guy to drive you to a little adult toy store just off the 309 near Wilkes Barre. You'll know it because there's a hotel, a custom car place, and a bunch of discount chain stores nearby. Maybe even a Salvation Army, if I remember correctly. He should drop you off and watch you walk inside. Bring *nothing* with you. From there, he should go to the hotel across the street and take a room for the night. It will be reserved under the name Fred Manford."

"What happens at the adult store?"

"You go to the back dressing rooms."

"And?"

"That's all you get, babe. Some parts of this plan still need work. Just get your ass there on Tuesday, and don't delay. Anything happens in-between then and here, I can't cover." He hung up almost as soon as he finished.

But I had a plan, which George was happy to help with. But I made him swear to secrecy. I made a few more calls, one to the police, to tell them about the car in front of the store.

A squad car drove past, and the car was gone within the hour. Trouble was, no one saw who got in it. That itch between my shoulders was full-out stabbing now. George made himself more than useful escorting us between vehicles and work, even going as far as driving us on more than one occasion.

Monday afternoon, I was in the back, tagging merchandise. A commotion up front sent George and a couple of the other men running to take care of it.

But it was too late. Cara was gone.

At the register, a single piece of paper was stabbed on the old memo spike we kept there. I tugged it off and my body washed cold. Scribbled on it was a Destroyers skull. Around it were squiggly lines. It was so poorly drawn I didn't understand it at first. Then I realized it resembled Shock's back tattoo. He had the Destroyers' patch inked there. Ringed around it were thunderheads and lightning.

I pocketed it. The police would want it, but what if they fingerprinted it? I'd held it. My sweaty hands were sure to leave a residue. I cursed my stupidity. Fingerprints were indisputable evidence that would get back to my husband as proof I'd been there.

He'd figure out the missing pieces and target Jackson this time. I was so dumb.

"Kate, the cops are on their way. Do you need me to take you anywhere?" George hovered, the concern making the frown lines in his forehead groove into deep mounds.

"Here." I dug out the paper. "My ex. That's his tattoo mark. He's probably got someone on payroll."

George studied the drawing. "Destroyers?"

"Yeah."

His dark brown eyes studied me. "You don't look like a biker chick."

"Why do you think I ran?"

His jaw tensed. "I got friends…"

"No. Use them to help *you*. I want nothing to do with gangs or bikers or anyone. I just need to—" The bell rang as the other workers filed into the store, all of them excited and angry. Mostly, they were upset that Cara was gone. I was, too, but also terrified of what would happen next.

Shock knew precisely where I was. It was a matter of time before I'd be taken in broad daylight, just like Cara. And if that happened, I was a dead woman. There would be no normal. Ever. And Shock was the kind of man to hold grudges. He'd keep me alive out of sheer spite as he tortured me into insanity.

George glanced at the paper again. His eyes filled with tears. He hastily swiped them away with his thumb and shoved the paper in his pocket. He blew out a breath. "I'll make a call for Cara. 'Cops won't know."

He disappeared into the back. When the police came, we all told the truth, as much of it as we could. No one had seen her. Not even the customers. It was as if everyone had amnesia or something. Which was absurd. But maybe George's friends could help Cara. I had to believe that.

That evening, I ate dinner with George. He'd taken me out for burgers at a joint in his old neighborhood. Five of his friends sat with us in a crowded booth. I squashed between the absurdly large men, eating what felt like my last meal.

Four of them openly carried handguns.

All of them had scarification or tattoos.

Not one of them said much about the silly white girl in their midst. They joked, talked about old times, and, every sentence or two, watched the door. I was making them a target.

"You shake any harder, I'm going to take it personally." George elbowed me.

"I'm sorry." It spilled out of my mouth on repeat.

He wrapped his arm around me, almost smothering me with his crushing side hug. "Ain't nothing to be sorry about. We got ya."

I shook my head. I wasn't safe here. That itchy knife was twisting. Like a clock countdown. *Tick tick tick.* My life was measured in seconds, maybe minutes. "We should get away from the windows."

To a man, they raised their eyes to the front of the hamburger shop. There was a nod and a tip of the head. Two men peeled out of the booth and walked outside for a smoke.

George kept me pinned under his arm. I could barely breathe.

Bam! Bam! The glass of the shop spiderwebbed but didn't break. Answering shots from the two men who'd stepped outside rang out. George dragged me from the booth toward the back door.

One of the men followed. There was a van in the alley, idling. George and I piled in while his friend ran to the mouth of the alley, gun in hand. He fired twice and then stood in the opening, staring down the street. Sirens blared in the distance, which drowned out the alarm bell ringing inside the shop.

"Stay down, baby-girl. BJ's motioning us to move."

The van rocked, and I held onto the bare wall. I marveled at the similarities between this van and the one Shock used to transport hookers from Pittsburgh to Skilletsville. This one reeked of pot more than that one, but in the end, I was still a victim. A statistic. A burden on society because a man—no. I used to think that way. But no more. I'd look ahead. Stay positive. I'd made friends who were helping. There was good in this world despite the ugliness of it. I'd be brave and smart and not let this defeat me. Ever.

We stopped outside a brick apartment building. The wings wrapped around a parking lot. I followed George from the van to a sedan.

"Gray?"

He laughed. "It blends in."

"Ironic, no?"

We left Trenton at five in the morning. Ate donuts and drank coffee in Wilkes Barre at eight fifteen and waited for the adult toy store to open.

"Tell me what he said again."

"He said leave early." I didn't like this any more than George did. I watched the traffic outside the donut shop pick up for rush hour. Customers came and went, grabbing coffee and food and not noticing the odd couple in the back booth near the bathrooms.

"Nine fifteen. It's open. You ready?"

Hell no. I hadn't slept a wink. I probably looked like shit again. "George?"

He looked up from his coffee. "Yeah?"

"Tell your friends, and tell yourself, thank you. I hope they find Cara."

"I hope so, too. I won't see you again, will I?"

I shook my head. "This time, there's no going back."

He frowned. "Run far, and keep running if you have to. I'm gonna say a few prayers for ya."

"Thanks." I didn't have the heart to tell him no one was listening.

CHAPTER 7

Wilkes-Barre, Pennsylvania, July 22, 2008—Jackson

Kate walked in twenty minutes after nine. She looked like hell. At least she'd put on some weight since I last saw her. She wore a simple flowered top and jeans. The top was wrinkled, and her hair was wildly frizzy. The circles under her eyes did nothing to ease my worry.

She looked around and spotted the dressing rooms. She randomly grabbed a negligee off the rack as she cut a beeline through the store. The gauzy outfit was deep pink, a horrible color for her. The green one I'd bought would bring out the color of her eyes.

I nonchalantly moved to the back. The woman at the register didn't even look up. I could be a predator, trapping Kate in a dressing room, and that bitch wouldn't know. My worry turned to anger. At least her ride had lingered long enough that she was inside the shop before the big Black man driving pulled away. As far as protectors go, she'd picked a good one.

Kate entered the dressing room but stood there, debating whether to pull the curtain. I made my presence known and held out the shopping bag of clothes I'd bought in the twenty minutes I'd been waiting.

"Thirty-two C. I remembered."

She pulled out the green bra first. The glance she sent me was mischievous and accusatory. "I'm supposed to wear this?"

"All of it. Leave your clothes behind in case someone got a tracker on you."

Her smiling eyes fell. "What about George?"

"The big guy in the gray sedan?"

She nodded.

"He looks competent. I booked the president's suite for him. He'll be okay."

"I'll thank you when we're gone from here."

"That's my girl."

I couldn't help it. She'd become mine almost the minute I locked eyes with her when she was cowering at Shock's feet. But now? That feeling was a tidal pull I couldn't ignore. And she was the moon. No other woman could compare. And I'd tried. But it was her in my dreams, in the taste of strawberries, any time of the day; I'd get a whiff of fresh air and I'd think of her. It was especially hard to ride. I'd given up escorting women on the back of my bike. I was tired of the grabby hands feeling my hard dick as I thought of her. Sunrise? Kate. Moonlit night? Kate. Balls deep and holding a nut? Kate.

She pulled the curtain shut and rummaged through the bag.

The shop-keeper finally noticed. "She's putting the shit on. Ya mind?"

I'd spent over a grand. She better not.

She smiled and went back to her phone.

"There's a dildo in here." Kate's voice was barely muffled through the curtain.

"That's for later."

She stuck her head out of the gap, taking care not to let me peek at what she did or did not have on yet. "*And* a vibrator?"

"I figured it's been a while."

Her face flushed bright red. "You…"

"Knave?" I wiggled my eyebrows at her and winked.

"That." Her eyes widened theatrically. Then she disappeared behind the curtain.

I angled to the side to line up with the meager one-inch gap. Her bare shoulder was covered in freckles. They were light orangish tan. Barely there, but so damn tempting against the backdrop of her peachy skin. Her hair was much longer now. All more one length rather than the layers she had before. I liked it. It made her look older. More womanly.

Speaking of… she turned to pick something up. I caught the flash of green. The cup gapped just a little, and I saw perfect, unmarred flesh. No nipple was visible, only that subtle slope and full-bottomed roundness that made me hard in my dreams. I stepped back.

There was shit to get done. Bad guys to watch out for. And a hell of a lot of driving to do. There was no time to deal with a hard-on.

The loud rip of a zipper told me she'd found the boots. That meant she had the silky leggings on. I pictured her ass in them and smiled, savoring the image.

"I'm almost done. How do I put on the wig?"

"There's a comb near the front, I think."

"Oh, here it is. Huh."

"What?" I tried to peek in the gap again, but she was on the other side of the dressing room.

"My hair is sticking out. Damn it."

More rustling. And cussing. She'd improved so much in two years.

"This is the best it'll get." She swept the curtain open.

From the tips of her ultra spike platform boots, up her long legs that were covered in shiny black satin, to her sweet thighs, a bangled chain belt that dipped in shiny silver arches, to the leather bustier where there was a peekaboo cutout for the emerald green of the bralette and silky lace cami, to her matching black spiked jacket, she was a knockout. The mounds of her breasts squashed upward, creating curves a stripper would be proud of.

But the icing on the cake was the fall of the silky white-blonde wig. That alone set me back four Benjamins. I brushed a stray clump from her face. I could see the reddish strands she was complaining about, but from a distance, no one would ever notice. They'd be looking too hard at her ass.

"You are fucking gorgeous."

She swallowed. "I need makeup."

"Hey!" I caught the clerk's attention. "My girl wants makeup."

The dollar signs lit up her eyes as she led Kate to various pots, creams, and tubes. She transformed from rose-golden waif to runway-worthy queen. If the runway was a strip club, that is.

I didn't mind. Kate was what every bad little biker aspired to have hanging on his dick, riding queen at his back, on her knees… *damn fantasies.* That's what she was. "Ready?"

"Your clothes." The clerk had helpfully collected them from the dressing room.

"Keep 'em, burn 'em. Don't give a shit. I'm taking this home." I laughed along with her, and led Kate to a luxurious sedan I'd parked off to the side of the lot. While inside, I'd kept an eye on it. This early, not much traffic bothered the naughty end of the mall. But the rest of the lot was gearing up for a day of normalcy.

I opened Kate's door, scanning for threats.

"How can you afford all this?"

"We'll talk on the road, babe." I circled the car and monitored traffic around us as I hit the freeway north.

She squirmed in her seat. "Take the shit off if you want."

That earned me a side glare.

"There's clothes in the duffel bag in the back seat. I picked up some yesterday."

"Then why make me dress like this?" She swiped at the outfit I stuck her with.

"Because, one, you look fucking kick ass in it. And two, if anyone followed me, they'd see me leave with a hooker, not you. Me with someone like you would raise flags."

"Someone like me?"

"Sweet, pretty without makeup, and off-limits."

Her mouth fell open. "I don't know what to address first."

"Don't then."

"I'm not sweet."

"No?"

"I'm not pretty without makeup."

"You're fucking wrong there. I know pretty, and you're fucking gorgeous."

The skin on her neck flushed pink. It took all my willpower to turn my attention back to the road.

"And, I'm not off-limits." She almost whispered it. "I filed for divorce."

Which was how that asshole found her. I was certain of it. "How soon after you did that were you followed?"

"The next day."

"Yeah. Off-limits." Poaching another brother's wife was a huge nope.

Her head dipped. The white-blond strands of her wig fell over her face. She brushed it back and then ripped it off. Her hair went in several directions. "I'm not off-limits."

Good to know. I kept my opinions on that to myself.

"I'm not." With that, she unbuckled and reached over the back seat. Her ass stuck in the air, and I couldn't help but look. That earned me a loud honk from the guy two lanes over who I almost side-swiped. "Watch the road, not my ass." Kate climbed over the seat and got settled in the seat behind me. I glanced at her through the rearview mirror.

"It's a nice ass."

"Knave."

I smiled. "You're doing so well, Kate. I'm proud of you."

She paused her rummaging to stare at me through the mirror. "They took a friend of mine. She and I were roommates at the shelter."

"They?"

Her breath stuttered as she inhaled. "Shock."

"You know that for sure?" He was out of territory. That carried repercussions. If those problems circled back, Skilletsville would be on the frontline of the bullshit wave.

Her nod was almost too quick to catch. "Whoever it was left a drawing of the Destroyers' emblem surrounded by lightning."

That would be Shock. Or one of his minions. "Didn't know any of 'em had artistic talent."

She scoffed. "They don't."

I laughed. Which was likely inappropriate, considering her friend was likely dead. "If she survives, it might not be…" for the best. I couldn't say it.

Her face was sad, pale despite the makeup. "I know. I'm kind of hoping she tells them everything and gets it over with fast." A frown, and then she returned to rummaging.

My sweatshirt went on first. From under it, she took off the bra, the bustier, and everything on top. Then she shimmied.

"Are your pants off?"

"Keep your eyes on the road."

Bossy. Just the way I liked 'em. "Yes, ma'am." I didn't mean it, but she couldn't hold me to that promise, could she? I mean, naked women had always intrigued me. Kate naked? Sweet Jesus Christ, that would be a marvel. "But you were the one who said you weren't off limits, FYI." I glanced in the mirror again. She paused her struggles to glare at me.

"I want to get to wherever we're going in one piece first."

Damn. If I were a less-controlled man, I'd put the hammer down and speed all the way there. But the main goal was to get Kate to a safe place without attracting attention.

Hours later, we stopped at a quaint little B&B along the Connecticut River. I'd taken a scenic route north to avoid all the congestion, traffic, and anything within a hundred miles of New York City. It was dark, so the red barn they'd converted to lodging looked almost black. The light outside went on as I parked.

"My ass is killing me." Kate rubbed her back and the aforementioned body part. Mine hurt too, but ogling hers magically diminished the ache in favor of the more forward-facing one.

"Can you carry the duffle? I got the other bags." I had a few things in the trunk that I didn't want her prints on.

The owner, a little gray-haired man in his late fifties wearing tie-dyed overalls, met us just inside and worked through the check-in process. I pulled out cash and handed it over.

He looked at it with confusion. "Not often we get cash anymore."

I shrugged. "I didn't bother to check to see if you took cards, so I came prepared. Sorry."

"Don't be," he smiled. "It'll save me the fees for processing. Thanks." He pocketed the cash and showed us to the room in the second-floor loft.

"We have live bands in the main room on Fridays and open jam sessions on Wednesdays. It's mostly a bunch of my friends and such, but you're welcome to join in if you play."

Kate looked at me, so I had to answer her obvious question. "I don't have a musical bone in my body. Sorry, man."

She smiled. "I used to play flute." She shook her head. "That was so long ago I…"

"My wife plays flute, if you want to join along tomorrow, we'd welcome you."

Her eyes met mine. There was panic in them.

I grimaced. We were supposed to be flying under the radar. I made up a lie that would sound convincing. "We're supposed to be at the resort tomorrow. Sorry, babe."

Kate's back was to the owner, and she mouthed a little "thank you" to me before turning and putting on her best smile and schmooze. It was brilliant. I couldn't have charmed him better myself.

"Breakfast is between six-thirty and eight. We put out a little variety." He accepted our gratitude with a smile and exited. We were alone.

Kate stared at the queen-sized bed. "How are we doing this?"

Her arms were clenched tightly around her chest.

It wasn't cold.

I tore the pillows from their nest at the head of the bed and flipped the covers down to expose the fitted sheet. Then I lined most of them up in a neat row down the middle of the bed. "I want you to take the wall side. I'll be by the door in case someone is an asshole. This," I plumped the biggest pillow in the middle, "is your fortress wall. Got it?"

Her nod wasn't convincing.

"I'm here to protect you, even if it is from me, understand?"

Kate's eyes flicked to mine. The seriousness and pain there hurt. Then she brightened and wiped all that anguish from my soul. She was getting better. This was helping.

And by God, she was beautiful, not just in face, but in spirit. I'd meant every word I said in the car. It wasn't blowing smoke up her ass when I said she was gorgeous. To me, she was…

Well, putting it mildly, trouble. And I *loved* trouble.

CHAPTER 8

A B&B on the Connecticut River, New Hampshire—Kate

If you told me two years ago that a biker could be kind and chivalrous, I would've thought you were crazy. Yet, here I was, alone with not just any biker, but one of Shock's "brothers," as he called anyone wearing a Destroyers' emblem on their back, and realizing my animosity toward all Destroyers and bikers in general was unfounded.

Sure, I trusted Jackson. He'd been the one to save me, twice. The first time, I thought it had been Regina who orchestrated my rescue. After all, she'd been the one to show me the phone number.

But then Jackson stepped up again. And I had to question why? Of course, I couldn't mistake the heated looks he swept up and down my body, but this was more than simple attraction. It felt *deeper.*

"Why are you helping me?"

His eyes were too curious, too knowing. They dipped again to where I'd crossed my arms over each other, desperately trying to be strong. "I can sleep on the floor."

"No." My protest came out a bit too needy. Shame washed over me.

"Are you sure?" His question held notes of caution and skepticism.

I cleared my throat. "I am. In fact..." Sometimes actions were louder than words. I tore the line of pillows from the barricade he made. "I can do this."

He picked up a pillow and brushed it off. "You don't *have* to."

There were no words to describe the gift he'd just handed me. By saying what he said, even if he didn't understand the importance of it, he gave me autonomy over my body and my choices, and in doing so, he absolved me of all the guilt and what-ifs I'd secretly whispered to myself for over two years.

"I don't have to; I *want* to." My pulse sped up. For the first time in too long, I did. I wanted. Which made little sense, but I couldn't explain it. Jackson should be everything I was afraid of, and by being that person but also being the person who saved me from a lifetime of torture, he became another person to me—one I desired.

He licked his lips. "Want." His eyes searched my resolve.

I moved the pillows to the edge nearest the door. "My fortress is you. But if you insist on having walls, you are on the inside of them." That was as bravely and boldly as I could say it without terrifying myself.

"I'm honored." He dipped his head as if to bow. Then his grin tipped lopsidedly and his eyes raked me from head to toe. "Very honored." One eyebrow arched to devilish angles.

The urge to fan myself was strong. But I resisted. Instead, I took off the clothes he'd given me. Except for the emerald lace panties he'd handed me in the store. I posed, pushing one leg slightly canted on tiptoe to the right. The stance flashed my inner thigh toward him. Maybe that was wrong of me, but I needed him to see I'd healed. More than healed. I was strong enough to trust him with this very vulnerable piece of me that extended past the physical form.

"Lay down and do that thing with your leg." His voice rasped with a breathy huskiness that hadn't been present earlier. "Show me all of it. I want to see you." His eyes glittered. Whether it was a quirk of refraction or my imagination, but in those pinpricks of light flared red-hot desire.

When I arranged my legs, I opened them wider, baring the darker wetness covering my crotch. His gaze lingered there. Then, carefully and methodically, he removed his clothes. He didn't drop them to the floor in slouched disarray, but took care to lay each piece over the antique chair in the corner.

As he slid his boxers down, he turned slightly. In profile, he resembled an erotic Eros, youthful in grace but possessing all the masculinity and temptation a man should. I couldn't take my eyes off him. Then he climbed over my pillow fortress walls. The heat from his skin clung to the air between us. It begged me to drag him close, but it also scared me. Could I do this? Would something go wrong? Would his closeness trigger a panic attack? I'd had a couple, but never pushed myself into intimacy like this before.

"Your safe word is butterfly."

"I don't need a safe word. We aren't, I mean, I'm not ready for any bondage or…" say it, be accurate. I swallowed. "I don't like S&M."

He had the nerve to laugh. Then he sobered. "Kate, I'd be sho—surprised if you did. *Fuck*. Let's lay it out. Say the fucking name. *Shock* has a reputation for being a sadist. I don't. And not only don't but *won't* go there. But, here's a hard truth, because of him, you need a safe word to tell me when you hit your wall. I can't know where it is. So, that word is *butterfly*. Got it?"

I nodded.

"Say it right now."

"Butterfly."

He blew out a soft exhale. "Gorgeous. Inside and out." Then he lowered his body until we touched. His lips brushed mine.

I kissed him.

His head reared back.

Had I done something wrong? Shock never let me kiss him. I braced for a blow or pain of any sort.

Jackson blinked. "You kissed me."

"I'm sorry." It was a mistake. I'd barely dipped a toe into the concept of sex and fucked up already.

"Don't apologize. Don't ever apologize to me. Ever." His hand cupped my jaw, holding me in place, but not bruisingly so. I searched his eyes as he searched mine. "You kissed me." He said again.

"I did." *Own it, Kate.*

"So beautiful." He leaned in. His breath warmed my skin as he finished those two words. His tongue touched my lips, and I raised my head to seal our mouths together.

And he reveled in it.

In me, in our connection—I was lost, unsure of how this was so arousing and empowering at the same time, but knew that I couldn't stop kissing him. I couldn't bear not making the connection stronger and deeper and, oh God… his hips canted into the cradle of my thighs, and the ridge of his penis pressed against me. I ached to discover if it felt that good inside. Like a flower pointing toward the sun, my body followed his lead and arched to find a connection.

Passion took over my reason, and I shimmied out of the last barrier between us.

The tip of his cock notched home. Instead of pain, I discovered joy. Bliss. But was this too fast? "Jackson?"

He froze. "Butterfly?"

"No." A thousand times no.

At the reassurance, he pushed in as far as he could until he was seated against me. I felt the twitch of connection shudder through him. And my answering clench of muscles caused him to blink. "Kate."

Was it a warning or a question? I didn't know. I nodded, absolving him, answering him.

He stroked out and in again, holding my gaze with his and then mirrored the slow rock of my hips.

"Talk to me," he begged. "Tell me what you need."

Just him. Just this. Oh, and that. I gasped as he rocked into me harder at the apex of a thrust. "That. I like that."

He ground his hips against mine. "This?"

Oh, fuck yes. I couldn't form words. But I also needed more. I needed him to hold me and tell me it was going to be okay, that he was never going to leave me and that I would never have to be scared again. But that was a promise he couldn't make. And I wouldn't beg for something I couldn't have. So I begged him to kiss me again, and again. And then I begged for him to hold me closer and tighter. Thrust harder…

And with a douse of realization, I wanted something more. But did I dare ask?

"You still with me?" His thrusts were almost bruising.

As my silence stretched, he slowed.

"Kate?"

Hesitantly, I met his eyes. "Can you?"

"Anything." His eyes were sincere.

"My neck is sensitive."

"Should I stay away from it or not?"

"Not. Just don't choke me."

His eyes narrowed for a fraction of a second. "I would never do that." He freed a hand and stroked down the ridges of my windpipe with his thumb. He didn't stop when he reached my collarbone. Instead, he changed directions and ran it up to my chin. With another change of directions, it skimmed down again. On the fourth slow sweep, it tickled. I flinched, but also wanted to beg for more. The sensations sparked to my toes and back.

I gasped.

"Found it." His lips touched that point.

More nerves lit up, and I began to quiver. "You did."

He breathed on my skin and ran his teeth along the path of sensitive skin that made me arch off the bed. In response, he pressed our hips together, getting his dick seated deep. And bit down with his teeth.

It wasn't hard, just a nip. But I lit up like a firework. My vagina fluttered, my clit snapping awake like a motor roaring to life, and I moaned. For the very first time, I wordlessly begged the heavens for this sweet torment to never end.

Jackson's thrusts grew harder, a counterpoint to the fluttering and pulsing and shocks sending me into ecstasy. He groaned, too. Our eyes met. "I can't hold…on," he said.

Power. I had power. "Come."

His eyes went wild for a moment. The agony in his guttural cry was one of victory and surrender rolled into one. In it, he cried one word, "Kate."

A trembling took over. I felt it in where he seated between my legs, and in his arms, and all the way down where I'd wrapped my legs around his thighs and locked us together.

He was so beautiful in this moment. Despite the stretched, open-mouthed, stupefied wonder on his face, despite the sweat on his brow or his disheveled hair, he was almost angelic in majestic masculinity.

Then he smiled.

It was easy to love that smile. There was no pain twisting it sideways or artifice crooking his expressive brows. This was the smile of a man who had nothing to hide. I wiped away a trickle of sweat from his brow. "Who needs a safe word?"

Instantly, the smile changed. Some of the pain inside him seeped out and his brow turned crooked again. "There's always round two for that."

"Really?"

"What? You think I'm a one-and-done guy?"

I shrugged. The motion jogged him loose, and a trickle of fluid seeped out in its wake. I froze. "You didn't wear a condom."

His eyes darted between us and back to mine. "Pill?"

"Implant."

That single-word exchange was a small relief.

"I'm clean." Two years and two rounds of antibiotics and I could safely say I was. Or had been up until ten minutes ago.

"Kate, I can see where your mind is going and I swear this is the very first time I've ever forgotten." His face turned red.

I traced the color from his chest to his cheeks. "Are you embarrassed?"

"No."

"You sure about that?" I tapped his warm cheeks.

He rolled off me. "Kate, I'll answer when I get back, don't get mad, okay?"

Don't get mad? I wasn't that much of a novice to know those words usually meant I *should* get angry. I searched for something to clean up with, but he beat me to it, bringing back a dampened towel. Instead of handing it off or letting me fend for myself, he held onto it.

"Let me."

"No."

"Kate." There was a soft warning in the way he spoke my name.

I acquiesced by letting my legs fall open. "How am I supposed to stay angry at you if you have your hand between my legs?"

"You're not supposed to be angry."

"Really?" Sarcasm dripped from the word.

He paused, putting a little pressure on the towel. "Since fourteen, I've only been with hookers. They bring their own condoms. I forgot."

There was too much to unpack in his confession for me to handle. "Fourteen?" I hadn't even kissed a boy yet at that age.

"Fourteen."

"How did you pay her?"

Jackson smiled. "I didn't. Dad did." The smile fell.

Oh. Wow.

Too much to unpack. Except... "How do you know about the towel thing?"

Another smile, this one quirked off to the side and devious. "Mom had the *Joy of Sex* on the coffee table for as long as I can remember."

"Huh."

His eyes twinkled with mirth. "She also had a fully illustrated Kama Sutra. Wanna see how much I remember?"

"You're dangerous."

His grin shot wide. "I try."

CHAPTER 9

Little Deer Island, Maine, July 23, 2008—Jackson

The old fishing town hadn't changed much. Hank, the town manager, had less hair, but the same wobbly hand wave and toothy smile as strangers drove past. I leaned out the open window and sent him a low wave back, with a "Hey-ya, Hank," to let him know I wasn't an out-of-towner, despite the out-of-state plates. Maybe he was just friendly or somehow remembered me, but he waved back strongly with recognition.

I turned right onto a pothole-filled road that cut across the center of the little island. There was a lighthouse at the end of the two-and-a-half mile road, and if you turned south a mile before that, lay one of the most well-kept secrets I knew. The fishing shack was formerly a home. In its time, it was likely filled to the brim with screaming kids, tired lobstermen, and frazzled mothers. But now it sat empty most of the year, except for the rare tourist brave enough, or cheap enough to deal with the antique stove, leaky roof, and overflowing hodgepodge of Maine fishing memorabilia. "Brace yourself," I warned Kate, "it ain't pretty."

I'd left the care of the property with the neighbor. She was a cantankerous witch, who squatted on one of the best ocean views I'd ever seen. There was a closer neighbor on this little dirt road, and he was the island's version of police. Not that he did much more than settle dock access squabbles or arrest the occasional drunk tourist. Because of that, he was also one of the few badge-wearing assholes I actually liked.

The door screeched on its hinges. The place smelled musty and kind of fishy. It looked much worse than I remembered. "Shit."

"Who owns this?" Kate eyed the three-quarters of a century-old tongue-and-groove walls and the piles of yellowed magazines.

"Technically or legally?"

She shot me a look that was easy to interpret as, "I'm going to murder you, Jackson."

"Technically, the island nature preserve. But legally? A corporation that maintains the upkeep of the buildings." Not that it truly maintained anything. It paid Crystal Dawn Hunnebaker a stipend to make sure the old shack didn't fall down. And Crystal Dawn didn't do repairs. She bitched for more money every year. Then, promptly spent that money on pot, not upkeep. I was thinking of firing her.

"Who owns the corporation?"

"Technically or legally?"

She threw up her hands. "I can't with you!"

"Maybe after I work my tongue up your pussy again, you will?"

That earned me a glare.

"Aw come on, you liked it." She did. You can't fake moans like that.

Kate sighed. "If the corporation can be traced back to you, I'm fucked, and not like last night. It would be in ways I wouldn't enjoy, okay?"

"It won't be."

This time, the sadness and the doubt in her eyes spoke to a much longer, more complex statement than was decipherable. But I felt it. Deep in my gut, I knew the fears she was trying to hide from me by obscuring it with anger.

And that was another thing. I wanted to dig deeper and find out more about her and the secrets she locked behind silent walls.

"How do you know it won't be traced to you?"

"Because, technically, John Hardy, the local sheriff, owns the company, along with your new landlord down the road." I pointed to the darkening trail downhill toward the cove. "John's is that farmhouse next door. Crystal's house is about seven hundred yards away."

"Crystal?" Her eyes narrowed.

"Crystal Dawn. A former hooker Mom helped out. She's a bit eccentric."

"How?"

"She's Wiccan and believes all sorts of stuff like the occult. In summer, she does local demonstrations, that sort of thing." Last time I was here, I caught her dancing naked in the trees. Should I warn Kate about that? *Naw. She'd find out sooner or later.*

"That's not eccentric."

Wait until you meet her. I kept that to myself. "She smokes a lot of pot."

That got her attention. "Who does she buy from?" Her posture stiffened, which was understandable. The Destroyers moved drugs. A lot of drugs.

"A local guy, he's a lobster fisherman with a grow lab in his basement. He's got a select clientele, John being one of them and Crystal being the other, so you're good."

"What's the catch?" She motioned to the house.

I stared at the room. The old place was an eyesore inside and out. "Keep the walls up. That's all. There's a fund for repairs, and Crystal gets a stipend for that, but I'll work something out with John that it becomes rent, and her role is landlord or some shit." I snapped my fingers. "One catch, no major upgrades, additions, or renovations. The building is historic, believe it or not, and needs to comply with the historic preservation rules. That could get tricky and expensive."

Kate scanned my face for lies. There weren't any to be found, but she spent so long doing it that I wanted to squirm. I continued so the silence would end. "There are jobs during tourist season. Most pay cash. Stockpile as much as you can during the summer months, and live frugally in winter. It's the best I can do." I wanted to tack on "sorry" at the end, but refrained.

"It will be enough. Thank you."

On the tip of my tongue were the words, "Don't thank me until you're safe," but honestly? This was the safest place I knew. John was a good man. He looked after the residents here like they were family. Hell, better than family. And Crystal? Despite the oddities, she was a friend. One of the first women I fell in love with outside of my mother. And in her day, she had been like a sister or an aunt to me when push came to shove. Three people knew where she lit off to when her pimp almost killed her. My father, who killed that asshole, my mother, who loved Crystal like a sister, and me. Dad was dead. Mom was completely removed from my current life; and my role in Kate's disappearance would get me killed, so there was no way I'd talk. My biggest regret would be never seeing the place again. I'd have to find another hidey hole to run to if the law ever caught up with me.

"Are you leaving tomorrow?" Kate asked.

"I should. I'll introduce you to John and Crystal, then head out."

The fear in her eyes grew.

"I swear by them. On my life." Saying that made me doubt. What if John had changed? What if Crystal was crazier?

"We have one more night." She picked at the stray threads popping up from the couch where it was worn through. Her head tilted as the devious and obvious flirtation flickered in that glance. But her cheeks flushed to a brilliant rose.

Oh. Sometimes I was a clueless son of a bitch.

She wasn't afraid; she was… something else. "If I'm not mistaken, there are two beds upstairs."

"We only need one."

Thank-fucking-God. I motioned to the stairs, but stopped, remembering the quirks of the place. "Don't drink the water out of the tap; it's from a cistern, and flushing is a bit tricky." I pointed to the bathroom under the stairs.

"That's… rustic. Where's the tub?"

Oh shit. "This way." I motioned to the kitchen. There was an old round barrel half in the kitchen with a hose that went from the sink to the tub. Another hose ran out the bottom where there was a crude spigot that clamped the contraption shut. The set up was simple. Turn the water heater on, wait two hours, fill the tub halfway, then uncoil the drain hose and run it out the back door when you were done.

"You've got to be kidding me."

I was beginning to regret this. "You had more at that shelter, didn't you?"

A scrunched expression of disgust flashed across her face. "At least I don't have to share this. Right? I don't have to share this, do I?"

"It's all yours." The sum extent of my wealth so far, except for the seed cash I'd dipped into hard for this trip.

She searched the room. There was a fairly new refrigerator, a freezer, a sink, the tub, and various shelves with all sorts of tins, containers, and cans. Then, her gaze landed on the stove. "Whoa, that's old."

"Really easy to use. Wood's outside. Load up the bottom, here," I pointed at the belly next to the oven drawers, "the heat goes up to the burner plates, or you open up the holes for higher heat. Smoke goes out the vent, and on this side, you can keep stuff warm or cook in the drawers."

"How do you know what temperature it is?"

You didn't. I shrugged. "Never used the oven. You might want to check for mice before you fire it up."

"Mice?"

Something between a groan and a squeak escaped my throat. "That's why everything stays in tins or sealed containers. Don't leave anything out."

Her hands went to her face and then she rubbed the tension from her jaw and moved farther back to linger on her nape.

"Let me." I spun her until her back was to me, then worked the knots out of her shoulders. "I hope you realize I'm not rich. I can't give you a mansion or much of anything at all."

She stopped me by turning quickly and covering my mouth. "I don't expect anything from you. You have been more than generous, and I don't deserve it."

It was my turn to cover her mouth and tell her she was absolutely wrong. "Wrong. What you didn't deserve, you escaped two years ago. Now? I *wish* I could give you more."

Kate lifted to her toes and pulled my face close to hers. "Thank you." Then her lips hit mine, and I forgot we were arguing. The closest thing to it was the way our tongues tangled. She made a noise that hummed in my mouth. I turned us to the stairs that cut the building in half. But in order to get up them, I had to break the kiss.

It was almost too difficult to do. I wanted to keep kissing her forever. But we were already at the unbuttoning stage, and I'd be damned if I took her on that filthy old couch. When I squeezed her ass hard, she gasped. I took that moment to break contact with her mouth. "Upstairs. Watch your head."

She didn't have to worry about hitting her head as much as I did. The sloped ceiling angled sharply at the end of the staircase. Walk more than one step on the landing and it entered the danger zone for me. Or was that the antique bed with barely room for both of us on it?

Kate took her shirt off as I shucked my jeans and dug out a condom. The non-perishables in the car could wait; this couldn't. I had a deadline to meet, or else I'd expose the connection here. Today, maybe tomorrow, I could indulge myself with her fair skin, the beauty of her sighs, and the soft way her smile filtered through her eyes after the pinnacle of ecstasy we somehow managed to reach together.

In that space, where breathing slowed and reality was an ambiguous thing, I found something I never had. It scared me. Thrilled me. Devastated me. This art we made was as fleeting as blowing on a dandelion puff. One minute whole, and in the next breath, a wish or a dream. And in its wake, the devastation of touching an intangible something that was flawless.

But I couldn't stop picking up another one and whispering that desire into my heart. Holding my breath and letting the gust of passion flow in kisses and sweat. Puffing again and again, gripping the last dregs of that desperation until the seeds floated away.

I traced her skin. My soul ached to tell her how I felt. But my words would kill her. That, I vowed, would never happen.

"I'm going to do whatever it takes to keep you safe, Kate."

Her eyes met mine. Hope lingered there. "Are you staying?"

No. "I can't. Shock will notice. Right now, I've got an alibi. But I'm going to have to leave soon. And once I'm gone, I can't come back. Ever." I worried about her. "Are you going to be okay?" Without me. Will you recover from the loss? Or would I?

Her fingers tangled in my hair. And she stunned me. "Are you?" They tightened slightly to shake some sense into my foolishness.

Should I be honest? I'd been altered by her. The man I was a month ago, or two years ago, was not the same one I was in this bed. Going back to that life revolted me.

But it was the only way I could protect her, so I lied. "I'll be just fine, babe."

CHAPTER 10

July 23, 2008—Kate

Jackson's fingers tightened on my hips. Not painfully, but hard enough that I felt the tremors he tried to hide. He'd stayed with me for three days. But this morning, the urgency in our love-making and the way his eyes scanned the horizon made me nervous. "Are you sure you'll be okay?"

"I'll be fine." I was lying, but he needed to hear those falsehoods. I could be strong, so he'd be safe. I knew there was a huge possibility that Shock would find me despite Jackson's plots. That didn't scare me as much as what would happen to him if he didn't leave. "You can go. I'm good." He'd introduced me to Crystal, who lived a half mile down the road. And to the local sheriff who lived literally next door. In fact, John stood on his front steps, coffee in hand, watching the road.

Perhaps he picked up on Jackson's nervousness, or perhaps he was just nosy that way. It was strange how much of a contrast this little island was from Pittsburgh. I'd lived my entire life in a city, never noticing how much people ignored your business. Until I needed help. Then that deliberate blindness became a nightmare.

Here? The connectivity was subtle. Like drinking coffee on your front steps. Or knowing everyone's first and last names. Where they lived. Whether they were born in this county or were from "away"—as they put it. Few of the latter group remained during the winter. Only three hundred residents remained on this island once the icy storms rolled in. On the bigger island, a mere thousand braced nature's worst. The bustle of the summer tourist season would vanish, and having people to count on like Crystal and John was necessary. The whole island was made up of brave, unselfish folks like that.

"If you have trouble with the generator or the—"

I cut Jackson off. "I'll talk to John. Right John?" I raised my voice, so he'd hear. He smiled and raised a friendly hand to wave. Agreeing without knowing what he was agreeing to—but that didn't matter with him. He'd do what was requested of him. It was comforting and scary at the same time.

Jackson kicked a ridge of gravel. "I can't come back."

"I know."

"You can't contact me." This was goodbye. His hands shook as he peeled them from me. "They'll kill me if they find out about this."

"I know." He'd whispered more than once how betraying a brother earned him a death sentence. Sure, bikers stole each other's women occasionally. Usually, it reconciled with a fist fight or maybe a long-standing grudge. But by doing what he did behind a chapter president's back and hiding me here, Jackson broke a code they lived by. Brothers trusted brothers. Even when they weren't trustworthy at all. It was a messed up and brutal life that I'd seen the ugliest side of. But outright betrayal? Deceit, to the extent Jackson would have to maintain, was an insult to all of them. "I'm fine."

His eyes raked my figure from head to toe. "Damn straight." One eyebrow quirked up into a crooked arch, and his mouth twisted into a smirk.

It fell, but before it could disappear entirely, he'd turned to go. He barely looked at me or John before backing onto the road and pointing the car toward the outside world.

Dust settled in his wake. Insects buzzed in the grass. A ways out, a boat horn echoed against the bluffs, signaling their departure from the harbor. A tourist, most likely. The fishermen had been up for hours already. I'd tuned to the life here. I had to; it was my home now.

John coughed once. "Morning." He waved again and disappeared into his house. Assured that I knew he was watching out but leaving me to my peace.

And a run-down shack that needed work.

I eyed the ugly shelves. "You're on my list."

But first was scrubbing the dated linoleum in the kitchen. As I dumped the dirty water outside, Crystal pulled into the driveway. She was on her way to her shop on the big island and asked, "Do you need me to pick up anything for you?"

"A job?" I joked. There were some to be had, mostly tourist-related, but nothing permanent. That, and I either had to depend on rides or find one within walking distance.

She stared at the rubber gloves on my hands. "You're cleaning?"

I nodded.

"Well. I *hate* that part of the job. You're hired. I'd gladly give you the fees for the next two months, and if you get done with this place sooner than that, it'll be a miracle. I want updates, and I'll pick up whatever groceries and supplies you need. Make a list."

"That's…"

"I was where you are. It's not easy finding an employer who doesn't ask for your social security number."

My breath caught. I hadn't thought that far ahead yet. Instead of focusing inward, I tried to lie to myself by asking, "But you got out, right?" Maybe I was reaching for hope.

Crystal went still. "If you call running a psychic shop on an island near the ass end of nowhere getting out? Yeah."

That sounded like paradise, but I wouldn't know the first thing about it. My thoughts resurfaced the fear I felt when Cara was taken. "I think I can't run a shop. Or be in public, yet."

My words caused Crystal's brow to furrow. "How bad was it?"

Bad. There weren't words to describe some of it. "Even after two years, he's got his club looking for me."

She thought for a moment. "Jackson needs to kill him."

"He can't."

"Would it start a war?"

"No."

Crystal got out of the car and met me on the steps. "I thought he, your abuser, was from a club?"

"*The* club," I clarified.

Her mouth fell open. "Oh." It was strange how she immediately scanned the trees surrounding us as if she expected an attack at any moment.

I took a leap of faith. If Jackson trusted these people with a secret that could kill him, then I had no reason not to either. "My h-h-husband is the president of the Pittsburgh chapter."

Her eyes snapped to mine. "Two years?" The thoughts racing through her mind echoed in the quick darting of her eyes and the myriad shifts in her face. "Did you ever see anything that could implicate him?"

"Aside from nearly murdering me, and gang rape, and drug deals?" That came out sarcastically. I shored up my emotions. "I'm sure I have."

"He'll want to stay married to you, so you can't testify."

That's where I'd gone wrong. It made sense now. Just disappearing was one thing; divorcing him was another. He didn't want me back. He wanted me dead. But the proceedings never happened. Perhaps if I stayed hidden, stayed quiet, and never got that divorce, he'd forget about me. "After I'm done fixing this place up, what kind of job could I get?"

She smiled. "By then, it will be Fall. There's a festival at the shop I need help with, and after the equinox and Samhain, there's more work, especially cleaning. Jackson's not the only person paying me to watch their place. If I had help, I could expand."

That was a plan. I had plans. I searched the quiet trees and empty road for hope and discovered that it was right here on my doorstep. "Thank you."

"Don't thank me yet."

Funny how her words echoed Jackson's.

* * *

Three months later, Crystal inspected my latest project and then commented on the bombshell I'd dropped on her. "Are you *sure* you want to live without running water for a month?"

"These pipes need to be redone, and you never know when it might freeze."

She sent me an admonishing glare. "You sound like one of them."

"Who?" I sanded the drywall in my bedroom.

"The locals. Always harping on winter coming."

"It is."

"It's October."

"Which leads to November, and … winter." I shuddered, my imagination trying to picture what the locals called "harsh." Probably ten-foot drifts and icebergs crashing into the shore. In other words, cold as fuck.

Her head shook. She stared at me for a full minute as I worked.

"If you're going to be here, sand." I handed her the block with 220 grit paper wrapped around it.

"I don't do hard labor."

She was lying. I'd come to realize she always had work somewhere. Whether it was running her store, delivering groceries to shut-ins, or maintaining the twenty, yes, twenty vacation houses on this and two other islands, she had more work than both of us could handle, which was great because it was much better than working a seafood shack on the shore for minimum wage. I'd made enough in the last month to pay a contractor to build a real bathroom in the place.

It even covered the extra fees that kept the building's historical charm without the inconvenience of historical living. But it also uncovered the issues with the well and pipes that forced me to go back to the cistern system. And like hell was I going to bathe in the kitchen all winter when I was so close to using my new bathroom.

"Indulge me." I pushed the bundle into her hand.

Crystal reluctantly scraped the block over a patch near the door. "You're going to help me with the Halloween festival, right?"

"Absolutely." Despite my upbeat answer, my heart rate picked up. "How big are the crowds?"

"Not as big as the lobster festival, and you did fine then."

I froze. "You noticed?"

"That you're a recluse with men issues. Yes."

"I don't have men issues." Just one man.

"You practically dove under the table when those bikers walked in."

They were bikers. Just not the outlaw kind. "They were wearing leather coats." I doubled my sanding speed to make up for the time lost.

Crystal sent me a look of pity. "They had HOG patches."

Harley Owners Group, HOG, was the civilian equivalent of bad-ass with about as much bad in that designation as a kitten. "I'm being careful."

She set the sanding block down and put a hand on my arm. "You're hiding."

I looked around the house pointedly. "Duh."

"And you're missing out on life."

Next, she'd ask me to smoke pot with her or something. "I'm not missing out on anything."

"Jeffery asked about you."

Said man was the owner of a seaside restaurant. He had kind eyes, but thick eyebrows. I didn't trust him because of that. "So?"

"You might want to go out on a date or something."

The thought made me queasy. A lot of things did. "No."

Crystal tried to infuse compassion into her expression, but I saw some pity in there, too. She proved me right when she finally said, "He's gone."

She and I both knew who she was talking about. "Obviously."

"And he's not coming back."

There it was. Spoken out loud in a room I was stripping, rebuilding, and completely altering because sleeping in it the way it was reminded me of Jackson. So did the kitchen and that damn tub. And the living room… stairs, and face it, this whole island. I couldn't look at the bay or the bridge and not wonder how it would be if he were beside me. I had "it" bad. It being obsessive lust disguised as passion and probably love. Or, at the very least, whatever was the opposite of a trauma bond.

I gestured to the room. "Good. Because I looked up his bullshit story about this being a historic property, and it isn't. I'm gutting this place one room at a time."

My dearest and currently only friend shook her head. "You're nesting."

"What?!"

It shouldn't have come out as a shriek. Nesting was something… No. I wasn't; I couldn't be. We'd used condoms, mostly, and I had an implant.

"When was your last period?"

"No." I waved my hands in front of me to ward off what she was implying.

"Kate," she put a warning note into her voice. "You've been sick every morning for the last two weeks, and you can't stand clams."

"That's not surprising since I puked up that bowl of chowder. Why would I like something that tried to kill me? Besides, I have an implant."

She sat on her heels. Puzzlement caused her face to twist into a frown. "How old is it?"

I thought back with some trepidation. "Four years, in August."

"Sweetie, it's October."

I knew that.

"You may want to get it removed and get tested."

"No."

"Kate, as your friend and as the person who will have to run your dumb ass to the hospital, you need to get checked out."

"I can't." That was the biggest thing holding me back from acknowledging what I didn't want to face. "If I use my real name, my social security number, or ID, he'll find me." My voice shook. My hands shook. My whole body shook. And the crackers I'd eaten for breakfast started back up my throat as clumpy acid. I shoved Crystal out of the way and ran down the stairs, skidding on the third to the last one that sloped downward, and catching myself on the landing before twisting around the newel post and racing to the bathroom. I tried to expel my soul through my mouth for a good five minutes straight, the dry heaves catching so bad that every smell from the moldy tile to the piney sap on the boards made my head spin.

Crystal held my hair away from the bowl. "You need to go in. We'll use the traveling nurse clinic on the island. She'll keep your name out of the records."

My breathing was heavy. "I can't run anymore."

"I know. You won't have to. We'll keep you safe."

"You got a mouse in your pocket?"

She smiled. "Ye of little faith. Us transplants stick together, didn't you know that? We might not be true Mainers, but when push comes to shove, we're just as ornery and insular." Crystal wetted a washcloth and wiped my face like I was a child.

A child, about to have a child of my own. What the hell was I going to do?

CHAPTER 11

Upstate New York, July 27, 2008—Jackson

I hit the Finger Lakes region at midnight. The cabin at about three in the morning. The dealer I'd dubbed "James Metfield" answered the door with a gun in his hand. He should have used it. But when he saw it was me, his shoulders relaxed, and he let the thirty-eight drop to his side. "It's you. What the fuck, man? I thought you said Thursday."

"I got delayed."

"I bet you found some hot chick and was banging the shit out of her, right?" He laughed and jabbed me in the arm with his elbow.

The truth could set you free, right? "She was smoking hot. I think I'm in love." It felt wrong to think of Kate right now. Already, I'd forgotten the smell of her hair.

James, not his real name, led me into the fishing cabin. What was it with me and properties that looked like shit? At least I didn't own this one. And the rental was under a fake name, and a face behind it that wasn't mine. Maybe someday in the distant future someone would connect his face to this place, but that was part of the plan. "You ready?"

"Fuck man, when you said pretend you're me, I didn't expect to like it so much. I could fish my life away."

What an unexpectedly *convenient* thing to say. "Did you do any night fishing?"

"Night fishing?" He shot me a look that clearly thought I was crazy.

"Yeah, about a half hour before dawn, the really big boys bite." I wasn't lying.

"No shit?" He was drunk. Evidence of his latest binge littered all over the cabin. Beer bottles on every flat surface. A bottle of whisky sat on the counter, almost gone. Missing lines of coke were outlined in the residue on the mirror that lay flat on the table. The little TV in the corner blared porn.

There were black panties on the easy chair. I picked them up and let them dangle from my finger. "You had guests?"

"Don't get mad at me. I went to the local strip bar. I picked up this chick. You'd do the same if you'd have seen her tits. She never even asked my name. Tits, man."

"How big?" I wasn't interested; I was just biding time.

He mimed the size.

I nodded with appreciation. "Big."

James snapped his fingers. "Speaking of big, let's do that. Biggest I caught all week was maybe a ten-inch trout."

"Fuck, man, that's smaller than my dick."

"Bullshit. You're such a liar, Jackson."

"Yeah, that's me. Come on." I swept up the poles and led him to the boat tied to the dock. While he busied himself with getting it loaded with a fresh case of beer and a cooler of ice, I went to the rental car. I pulled out a duffle from the trunk. The one I'd put in there over a week ago.

I set it under the seat of the boat and helped James push off from the dock.

"We forgot the running lights."

I scoffed. "This hour of the morning, no one's going to care. Besides, we'll keep to the shallows, go over there to that point." I knew this lake. It wasn't shallow there at all. Locals sometimes used the cliffs to dive from. But dumb James didn't know that. I rowed for a spell, pausing in open water, just past the point where the weedy shoreline dipped drastically from about twenty feet to over seventy. "Fuck. Rowing sucks."

"You're the one who didn't want to use the trolling motor." James's laugh echoed in the night.

It pissed me off. "Grab me a beer."

He had to turn around to reach it. The little boat rocked with the motion. I mirrored the momentum with my body, becoming one with the boat.

"Hey, stop rocking. You're going to tip us over." He braced on the gunwales, turning fish belly pale.

I let the boat settle. "Switch places with me. I'm tired of rowing."

"Fuck you."

He forgot who he was talking to.

"Switch places." It wasn't a request. And I made certain he heard it wasn't.

"Just use the motor."

"You owe," I reminded him.

His mouth worked. "You said the debt would be paid if I just hung out here and used that credit card you gave me. I showed my face around the town like you asked."

"That was *my* debt. Now let's talk about the one you have with Nonno."

He glanced around, realizing maybe for the first time how isolated we were, and how far out we'd drifted. "You sure you want to do this?"

He was funny. "It ain't like *that*. We're just talking. And fishing. Hand me a beer."

Warily, he shifted positions again.

No sooner than his back was turned, I struck hard. The boat rocked but didn't tip nearly far enough to dump us in. Which gave me time to cut off his life jacket and tie his leg to the duffle bag I'd put under the seat.

To drown a man, you needed two things. First and foremost was the will to kill. Second, a moonless night, a lake deep enough, and enough weight to sink the body. Oh, and a knife to open up the gut so gases in the stomach didn't build up and push the body back to the surface.

If the water was deep and cold enough, at a certain point, the corpse would sink and never resurface. The density of the water overcame the buoyancy of the corpse. But most freshwater lakes simply didn't have that perfect combination. This one did.

I shoved poor James's body over the edge. He was likely still alive, but knocked out so hard, filleting his body didn't even produce a scream. I turned on the little trolling motor and pulled back up to the dock. Blood coated the bottom of the boat, the cooler, the fishing poles, and my hands. I rinsed them off in the water and cracked the drain plug. Then, I rigged the trolling motor to drive straight toward the center of the lake. It veered after a few feet, barely making it to open water before the whole thing swamped. The tiny electric motor sparked out with barely a sputter.

In less than a thought, there was nothing. Not even a wake or the lapping of waves. The night had hit that sweet spot where the world held its breath as it waited for the dawn to get its ass in gear. An early bird cheeped twice. Soon, a bullfrog echoed it. Then another cheep from the treeline signaled the world was about to rev into gear. I showered in the cabin, cleaned the drain with the supplies under the cabin sink, and drove away from the dawn breaking over the horizon.

I hit a motel in Buffalo at eight. Slept for a good nine hours and then ate a hearty dinner at a local place where the waitresses dressed in skimpy little skirts and the owners were assholes like me.

Nonno joined me as I sipped a whiskey and admired the night's opening act.

"You're late."

"He ran."

Nonno frowned. "I thought you said you could take care of it."

"I did." I dug out one of those cheap digital cameras and showed Nonno the photo I'd snapped of the dearly departed "James Metfield," otherwise known on the street as "Tercel Timmy." He was a two-bit coke dealer with a bald patch and a big ass mouth. He'd flipped a dime on more than one dealer in his career and was rumored to have turned State's evidence on the local Destroyers.

Of course, he claimed those stories weren't true, and swore he'd make amends, but that didn't matter anymore.

Because he was fish food.

"Huh. Better get rid of that."

No shit. I tucked the device back into my pocket.

"Back in the day, your father was a good man."

I sent Nonno a side-eye. My father taught me every bad thing I knew, including how to make bodies disappear. "Yeah?"

His eyes traced the movements of the stripper on stage. "He never fucked around or missed a deadline."

"I didn't miss it."

"Shock says his wife is missing."

I snorted. "Which wife?" He'd replaced Kate almost as soon as she disappeared for the first time. Rumor had it the current squeeze was a hot little Puerto Rican chick.

Nonno slanted his gaze at me. "*The* wife."

I screwed up my face, hoping it looked like confusion. "Didn't that one go missing like… two years ago?"

His gaze lingered on me too long.

I held my hands up to nudge him into an answer. "Well?"

"She resurfaced. Jersey, he says. He's looking eastward to see how she slipped his net."

A little huff came out. Whether it was the right thing or not, I couldn't help it. "East, huh? He stopped by Skilletsville with that girl once. That's the night his *wife* puked on his shoes." I danced around Nonno's unspoken accusation. "She was a sack of trouble."

He squinted at me. "If I recall, you like trouble."

I tsked. "Not like that. I like good trouble, not bad." I pointed to the stripper, who was upside down on the pole. "That's good trouble."

It was a brilliant distraction and broke Nonno's hard stare. "She's available."

My heart skipped. But I plastered a shit-eating grin on, anyway. "Really? How much?"

I licked my lips, hoping he'd name an outrageous amount, so I'd have to beg off. I'd done this job as a "favor" to Nonno, which meant I had to be strapped for cash.

"Consider it a perk of a job well done, even if it took longer than expected." He slapped my back and motioned the girl over.

She made the mistake of looking around the audience rather than coming directly after being called, and Nonno turned his angry glare toward her. She faked a grin and shimmied her ass off-stage to swagger over to the private table.

I wiped any traces of food from the scruff on my face and smiled, acting as if she was a rare treat. Because, face it, she was. Nonno liked cash. He hated giving stuff away for free. Even getting road money to off a narc for him was like pulling teeth. But it was a good thing I'd been watching the nearby chapters for holes to exploit. Because when Kate asked for help, it took just a few days to arrange a hit, figure out an escape plan, and trick Nonno into letting me take the job. "That's a pretty bonus. But…"

His sharp glance skewered me.

Think fast. "…I was hoping for a promotion, not pussy. No offense, baby, but I can get gash any time I want. Maybe not as fine as yours, but…" I grinned at her with one eyebrow tipping an appreciative nod of approval her way. I let my eyes linger on her crotch for long enough that Nonno's death glare fizzled.

"You keep doing good work, I'll think about it. Meanwhile, *take* what you're given." His hand landed heavily on my shoulder as he used it to stand up. Before he let go of me, he leaned over, squeezing hard, and whispered in my ear, "And stay away from what is *not*."

Aha. That deserved a true One-Eyed Jack sneer. The kind that started fights and make the guilty damn uncomfortable. "Nonno?"

He turned, his attention piqued, and his hand curled into a fist. "Yeah?"

"I'm One-Eyed Jack's son. I'll take anything that's not nailed down." I held his eyes and let some of the violence I'd grown up with shine through. "Including roles you need *outside* help with." I licked my lips again, showing him I was hungry for power. Maybe too hungry.

Then again, I had to convince Nonno that we were talking about two different things here. On my side of the conversation, it went like this. *"I want to be president of my own chapter. And I will kill anyone and anything that stands in the way of that. You'll reward me for being your dog. Got it?"*

On Nonno's side, he was silently warning me not to make waves. To play the good biker brother and keep the peace internally. What that told me was that he was a scared man. One who was almost as hungry as I was but also one who had to be much more cautious. He wasn't the top dog yet.

I sent him a nod to tell him that I heard his fear loud and clear, but also that I could be counted on to do the hard thing when it mattered, maybe even help him become top dog. Because he was a coward with a lot to lose. I wasn't. I was a dead man with a lot of life to pack in the span between now and a knife to the back, and I wasn't going to let anyone cow me into submission when there was too much I desired. "Don't forget that." *And don't forget me.*

"Take what you're given. Faye? Make sure he takes."

Damn. Maybe Nonno wasn't as cautious as I thought. Or maybe I'd betrayed myself somewhere in that exchange. I didn't think I had, but any slip now would put the cross hairs on me. Somehow, Nonno knew I had secrets. And one of them was Kate. I'd have to do a better job of acting to prove she meant nothing to me and that Shock was delusional.

Nonno had done me a favor by walking away. He'd given me just the alibi I needed to prove Shock wrong about me. I'd do whatever it took to show the world that women meant nothing to me. That the rumors Shock was spreading were baseless.

"So, Faye, is it? How fine is that pussy of yours? Care to show me?"

CHAPTER 12

Maine, October 21, 2008—Kate

Pregnant. Phrases like *one in a thousand* and *limited effectiveness* swam in my head. One in particular stood out. "Certain depression and anxiety medications can interfere with your birth control." Damn Shock all to hell for getting in my head after over a year of work. No sooner than I filed for divorce, the nightmares came back. Along with it, the need to return to medication.

And because of that, and finally feeling safe with Jackson, I was in this situation.

Even scared out of my mind, alone, and waiting for Crystal to come back to pick me up, I had one hand over my lower stomach as if to protect the potential human in there from what was to come.

It. Him? Her? I wouldn't know for a while. Would they look like Jackson or me? Was this even real? My breathing was shallow, but slow. Paced in such a way that the panic was a low ebb of waves like a gentle shoreline. My freakout was filed away as happening, yet I answered questions, knowing underneath it all I wasn't there. I was shut away, maundering in that limbo between reality and terror. Crystal pulled up in her truck.

Where would she put the car seat?

"You okay?" She helped me in, instinctively knowing there was something wrong with me.

"You're right."

She waited for me to say more. To confirm a fear no woman isolated and near penniless wanted to have. I could barely take care of myself; how would this work?

"Should I be sorry about that?" The words were harsh, almost accusing.

They shocked me out of the panic and fear into anger. "No. It's my own damn fault."

She nodded sharply. "Technically, both of your damn faults."

I glared at her.

"It takes at least two, you know. Are you going to tell him?"

I couldn't. Even if it was the right thing to do, he'd explicitly warned me to never contact him again. "I'm not supposed to contact him."

"Bullshit. He'll want to know."

"You know this how?"

She shifted the truck into gear and began the slow trip back to the island. Just before the bridge, she admitted one of her secrets. "His father, One-Eyed Jack, was the kind of man who tried very hard not to get any of his girls pregnant. But was one hundred percent vested as soon as possible. Only Jackson survived to be born, though."

That was... horrific. "His father was—"

"A biker, a pimp, one of the girls' biggest customers. And, overall not a bad man, despite all the murder and shit."

I blinked, not believing my ears. "Wait a minute, Jack's son... Jackson? Oh my fucking God, I don't even know his real name. Damn it." He'd made up names so easily. Bill, James... Ugh.

Crystal was kind enough to keep her laughter silent. But her shaking shoulders gave her away.

"What is his real name?"

She sighed. "Honestly? I don't even know if his mother remembers it. Everyone's called him Jackson since the day he was born. One look at him, right out of the womb and that damn eyebrow was right there staring everyone in the face."

I knew exactly what she meant. I'd traced it one night, marveling at the clean angles of it. "Not even a hint?"

"Nist. That's his last name. Like list with an N. Not many of them around."

That tidbit got filed away. "Was his father Jack or John?"

"John. John Edward Nist. John named him James. James Campbell Nist."

More trivia to bury deep inside should I ever need to dig it up. I labeled that with "Break glass in case of emergency."

"You're keeping it, ain't ya?"

At first, I didn't move, but I nodded slowly as it sunk in. If I could get angry at Crystal for being sharp with me, I had enough fight in me to see this to my grave. No matter how long it took, this child would know my love, the love of this tight-knit community, and maybe grow up to be… I pondered over that. Would I be the kind of parent who pushed her—wait, him, they, them— face it, I wanted a boy, but knew my life and luck would make it a girl. So, her. Would I push her to be something she didn't know whether she wanted to be that person, or would I let her discover it on her own?

I never wanted to be the person I'd been. My father pushed me into it. That was quite enough to solidify my plan. *She'd* do whatever she wanted, when *she* wanted, and get one hundred percent support from me no matter what.

"You're thinking awful hard over there."

For that, Crystal got a smile. "Is it better, as a parent, to try to mold a child into what they can be or let them be who they want to be?"

"I'm team let them be who they want."

"I think I am, too."

She had to concentrate on the bridge traffic, so she was silent for a minute. That continued as we weaved through the little Main Street of the town at the bridge's feet. Crystal waved at the mayor. I did, too, sending him a cheery "Hi, Hank" as we passed. He smiled and waved back, leaning a bit forward from his perch outside the local ice cream shop. One day my daughter would hang out there. And maybe Hank would still be mayor.

"Wait til he hits his teen years; you'll regret that decision."

"What if it's a girl?"

"God help us all. A girl with One-Eyed Jack's blood. Poor kid. She'll be running this town by age twelve."

It wasn't difficult to imagine that.

"It's a good thing you live right next door to the sheriff. He'll know where to drop her off when she gets in trouble."

The sly way Crystal smiled at me was annoying. But the worst part of it was that I could also picture the scenario she conjured up. "Okay, maybe not team freedom."

"Balance, like nature. Find the right blend of discipline and love and freedom with boundaries; she'll be fine."

She. My hand stroked my stomach.

I happily pictured that for a minute or two, but Crystal was too quiet. "What's wrong with you?"

She stopped outside my house-shack. "Better wait to tell him. Just in case it doesn't make it."

Oh.

We sat there, each weighing the risks, choices, life, death, and all that lies in between. "Okay."

I hopped out of the truck and planned the next remodel. Winter would be here soon. And then… April.

Too soon, it was a capricious, nasty, tricky spring in Maine. Fifty degrees one minute, snowing the next. Icy, sunny, spitting rain and freezing cold, or almost balmy. I'd finished remodeling everything but the living room. In the gut of the bathroom, the bones for a decent kitchen were born, and I had a real tub with hot and cold running water, but still relied on the wood stove in the living room. Which meant keeping the haphazard bookshelves, antique paneling, and ratty carpet until I could find time and energy to rip everything up.

But mostly, I was just too cumbersome to do more than fix the petty stuff within reach. I couldn't even accompany Crystal to check on the mansions near the lighthouse. Doctor's orders. Or in this instance, traveling nurse's orders. I was due any day now, and had been since April 15th.

Zoe, the baby girl in my womb, was alarmingly big, kicking hard, and taking her sweet time in dropping. But last week, everything shifted and changed and now it was a struggle to waddle. Or sit. Or stand. Or pee. Or not pee.

"I hate your father right now," I told the empty house and the child who wouldn't understand. But in an odd way, or maybe because Zoe was Zoe, she took that as a cue to kick.

"Good one. Now I have to pee again." Or change clothes. I stuck my hand between my legs to hold the water in. But there was too much. And a bit of pink.

"Shit. Shit-shit-shit-shit-SHIT." That wasn't pee.

My instinct was to call Crystal, but she was at least two miles away on twisty, icy roads.

John. Right. I dialed nine-one-one, hoping to be patched directly to my neighbor next door. I'd barely explained my predicament when the squawk of radio chatter was outside my door. I grabbed a towel from the bathroom and a blanket to wrap in and whipped the door wide. "I'm in labor."

He had the radio in one hand and the other raised to knock. His mouth was open, but I didn't give him time to talk.

"Move," His car was just down the street and I was determined to get my ass in it.

"Hold on, it's icy." He stuck his arm out, radio and all, for me to brace myself on.

Which worked for the steps I kept meticulously salted, but as soon as I hit the road, I slid.

He came down with me and slightly under me so I hadn't landed hard, but it tore something loose. Cramps that wouldn't let up started at my back and shot right to my crotch. "John?"

"You okay?"

"No." I fought to keep the tears inside. I was going to die. Zoe was going to die. "Help."

He tried to stand up and offered a hand.

I shook my head. "Get the car right here, help me in the back. Get me to the hospital as fast as possible with these damn roads." I spoke each word carefully and didn't yell, but you'd have thought I did.

Twenty miles an hour was the maximum speed. On the bridge, he hit his lights so people would move out of the way for us.

I breathed like I was supposed to and held on for dear life with the single intent of getting to the hospital without screaming or hysterics or anything. But I was freaking out. The hospital would take my name into the system. Shock would find me. He'd take Zoe. He'd kill Jackson. "John, do you have any cousins who are terrible?"

"What?"

"Cousins, relatives, something, someone I can blame this on and use their last name for the hospital. Shock is going to find me."

Crystal and I talked about this at length. She'd told me about her third cousin, Barry Hunnebaker, who was a drug addict with little memory. Blaming him with her say-so was our plan. But something about giving Zoe a mouthful last name like Hunnebaker killed me inside. I wanted something shorter. Fewer syllables. "John?" I searched the mirror to see his face.

His eyes met mine. "You're asking me to lie."

I was. A cop, my friend, my neighbor. One of the few people who gave a shit about me. "I'm sorry."

"No, I get it. I did some digging on your ex. He's a piece of work."

That was an understatement.

"Back in the day, there was this guy who'd come fishing every summer. He brought his kid with him."

Was he talking about One-Eyed Jack? I panted and listened as hard as I could.

"Every year, he'd make up a new name. One year, he was Johnny Van Zandt. But I knew some Van Zandts and called him on it. Said at least change up the name a bit if you're going to pretend you're someone famous. Ol' Jack laughed at that."

"The point?" We were about five minutes from the hospital despite the slow speeds. The roads here were good, barely icy at all. The rain was just that, rain.

"Point being, pick your favorite rock star."

"I don't have one." Those damn posters flashed in my mind and made me ill on top of everything else.

"Country singer?"

"I hate music."

"Pick any name then."

Jackson, Zoe Jackson, echoed in my head. I searched for a name that wouldn't tie to her father so tightly. "Brown. Last name Brown, first name…" I was at a loss.

"Jackson Brown, huh?"

He'd seen through me too easily. I had to throw him off track. "*Dick*. Dick Brown."

John snorted. "That's awful. But okay. Richard Brown it is."

Zoe Brown. Not ideal, but easy enough to throw someone off track, right?

Zoe Regina Brown was born at four-fifteen in the afternoon on April 24th. Her father, *Dick* that he was, was out of the picture. And I, one Katherine Jackson, with no insurance, was glad of it. Everything about her paperwork was a lie. One corroborated by an upstanding member of the local police force, so no one questioned any of it.

Crystal sat with me, holding Zoe as she slept. "You tell him yet?"

Him. "I will."

"You have to, as soon as possible. He's going to flip out if you keep it secret. He's got too much of his father in him not to." She cooed at Zoe and traced her eyebrows. One sweetly curved with a little perfect arch, the other crooked and angular, just like too many men in her family line. It gave her a puzzled look. Like one that asked, "What the fuck have you gotten me into, Mom?"

A mess, that's what I'd gotten her into. One I intended on cleaning up, hiding, or burying as soon as I could.

CHAPTER 13

Skilletsville, April 24, 2009—Jackson

Pinner held his baby girl, Lily, with great care. His gaze locked on the practically perfect little human with blonde hair like his own, and the good fortune to take after her mother in most other features. A year and a half old, and spoiled as hell. I felt bad for him, and the whole situation.

No sooner than the whore, Jewel, announced she was pregnant, Pinner's wife left the state, hell, the continent, moving back to Hawaii to be with her parents. And she took Pinner's oldest daughter with her. Now the old man was doting every ounce of his love on this baby because if he didn't, he'd kill something.

But a biker club was no place for a child. Especially since we had church tonight. Every Friday night like clockwork. The junkyard office would shut down promptly at six, the floors swept, then the beer flowed, and the gavel pounded. And with this gavel pound, I knew today was going to be the best day of my life yet. Rumor had it Toro was pissed at Kush for something or another and needed a new vice president. I intended to be that man. I'd worked hard to gain the trust of the officers, the members, and any motherfucker who held influence in the region. Even Nonno said I was a shoo-in.

There was one man who didn't hold that opinion, though. And since this was an election meeting, the nearby clubs were present and vocal.

Shock walked past me as I manned the counter and stopped in his tracks. He pointed his meaty finger at me and said too loudly, "That's the only position you're qualified for." Then he laughed and shut himself in conference with Toro.

"Toro won't listen to him, he'll listen to us." Pinner said as he rocked Lily who was mostly asleep.

I wasn't so sure. I was so close to having it all. "He's an asshole." I spoke quietly enough, so only Lily and Pinner overheard. Days like this, I knew better than to say a bad word about any ranking member, but I hated Shock with a fire that wouldn't die. And he returned that hate with a grudge of his own.

"He's always going to think you stole his wife."

I shifted, not willing to rehash old news. "He's an idiot on top of being an asshole."

Pinner laughed quietly. "You talk to Sprout?"

"About what?"

"About keeping his big trap shut."

I glared at Pinner. "I didn't hand him that phone, you did." Lie often enough and long enough even innocent people believe it.

Pinner smiled. "Damn straight." He jiggle-walked a pace or three away. "You hear from her?"

"Who?"

He turned and shot me a look that said, "Do I look stupid to you?"

So, I fired my answer right back. "You look dumb as hell, holding a kid."

"There ain't nothing like it. Looking down on that pretty little face and seeing parts of you there. One day, Jackson, you'll get that. Hopefully, it won't be taken away from you like my oldest. You need something like a baby girl to keep your ass honest."

"Get the fuck out of here with that shit." He was talking out of his ass.

He shrugged. "The way you whore around, I'm surprised you don't have five kids toddling around here." He began to count and point and name names. "There's Jackson's son one, and Jay two. Over there, Jay three, and four, twins, you know?" He laughed.

"Shut up." I glanced at the door, suddenly uneasy, like there was a target on my back. I shuddered. It was almost closing time.

He kept making up names, giving me shit.

The phone rang, saving me from Pinner's idiocracy. "Your dime, your funeral," I answered.

"Hi, I'm looking for a part, but don't remember the name of it. I talked to someone about it a while ago." The woman on the other end was timid. But it was a woman. Which meant I turned on the charm.

"Do you remember who you talked to, pretty lady?"

"A man named Jackson."

I smiled at Pinner, who rolled his eyes and mouthed something vulgar my way. Then he pantomimed getting a phone number along with a quick thrust of his hips twice. Too bad Lily in his arms made the action terrifying. Otherwise, I'd have laughed. "You got him, darling." I didn't remember talking parts with this voice, but she did sound vaguely familiar, so I probably did.

"Do I?"

There was a sharp note in her tone. A chill ran down my spine. I knew that voice. "Remind me when we talked last." I checked on Pinner to confirm his back was to me and fiddled with the computer to make this look legit.

"July."

"Uh-huh. The '05 Ford Fiesta with the sticky third gear problem. I remember you." I strode into the shelves of parts, bullshitting my way in a one-sided conversation until I was sure I was far enough away to not be over-heard at all. I still lowered my voice to a whisper. "I told you not to call me."

"I had to."

"Bullshit." I didn't need this fucking crap today. *Fuck*, Shock was right next-fucking door. "I'm hanging up."

"No, please, I just had a baby."

"The fuck?" I stared at the phone in my hand. Was I hearing things? That shit with Pinner was messing with my head. "Kate?"

"Her name is Zoe. She was born this afternoon. Crystal said you'd want to know. And we're fine. I'll hang up now."

And she did. I stared at the number. Maine. It might as well have been the other side of the planet. A girl. *My girl, Zoe.* I leaned against the rack, dislodging a box of hose clamps. I quickly straightened the mess and tucked the phone away. Then thought better of it. I went to the call log and deleted the number from the history. Covering her tracks as best as I could.

I was a father.

Pinner came around the end of the aisle. "Yo, church is starting." He bounced Lily in his arms and smiled down on her, a light on his face not many got to see.

One I'd never have on my face. *Ever.* I vowed that. Kate would be my one and only, and Zoe would be my one and only. And that's the way it was meant to be. A biker clubhouse was no place for a baby girl. Or love, or weaknesses.

The vote swung my way easily. Toro whispered in my ear that Nonno approved me personally, despite Shock's bitching. I celebrated. Drank, fucked, toasted the patch and my brothers, and even raised a glass with Shock. All the while, trying to forget that this was the last best day of my life. There would be no other day I'd remember more. Even if they someday voted me president of the entire region. This was it.

About midnight, the spell broke. Shock came at me, bitching his usual rant about stealing his wife. He had the hooker I'd fucked earlier under his arm. She didn't want to be there. It was plain on her face. The lack of smile, the fear in her eyes, the marks on her skin. And she was one of mine. Ours. Whatever. Skilletsville's stable, not his. "Take your hands off her."

"I beg your pardon?"

I stood up and wavered slightly from the heatwave of whiskey fumes trying to overpower me. "I said, take your hands off her."

Shock's eyes narrowed. A grin spread across his face. "How does it feel?"

"How does *what* feel?"

"Seeing me steal your woman. How's it *feel*?"

Terry wasn't mine, except in the protective sense. But if that's where Shock was going with this, I was in a mood to play along. "Take your hands off of her, now."

"You ain't no president."

"Yet. But this is my club. The club's girls. My officer patch means it is my responsibility. So, hands fucking off our property."

"She's Destroyers' property. That means she's mine."

He was goading me, trying to get me to pop off hot-headed and admit I stole his wife. The whisper made me smile. It wasn't a nice one. "She's here for everyone, not just you. But she's done for the night, right, Terry?"

The girl nodded and slipped out from under Shock's arm. I held his bloodshot stare with my own.

"Everyone? Is that what we're doing here? Sharing?"

I blinked. "I had her first." Sending a little nod in Terry's direction.

"And I had Kate first," Shock stated.

There was a sheen of drool at the corner of his mouth. His beard covered where the rest dribbled off to hide. I focused on that. He was drunk. Easy pickings if I wanted to throw a punch. Cause a fight, bring him down, snap his neck. He was weak. "Your problem is, you don't know how to balance." I could have been talking about the list in his stance or the way he ran hot and cold. Or his books or payments to nationals. But we both knew I was talking about Kate and his possessiveness. "Treat women nice; they come back. Treat them like shit; they run. Terry will come back to me. Maybe even later tonight. But Kate? She ain't ever coming back. She ran because you are an asshole who can't balance."

His fist shot out.

I blocked it and tucked his arm under mine, trapping him close. I had a knife to his throat. "I'm an officer, and this is *my* ground. You fucked up, Shock. Leave."

He leaned his weight on me. "You fucked up, Jackson. She's mine. Kate's mine."

A weakness. One I couldn't exploit without jeopardizing her, or...*oh shit*, my baby girl. That sobering thought had me push him away. "Take Terry with you. I don't give a fuck."

His eyes glittered. "One day, I'm going to catch you. You can lie all you want, but I'm going to catch you in those damn lies and bring you down."

"Yeah, good luck with that. It's nice to know you care so much."

"I don't care. I *hate* you."

That's where he was dead wrong. "You gotta care enough to hate. See? I don't hate you because I don't care. Have a fun time, Shock." I slapped him on the patch as I strolled past, looping an arm around another hooker so I could go upstairs and get some fucking sleep. Who gave a shit about anything? This place, this club, this life I'd carved out? It was one big pile of lies I'd have to keep cultivating forever, like a poisoned garden.

I fell onto the mattress. I don't even remember putting a condom on, but it was there after it all. Still intact, whole, and slimy. I'd get a vasectomy. Schedule it for tomorrow. And keep my shit tight from now on while playing it fast and loose. Win with a grin and bury my enemies deep, just like dear old dad. Shock didn't know who he was messing with.

One-Eyed Jack was a biker all his life. He held officer ranks from secretary to president and everything in between. He taught me at his knee, carried me into meetings before I could even talk. He taught me how to lie, steal, and murder my way to the top and beyond. Men like Shock? They didn't have the education I had.

I lay awake, listening to the dark-haired hooker snore, and letting all the echoes of past, present, and future bounce around my thoughts like a whirling carousel of color. It was a puzzle to figure out. Find the pattern. The thing that repeats—anticipate when it comes around next. Plan. Let another piece fly by, set the pattern as it filled in piece by piece until the entire crazy picture was laid out as if it were standing still. Once you did that, you were invincible. No secret in the world would bring that ride to a halt. I built my kingdom in the dark. Bit by bit, horse by horse. Laughing rider by laughing rider. A machine that would live long after some asshole shivved me in the ribs.

Maybe it was the whiskey? Or maybe it was intuition.

The best day of my life was gone. I couldn't expect another like this again. A tear slipped out of one eye. I let it fall. Let the salty trail dry until it was crusty and stiff.

I was a father. It was about time I started acting like one.

Or, at the very least, begin stepping into the ruthless shoes One-Eyed Jack left behind.

Terry's body washed up on the banks of the Ohio River, miles from Skilletsville. I saved the newspaper clippings in a locked box I kept stuffed under a junked-out RV we sometimes used as a place to crash. It didn't matter if the elements ruined it. I memorized the date and the headline. I could reconstruct it later if needed. Two months after that, I collected another trinket.

A smuggler who ran the border told me how he despised working with Shock. How it felt like the man couldn't be trusted. I laughed at him and flat-out told him I couldn't be trusted, either.

He winked at me and smiled. "But at least with you, I know where I stand. You're in this for the long haul. Shock can't think that far ahead. And I can't work with that. But I'll work with you. You can make me the connections I need farther up the lakes."

And that was how I gutted Shock's pipeline and became the hub Pittsburgh had to go through to get product. Each were little trinkets of businesses or people with power. I collected them like a magpie. Because one day, Shock would fall. And I'd be there to make sure he never got back up.

CHAPTER 14

Maine, Present Day, June 10th—Kate

It's just a summer job. All teens got one. It was a normal part of growing up. Each sentence clawed at my heart. "Why the ice cream shop?" It was one of the major tourist stops quaintly situated at the end of the bridge on a very picturesque part of the harbor. No matter where you sat outside, you had a view of the islands and ocean.

Where everyone could see you.

Zoe looked at me like I was an alien with two heads. "Mom? It's an ice cream shop. It's not some hotbed of organized crime or even a place that that kind of people frequents. I'll be safe and Mayor Hank is right there."

That was a good argument. Hank waved from his rocking chair parked out front. But I had to try one more time to dissuade her from taking such a public-facing job. "I suppose your boyfriend is working there."

Gah. Sixteen, a boyfriend, and slowly but surely flying away from the little nest I'd built for her and me to hide in.

Her face flushed red. She got that from me. "Sometimes, but it's a real job. I'm not taking it to flirt with him."

"You have a real job that lets you take off summers," I reminded her. Maybe I shouldn't remind her of that. So far, I'd lucked out and had a wonderfully obedient daughter.

"Checking on houses isn't a real job."

"I beg your pardon?" Crystal and I made a decent income by "checking on houses." The more people discovered our pristine little island, the less pristine it got, but the more money we made. So far, growth had slowed to a few dozen mansions on the south-facing coastline. There was one practically in our backyard. Two more stood on the point by the cove. But there was a plan for about seventeen developments in the next five years which would hem us in on the east. That I didn't like. It felt like there was a noose slowly wrapping around my neck. And I got more nervous with each new stranger. But short of moving to climates even colder than this, it was the plight of every coastal town, eventually.

Global warming couldn't come fast enough. And with that morbid thought, I addressed Zoe's biggest issue. "I don't want you walking to and from there alone."

"I've got my intermediate license. Let me borrow the car."

My heart skipped. "That leaves me without one."

"Duh."

What if we have to run? I swallowed that fear down. "I should drop you off and pick you up."

"No! It's only for this summer. I'll have my own ride next summer, promise."

My motherly radar blipped on a target. "Oh, I get this now."

"No, you don't."

"Oh, yes, I do." Chris had a motorcycle. And like most things inherited, Zoe loved that more than her boyfriend. Although, maybe the whole falling for biker bad boys was my fault.

"Mom…" she warned.

"Zoe," I countered and then clarified. "A motorcycle is not a mode of transportation I want you on with or *as* an inexperienced driver. Especially not during tourist season. Even the best riders get blindsided by stupid people."

Her face settled into a silent, fuming mask that reminded me of Jackson so much it hurt. I could still remember that expression when he talked about going back. It was something he hated, yet resigned himself to doing.

Or maybe I was making up that memory, and he really was angry with me for keeping him too long. I didn't know. He hadn't been around to ask.

There was a compromise needed here, and I had a feeling that no matter what I did or said, it would be a losing battle for me. So, I had to lay out rules. "My car, three days a week, on weekdays when traffic isn't so bad. Weekends, I drive you there and back, no exceptions." Freedom with boundaries. "And don't cross the causeway or the bridge." Both were dangerous for a new driver.

Zoe frowned. "I use the causeway all the time. You taught me on the way to school."

"Excuse me? Did I stutter?" Damn. That was right out of Shock's vocabulary. I shoved that uncomfortable thought into a pit of flaming ashes.

"Mom, what if I want to have some fun with my friends?"

Of which she had few. Why? I didn't know. All I understood was that Zoe held grudges for a long time. The children she went to school with not only teased her about being an only child, but illegitimate as well. Which was stupid because quite a few of them were from broken families. I'd only bypassed the whole divorce factor. And if you had to parse facts, technically, Zoe was born from a married woman. But that was my secret, and I'd take it to the grave and pull a few in with me if forced to admit it.

Maybe she was making more? "Do I know them?"

"Maybe."

That was a bad answer. "Local or out-of-towners?"

Her thin scowl told me that answer. "When they leave, what happens then?" I didn't give her time to answer. "They go back to their regular lives, which may include very real boyfriends and or girlfriends and you, my dear, are shelved somewhere with a summer memory."

She glared at me. "Was that what Dad was?"

"Zoe," I warned. We talked about him occasionally, but in the "yes, you have a father, and no, he's not in the picture" sort of way.

"Is that why you're so angry and worried about out-of-towners, because I was a summer fling?"

I swallowed. Technically, she might be correct. It was barely four days. Four amazing, sexy days when I didn't feel scared all the time because Jackson was right there. "It wasn't a summer fling." It was a wild ride, a blip in the messed up nightmare of my life, and a shining memory I would never forget.

"Why isn't he *here* then? Why doesn't he visit? Why don't I know *my own father*?" Her tirade hurt my ears. I fought the urge to cover them.

"He lives far away."

"There's this invention called airplanes, Mom."

"The nearest airport is Bar Harbor." Funny the things you learn when researching escape routes.

"Car rentals."

"Zoe."

"Mom." She fired back at me, mimicking the warning tone I put into her name. "I want to know the truth, okay?"

This day came too soon. I always thought it would be a school project or bullying, or later, when she was an adult and finally tracing her history. But not in the middle of an argument. Not when I was already defensive and frightened.

"I was raped." That came out wrong.

She paled.

"Not with you, or that's not how… oh geez. What I'm trying to say is your father saved me."

The hope on her face killed me. Not because I hated it, but because it mirrored everything I wanted but had lost.

"First, he set me up with a shelter in… another state. When my… husband, who is a horrible man, mind you, found me there, your father helped hide me again. So, you see why he stays away?"

"No."

I took a step back, blindsided.

"That doesn't make sense, Mom. He hid you but didn't stick around?"

"If he had, he would've led Shock right to us. And, he'd be dead. We all would be. Maybe. Or worse, not dead. That's definitely worse." I couldn't look her in the eyes. My cheeks were overly warm. A dead giveaway that they'd flushed red in shame.

"Wouldn't he—Shock—what kind of name is that?"

"A biker name. Keith Shock Weaver. Of Pittsburgh."

She blinked at me. "Your last name is Brown."

I shook my head. "It's an alias."

Her face went from confused to scowling. "We live next door to a cop. He's my godfather."

"John knows. He helped me pick your last name."

"Our last name."

"Yes, *ours*." Calling myself Katherine Jackson was too close to the truth, so I had to give up that name almost as quickly as I'd used it.

She mulled that over. "I have a social security number."

"Yes."

"Do you?"

Zoe deserved an honest answer. "Not one that I can use. I'm sure he'd track it down."

"That's why you work for Crystal."

I nodded.

"Does she know?"

"Yes, she does. She knew your father when he was younger."

The shift in her demeanor was unnerving. "How well?"

That I could not answer. Crystal hinted at sleeping with Jackson's father, but she didn't stop there. When I first suspected, it put up a wall of distrust between us. And she noticed. He'd gotten his experience from his mother's hooker friends. That circle included Crystal. We both decided not to delve into details to maintain our own friendship.

"Ew, Mom."

"Zoe, don't. Crystal is a good friend. Just because she wasn't a saint doesn't mean you need to yuck on her. I'm not a saint, either."

At my admission, she measured me with her gaze. "Was Dad a biker?"

"Is. Another reason he can't be here. They're in the same organization." I used the word deliberately, as in organized crime organization.

"Which one?"

"If I tell you, what will happen? Will you ask questions, lead them here?"

"No. God, no."

"I want you to be careful around *all* bikers, okay? Especially those who wear club patches on their coats, three-part rockers. Do you know what I mean by that?"

She nodded. Despite being tucked away on an island in Maine, we weren't isolated completely. There were clubs and problems occasionally. Mostly farther south in urban areas. But every once in a while, riders would loop around the islands and check out the scenery. Most of them were just average everyday people with a love for riding. I couldn't fault them for that. Before Shock, I'd enjoyed riding on the back of my high school boyfriend's bike. But that was exactly why Shock noticed me. We went to the wrong party when it was the wrong time because my father owed him a favor.

"Would he ever come up here? My dad, that is."

"No. He said he'd stay away so no one would connect him to this place."

Zoe frowned. "I want to meet him someday."

That would be *never*. "It's not safe." And she might not like him. I had no illusions that he was rough around the edges. For four days, I found that charming. My poor, abused heart wanted to love him so badly that I ignored all the warning signs.

"You're always saying that. This isn't *safe*, that isn't *safe*. Mom, live a little."

I perused her from head to toe. "That's how I got you."

She fired back, "Low blow, Mom."

"The best thing I ever did was live just enough to have you. But I'm scared to death of losing you." Despite all my good intentions, I was trying too hard to keep her in a bubble where she could never ever be hurt. And even knowing that, I had an overwhelming urge to pack everything up and flee. Sixteen years of safety, and it wasn't enough. Nothing would ever be enough as long as Shock Weaver was still alive and kicking.

Unfortunately, he was. I subscribed to online Pittsburgh news outlets to watch for his obituary or news on the Destroyers. He'd been arrested for battery a year ago and was released without charges. It made headlines because while the police did their jobs, so did my father. Shock got off on a technicality.

She shifted subjects. "You're a sap. Weekdays, huh? That means I can use the car tonight to go down there for orientation, right?"

I bit my tongue. "No," was right there. Instead, I capitulated. "Be home before nine-thirty."

"Mom."

Oh God, that tone. "Zoe, it's a weeknight and—"

"And school's out. I can drive until midnight, you know."

"Not with my car."

She made a face and muttered something that sounded like, "Fine" but I wouldn't put it past her to change up the words to fit her agenda. "What was that?"

"I said, fine. Nine-thirty."

Thank goodness. "I love you. And I'm proud of you. But I'm still scared."

She shot me an odd look as she grabbed the keys from the hook. "I love you, too."

A quiet house was something I wasn't used to. School days, I'd drop Zoe off and go to work. Or if she was with friends, I'd start another renovation project. But this silence was different. Almost taunting. I puttered around, picking up and deciding what needed the most urgent fixing. But I'd managed to fix almost everything I could in sixteen years. The place wasn't the same. And my baby wasn't the same either. She was almost an adult. I marveled a bit at the things I'd managed.

One of Zoe's socks was under the coffee table. I grabbed it and went upstairs to get a load of laundry from the rooms. Zoe's room was in the front of the house. As I collected more strays from under her bed and straightened, I looked outside. John stood in front of my house, staring at the road.

That was odd.

I went downstairs and dumped the armload of clothes into the basket in the laundry room and went outside to check on him.

"Hey, John. Is everything okay?"

"I don't know." He stared both directions at the road.

My pulse sped up. There was something prickling at the back of my mind, nudging my instinct to run. "That's a first. You usually know everything." I tried to keep my voice light.

He held out the large envelope in his hands. "This was on my front step, but there's no postage or barcodes."

Oh, that *was* odd. "Maybe one of the neighbors dropped it off."

"It's addressed to you. But not Kate Brown. Kate Weaver."

John held the envelope out, but we were too far apart for me to take it. In bold Sharpie, my name was scrawled across the tan paper. I took a step back toward the safety of my house.

As I did, John said something about going to grab gloves before we opened it together. My whole body felt numb, and I moved on autopilot to enter the house, grab my suitcase and the three duffle bags I'd squirreled away in the hall closet. I filled the bags methodically. One with toiletries, towels, and the first aid kit. The second with three sets of clothes, a sweater, and a hoodie for me. I went to Zoe's room, furiously trying to scan it for anything valuable and memorable and stuffing it into the third small duffle while filling her suitcase with clothes and shoes and whatnots she'd need.

"Kate, where are you?" John's voice echoed in the house. I gave up on the suitcase and started down the stairs. There were two photos of Zoe hung on the stairs. The rest depicted places we'd been without any images of her in them. I began to take them down and rearrange the pictures to cover the blank spaces, so Shock wouldn't find them.

"What are you doing?"

"He can't find out about her."

"Kate, we don't even know it's from him until we open it."

John was right. I was being paranoid and overreacting. "Okay, open it." My knee bounced as I tried to project calmness.

He sent me a look that was one part speculation and the other part admonishment for jumping to conclusions. Then he donned plastic gloves and set out a series of large bags. "If it's from him, everything goes in a bag first, then you can look at it."

I nodded, squeezing my hands together so I wouldn't touch something.

He cut open the top of the envelope. Very carefully, he used the knife tip to prop open the edges and peek inside. "Newspaper clippings."

That wasn't awful, was it?

He pulled out the stack and slipped them one by one into the plastic bags, taking care to label each one in the order they were piled. In between them was a hand-written note. John took his time reading it before placing it in a bag of its own. I picked up the first clipping. It was the trial I'd read about online. My father's face was prominent on the page. Since I'd already seen it, I scanned for any notations or indications of why it was important. But there was nothing new. The second one was a clipping from a week ago. A major drug bust in a neighboring town. Several arrested. Good. Again, no notations or commentary.

The third was the handwritten note. John took that from me before I could read it. I only caught the stationary heading, recognizing the familiar logo and address of my father's law firm. John handed me the third clipping.

It was an obituary.

I read it twice before the words sank in. My brain tripped up when I read the phrase, "loving father." He was anything but. Dad was a piece of shit. A *dead* piece of shit.

"This is a homicide report." John stared at the stack of papers accompanying the clippings. He handed me the top page and pointed to a couple of salient facts. "He was shot in a parking lot."

The address matched his work. "That's outside my father's law office. The victim was my father." I showed John the obituary.

"I figured as much." He scanned a few more pages. "This shouldn't be anywhere outside the investigator's office. I'll take these in and make sure they get back to where they need to be." He shuffled the bags into order and placed the note underneath the stack.

"Stop trying to hide that from me." I pulled it out and read the sloppy printing. Shock never could write worth a damn.

I read his words out loud. "'Dear Kate, I want you to know what a piece of shit your father was.'—*No*, really?" I scoffed at my editorial comment and read on. "'He got me off a charge two weeks ago, but thanks to him and his fucking habit, he cost me a million-five. But I'll forgive him for that because he left me two great things. First, you. My fucking wife. Second? An address in

Maine. That motherfucker knew where you were and didn't tell me. I'm glad he's dead. You're next.'"

My dad handed me to Shock gift-wrapped. *Again*.

CHAPTER 15

Skilletsville, July 19th (Present)—Jackson

Working hard to make money is a fucking scam. There's a certain tipping point where all that hard work can't get you any more scratch than the day before. That's when you look at that bank account and wonder where the fuck it's all going. Worse? You look at the suits on the banker holding your cash and realize, *there*. That's where it's going.

Hickey and Skinner droned on about the club's investments. Time was, under men like Kush or Pinner, the highest money maker outside of drug and gun running was this fucking junkyard. Now, it barely kept the doors open.

When did ten grand become a small amount? I pondered that while the geek squad of bikers got hard over spreadsheets. I didn't care much for the particular details, just the paycheck at the end of the month. And this month, it was down. Sprout's construction business was spending cash building houses that weren't selling, the waterfront project was on hold because of one bullshit thing or another, and the cam girl business was flatlined because Grace couldn't keep girls happy because she was unhappy. And when your boss is a bitch, well...I didn't blame them for finding a new boss.

A tentative knock at the door saved my ass from murder. "Knock like you fucking mean it, or don't fucking bother." I yelled, quieting both my treasurer, Hickey, and Skinner, who was damn good at computers.

A prospect shoved his face in. This one was supposed to be working at the desk at the junkyard. Which at least was making money. That was *if* someone was there to answer the goddamned phone.

"What!?"

"One of your hookups is calling for you again."

My heart stumbled before picking up pace. "They're always calling."

He turned to go, but I stood up and snapped my fingers. "Give me the goddamned phone. Hopefully she's got good phone sex. I'll send her Grace's way." I shot the last at Hickey, who didn't find it amusing.

"Yo. Jackson here."

"Tell me where you were on Christmas Day, 1984."

I stared at the phone. This wasn't some bitch from the strip club, or one of the hangers, or even one of the hookers, not mine anyway… "Give me a minute, I gotta kick some assholes out before I get revved up on your sexy voice." To the geek twins, I said, "Scram. We'll finish later."

Once the commotion of their collecting papers and laptops ended, I turned back to the call. "I was at your trailer that Christmas because Dad was on a job somewhere west and Mom was in a snit. Why are you calling, Crystal?"

"First, they're gone."

They. Stick a knife in my heart, will ya? "Where?"

"I don't know. And I'm sure that's on purpose."

She said *first.* "And?"

"And John's in the hospital. *They* shot him. Why?" Her voice was laced with pain.

I should ask a ton of questions. I should be getting my ass on my bike and riding somewhere to make solutions happen. But this was what I told Kate to do. Run and don't stop. Don't call, don't contact me, and don't look back. "When was this?"

She sighed. "It started over a month ago according to John. Kate had a package. It was delivered to his doorstep on accident. It had shit in there about her father's death and a threat from that asshole. Then it escalated."

"Escalated, how?"

"John dropped Kate off at the ice cream place, you know, the one at the bridge?"

I knew the place. Hard to believe it was still going strong after twenty-some years, but that wasn't the point. "Why there?"

"Zoe just got a job there. You know about her, don't you?"

"I do."

"Good, I don't need to tell you how well that all went down, then. Kate had bags packed, grabbed Zoe, and took off. But someone must have seen her get out of John's car. They followed him around, harassing him and being a menace for a bit. But mostly held off because he called in reinforcements from the mainland. We thought it had blown over, but last night, they broke into his place and shot him. Luckily, he had his shotgun and service revolver."

"Any of the assailants die?"

"Two."

I needed that info. Nonno needed that info. "Have they been identified?"

"One of 'em. He was from a local club. The other one isn't in the system, so it's taking longer."

"Tats?" I asked, knowing it was a long shot that Crystal would have that information.

"I don't know. I'll ask."

If there was a plant locally, she shouldn't. "Don't. I don't want them targeting you, too."

"Where would she go? I was hoping she went to you, but if she didn't…"

"She'll be fine," I lied. Running scared and for over a month straight with a teenager, no matter how much Zoe might know or not know, had to be rough, but without family or friends—hell. My mind flashed back to a glimpse of the driver and the tattoos that I'd logged to memory. I knew where she was. And if I did, so did Shock for obvious reasons. I hoped Kate was smarter than to go back to New Jersey.

"Jimmy," Crystal started.

"Stop, you know better than to call me that. It's Jackson."

She cut me off. "I *need* you to find her. She's a good woman, and Zoe? She's like a daughter to me. You'd be proud of her."

"Crystal Ann, I told Kate to leave me out of this. I can't."

"Can't or *won't?*" Her voice was hard.

"Can't." Even saying it, I knew what my next step was. After making a few calls and raising some stink, or maybe even pulling in people who would have my back on this. Of which, there were very few. I'd lied so long and well, it was a crap shoot if anyone would listen, let alone not take offense for being misled by a brother. But saying the word "can't" made my hackles rise. There was no can't. It was only a challenge I hadn't conquered... yet.

"Anything I can do to help?" she asked.

"Stay safe and stay out of it. Lay low. That's all."

The line went dead. Crystal knew she wouldn't get more out of me than what she already had. But she'd managed to twist me around her finger almost as well as Mom did with my father. Funny how well both of them knew how to do that shit.

I stared at the paneling of my office and wondered which string would be the thread that unraveled everything. Pull too hard, and my life was over. Not just here, but permanently over. I dug a folder out of my desk. One I'd sealed and hidden under a fake bottom in the lowest drawer. Some time ago, I had a club member with government connections. He helped me create a fake identity for myself and two women. I stared at the envelope, still sealed, and never even looked at. I shoved it back under the veneer plate and fixed that in place. I wasn't the kind of man to run. Moreover, I couldn't trust the information wasn't already compromised.

Which meant I needed to face this head-on.

"Sprout!" I yelled. There was always someone outside at my beck and call. In under a minute, the door of my office opened, and Skinner popped his head in.

"Hickey's tracking him down."

I motioned for him to come in. "Call Wolf in." I made the hand gesture to indicate Hickey's phone. My VP needed to be the first to know. Maybe his wife would have ideas on how to hide Kate better. She rode with a bunch of bitches who made it their life's work to mess with assholes like Shock. "Tell him that Tits needs to come with him."

Skinner's eyes went wide. Me asking for Tits was a minefield, and everyone knew it. She wasn't sane by a long shot, and getting her involved in Destroyers' business was one of those unavoidable but forbidden actions we all tiptoed around as much as possible.

But she owed me a favor, and this time, I bet she wouldn't hold that over my head. If I handled it right. "I need you to track down street gangs in Trenton. Black clubs established for at least sixteen years."

"Should I ask why?"

Skinner was on dangerous ground. "No. Just do it. I need it in two hours."

His jaw shifted, and the gears turning in his head were reflected on his face. "That was some different kind of phone sex."

"Fuck off. One hour and fifty-nine minutes, asshole."

While I waited for Wolf to arrive and Skinner to track down the information, I made a call south.

"Who's bleeding?" Disney needed new material.

"Yo momma," I shot back automatically.

"Hey now, leave her out of this. What do you want?" In the background, there was the distinct shuffling of his bulk and the click of a door shutting. I counted on his discretion and he wasn't failing me.

"First, I owe you an apology."

"Ho-lee hell. Let me find my calendar. I gotta mark this date for posterity."

"Those are awfully big words for you." I turned in the chair, unable to sit still.

Disney laughed. "Sue me. A couple of my men snagged up some smart women, and they're giving my Mary-Cherry a run for her money. She's started one of those word-of-the-day calendars."

I chuckled at his pain. It was either that or admit the truth. It was a rare treat to find smart women, and in this life, practically impossible. The rare few, like my VP's old lady, were forces to reckon with. Disney had more than one in his circle, marking him as a rare leader who'd tolerate that shit. Which was exactly why I needed to be up front with him. "About eighteen or nineteen years ago, I'd gotten a favor from you."

He made a noise that must have jiggled his memories. "Right. The hookup while playing hooky."

Damn it. He remembered. "Yeah."

"How bad is it, damage-wise?"

Thank God I didn't have to explain myself or my actions, and he homed in on the precise issue. "It could take you down. So, if Nonno, or Big G asks, tell them the truth. If Shock asks, tell him to fuck off."

There was an uncomfortable space of silence. Disney was thinking too hard. "This has something to do with that wife of his who disappeared, doesn't it?"

If I told him the truth, I was dead. If I didn't, I wouldn't have an ally. And I needed allies for Kate and Zoe. I skirted the truth. "You're a smart man."

"And you're a dumb ass. Jesus. She's still alive?"

"I hope so." With every fiber of my being.

He huffed out a laugh that didn't sound amused. It was more akin to dumbfounded fear than anything. "All those years. Damn." He took a breath.

Oh great, here came the pearls of wisdom from a fool. If I wanted that, I'd talk to Sprout, who miraculously slipped in and stood against the wall, waiting for me to finish my call. Damn six-foot-seven-inch ninja. "What bullshit are you going to beat me up with?"

Disney spoke, "Two things. One, you love her. You might not think you do, but you do. Otherwise my bullshit wouldn't be needed. Two, a birdie told me that Shock's crew got in trouble up north."

I glanced at Sprout who was making a point to pretend he wasn't listening, but those big ass ears heard everything. "Where?"

"Catch this, Maine. What the fuck is in Maine?"

"Lobsters. Clams."

"Fish?" Disney asked.

I sighed. "Yeah, those too." For the millionth time, I regretted not recruiting him and losing him to his own chapter.

"What's the plan?"

He didn't need to know my next move. Knowing him, he'd try to help and get his ass in worse trouble than I was in. It was one thing for a man like me to lie to everyone, but a man like him? Jesus Christ, he'd make mortal enemies, and was the type to take it personally. "Your plan is to keep your head down, stay out of the crosshairs, got it?"

"That's going to be difficult if Shock wants blood and starts sniffing around the edges."

"Well, I'm making sure it isn't yours. Got it?"

He grunted. "Huh. Here I thought you didn't like me."

"I don't like anybody, you asshole." With that, I hung up. He was baiting me to cut him in. I'd be damned if I did that. He'd already grabbed territory from me. I didn't need him taking over my thinking.

"Sprout, you're good at playing dumb, right?"

He made a face that normally would make me laugh. But today was not a good day for that kind of fuckery. "I need you to crank that shit up to a-fucking-hundred."

"Why?"

That door was unguarded and unblocked. I motioned to it with my head. "Make sure that stays shut for one minute."

He dipped his head, picked up a nearby chair, and propped it under the handle. Some days, I wondered why he wasn't running this joint. Then he opened his big ass mouth and quipped, "I'm all ears." Then, with practiced art, he tucked his mess of curly hair behind both, making them stand out like a fucking elephant's.

"I fucked up, and Wolf might be president in anywhere from an hour to a month from now."

He straightened to his full height. "How?"

I glanced at the door again, waiting for the wrong person to bust in. "Shock found Kate."

His brows furrowed for only a moment. "The puker?"

Sprout's memory was even better than mine. "Yeah."

My confirmation made his face go dark. "Ma helped her."

"Jesus, you're fucking right." I'd forgotten about that. His mom was one of the smart ones, but too damn helpful. Sprout shook his head slowly, digging my grave even deeper. "Damn it. She wasn't supposed to stick her neck out."

"Well, you know Ma, she'll defy the devil if someone needs her."

It was my turn to thwart the tragedy coming our way. "Isolate and insulate her, Danielle, the business, and anything—I'm talking anything not attached to the club. Got it?"

He nodded. I'm sure he'd already done a lot of legwork to protect his wife's fortune, and his budding construction business that supported half this club. But what I was warning him about right now would topple the whole thing.

"If anyone other than me takes heat on this," I shook my head.

"Walt's right." He called Disney "Walt" because that was his real name. I never did. It would imply we actually liked each other rather than keeping a wall of mutual respect, distancing my shit from his. Sprout didn't have to do that sort of thing.

"How's that?" Them damn big ears. I vindictively hoped his future kids got them and were ugly as fuck.

"You love her."

Sprout was so wrong. "I'm *covering* our asses. Show some respect."

A knock interrupted whatever he was going to spew out next. Wolf and his wife were waiting for me to fill them in. "Leave."

"Your funeral," he joked and swept off his imaginary jester hat at me with a wide smile.

"Guard the door from the outside," I yelled at Sprout. He made a display of spinning around and sweeping up the chair to plant his ass in front of the open door. Added a bit of twerk in the antics to rub my face in the order.

Wolf shut it on him and held a chair for Tits before sitting down himself.

That was one of the things I truly appreciated about him. He was power hungry, but courteous. A great combination for leadership. Especially when leading a club sandwiched between Shock, Walt, and a growing outlaw club to the east. Not to mention we were sitting on millions of dollars. The pressure on me to walk that tightrope was immense. I needed someone with brains to replace me, but until Wolf, I hadn't found the right man.

Trouble was, Wolf had a permanent disability. He'd lost his foot and most of his lower leg a few years back. It hampered him in a fight. And for what was coming, he'd lose. With me dead, they'd question his ability to lead. I should have replaced him a year ago or more. But, it was too late for that now. He was going to have a target on him, and it was all my fault.

CHAPTER 16

Trenton, New Jersey—Kate

New Jersey wasn't the same as I remembered. The shelter I'd stayed at sixteen years ago was now an apartment or condo building, and the resale shop I'd worked at was completely restaffed. I didn't recognize anyone.

The restaurant was a long shot. The neighborhood it was in was almost worse than I remembered. Zoe shot me incredulous eye daggers every step of the way. Luckily, she stayed close and quiet. We walked in, gathering more attention than I cared for. I went to the counter, barely scanning the menu, and asked for George.

Of course, the staff didn't know anyone by that name. Discouraged, I nudged Zoe to pick something for dinner. We hadn't been eating right since we left Maine, and money was getting tight. But I had to spend something here or risk standing out further.

"I'm not hungry."

Her attitude was grinding my patience to a stub. "Get it for the road then." I redirected my attention to the cashier. "What do you suggest will keep for a couple hours?" My nerves were shot, and I needed safety. But I also needed answers. How had my father found me? Did Shock go after Jackson already? Was anyone I knew safe?

"You lost?" the cashier asked, too loudly.

"Yes," I admitted, despite Zoe's violent shake of her head and the death glare sent my way.

As the cashier gave me directions to the interstate, I pretended to pay attention. I knew four ways out of this town. Each way was worse than the last. North? I'd run the risk of running straight into Shock's minions. East? I'd run out of country and be trapped against the coastline. South? We'd were pointed that way. Continuing on that path was predictable.

And the remaining compass point was where I wanted to go, but also needed to avoid at all costs. Both Jackson and Shock were in that direction.

One of the patrons stood up and Zoe moved so close I thought she was trying to meld into me.

"Excuse me, ma'am. Did you ask for a man named George?"

I glanced his way and caught the aged marks on his hands. "Yes, George Williams, he'd be about fifty-seven now? I think."

The man nodded and grinned. His capped teeth flashed. "Old George always had a weakness for pretty ladies." His eyes dipped southward, and I told myself that this was expected. I shouldn't take offense or make a big deal of it until absolutely necessary. But my fears screamed at my impulse to run.

"I used to work with him at the resale shop."

The stranger's eyes flashed back to mine. "I remember you."

Oh shit. Did I know this man? I tried to match his face to the two years I lived here, but came up blank. I very cautiously said, "I'm sorry, but I don't remember you."

He smiled again and held out a hand. "Name's Romeo."

I bet it was. "Nice to meet you." I shook his hand and slipped out of the grasp before it could linger too long. "Is George still around?" My heart picked up, predicting an answer I didn't want to hear.

Romeo shook his head. "Died. Shot in his home about a month ago."

Zoe sucked in her breath. "Mom?"

Since I'd already braced for the worst, I had no external reaction. But inside, it felt like someone sucker-punched me and pulled the rug out from under me. I truly had no where to go now.

Except there.

I squashed down the insidious whisper. That wasn't an option. "Who shot him?"

Romeo motioned for me to come closer. I did, but the shuffled step and lean forward proved to me I wasn't a brave person.

He whispered, "Your biker friends did it."

"I'm not friends with bikers."

His eyes dipped to Zoe. "Where'd she come from then? George said a biker picked you up from that place he dumped you at."

George had a big mouth. *Had* being an important word that slapped me upside the head. "Sixteen-plus years, Romeo."

His smile cocked sideways. "You looking for a new sugar daddy?"

It took everything I had to not scream or lash out. "I never was looking for one. I won't start now."

His face softened. "Had to try. George took a shine on you, you know that?"

Apparently, I'd missed that. "We were just friends."

Romeo frowned. He bent over, pulled up his pant leg, and pointed at a puckered scar that twisted his calf muscle into a knotted depression. "I took a bullet for you. Least you could do is say thank you."

"Thank you." I meant it sincerely and as a punctuation point to this whole conversation.

"Your food's ready." The girl at the counter held the bag I'd ordered. I took it, left a cash tip in the jar by the register, and collected Zoe under one arm before addressing Romeo.

"You and George saved my life. I do appreciate that. Thank you again. I won't burden you any further."

"We could work out a deal." Again, his eyes raked down my body and back again. His eyes drifted to Zoe.

I didn't answer him. I tugged on Zoe and walked away. Something I should have done a long ass time ago. Like before Dad saddled me with Shock.

Every eye in the place followed our departure, and I'm certain more than one person noted the plates attached to my little Honda. But that detail didn't matter. They were stolen. I'd parked in a busy Walmart and taken them in broad daylight. Sure, there were security cameras and customers walking to and from the store. But no one questioned a woman and her teenage daughter as I swapped out the plate holder I'd purchased cheap.

Jackson taught me that trick. One of many I'd used to get away this time. But now, I was out of ideas.

I pulled off the highway in Wilmington, knowing it was the last opportunity to turn back. The car ticked as Zoe and I sat in silence.

"We should go to a library," Zoe suggested.

"What?"

"Free internet. I think they ask for an ID, but I can show them mine."

What was she up to? I turned to figure out what she was plotting. "And what would we use the internet for?"

She ticked off her list on her fingers. "First leave a message for John, if he's alive. Second, try the store's email to contact Crystal and let her know we're okay, but not leave a trace. Third, download some maps and figure out where to go."

Great ideas. I mulled them over. Contacting Crystal was not a good idea. John likely had ways to avoid his email being hijacked, but Crystal didn't.

"Or, we could find out if my dad is still alive and go to him." She side-eyed me as she spoke.

"I regret ever telling you about him."

"I don't. I want to at least know if he's alive. Everyone else seems to *die* around you."

Her tone was bitter. I didn't blame her. Two days ago, I tried to contact John through his district office. They informed me he'd been shot and was in critical condition. Unfortunately, I'd had the cheap prepaid phone on speaker, so Zoe heard. "John isn't dead."

"That you know of. We could find that out, too."

The sigh that leaked out of me was angry. "Fine."

"And you could let me do some of the driving so you're not so tired all the time."

"No."

The glare she shot me clearly had that tone. The one that screamed, "Maaawmn."

"Not until we're away from the congestion." I indicated the miles of paved streets and highways and people. Too many strangers everywhere I looked.

"Promise?"

As much as it terrified me, I gave in this time. "Fine. Yes, I promise, but only on the back highways and only for two hours at a time. And if I ever get the feeling you're getting tired, I'm taking over. Got it?"

"You've been driving tired for almost a month now," she shot back.

I had, but that was beside the point. I was the one responsible for this mess, and I intended to shoulder the burden alone. And after finding out George was gone, it was truly alone. Everybody I'd confided in was either hospitalized, missing, or dead except Crystal, who was savvy enough to keep a low profile due to her intimate experience with this type of situation.

And Jackson.

I refused to think about him. He'd told me to stay away, and I promised I would. No matter what.

Changing the subject, I asked Zoe to keep her eyes peeled for a library sign as I puttered down the business highway I'd chosen at random.

"Left, Mom."

Shit. It was almost as if the building materialized out of nowhere. I circled the block to park in the lot.

"Okay. Hopefully, they won't ask for my ID."

Zoe stared at me with a scowl. "I've done this before, Mom."

"What? When?"

The silent "duh" was almost audible. "Since I was six. They taught us how to use a library in school."

"Right." I shook the cobwebs out of my head. I needed to stay sharp to not only evade Shock, find a place for Zoe and I to hide, and keep at least a half-step ahead of my daughter, who was becoming more and more like Jackson every day. Why hadn't I noticed that before?

She broke into my scattered thoughts. "Find a book and read, or stay out here and sleep. I'm going to print out maps."

"To where?"

She shrugged, and there was a bite to her reply. " I don't know. I'll improvise. Why not make a real road trip out of it? Find a liquor store and go full Thelma and Louise."

That attitude was definitely inherited from her father. "They died, remember?"

"Well, we leave killing someone and getting chased by cops off the list, okay?"

I stared at her, too wiped out to process where this was coming from. "Killing someone is never a good idea."

"Killing Shock would be," she muttered.

Holy shit. That woke me up. "What? No. That's a bad idea. Not only is it illegal, but we'd have the entire Destroyers nation coming after us, not just one or two clubs."

"You need a hobby."

"I can't have a hobby; I'm a full-time mom to *you*." That was an awful thing to say, and I opened my mouth to apologize but didn't get the words out because Zoe laughed hard.

"Finally. Let it out, Mom. Tell me how you really feel."

Her laughter was contagious. But her words dug in. "I love you. And I would drive a million miles to keep you safe. I'd steal; well I think we've proven that already. I'd lie."

She snorted. "I'd bet you'd kill someone, wouldn't you?"

That was questionable. "I don't know." But I did. I looked at her. "If it was a choice between losing you to Shock and going to prison for murder one, I'd take prison. I know I would."

Her hand crept over the console between us. "Ditto, Mom."

I shook my head. "I don't want that for you."

She squeezed my hand. "I know." Her eyes drifted to the building. "I bet it's air-conditioned in there, and they have a bathroom. It might even be clean."

"Let's find out."

While I browsed the romance stacks, Zoe talked the librarian into helping her with her "homework." I overheard her joke, "Even on vacation, Mom makes me work." Of course, the librarian was more than happy to get her signed in.

I settled into a comfy chair and started reading a thin novel. I couldn't tell you what the title was, or the story because it quickly became background to a lucid nap. Funny how I remember people walking around, Zoe in my peripheral quietly tapping away on the computer, and the various noises, but I dreamt of somewhere else. A place where the tension of hiding and concealing my identity vanished, and I could check out whatever books I wanted. Maybe even have a library of my own again.

Zoe stood over me, a stack of papers in hand. "Ready, Mom?"

Had I slept? I looked at the book in my hand. Page thirty. Man, that was pathetic. I must have fallen asleep. "I guess."

"Keys, I'm driving." She shook the stack of papers in hand. The colored maps had turn-by-turn directions gracing multiple pages.

"I thought your generation didn't do paper maps."

"Only the funky folded kind. Although, if we find any somewhere, you can teach me how to be a true pirate and do that fancy origami shit."

"Stuff," I corrected.

"Shit, Mom. I'm sixteen."

I stood up and glared at her. "We're in a library." I pointedly shot a look at the kiddie section.

"Whatever. We be off on a bonny adventure. And I be yer capt'n." Her pirate-ese needed work.

As I put the book back on the shelf, I realized I'd grabbed one of those kidnapped pirate princess titles. Zoe was smart enough to use my weakness against me.

God help me.

CHAPTER 17

Skilletsville—Jackson

"You did what?" Wolf grabbed the desk edge to push himself to standing so he could tower over me.

Tits grabbed his arm. "Hear him out."

"Fuck no. It's bad enough my wife is still sticking her neck out—"

"Wolf," I warned him. But he kept going.

"—every goddamned time there's a fucking sob story on her club's doorsteps, but now I gotta deal with the same shit from my fucking president?" His face screwed up with disbelief as he flung words at me. "You? The king of love 'em and leave 'em? What the fuck is next, Sprout is actually a savant?"

Considering he knew about my secret this whole fucking time, I wouldn't doubt it. But right now, Wolf had dug a grave and stuck a headstone in the churned-up dirt right next to it with his name on it.

Tits fumed. "Tell me what you really think."

He blanched. "Babe, I'm … sorry."

Her face was stoic—in the way a teakettle hides the boiling water inside. I waited to watch it whistle.

"I thought you were okay with my work." Her voice was quiet but deadly sharp.

Wolf opened his mouth and wisely shut it before saying something stupider. It was time to save his ass without actually sticking up for him.

"I need an introduction to one of your connections."

"You're looking at her." Tits flashed a hand down her upper half.

Sue me, I kind of got stuck on her namesake. It was a hazard I should have been immune to by this point when dealing with her.

And for that, Wolf turned his vitriol on me. "Jackson, you're going to take us down with this bullshit."

"Trust me, I'm trying to avoid that."

Tits broke in. "Has Kate contacted you?"

A great question. In fact, probably the best question anyone had asked so far. "No."

She leaned back, putting a hand on Wolf's arm as she did. The action turned him toward her and he deflated into his chair. Their hands stayed connected in the end. "You're setting things into motion as a back-up, I take it?"

"Yes. In case she shows up here or calls or anything, I want a way out for her." *And Zoe.*

Tits nodded slowly. "How far away should I reach?"

Another excellent question. One that Wolf pounced on. "Try Timbuktu?"

She shot a glance at him, quelling his joke.

"As far away as possible. Preferably somewhere Shock can't find her, ever."

Wolf didn't hide his bitter head shake.

I addressed that. "I know it's not going to be easy."

"Why did you lie to Nonno?" He caught himself and corrected the statement with an addition, "Fuck, you lied to Big G, too. Christ!"

Yeah, he was a smart man. He was beginning to see the disaster looming.

Another thought dawned on him. "You're going to have to step down."

Right. And nope. No way in hell was I doing that until forced. "And what? Leave her swinging without an ace up the sleeve? No fucking way. Until I'm pushed out, I'm staying right here or climbing higher."

He stared at me. "You have a fucking death wish, don't you?"

"If it keeps her safe and the rest of you idiots out of the hot seat, yeah!" I pounded my finger on the desk, punctuating my words. "Think about this. If I'm out, and you're still protecting me? You're blamed. Any single one of you steps up for me, you're a target. I'm doing you and all of them a favor by being glued to this chair."

"He's got a point," Tits commented. Her eyes pleaded with Wolf to see reason.

"He's an asshole who fucks a brother's old lady. At least that's how everyone else is going to see it."

Tits indicated me with a toss of the hand as she spoke. "Everyone *knows* he's an asshole."

"Hey!" That was uncalled for.

"True." Wolf tipped his head to concede.

"My own fucking VP. *Cold*, man."

Their smiles mocked me.

A tap on the door interrupted my tirade before I could get it started. "What?" Fucking Sprout.

"Boss? I think you're going to want to see this." He held up the fancy smartphone he used for the multiple businesses he inherited with his wife's money. The white screen wasn't a message thread or anything on social media. I motioned for the device, resigned to whatever dumbass shit he'd drummed up to break the tension in the room.

His gift, my curse.

I stared at the short email. "Who the fuck sent this?"

Sprout shrugged. "Dunno."

Wolf leaned over to try to read upside down. I gathered the phone closer to my vest to keep his prying eyes away. Sprout was smart enough to figure out that the sender wasn't Kate, but not smart enough to see who it really was.

But I knew.

There was only one girl on this planet who deserved the moniker *Knavette*. Which was her webmail handle. I hoped like hell she'd learned enough to cover her tracks; otherwise, Shock's goons would sniff that shit out faster than a cadaver dog. The note was simple.

We're coming to you. Four hours, max.

Four hours. That put them in a radius from here to Trenton, or maybe a bit farther out. Unless they were taking back roads, which could mean they were within touching distance.

Or, my heart shriveled a bit, they were in Pittsburgh.

Sprout glanced at Tits and Wolf. His eyes flicked to mine. He'd read the email. Seen the clue staring him in the face, and kept it quiet. I locked gazes with him for a short moment, quietly warning him to keep his mouth locked. If he could.

Which there were zero guarantees of. I handed the phone back. "Thanks for the heads up. Go back to guarding the door."

"I'm not a fucking prospect anymore." He'd used his low register voice, not the usual clown tones.

"I know that, and trust me, it can't be a speck this time. It needs to be someone Wolf and I trust, understand?"

His measured nod reminded me of his father. It was a damn shame that man was gone. Old Jolly would be a godsend right now. I'd tried to replace him for years. But my efforts were likely in vain. We were getting soft with good living and a bankroll that didn't rely on illegal activity. No matter how many quality killers I found, I failed to hire the right kind of killer who wouldn't question the cost.

Which brought me back to the current issue of getting Wolf on board, now with a deadline. "Here's the issue. The shit storm is coming. Now."

Wolf smirked.

Tits, much smarter than her husband, jerked her focus to me. "Now?"

I nodded. "It will have to be you. Wolf, please understand I didn't want that. I just wanted an introduction so I could keep you both out of my mess, believe me."

He blinked. "*Now?*"

"Four hours. Or less."

"Jesus." He searched for an exit I hadn't discovered. "We're fucked."

Not if I could get her and Zoe gone fast enough. "Take Tits wherever she needs to be. Wait for my call."

Wolf shook his head. "No."

"What do you mean, no?"

There was a moment where I swear those two were telepathic. Tits raised her eyebrows. Wolf tilted his head. Their hands squeezed so tightly their knuckles turned white.

"I never saw you as a man who runs," Tits started.

"I don't."

She nodded and sent another look to Wolf. He shook his head, still arguing with her silently. Apparently, Tits was having none of it. She turned to me and asked, point blank, "But your woman is? I don't believe that."

"I told you her history. You both weren't there, but it was bad, even for Shock."

Tits flinched. She'd witnessed far worse in her life, that I was certain. I used that to my advantage.

"He might not be as powerful as some, but he's powerful enough."

"A bullet or two fixes that." Wolf squinted at me, remembering exactly how he and Tits managed to bury the ghosts of her past.

I stood up and leaned over the desk, examining the leg he'd lost. "And there's a price if you or anyone in the club does that. One I'm not letting *you* take, got it?" I included Tits in that declaration. "Find me a connection. Work fast. It's going down."

She stood up, pulling Wolf with her. "Are you sure? Because if she goes into my club's protection, she's never coming out. And you'll *never* see her again."

This was something I had been deliberating over for sixteen years. With every glimpse of happy families, especially ones with little girls, I ached for a better way. I wanted my family with me. I wanted Kate in my arms and Zoe under my roof.

Which would be their death sentence. Or worse. "I'm sure." It hurt like hell to say those words.

She read my face. "No, you aren't."

Wolf shot her a look. His lips tightened. "She's calling your bluff."

"Who says I'm bluffing?" I had a shit hand. One I knew better than to play. In little over four hours, I'd finally see my daughter. And then I'd have to give her up. Forever. There was no salvaging that. No happily ever after. It would gut me. I'd be a shell of a man waiting to die.

Which was what life was truly like; you lived to die, and it was just the way things worked in a perverse way. I wasn't the kind of man who deserved the fortune I got. I was a murderer and a liar, and had stolen a sworn brother's woman. Wife or not, that shit didn't fly. And for a possessive yet powerful man like Shock, a beating wouldn't be the end of it. He wouldn't stop until I was dead.

"You better talk to your woman, Wolf. It's going down like that."

I turned my back to them both, motioning for them to get their asses gone. I stared at the window in the wall, not seeing the trees or the piles of junk outside, but rather wondering where and when my life took a wrong turn. It likely wasn't even my fault. It was a birthright. The son of a hooker and a killer would never live easily. That was a fact.

Sprout made a noise, so I knew he was behind me.

"What the fuck do you want now?"

The door snicked shut, and he cleared his throat. "We?"

Fuck. Sprout was too damned smart. I closed my eyes. "Yeah."

He sat in the chair, clothes rustling and leather coat creaking. I took my time to push all of my fears and hopes out of my expression before turning to see what kind of insanity Sprout cooked up.

"Well?"

He tapped his fingers on the padded arm. "Shock's?"

Sprout was a hell of a lot smarter than I knew. "No."

He visibly relaxed. "Cool."

"That's it? Cool?"

He grinned, the gape of his mouth widening and taking over more space on his face than was natural. "I can't wait to be a Dad. What's it like?"

"How the fuck would I know?" I hadn't even met my daughter. And she was almost an adult.

His grin grew impossibly wide. "Oh, you *know.* Good thing it's a boy, right?"

Whatever amusement I had left dropped into my shoes. "I'm fucked."

Sprout's smile wilted like wet toilet paper. "You've got to be kidding me. A girl? Holy shit. You *are* fucked." His laughter shook the panes in the glass.

"I hope your first born is a girl, too, damn it."

He grinned again, softer this time. "She'd look like Danielle, or Ma. We'll know next ultrasound."

I buzzed to cut him off. "Nope, she'll have your big ears and gangly limbs." That made me smile maliciously.

But Sprout was undeterred. "That would be amazing." His smile quirked up to one side, and the lines around his eyes deepened while the worry marks on his forehead eased. I recognized that expression. I felt it mirrored in my heart. If Zoe looked like me, God…

"What's her name?"

"Zoe." My voice was a reverent whisper.

"Fuck man, that's a good name."

It was. And I had nothing to do with it. Just like I'd have nothing to do with her future. I wouldn't be there to cock-block assholes when she started dating.

"Oh shit," I whispered, my thoughts already screwing with me.

"What?"

"She's sixteen."

Sprout's horror morphed into a puckered face, and then he guffawed. "Oh *shit*, boss. You're going to go gray overnight once we collect her. Brace yourself for your ultimate nightmare. You're not only going to be a dad in a couple of hours, but a dad of a teenage girl. A little female clone of you."

My head dropped, and I rubbed the budding headache from between my brows. And emotion hit me hard. I didn't want to give her up. Not ever. And I certainly didn't want her going off to God-knows-where. A place I couldn't be her protector.

Tits was onto something. I was *not* certain about giving them up. Moreover, I wasn't the kind of person who ran. Sure, I lied, I evaded, I flexed reality as much as I could to mask my crimes. But I also was not a man afraid of tackling a tough problem and meeting it with force. I'd spent years building the club, picking fearless men. My immediate brothers didn't shy away from challenges. And they could not be ruled, except by the High King of Fools. Me. Their brother. The one guy who made sure this madhouse had walls twelve feet high and enough killers in the ranks to wage a regional war.

I texted Wolf. It was short and sweet.

Tits is right. I'm fighting for her this time. Brace yourself.

CHAPTER 18

Kate

The drone of tires on asphalt and the puttering of the engine slowed. The trip started with good intentions, watching Zoe carefully, monitoring her speed and her distance, making sure she wasn't swerving or not in control. But when she proved herself as not only a cautious driver but a steady one, my apprehension faded. With it, my ability to stay awake. I hadn't been the passenger in so long that the lack of vigilance lulled me into much-needed rest.

"Where are we?"

"Getting gas." Zoe pulled up to the pump and maybe hit the brakes a little harder than I would, but otherwise, she handled the entire event well. "I'll go in and pay." She held out her hand.

I dug into the petty cash that was dwindling too quickly. We'd have to go to ground soon or risk running out. As I handed it off, I blinked to clear the fuzziness out of my eyes.

A sign in the distance marked the fast-food restaurant down the double-lane highway. I squinted because there was a large road sign indicating a major highway. And it was too familiar. I got out of the car so I could see better and immediately knew my competent daughter was too damn competent. She came out of the store with a receipt in hand.

"Here." She handed it off and began pumping gas. We'd need that full tank of gas to get as far away from this place as possible.

I waited until she returned the spout to its cradle. "Keys."

"I got it, Mom."

"We're in Pennsylvania." The keystone circling the highway number gave it away.

One shoulder went up, and I waited for her to match it to the "So?" in her eyes. But she didn't say it. Instead, she squared up.

When did she get taller than me?

"We're going to Dad, and if you throw a fit, I'm going to toss one right back." She motioned to the busy station.

Under my breath, I hissed out, "Do you know how dangerous this is?" To punctuate my warning, a motorcycle roared past. I didn't dare look because I'd truly freak out if I saw Destroyers colors on their back. Fit or not, Zoe and I were leaving this goddamned state as fast as possible. "Keys."

"No." She pushed the lock button on the car. Its chirp caught the attention of the guy pumping gas on the next island over. He smiled and did a little head nod, then continued filling his truck as if my daughter and I weren't having a standoff in the middle of the lot. However, I couldn't count on that if Zoe started a true tirade. She'd fooled me earlier, and I had no doubt she could fool complete strangers into doing her bidding.

"Let's talk in the car." I motioned for her to unlock it again.

"No."

"Zoe."

She shook her head and started for the store instead. God knows what she'd say to the clerk in there, so I followed her to mitigate the damage as much as I could.

And caught her with my prepaid cell phone to her ear. "What are you doing?"

"Calling Dad."

"You don't have his number."

She glared at me. The clerk looked conflicted.

"Is everything alright?"

"She's being stubborn," I said.

"So are you," Zoe shot back.

I prepared to fire something back, but the call went through, and Zoe started talking. "James Campbell Nist. They call him Jackson."

In the pause, I marveled in utter horror and amazement at my daughter's resourcefulness. I'd never uttered Jackson's real name. How in the hell had she found that out?

She tapped her foot and raised that eyebrow at me. I shook my head back at her.

"Hey… yeah, you got her."

If I hadn't glared at her, I might have missed it. The water in her eyes as she teared up. Pain clutched my heart. What if he rejected her? How would she ever recover? I'd been an idiot to build him up to be some sort of savior when, in truth, he was just another asshole biker. Now she was paying the price for my stupidity.

Zoe turned her back on me and mumbled our location. "Yeah, we will."

She ended the call and wiped her eyes, still trying to hide the tears from me. I put an arm around her shoulder, pulling her close. "I'm sorry."

She sniffed. "For what?"

"Everything? I love you."

"I know."

I squeezed her tightly. "Pick whatever you want, then we'll get on the road again."

"We're not leaving."

What? "I… I'm sorry, why?"

"Because Dad's going to be here in twenty minutes, and if we're not here, he said he'd tear Hell apart to find us."

Holy shit. I wanted to be cautious, but my heart leaped out of my chest and was dancing with glee. He cared? He wanted us back? Or was he possessive like Shock? The elation I felt was mixed with terror. "I hope that's not a trick."

Her eyes met mine. "It won't be."

Oh, Zoe. My heart went out to her. So young, so hopeful. "Let's *please* be careful, okay? I can't lose you. And I don't want to see you hurt." And I had an intimate understanding of how much it hurt when he was gone.

Too soon, a distinctive rumble of multiple motorcycles made the cashier crane her neck out the windows to see what the thunder brought her way. The nervous way she emptied the till made me check the clock on the phone Zoe relinquished. It hadn't been twenty minutes. And from the rapid approach, either the whole pack broke the sound barrier, or it wasn't Jackson.

I grabbed Zoe and pulled her away from the window. "Go to the back, find an emergency exit. Now!"

"It's probably him."

"If it isn't, I need you gone, got it? Don't talk to anyone, not the cops, not a stranger, and definitely not a biker." I pressed the phone into her hands. "Call John if we get separated; he'll figure something out."

I hoped like hell there wasn't a way to track a prepaid phone, but I'd been away from the realm of criminals for so long that I had no idea anymore. Zoe hit my back, giving me a crushing hug, then followed orders and hid out in the back hallway. The cashier saw it, met my eyes, and nodded.

Four bikes pulled in almost simultaneously, and at least seven followed. There was a range of machines, from shiny to one that barely looked road-worthy. Every single rider wore face masks or full helmets.

The Destroyers Skull on their back was unmistakable. The sight of it made my legs shake. I'd only known that ugly logo in terror. I swallowed and stood my ground near the door. I was ready to bolt if needed, but if it was Shock, my running was done. I'd gladly step back into his deadly clutches if it meant Zoe was out there, free. A straggler driving a van joined the group, bringing the total up to twelve. The lead rider barely acknowledged the final member, opting instead to swiftly park the bike and, *oh my God*, pull out a gun.

He didn't even bother to take off the mask or wait for the mohawked monster at his side. But I took a small comfort in not recognizing the soldier flanking the leader. Despite being almost as large as BamBam, he carried it differently. More in the shoulders and in raw power than a quarter ton of weight. And the leader was most definitely not Shock. He was too lean, too tall, and despite the ambiguity of not seeing his full face, I recognized that body and that walk.

I burst out of the station, motioning behind me to indicate to Zoe that it was him.

Jackson had come for her. I screeched to a halt, realizing that he might be angry with me. And that gun was dangerously visible.

"Is that her?" His Sergeant-at-Arms' name tag read, "Bear." He pulled off his riding goggles and scanned me from head to toe, but not in a lecherous manner, more like he was searching for threats, weapons, or anything that marked me as a danger to his president. I held out my hands.

"Jackson." I could hardly meet his eyes. Those piercingly familiar eyes Zoe inherited narrowed.

"Where is she?"

I sucked in a breath and braced. I was a fool to think we meant anything to each other anymore. "Inside."

To prove me wrong, the door at my back swung open, and Zoe raced past me too quick to catch. "Daddy!" She hit his chest and bounced as he stepped back, both arms out.

My heart hit the pavement. He wasn't hugging her back. And in that brief moment, I wanted to grab that gun out of his hand and kill him.

"Bear, take this." He held the weapon out stiffly.

Zoe's arms dropped to her sides, and she took a step back to look at her father. "Dad?"

Jackson's jaw worked, but no words came out.

I stepped in, ready to do battle for my baby. "Yes, Zoe. That's him." I put a hand on her shoulder and inserted myself firmly at her side, just in case I had to pick up the pieces.

His eyes met mine. "Kate," he breathed.

It was as if someone had stolen his voice. "Hi." I glanced nervously at the crowd of bikers and tightened my grip on Zoe's shoulder.

An extremely tall biker with wild, curly hair stepped forward, leaning a little to examine Zoe and me. "She's got your eyebrow, boss."

Jackson's backhand caught him in the gut. "Not the time, Sprout." He acknowledged both of us with a tip of his head. "Zoe." Then he blinked as if clearing his eyes. His now empty gun hand lifted, grasping at air. "I never…"

He turned to me. "Kate?" The anguish on his face furrowed between his brows. "I told you—"

"I know. It wasn't—" I caught myself, I would *not* blame Zoe. "I'm sorry."

He shook his head. "No." The gesture became more forceful. "No. I'm the one who should be sorry. I never should have told you to stay away." He swallowed. The movement drew my attention to his bare throat and the leather vest on his chest. The president's patch mocked me. How? When? And the biggest question: how could I ever deal with this version of him?

"We need to move, Jackson. Get her and the kid somewhere safer."

It was shocking to see a woman with them. She didn't wear Destroyers colors, and it was her bike that was the ugliest one. But she certainly fit with these men. Something about the wary way she scanned the lot and the road beyond told me she was more than competent. And, I had to admit, she was much prettier than I could ever be. Her white-blond hair and perfect skin belonged on magazine covers, not in the middle of a biker gang. The gun in her hand fit, though.

"She's right. My car's right there. I can follow."

Jackson held up a hand. "First things first, Zoe?" He motioned to her.

My daughter shook off my grip and stepped forward. She stopped barely a stride away and looked up at him. He tilted his head to search her face.

"You took an awful risk today."

"I had to." Her fingers curled into fists, but she didn't break eye contact.

Jackson's hand lifted. I cringed inside, worried this was going to be a nightmare. Instead, he held it inches from her face.

"May I?" Asking if he could touch.

Zoe nodded.

At first, it was light. A tentative brush of her eyebrow. Then his hand fell to her shoulder, and he pulled her in for the hug she deserved. His shoulders shook, and I knew, despite his face being buried in her hair, he was crying.

Bear turned away, scanning for threats and ignoring his leader's weakness.

So did the woman, and the tall one named Sprout. The latter didn't stay quiet, though. "What are you assholes waiting for? Gas up. Fuck. Y'all act like a bunch of fucking prospects."

"Watch it, Sprout." A long-haired man who looked like a Viking in biker leather limped up to the woman and whispered in her ear. The quiet command got her moving to her bike and filling up with the rest of the group while her man examined me. I caught his name patch and the VP patch.

"Wolf." I held out a hand. "Kate..." I didn't want to lie to them, but would not say my full name if I could help it.

"Kate Weaver." He didn't take my hand. "I know." He tipped his head toward Jackson. "Didn't know about that, though." He frowned. His eyes flicked back to mine accompanied by a slight shake of his head, warning me I'd better not fuck up. Or that he didn't like the situation one bit. I couldn't blame him for it. I'd brought a war to their home. "Keys." He held out his hand.

"Zoe has them."

His shock turned to a scowl. "He's got a kid who drives?" A curse hissed out of his lips before he could stop it. Then the damnedest thing happened. It started with a slight tremor in his shoulders and turned into a full bellow of laughter. "Jackson, you fucking dog."

"Fuck off, asshole."

"She's old enough to drive. You know what's next, old man?"

That got Jackson moving. "Enough. Zoe, give the keys to Wolf. You're riding with Sprout. Hey, dickweed, do you still have that vest for Danielle in your bags?"

"Yup," Sprout answered. He dug through the bag nearest and pulled out a velcro-strapped vest that looked like John's body armor. He handed it to Jackson with a quick tap on the front and flipped it over to tap the extra panel on the back before letting it go.

Jackson strapped it around Zoe. "Precautionary. You're riding with the village idiot, but don't let that scare you. He's been on two wheels longer than he's been walking. I wouldn't trust you with anyone else, understand?"

"I guess." Zoe patted at the heavy panels now snugly encasing her. I breathed a little sigh of relief, knowing she was safer. Maybe not as safe as a car, but protected from Shock just a bit better.

"And you," Jackson's finger moved, trying to reel me in. I resisted and crossed my arms.

"I told you, I can follow."

He shook his head. "Absofuckinglutely not. You're on the back of my bike and you ain't never leaving it, got it?"

It took everything in me not to cry. It wasn't every little girl's dream, and certainly hadn't been one of mine nineteen years ago. But today I was surprised to discover there was something I longed for more than safety. And that was to wrap my body around him again.

CHAPTER 19

The Clubhouse—Jackson

Sprout's legs were too long. He matched my hurried stride as I crossed from the staircase to the meeting room.

"What are we doing with them?"

I grunted and scanned the bar. It wasn't evening yet, but a couple of the hookers had shown up. "Take the night off, ladies. Upstairs is off limits."

"Boss?"

"Not now, Sprout."

"Boss."

I stopped, almost exactly in the center of the room, where nineteen-ish years ago Kate puked her guts out. "What?!"

"They can't stay here."

"Like hell they can't."

He opened his big ass mouth, but looked around first. "If you haven't noticed, this is a biker clubhouse, complete with whores, set inside a junkyard."

My glare should have had him ducking for cover. But fool that he was, he kept talking.

"I know if it was my Danielle or Ma, I'd want something better."

"You got a castle you can pull out of your ass?" *Complete with a moat, guards, and a fire-breathing dragon?*

"I've got three showcase houses, and I only need one. Maybe two."

I blinked.

Somewhere between that email and holding Zoe in my arms for the very first time, I'd forgotten all about the club, the businesses we ran, and the sometimes competence of it all. "I wasn't going to ask."

"But I'm giving."

If it were any other man, I'd ask what was the catch? But this was Sprout. He was born into this shit. His grandfather was a member. His father died for this club. He shared millions of dollars he didn't have to share because he believed in us. It was about time I showed some faith back. "I appreciate the offer. But you know Shock might fuck it up."

He shrugged. "They're insured. And right now none of them are making me any fucking money. So, that might be a good thing."

I slapped the top of his head. "And while it's getting fucked up, my woman and daughter are there. No. It ain't a good thing."

"But it's better than this." He motioned around at the squalor.

Reluctantly, I had to admit it was a valid point. "I don't want to…" I didn't want to what? Get their hopes up? Play house, and then have them find out I was an utter asshole? Better they find out exactly who I was first and then see a better side of me later.

Or else it would all be lies. I'd had enough of those.

"Get everyone who was on the run in the fucking meeting room. We gotta put a lid on this shit immediately." Before Nonno or Big G, or God forbid, Shock, found out.

"On it." He whistled, "Prayer session. Specks, you heard Jackson, the girls gotta get out. O.U.T. Now."

One of the hookers complained. As did a member who must have shown up while we were out.

I bitched right back. "Baldy, shut the fuck up and get your ass in that room. Smoke, you can keep a lid on this shit out here, yeah?" Smoke was almost out of his prospect phase, and already shacked up with an ol' lady. He'd done a stint in prison between his first two years as a prospect and this final year. He was one of the few I believed in to lead this group of misfits. And he'd already proven to be an asset.

"You got it, boss." He personally helped one of the women off their barstool and pointed her to the door. The other prospect, who hadn't earned more than the name "Speck" was doing a piss-poor job of corralling. He would not make it. I didn't see the fire in his gut. He was strictly here for the money he'd get someday.

I had enough of that type of asshole. With Kate and Zoe here, there were going to be no more free rides for anyone. "Sprout, put that one on the list."

"The shit list or short list?"

"What the fuck do you think?"

He tipped his head and forced a comical frown on his face. "I don't know, we don't have anyone to replace him yet. But you do you."

"Who runs this club?"

He grinned. "The ol' ladies, of which, I think we just got another one."

That didn't deserve a response.

Neither did the jeers and bullshit my men gave me in our little "prayer" session. Then again, at least they booed down Wolf's suggestion that I take the women and run. Maybe those fuckers wanted to see me dead? Whichever way you sliced it, the club knew about Kate. And worse, they knew about Zoe. From that point on, it was an endless stream of "how old was that hooker you had last month," to "Gee, Dad, a couple more years and you'll be a grandpa."

The noise followed me out the door.

Smoke had one of the hookers by the arm, a deep frown on his face, and if I wasn't mistaken, a war storming behind his eyes.

"Why isn't she gone?"

"Not my fucking idea," Smoke grumbled.

The hooker, Tina, talked over him. "Shock's been trying to pay us for info on you about Kate."

"Trying or succeeding?"

Her eyes hit the floor. Just like I thought.

"And?"

She rallied. "And sending the rest of them home before laying down the law was a mistake."

I motioned for Smoke to let her go. There were red marks on her upper arm. Luckily, they faded quickly, otherwise I might have lost track of the conversation. "Sweetheart, Shock's going to find out sooner or later. It wasn't a mistake. If I wanted to hide Kate, I would have."

Her mouth softened. "What about the other girl?"

My eyes flicked to Smoke's. He wasn't the right man for this. I needed Wolf or someone brutal standing behind her. But apparently, Smoke saw enough in that quick glance to grab her by both arms and demanded. "What other girl?"

He squeezed her biceps until she winced.

I repeated his words, "What other girl?" Mine was kinder, good cop, bad cop, except of the two, I wasn't the good cop at all.

"Is she Shock's daughter?"

I laughed. My brothers laughed. Smoke let go of Tina and waited as I got it out of my system. Finally, I wiped the moisture gathered at the corner of my eye. "Tina, you can tell Shock yourself that the other girl is my daughter. Mine. No doubt whatsoever. And if he wants to come fuck with what's mine, or what he lost? He's a dead man. Got it?"

Her face blanched slightly. "Are you serious?"

"Everybody keeps asking me that. And I'll tell you what I told them. Yeah. I'm one hundred percent serious about this. She's mine. Her mother's mine."

Tina's eyes dropped again but flickered up with a tilt I could read a mile away. "But is she on board with this? Or is she just using you like she used Shock?"

That's what she thought this was?

I lifted her head by the chin and got real close so she'd hear me loud and clear. "Pack your things. You can tell Shock in person. And after you're done ratting on us? Don't come back."

She scrambled to the door. I made Smoke confirm she was gone.

"What's this? You got an ol' lady and we can't fuck anymore?" Baldy stuck his ugly mug in my face.

Sprout was right, damn him. "While Kate or Zoe is here, you keep that shit out of sight. I'm moving them tomorrow."

I flicked a nod toward Sprout to make it happen. As much as I dreaded the danger they'd be in, tucking them into a brand new show model house in the fancier suburbs we were building was the right thing for the club. And since they'd lived in squalor for so long, it would be fitting for me to give them luxury finally. At least until the hammer fell, and I was dead. Then they'd get it all. That had to be better than a junkyard and a death sentence. Although it was debatable if the latter ended with my demise.

Tina wasn't the only hooker in our corral on Shock's payroll. I could feel it. Which meant I needed to perform damage control, fast.

On the way up the stairs, I dialed Nonno. Big G was on my list, but not immediately. He wouldn't give two shits about Shock's complaints. But Nonno had to listen. That was his job.

Loud music blared through the phone's speaker. "I'm busy Jackson."

A good fisherman knows bait. "Too busy for an apology?"

There was a moment I thought he'd hung up on me. I waited at the top of the stairs to give him time to speak.

"What kind of stupid do you take me for?"

"I don't. You wouldn't be where you're at by being stupid." Just greedy, which, as a character flaw, he had in abundance.

"Shock told me what you did."

There were a million things Shock could have told him. "Did you happen to hear what he got in trouble for up in Maine?" It was a long shot. All I had was a hint of a rumor through Walt.

Silence.

"It's related. But I think you know that." I was bluffing.

"Hang on." There was a low rumble of voices and the music in the background faded. "I've got guys from an Eastern New York feeder chapter bitching at me because two of their own are facing attempted murder of a goddamned cop. I've got you calling and being all cryptic, and I got a fucking shit show brewing in Pittsburgh. Tell me you are not to blame for all of this."

"I'm not. Shock is."

"Goddammit. You're like a couple of fucking kindergarten punks fighting over a damn toy."

Ah-ha! I was right. Shock already knew about Kate and he'd filed a complaint against me.

"Well, I've got the toy now, and she ain't going back."

"You motherfucker. She's Shock's wife."

"She's a human being, and trafficking will get you twenty. She's got all the evidence to bury our guy. So tell me, why shouldn't I keep her safe, happy, and quiet?"

The door at the end of the hall shut abruptly. I'd been eavesdropped on. Either Kate or Zoe heard me and probably caught the worst of it. I tacked another to do tick box on my list. Fuck it, I was going to handle two problems at once. I strode to the end of the hall and entered my office. Kate was there flushed all blotchy and breathing hard. She scurried to pack everything they'd brought with them, and an irate Zoe was in my office chair deliberately not helping.

Nonno was done ruminating over my proposal and spoke, "This shit is your fault."

"Well, I'll admit some fault and say sorry for some of it. See, I took a woman who was scared to death, almost dead, and ready to turn state's evidence on your golden child; and I placed her somewhere she'd be safe and happy. That's on me and I'm not one damn bit sorry for that part. What Shock has been doing to women is wrong. You and I both know that."

"She's his wife, asshole!"

"Wife or not, she's got a mind of her own. And she'll do whatever it takes to stay clear of that asshole. And the only thing I'm sorry about is the fact that I got fucking caught. That's it. I'm sorry I got caught helping. Such a damn shame." Nonno wasn't going to be happy with me no matter which way this went. I might as well own it.

Kate froze mid-stuff and stared at me open-mouthed.

"Nonno, get mad at me. I don't give a shit. But she ain't going back to Shock. If I have to help her find a hole in Timbuktu where she'll never have to see that asshole again, so be it."

The connection ended. Nonno was going to set stuff in motion that would seal my fate. I'd fucked up royally.

Yet somehow, it wasn't the end of my world. I was staring at the end. This beautiful, courageous woman, with her hair mussed and her face a mess of emotional turmoil. She was my future. Destroyers club or not, I knew my dying breath would be for her. "Hey, Kate."

"Who was that on the phone?"

"The national president for the Destroyers."

Her eyes went wide. "You stuck up for me against the—I'm still not staying. I'm sick and tired of being caged up even if it is for my own protection."

Zoe talked over her. "Dad, Mom is going to leave again. I'm not going. I'm staying here." She hit my side and wrapped her arms around me.

There was a split second I almost reached for my gun. Kate's eyes flicked to my hand.

I wiggled my fingers to loosen them and wrapped my arms around Zoe. "You are more than welcome to stay. But to set the record straight, your mom's upset because she heard part of a conversation, not the whole thing. But that part was bad, got it? Any sane woman would do exactly what she's doing right now." I pried Zoe off me and looked her square in the eye. "You're too old to play games like you're doing with me, though. I see you."

Her eyes were almost a match to mine. Instead of the clear green of her mother's, my mud-splattered blue ones glared at me. "I'm not playing games."

She was a damn good liar, too. "You barely know me, and you're hitting me up with hugs to try to get your way. I grew up knowing every game a woman could play, and trust me, I *see* you."

That glare turned ice cold.

I laughed. My girl had a killer instinct. I loved discovering that. I asked Kate, "How did you deal with her for sixteen years?"

She set the bag down. Her eyes wandered to Zoe. Her words were barely a whisper. "I loved her every day." Then she pinned me with a glare of her own. "And that's why she hugs. I'm a little pissed at you for thinking she has an ulterior motive."

Another laugh barked out of me. It didn't go over well. "Sorry. I'm not used to it."

Kate blinked. "Like being kissed." Her eyes searched inward for answers.

Damn. She remembered that about me?

"Exactly." I closed the gap between us and nudged her to get her attention. "*Your* kisses." My gaze fixed on her lips, and I forgot about anything but kissing her again. It had been so long since—

"Wait…ugh. I don't wanna hear more of this. You two are disgusting." Zoe plugged her ears and began that annoying "la-la-la" kids see in videos.

Kate's spine straightened, and she brushed herself off, as if to dust off memories. But mine weren't so easily forgotten. How could I? She was the only woman I'd kissed in the last twenty years. My one and only. The woman who gave me a smart ass little girl who liked hugs. *Damn.*

"Zoe, get over here."

She unplugged her ears and stopped chanting. "Why?"

"Because you caught me by surprise earlier, and I wanna fix that. Hug?" I held my arms out, hoping like hell I hadn't ruined a good thing. Sure, it was a shock to the system, and my first instinct was to grab my gun and shoot whoever was attacking me, but once it sunk in that this was my girl—my baby I never got to hold? Well, my whole soul missed what it never had.

Zoe wrapped around me and squeezed. I checked with Kate before wrapping my arms around my baby girl. She nodded, giving me permission to hug back.

Like a flood, emotions I didn't know I had pushed up out of my gut and clenched my heart hard. I barely felt Zoe in my arms. I squeezed her just a little to ground me. Kate joined us, wrapping an arm around Zoe and one around me. Her breath brushed my neck as she tried and failed to bury her face in my shoulder.

Her body shuddered with a sob.

And I couldn't let that go. "Sorry, kid. Mom's turn." I let go of Zoe and wrapped Kate up tight, pulling her into me like I had those too-brief nights we had together. "Shh. I'm here. It's going to be okay."

"You don't know that."

"I don't. But that won't stop me from trying to make it okay. You gotta trust me on this."

Kate searched my eyes before speaking. "I don't want to stay here. It holds bad memories for me."

I understood why. "Only tonight. I'll set something else up for tomorrow. No cages."

Kate relented and curled back into my chest.

I looked over her head to check on Zoe.

She mimicked her mom's move earlier and wrapped around us. We were one, finally. A family. Even as fucked up as the situation was, we were whole. I kissed Kate's hair, then her cheeks, which were wet with silent tears. And held on tight to see her face and feel her warm skin in my hands. She was kissably close. But I hesitated, knowing I didn't deserve their love.

Kate's lips hit mine. It was almost as much of a shock as the hugs. But I remembered this. I remembered every second of passion and torment and treasured that blissful fall into a peace so deep it was like the perfect sunrise every damn day. She was *mine* in that kiss. And I was hers. Wrapping it all together in perfection was Zoe. The cutest damn teenager I'd ever seen. I broke the kiss and held Kate close so I could check to see if we weirded the kid out.

Zoe rolled her eyes, but her smile quirked off to the side, just like mine. I raised a brow in a silent question. *"You okay with this?"* I asked.

Her matching eyebrow went up, just like mine, with one eye squinted and the other drilling into mine to make the point clear. She skewered me with a command that was easily read. I'd seen it too often in the mirror and from my father. *"Don't screw this up,"* it said.

I shook my head. I'd move heaven and earth to make things right. She had my vow on that.

Zoe smiled and squeezed us both.

I wasn't a good man, but one of the luckiest sons of bitches ever because of the two beautiful women who trusted me. I would *not* screw this up.

CHAPTER 20

Kate

Deep into the unlit hours before dawn, I snuck around Jackson to use the bathroom attached to his domain. While not a castle, it was a private suite of three rooms. It included an office with space for at least five men to sit if you didn't count the chair behind the desk. From that throne, Jackson ruled these miscreants.

Attached to the office was a small bedroom with a queen-sized mattress, two mis-matched dressers, and a trunk overflowing with motorcycle gear. On the other side of the office was a private bathroom, complete with one of the smallest showers I'd ever seen. And for a woman who survived with an in-kitchen tub for over six months, it was one of the worst things I'd ever seen. But it was much better than the one I'd noticed on the trip to this little retreat.

Why? Despite the larger size and amenities, that bathroom reminded me too much of the one at Shock's headquarters. The one the hookers used. Judging by the series of three doors along one wall, Jackson kept hookers here, too.

Was I okay with that?

He'd told me his mother was one. Could I possibly be judgmental of him knowing about his childhood? I shook my head. No. That wasn't what bothered me. It was deeper than that. A fear that he was going to be like Shock. My hands trembled. I stared at them, trying to will myself to be stronger. I had to be. Zoe needed me.

Of course, she had her dad now.

With that thought, a pang of sorrow sliced through my heart. I was deathly afraid of this. Not only losing my daughter, but possibly to a man as evil as Shock. Worse? I didn't know if I wanted to escape from Jackson should the depths of my imaginings come true. Nor could I count on Zoe to see reason if escape was necessary.

Thank God for John. He verified my story with Zoe, giving it the gravitas needed to convince her to leave with me.

And they'd shot him. Shock did that.

Not Jackson…yet.

A soft knock tapped on the door. "You okay in there?" Jackson's voice was quiet, barely discernible over the constant thrum of noise from the jukebox a floor below. Didn't these assholes ever sleep?

"I'm fine."

He cleared his throat. "I'll believe that when you get your ass out here."

Spoken differently, it would have scared me. But he said it so kindly, I had to wonder if I was wrong to worry. Then again, I'd been proven utterly wrong with my father. "Give me a minute."

I washed my face and hands and nudged a half-hearted pep talk into my backbone. But the effect was fleeting. I had no strength left to fight.

"Babe?"

That soft prompt made me open the door to glare at him. He smiled.

Shock would have hurt me for that defiance.

"I'm scared."

Jackson blinked. Then opened his arms. "Come here."

I wanted to. But this was not something solved by a hug. Shock would kill him. Despite Jackson's position or his club as guards, I had an acute understanding of the vindictive evil aimed at us. "Shock is going to kill us."

He dropped his hands and sighed. "He'll kill me." His face turned grim. "Once that happens, you and Zoe…"

Yes. I knew the dark place his words had trailed off to. I'd lived it. I'd survived and fled. In doing so, I'd killed at least one man, and gravely wounded another already. Not to mention Cara, who never resurfaced.

"I'm not going to let that happen."

He was delusional. "It's going to happen."

Jackson grabbed me and pulled me close. His fingers cupped my chin, but they weren't bruising like Shock's would have been. "Listen to me. I will move the heavens for you and Zoe. No one is going to get through me. But if they do, I've got plans for that."

"Like?"

His jaw tightened. "My VP, Wolf... he's got a wife who works with a group who can move you, hide you, give you a whole new identity. Her name is Tits, but don't let that fool you. She's a badass with expertise in making that sort of thing happen. She knows how to keep you and Zoe safe."

While it was a relief to know there was a plan, it still meant he'd be dead. "Jackson..."

The arm around my waist tightened, and his grip on my chin turned into a caress. "I don't want to die. I want to live... for you. For Zoe, too, but mostly you. We deserve this. We deserve *happy*."

Which was why it wouldn't happen. The perversity of fate meant two people like Jackson and I wouldn't ever get a happily ever after. Eventually, the life we were tangled with would eat us alive.

"You deserve happiness, Kate." This time, his sigh sounded defeated. "You're right. I don't deserve happiness. But you... my God, Kate, you were born to be everything happiness is. You're beautiful, so damn beautiful, and you're not a bitch about it. You could be. But instead, you hold yourself with such grace and strength that I'm awed. You've become a wonderful mother and person. I can't compete with that."

"Shh." I put a finger on his lips to stop him from demeaning himself any further. If anything, that proved to me he wasn't like Shock at all. Jackson may be the leader of a motorcycle club and all that comes with it, but he wasn't soulless like Shock. And for some reason, I wanted to be at Jackson's side through the good and the awful, rotten, criminal bad. Because no matter what he'd done in his career as a member of the Destroyers, he simply wasn't the evil man my husband was.

Jackson's lips puckered on my finger. He broke the kiss with a warning query. "Kate?"

"Make sure Tits has a plan for Zoe. I'm going down with you."

He shook his head, disagreeing with me but not fighting me. "With you at my side? I'll fucking move the goddamned universe. Wait and see."

The familiar quirk of his cocky grin flicked upward.

I kissed it for no other reason than to see what it felt like against my lips.

Which was a… mistake? One I simply did not regret as our tongues tangoed, and he pressed me against the wall. I made a noise as he slipped his fingers under my sweats and into my panties.

"Shh, Kate. Zoe's sleeping in the next room."

"Which is why we shouldn't—" His mouth smothered my words and my resistance. I wrapped one leg around his hips to give him easier access to my clit.

Jackson did not fail me. His finger circled the nub, adding quick brushes against the apex as he swept over it again and again. I whimpered for more. I needed to feel again. I hungered for the slide of his cock in my vagina. With a few kisses and masterful fingering, he'd resurrected the passion I'd buried when he left that morning so long ago.

"Bed," I demanded.

Or mattress, *whatever.* He'd given up his queen-sized bed for a much smaller mattress dragged from one of the hooker's rooms into his office. It was slapped down in front of the door to his bedroom. I tugged at him to give me space to let me drag him over to it.

But he lifted me instead.

He carried me to the desk and set my ass on the edge. With a shove, he sent the contents to one end. "I'd send it to the floor, but I don't want to wake up Zoe, so—"

I stopped his words because I had a question that was extremely important to me. "Have you ever had sex on this desk before?" *Please, dear God don't say yes.*

"Hell, no. The desk is sacred."

And my butt was on it.

He must have read my face. "Only you. Lift up; I want your bare ass kissing it *now.*"

Tingles of arousal and a small amount of fear shivered through me. But I did as asked, knowing deep down I wasn't in danger. But it did cross my mind, which was too close to that threshold of terror to be benign. He stripped me easily and, with another lift and maneuvering, laid me on my back.

"Pull your shirt up, I need to see those tits."

My breath came in short gasps. My pussy was soaked. He pushed down his jeans, baring his penis. I tugged my shirt to my neck to expose my breasts, but didn't take it off because I needed to see him.

He tapped his dick on my pussy.

His *bare* dick.

"Condom!" I glanced at the bedroom because I might not have whisper-shouted that.

Jackson grinned and dug a packet from his jeans. "Not that I need it with you, but… if it makes you happy…" He rolled it on.

"What do you mean you don't need it? I'm not on the pill or anything." This time, I remembered to keep my voice down.

He sent me a look. One I couldn't decipher. So I shot him one back.

Jackson raised two fingers in a quick scissors motion.

"Oh." Oh. Wow. "When?"

"Right after you called me to tell me I was a dad."

Well. I tried to close my legs, but he'd already snuck between them again.

"What? You mad at that?"

With a hastened debate, I decided not to be. I didn't want to be a mother again. Not that raising Zoe was awful, but because of her age, and my age, and heck, to be utterly honest with myself, I was looking forward to life after twenty-four-seven mom life. Zoe would always be my baby, but part of the deal was making sure she became a functional adult. I hadn't had that option. I was seventeen, sold, raped, a fugitive, then a mom so quickly, I didn't know that life.

Jackson leaned over and kissed my breast. He settled his chin between them and stared at me. "You with me?"

I nodded. "I'm with you."

"Good." His lips locked onto my nipple and sucked just hard enough to send a wave of lust through me. I arched into his attack and relished in the ecstasy.

In reward, his fingers pinched at the other tit, and that was even better. But most of all, his crotch pressed hard against mine and with the right upward rock of my hips, I aligned with his shaft and worked against it, spreading a rush to every part of my system.

He broke the suction and reached down to insert himself. In a masterful thrust, he seated inside me.

I moaned.

He clapped his hand over my mouth and pumped into me furiously. "Shh, Kate. Hold it in."

I tried. He wasn't making it easy with the hard slide of his dick in and out of my pussy. I was lighting up from the inside as his neck turned red.

"Hold on to it. I'm almost there."

I was, too. I gripped his waist and tugged with each inward thrust, adding the silent urge to pound into me harder.

His hand slipped from my mouth and planted on the desk by my head. I gasped for air, but kept the keening demand to scream locked deep inside. "Soon, harder, but soon."

"Oh, Kate." His words strangled, and he sunk deep and hung there, his fingers grasping my shoulder and hip almost painfully. Connected as we were, the pressure of his body against mine, and the frantic cacophony of my nerves, all of it combined with the heady memories of our nights and this one. My body clamped onto his, throwing me into an orgasm so hard I almost forgot to be quiet. A tiny cry of ecstasy squeezed out, and I held my breath to ride it to the final throbbing bliss too many years denied.

Over me, Jackson grunted. His eyes met mine. But there was a madman inside, not the collected leader who made plans. This was the wild soul that lived inside him. Glorious and untamed, unleashing itself in the twitching pulses of his cock.

We were breathless and Jackson's body bent over mine. His grip relaxed, and he followed the collapse of strength down, barely catching himself above my body. "Fuck. It's been too long for us."

I had nothing profound to say to that, because it had been too long. "Next time we'll last longer."

He laughed in a quiet gust. "Next time, we'll be in a bed. Promise."

I ran my hand down his sweat-slicked neck. "What's that over there?"

He looked to his left. "Damn, part of a bed." His smile was contagious. But my quiet laughter caused him to slip out. I regretted it instantly.

It had been too long. And I needed more as soon as possible.

"I'll be right back. You're on the side against the wall, got it?"

A memory resurfaced. "That way, they shoot you first?"

He stopped, his grin uncertain. "You remembered?"

I nodded.

Such a bittersweet remembrance. This time, the threat was all too real. But I wasn't a coward. Logistically, a bullet would pass right through Jackson's body shield and into me. Which was exactly how I wanted it. If he went down, I'd be right there with him. "Against the wall, got it." I smiled at him to convince him this was all going to be okay.

I lied.

But we both knew I did, so it didn't count.

CHAPTER 21

Jackson

Practically our whole clubhouse barn could fit into the monstrosity Sprout grinned like a lunatic over. Kate and Zoe hesitated behind me, but they'd exited the SUV and were now targets. I motioned them to follow Sprout inside.

He hung in the foyer by the door, waiting for Bear and me to get our asses in gear.

"This ain't small, Sprout," I scanned the double-wide arched brick of the foyer.

"Funny. That's exactly what my wife said last night," Sprout joked.

Hilarious.

Kate and Zoe were in the great room by the fireplace.

"There's too much glass." I pointed to the windows lining the space. Two facing the street and a whole bank of them in the back so you could see the covered patio. It was a criminal's wet dream. The place screamed, "rob me!" Double doors in the front and back. No reinforced beams between them, either.

My head shook from side to side as the girls went from one room to the next. They oooed over the marble countertops, the wood floors, the vaulted ceilings, and each artisan pendant lamp that I was certain held non-tempered glass that would shatter everywhere if someone started shooting up the place.

"It's a fishbowl, right Bear?"

He grunted. "You've seen Sprout's house, haven't you?"

True, but wrong. I pointed at the backyard, which I could see plain as day. "Sprout doesn't have to look at his neighbor's upstairs bedroom over the fence."

"You haven't seen the best part." Sprout motioned for us to follow him.

That side-to-side motion of my head kept going. There was a window right next to the tub. I pointed it out to Kate. "Better not stand up; the neighbors will get a show."

She blushed.

"I kind of hate tubs. Especially ones in exposed areas…like *kitchens*." She sent me a crooked grin.

Oh, yeah. I remembered. A chuckle escaped, which caught Bear's attention. He wouldn't understand even if I explained it to him.

"Let me show you the closet." Sprout led us through the bathroom, past the fancy tub with the huge ass window next to it, and tapped on the closet door.

His finger thunked mutely. "Reinforced. The entire walk-in locks down as a safe room. There's a gun safe in the back." He flipped open a hidden panel, revealing a full-sized steel cabinet with biometric locks.

Now we were talking.

"Does the other closet have one?" This beast had two walk-in closets in the owner's suite.

He shook his head and squeezed past me and Bear to lead us through the maze of rooms and back through the main area to the other wing of the house.

"Office, full bath, two bedrooms with walk-in closets." He pointed out each detail. Zoe parked her ass in the bedroom on the right and bounced on the bed.

"This is my room."

I eyed the street through the window behind her. "The hell it is." I pointed through the window. "Bear? What's the range of a nine-mil with hollow points?"

He tipped his head and scanned the sightline from the curb to Zoe's closet. An un-reinforced one. "At least double. Half-aimed with spray, she's done, boss."

"Let's look at the back bedroom."

"Dad!"

"No, Zoe. Do I have to park Bear on the street and have him point his 50-cal at us to prove why? Jesus."

Kate blanched.

That side-to-side shake of my head was back. "Ground floor, windows, cheap ass fucking locks. I hate it."

She glanced at the decor. "It's too open."

"Mom, it's huge. I love it."

"It's the first place you looked at. Sprout, let's see what else you got."

The next model home was a two-story with garage doors gobbling up the curb appeal. I liked it already. I could ride up to the smaller door, slip the bike in, and lock it down without exposing Kate's car or the SUV to thieves. The windows facing the street were higher and smaller, exposing much less of the life inside to someone casing the joint.

The door had a reinforced kick plate. I tapped it as Sprout led us in. "Much better."

The foyer opened up on the right to a compact office. Beyond that was the great room and open floor plan kitchen and dining. The space was much less ostentatious, with fewer windows, subdued stone counters, not the garish black and white of the other house, but it still managed to pack a lot of space in the tighter frame.

Bear pointed at the yard behind the house. It was walled off, with no neighbors. Trees lined the sightline along with old-growth vines that would make most snipers groan with frustration. I'd have to get Wolf's old Ranger buddy up from West Virginia to check it out. But it felt safe. *Safer.*

"Pantry, mud room that attaches to the garage…" Sprout led Kate and Zoe through the tour of the main floor before leading us to the stairs we'd passed on the way in. One side went down, the other up.

"This reminds me of the house in Maine." Kate smiled at the open banisters and ran a hand over the railing.

"Except it's a *lot* bigger," Zoe commented.

"The stairs aren't nearly as steep."

"Or as narrow."

Their commentary bounced back and forth as they pointed out the similarities and the differences.

The staircase opened to a common area at the top. Sprout's decorator feathered it with a huge ass couch and sweet big-screen TV.

Zoe ran to the couch and picked up the remote. "It's got movie streaming!"

I scrutinized Sprout. "You keep a model home wired?"

He shook his head. "I had Hickey set it up last night after the meeting."

"Did you wire the other house?"

Another shake of the head.

"Bastard," I muttered. He arranged the showing in the order he did on purpose. He knew I'd turn down the first house because of the security issues. Most people thought he was a dumbass. Things like this were why I kept him around.

"This one could be a guest room." He motioned to the bedroom next to the stairs. It had double windows facing the street. "This one is harder to target." He led us to the doorway to point out the smaller space. The single set of windows above the garage was tucked into a dormer. Bear scanned the view.

"Bitch of a shot. The overhang fouls everything up."

I nodded and silently conferred with Kate, tossing the ball into her court.

"Zoe's," she agreed.

Perfect.

"Now for the money shot..." Sprout was finding too much pleasure in this.

And yet, he was right again.

The vaulted owner's suite was large enough that the king-sized bed fit nicely. There was a set of double French doors along the back side.

"What is that?" A security risk.

"Balcony. A private balcony."

Well. That might be a deal-breaker.

I let Bear check it out first. Meanwhile, Kate ran her hands over the marble counters in the attached bath. I pointed at the freestanding tub. The window next to this one was smaller, less exposed, and still kinky enough to make me wiggle an eyebrow at her.

"Boss?" Sprout called from the attached walk-in closet.

I peeked inside. "Reinforced?"

He nodded. "But the main safe room is in the basement." He waited for me to step out of his way to lead us down both flights of stairs to the family room.

"A bar should go over there," Bear pointed to the far corner.

"This ain't your house," I reminded him.

He shrugged. "Figure I'll be here often enough."

Damn it, he was right.

There was a simple bedroom off the hall flanking the stairs. Near the end was a bathroom. And at the very end, a closet. I didn't see the promised safe room he mentioned and was about to bring it up when Sprout reached inside the closet and flipped open a hidden panel, revealing a whole extra bedroom complete with gun storage, and an ultra-secure panic room.

"Sold," I said. It was perfect. A house, big enough for at least a handful and a half of my men to visit, and small enough that I didn't feel like a walking target. I looked at Kate for her sentiment.

"It's too big for just me and Zoe."

There was so much wrong with that sentence. "Bear? Check on my girl and do a circuit outside. Sprout?"

"Don't have to ask me twice. Zoe probably needs help bypassing the child locks for the porn channels."

"If you show my daughter porn, I will personally bury you alive."

He had the audacity to laugh at me as he took the stairs two at a time.

Then it was just Kate and me.

She read my face.

"You can't honestly tell me we're going to live here *together*. We don't know each other that well."

As far as arguments went, Kate's sucked. "My dick was in you last night. Your bare ass was on my desk."

She frowned. "That doesn't mean we're just going to play house all of a sudden."

"Yes, it does. You're mine."

Her back went straight. "Don't."

"Don't what? Lay my claim? I did that sixteen-plus years ago when Zoe was born." I pointed to the stairs.

Color stained Kate's cheeks as she cleared her throat. "Your claim? I'll remind you that the last man who laid a claim on me shared me with his entire club. Are you going to do that, too?"

"Hell no."

"Are you going to conveniently forget I'm still technically married?"

Fuck that. "You're getting a divorce." I'd sic the club's lawyer on it right away.

Her eyebrows rose. "Do you honestly think it's that easy? I've been a missing person for eighteen years. I'm probably legally dead. I can't just pick up where I left off."

"If you're legally dead, Shock ain't got a husband claim, does he now?"

Her open mouth froze in place before she could utter her next argument at me. It shut as she thought about my statement. "If I'm legally dead, Shock got my trust fund."

"*You* had a trust fund?" Everybody and their fucking cousin seemed to have one of those. Except me and all the other dumb, working-class schmucks in my club.

"Had. Dad's father. He was a circuit court judge."

How to put this as kindly as I could? "You ever think that's *why* Shock targeted your fucking sperm donor and his fucking coke habit? And maybe why he stuck a ring on it when that *isn't* his M.O.?"

Maybe that wasn't delivered with the finesse it should have been?

"Trust me, I thought about that a lot." Her tone was acidic.

"Well, if you're not dead, we should sue Shock for it." I hadn't heard of any rumors about a trust fund, but that wasn't something I'd considered before.

"We?"

"You and Zoe. I'll help. That *we*." With a trust fund, she could have a life again. Maybe one without me. I rethought my offer but kept my mouth shut. If worse came to worst, and Kate and I couldn't stand each other outside the bedroom, then I'd take my lumps and demand visitation. Because I wasn't about to get cut out of Zoe's life again. I'd just begun to dislike her as a teenager, and someday, she'd be an insanely strong-willed woman like her mother. No one was going to deny me the opportunity to see that to fruition. "I've got a lawyer on retainer."

Technically, a whole firm because the club's legal issues got a shit-ton more complicated a few years back.

"How can you afford that? And this?" She motioned to the house. "You had a shack in Maine."

"Yeah. And you saw how I lived until this morning. I had a room with a tiny ass bathroom above a biker clubhouse. Every dime went into making money." For the club, mostly. But also got socked away for legal fees and my Justin Case Charity Fund. As in, just in case my evil doings caught up with me and I had to run. Once Sprout married Danielle and started using the inheritance from his wife's grandmother to start a construction company, that fund got bigger fast.

Her scowl confused me. "Why the face?"

"Illegal money?"

I tipped my head to the side and tugged on my ear as if I hadn't heard her correctly. "Huh?"

"Who was I married to?" Her eyes narrowed.

Ah, right. She'd have seen ten times worse than the typical shit we got into here in Skilletsville. But that didn't include my extracurricular activities, which ensured that no fewer than a dozen clubs around this country owed me a blood debt. Not even Wolf knew about those. But Nonno did.

And if he and Shock were cooking up a way to bring me down, it would be too damn easy to pin at least one of those murders on me.

Except that would also implicate Nonno, who ordered one of the hits. I stuck a mental Post-it on that memory to revisit later.

"About six, seven years back, the mayor of this little sphincter of a munici-pality saw the error of her ways and set us up with a lot of money and property."

"Legally?"

"Yeah, all legit. Long ass story short, we had to protect her grand-daughter. Sprout ended up sticking his dick in it, and they're having a kid come December."

"It's hard to believe that gangly kid is going to be a father." Her mouth lifted in the corner.

"Do you remember Ma?"

"Gina? Oh my God, yes. She saved my life."

It was official. I was wounded. "So did I."

Kate shot me a look that clearly said, "duh." Or maybe something a little more complicated than that. I opted for simple. But I also had to warn her. "You didn't tell anybody that, did you?"

"What? No. Shock would kill her, biker mother or not."

If Shock killed Sprout's ma, nothing would save him from the hell that would rain down.

"Good. Keep that in mind when you see her tonight. I'm going to get the prospects to bring your shit here. We'll have a party to break the place in."

"A party?" Kate was not enthused.

"It'll be fun. Trust me."

CHAPTER 22

Kate

"*It'll be fun. Trust me.*" I cursed Jackson under my breath as I mopped yet another spilled beer from the still so new it smelled like a factory, wood laminate flooring. I did not know if it would stain or not; having zero experience with the particular brand they'd run from wall to wall lengthwise through the open floor plan, but I remembered the work it took to strip the floor in the house and did not want to face that again.

At least it wasn't carpet.

The rug in the living room would never be the same.

Jackson was in the backyard, testing our new neighbor's hearing with loud music and no fewer than five bikers swearing and laughing and being assholes in general.

I opened the pantry to put the mop away and stopped short.

Baldy, who came in with the second wave of bikers, grinned at me.

The girl kneeling at his feet hadn't noticed the open door at her back yet... being too busy slobbering on his knob.

His fist was buried in her hair. The tattoos on his hand stood out against the white-lined tension in his grip.

Almost twenty years should have been enough to erase some memories. But as I shakily handed Baldy the mop, I realized that I still hadn't recovered from all of them.

I closed the door on them and stared at the pristine white shaker-style molding. Her moans and the wet sounds of mouth on cock echoed in my head louder than the stereo thumping away at a heavy song I didn't recognize.

Laughter from the backyard.

The clang of the grill lid.

Snatches of the TV upstairs where Zoe and some of the younger women of the club watched movies.

To my left, one of Jackson's crew embellished a story about sex. It layered upon the memories and added fresh new grooves of trauma. I searched the room for a friendly face. There was Skinner, the too-thin tech guru who Jackson recruited from Hagerstown. Next to him was Hickey. He was also thin, but taller and more muscular. Both liked computers, but Hickey was also good with money and therefore voted treasurer for the last eight years. On the couch, almost taking up a section by himself, sat Bear. He had a woman on his lap, but she was too busy rolling a joint to care that he was deep in discussion with the guy to his right. That was Coop, or Chickenman as sometimes called. He also had a woman. Jelly. She was dancing near the fireplace with Hollywood. His name patch declared his road name was "Trout." But the Hollywood moniker was due to his recent stint in amateur porn.

The club made porn movies. And ran a sex cam business. They had whores.

They smoked pot and sold cocaine.

What was I doing here? One of my two best friends was a cop. Wait, my other best friend used to be a hooker. I had no right to judge anyone. My father died a crack addict.

I'd been forced to give blow jobs to the officers of Shock's court.

That's what was really bothering me. I turned to look out the glass to see if I could catch Jackson's attention. But his back was to me.

Slowly, I crossed the house to the stairs. I remembered to smile and nod when greeted. Pretending to be happy was a skill I'd never really lost. In fact, I'd perfected it over the years between then and now.

The music almost drowned out the TV, despite the volume being too loud to hear yourself think. The women scattered on the large L-shaped couch were from various backgrounds. My daughter sat next to a girl named Lily. She was nineteen and going to college a month from now. She'd had a rough start in life, being Jewel's daughter. But the young lady she was becoming impressed me. It struck me as odd to know exactly how she came to be, seeing the before of Pinner's relationship with Hilea in Poppy, the woman sitting next to her, and remembering that lovely child who somehow remembered me from that life. Next to Gina was her daughter-in-law, Danielle. She was an heiress. Her grandmother once ran this town for at least two decades. But now Danielle was Sprout's wife and expecting their first child.

I took the empty end next to Poppy. The subtitles were on, so I began scanning them to take my mind off downstairs.

Gina lifted an eyebrow. "Did you finally give up?"

"What?" It was difficult to make out her words.

"Trying to corral the looney bin."

Danielle glanced over. "I lasted exactly five minutes. Jackson had a party going before I could even open my mouth."

Gina wrapped an arm over her daughter-in-law's shoulders. "Don't let her fool you. She's got Sprout wrapped around her little finger."

Danielle put a hand over her stomach. "It helps that I can play the pregnancy card now." A secret smile tilted at the corners of her mouth.

"Face it, you either fight it or join it. Or you do like we do and stake claim on a section of the house and make it a testosterone-free zone." Gina indicated the stairs and the bedrooms.

From my vantage point, I could see the open doors for each one. They were empty.

If this had been Shock's house, they wouldn't be. I took comfort in that.

"What was the tipping point?" Danielle asked.

My eyes darted to Zoe and then I sent Gina warning in my silent "don't get me started" expression.

Danielle's mouth opened with a little gasp of understanding.

Gina, however, had no filter. "Was it the drugs or sex? I haven't heard any fights yet."

Of course, Zoe perked up and heard that.

"Gina!"

"Everyone calls her Ma," Zoe observed.

"That's because most everyone is young enough she *could* be their mom," Lily stage-whispered.

"That's enough out of you." Gina clamped her fingers around the air to shut her up.

"Jelly's older." That was sweet of Danielle to stick up for Gina that way.

"I'm not calling her, Ma." I sent a stream of gratitude to Gina. I wished I could tell her how much I appreciated her help. I opted for a partial truth. "She was one of the few people who were nice to me a long time ago."

Poppy wrapped an arm over her half-sister. "Was that the night I met you? Mom said you were sick."

"It was. Old Toolbox gave me some antibiotics and stitched up my head wound." I'd almost forgotten that. When Shock clobbered me in front of the entire Skilletsville chapter, he'd opened up a cut I'd gotten the week before when Shock threw me into the corner of the dresser. It was infected. Which meant, even if I had gotten free, I'd probably be dead now.

Gina looked uncomfortable.

"Who's Toolbox? I don't remember him," Lily wondered aloud. She looked to Poppy for insight.

Behind Danielle's head, Gina slashed her hand in front of her throat, warning me to kill the trip down memory lane. *Interesting.*

Lily directed her question at me.

I shrugged. "A doctor, I think. Maybe." Shock had a horse trainer on call. Their go-to for everything from stitches to syphilis was addicted to gambling. "They find someone with debts, usually."

Gina's eyes bored into mine.

"Shock's guy had a gambling habit and used to give us horse medicine." I scratched at my nose nervously. My hand shook, remembering the times he doped me up with ketamine.

"Mom?"

Zoe's soft question broke me from my fugue.

"I'm okay."

She frowned and got up from where she was sandwiched between Danielle and Lily to sit on my lap. I wrapped around her almost as tightly as she wrapped around me. But I didn't cry. I wouldn't. I was the strong one here.

"Do you still have a scar from the stitches?" Zoe searched my face for answers to all the questions in her eyes.

I led her hand to that ridge about an inch under my hairline. It was behind my ear where the skull got boney and thick. Luckily, it hadn't been lower. I would be dead. At the time, I didn't think it was lucky at all. But holding Zoe made me look back on things a bit differently.

Her expression was one of pity mixed with fear.

It was *real* now.

Not just a story from someone else.

"I love you, Mom." She threw her arms around me again and squeezed hard. I squeezed back, savoring the moment for all it was worth.

Poppy's arm tightened around Lily, and Gina put a hand on her daughter-in-law's back.

The sweet moment was too good to last. A sound louder than the TV and the stereos erupted from the backyard.

"Oh shit. No one invited Hagerstown, did they?" Gina jumped off the couch.

I joined her, motioned to my bedroom, and led her to the balcony so we could see what the hell was going on.

The grill was tipped over, and there were no fewer than four men patting at the embers stuck to Sketch's coat. Half of them were doing more laughing than fire prevention.

Sprout released the fire extinguisher on the pile of coals, scattering them into the grass.

"Get the hose." Jackson motioned for a prospect to spray the grass.

Gina yelled down, "What the fuck are you idiots doing?"

Sprout looked up. "Hey, Ma."

"Don't 'hey, Ma' me. What did you do?"

"Me? Nothing. Bear bet Sketch fifty bucks he couldn't climb to the balcony. But I greased the pole earlier."

As they spoke, Danielle joined us, followed by Lily, Poppy, and Zoe.

"You greased the pole?"

"Yeah. Security risk, ya know?" He noticed Danielle. "Hey, babe. You're looking fine tonight."

Gina shook her head. "Never a dull moment. Are you sure you want one like him?"

Danielle smiled and covered her stomach. "I think he broke the mold."

"You better hope he did."

Sprout called out to Bear. "Yo, dipshit, do I get Sketch's fifty if I make it up there?"

"Go for it," Jackson said and dug out his wallet. "Fifty more says he lands on his ass."

Money changed hands quickly.

"Do they always bet on stupid shit?" I stage-whispered to Gina.

Zoe overheard me and snickered.

Lily downright laughed. "Always. You better get used to it."

Sprout took his time kicking any coals or ashes from under the balcony and stepped back a good three strides. He took a short, running leap at the house.

His hands hit the flooring, and he hung there, suspended and swaying from the momentum.

"Damn it. He's going to make it." Jackson said.

Bear answered back, "It's that fucking reach of his. He probably wouldn't have had to jump. He's built like a fucking ape."

A foot hit the edge and slipped. With it, his left hand tore loose.

Danielle leaned over the edge just in time to say, "Don't fa—"

But he landed before she could finish. Flat on his back.

"Are you okay?" she called out.

Ma leaned over with concern on her face.

Sprout wheezed out a small, "Ow."

"Oh shit. He's hurt!" Danielle hesitated for a moment. "I'll be right down."

"Okay. I love you, babe." Sprout's reply was a bit stronger.

"He's milking it." Gina stepped away from the ledge to lead her daughter downstairs.

"Smoke, get your ass over here and try getting up that pole," Jackson ordered.

"Hell no. I ain't stupid," he said.

"Not even for Poppy?" Bear joked.

By this point, Sprout was sitting up and twisting the kinks out. Danielle took his side and helped him up. Smoke helped on the other side. From his vantage point almost directly under us, he yelled up. "My beautiful wife wouldn't let me, would she?"

"Damn straight, I wouldn't."

"Party pooper. I bet Smokey-Pop could do it."

Poppy turned to her sister. "Oh, I know he could. But I don't *need* him to."

She followed Gina and Danielle. Soon, it was only Lily, Zoe, and me left.

"I'd do it." Jackson moved Smoke aside and studied the pole.

He took a step back, similar to what Sprout did, and I got scared. "Don't."

"Babe. Trust me. I have a plan."

I don't know what came over me, but I yelled down, "The last time I trusted you, I ended up in Maine. Pregnant!"

Bear laughed and slapped Jackson's back. "You dog."

Jackson shrugged him off. "I'm coming for you, Kate."

He never took his eyes off me as he unhooked his belt and slid it out of the loops. At the very end, he flicked it loose with a *crack*.

Behind me, Lily breathed, "Whoa. That's sexy as fuck."

I shot her a glare because Zoe was right between us.

He wrapped the belt around one fist and stepped forward.

I leaned over, mimicking Danielle's position earlier. He glanced up, one eyebrow quirked. Then he whipped the belt behind the post and caught it with the other fist. A couple of tight twists later, he reached high on the post and notched the belt in place and tugged to see if it would slip.

It didn't. He planted a boot edge high on the pole and almost started up. But before he did, he leaned away.

"Bear, get your ass under here. I do not want to fall on my back. You're going to catch me."

"You got it, Boss." He was laughing, but stood behind Jackson.

Sprout yelled from his spot in the lounge chair, "No cheating. Bear can't touch you until you fall, asshole."

"No respect." Jackson frowned. He looked up to where Zoe and I stared down. "My girls. If that ain't incentive, I don't know what is."

He planted his boot and leaned back, letting the belt in his hands hold his weight.

The third time he planted his boot, it slipped. He caught himself with a grunt.

I winced in sympathetic pain. "Are you okay?"

"Just fine. Fucking grease… 'Saw a stripper do this once." He wrapped a leg around the pole and hooked his feet together. Then he hooked the belt higher, almost at the eaves. With another leg wrap, he hooked the belt on the top and secured his position.

Bear hovered below, no longer laughing. Jackson reached a hand up and caught the railing. I had the strongest urge to grab him and pull him over the edge, but the teasing and jeers were louder now that he was close. Sprout cupped his hands and yelled, "No helping!" I don't know if that was a reminder for Bear or for me. I snatched my hand back and gripped the rail as if I had a fist in his shirt.

Zoe was white-knuckling it, too. "Be careful, Dad."

He glanced at both of us. A grin washed over his face. The other hand, still wrapped in the belt, hit the railing, and he let loose with his legs. His whole body swung like Sprout's had.

This time, I did grab his shirt. I didn't give two shits if someone said it was cheating or not.

With a side-to-side rock, Jackson walked his free hand halfway up the rail, hooked his feet underneath the overhang, and pushed up.

His arms wrapped over the top rail and he hefted himself up to the ledge. He rested his chin on his arms. "Do I get a kiss for making it this far?"

Hell yes. I kissed his mouth. Zoe wrapped her arms around him and laid a smack on his cheek.

Lily laughed at us both.

Jackson hung there for a moment longer. "When I get over this ledge, you're mine, Kate." He let the belt slither to the deck and crawled over the rail. Once firmly on our side, he leaned over to yell at Bear, "I want something better than grease on this tomorrow. And the rest of you assholes, keep it down. I'm going to bed with my woman."

"No, you're not," I hissed at him.

"The hell I'm not. Zoe, Lily? Hole up in Zoe's room. And shut the door behind you." He motioned for them to scram.

"You're not staying here tonight," I told him.

"I'm staying here every night from now on."

That sounded serious.

And I'd just witnessed proof that Destroyers take their fun very seriously.

CHAPTER 23

Jackson

There was something in Kate's head that was shoving me out. Charming her pants off wasn't going to be easy. I figured a direct approach might be an option. But first, I needed to ensure we wouldn't be interrupted, and that there'd be no need for Kate to leave this room. Luckily, giving orders was second nature to me.

"Bear! Stick someone on the stairs. Upstairs is off fucking limits to anyone with a dick. That means all you fuckers, except Sprout, so fuck off."

Despite the ultimatum to protect her and Zoe, Kate glared at me.

"What?"

She broke eye contact and blew out a breath. "I want to be alone."

"How's it feel to want?" No sooner than I said the words, I cursed my smart-aleck autopilot.

"What?!"

"Babe—" I'd spent the better part of the day getting teased and questioned about Kate and my plans to keep her in my life. Getting shit about it from her hurt.

She stuck a finger up in my face. "No. You do not get to dictate what I want. I distinctly told you I want to be alone. I told you last night that I don't want to be in a cage. I told you. No."

Ah. Right. "Was that before or after we decorated my desk?" I knew it was after. But couldn't stop from sticking my foot in my mouth.

"Fuck you!"

She meant that. And not in a good way.

"Kate?"

"No."

She'd closed herself off, hugging her body tight. And I was an utter asshole. I softened my tone.

"I'm not Shock."

Her mouth opened and shut. Her color shifted from flushed to florid. With that shift, she figured out what she wanted to say. And she did so quietly.

"There are similarities. You're both bossy. You have to be to run a club like this. However, I do understand the difference between you two. I would have been backhanded for telling Shock to fuck off. Part of me remembers that vividly. Another part of me is damn certain I never want that to happen again. And that part? She's telling me to get the fuck away from you right now. And it isn't because I'm scared of you or I think *you* would hit me. It's because I'm deep in protective mode right now.

"I'm fragile. Yet I can't be fragile because there's no breaking allowed for me. There's no *time* to break. I have to be Zoe's mom. I have to be the survivor. The one who doesn't wallow in the pain. And do you know *why* that is?"

I had the feeling if I stayed quiet, she'd tell me. And another feeling that if I didn't stay quiet, she'd get angry with me. "I'm listening. Go on."

Her chin wobbled. Her words came out broken and hoarse. They barely were above a clogged whisper.

"I was property. His property, the club's. They even gave me a vest, saying I was theirs. The only person I could count on was me. I know you helped me get free. I *know* that. But if I hadn't taken the chance, it would've never happened. Deep down, I know the only person who *really* got me out of there, was me. Not you. I..." She paused to collect her voice.

"You needed help. And I gave it freely. Not because I wanted something or because I had a beef with Shock. It was one of the rare times I didn't do something for a reward. But you gave me… I can't tell you how much I'm in awe of you."

"Don't be. I should have run sooner."

My fists curled in rage at the torment she endured to get free. I remembered the bruising, her raspy cough. "Stop—"

Her eyes flashed to mine in question. There was fear in their depths.

I clarified. "Stop beating yourself up. You've got help now."

I needed her to work with me, not against me.

She wasn't seeing the big picture. I needed her to realize if I wasn't in this room the entire night, Shock would use that against us. He'd isolate her. And it would make it much easier to break her this time.

"You got a whole club of somebodies to turn to. I hope you realize that."

"Do I?"

Her hands were shaking. I'd missed something.

"What did I miss? What happened to make you shake like that?"

She stared at her hands like she'd never seen them before. "I…"

I had to tread very carefully here. She spoke the truth when she said she was fragile. And yet, it was also a lie. Anyone who can hold themselves together when their body is literally trying to shake them apart had to be the strongest person in the world. "You can tell me… I mean, you don't *have* to tell me, but you can if you want."

"Jackson." The tears she was trying to hide clung to her eyelashes. She fought them back with sniffs and swallows until she found her balance. "Baldy was getting a blow job in our pantry."

I tried not to smile. She'd said "Our."

"It's not funny."

"No, it's not that—" Unbidden, the image of Kate opening the door on that asshole with his pants down around his ankles and some bitch slobbing on his knob flashed in my head. I snickered.

"Jackson. Our food is going there. Your daughter's cereal."

"What kind of cereal does she like?"

She glared at me like I was an idiot.

"Kate, love? Help me out here. I can't get the picture of that hairy asshole getting his dick spit on out of my head now, and I need something to distract me. Anything? If not Zoe's favorite cereal, tell me why were you looking in the pantry?"

Kate shook her head. Then she started laughing silently. It turned into a snort that shook her whole body. "I was putting the mop away."

"And?"

"And… I opened the door. There he was. And I just… handed him the mop." Her giggles turned into sobs. "I thought, what if Zoe had caught that? Would she be safe?"

Oh shit. Now I wasn't laughing. Because while I could order my men around, there were certain things some of them did that were right on the cliff's edge of things I'd kill them for. And while I could guarantee Zoe would be safe if she interrupted Baldy and some whore; she shouldn't see shit like that, nor could I vouch for all the whores Baldy messed with. They might start shit. But I could promise Kate one thing, I'd do my damndest to let the entire club know that Zoe and her mother were first in my heart. "He won't do that again."

"You can't guarantee that. Even if you could, there was…is cocaine on our coffee table. If the cops come, we'll get busted for that."

Unfortunately, she also had a point there.

"And then what happens to Zoe? Who takes care of her?"

"First things first, are you mad at me, or just all things biker?"

She closed her eyes. "You haven't heard a word I said."

"No, I'm hearing you. I'm hearing that this party was a trigger for you. That it was too much too fast. But I'll tell you why it had to be that way if you *please* let me try to explain?"

"What is there to explain? You party. You drink, your friends do drugs, I—I can't say I'm surprised at all. I saw ten times worse at Shock's, and I hated him for it. I don't know why I thought you'd be different."

Fuck. This was going south fast. "Who drove three hours in the snow to pick you up from a hospital?"

She didn't answer.

"Who... stole you from a patched brother? Who risked their life, their future for you?"

This time, I didn't wait for her to think.

"I invited *every* member of my club tonight. And they showed up. They had to see you and Zoe to know who they're fighting for. While I'm sure they probably didn't see the best of you, they sure as hell didn't see the worst of you, either. What they did see was *you* as a person. As a survivor. As *my* woman. The only one I've ever gone out on a limb for like this.

"I know that sounds egotistical or like I own you or something, but I'm giving it to you straight here, sweetheart. Those men may have shown up to party. But they also saw something they'd never seen before. *Me.*"

"That's not egotistical?"

"Let me clarify. They saw *me*, in love."

That statement didn't exactly wow her.

Goddammit. She was going to make me say it. "I love you. I love you so much, I'd do anything to make sure you are safe."

"Safe isn't happy."

"I want that for you, too."

The silence between us felt like a showdown that started wars. I'd said my peace and had to wait her out. There wasn't a problem I hadn't been able to solve, fight, or bide my time on.

"Fruit Loops."

I tried to catch up where that made sense in the conversation. Was she calling me nuts? Wait. She was letting me in. I'd asked about my daughter's favorite cereal. "Zoe's?" I asked to clarify.

Kate nodded. "We'll need milk, bowls, bleach, towels, and a whole lot of stuff..."

She still hugged herself as if holding the seams together. Or shutting me out. "Will that make you happy?"

I got the evil eye for saying that. "What?" I threw my arms out.

"Taking care of Zoe makes me happy. Seeing her happy makes me happy."

Ah. This was great insight. And it also *sucked.* "You aren't just her mom." I braved a step closer, then another. "You're allowed to have something that makes *you* happy." I brushed a finger over her hand. Her gaze locked on me, searching my face for clues. Or gauging how far she should trust me.

The corner of her mouth twitched upward.

"Happy." I reminded her.

Kate's fingers slipped into the belt loops of my jeans. "What about you?" She tugged me closer.

"I'm always happy." When I was with her. Unless she was hurt. But even then, there was the unexplainable "rightness" to the things I did to help her. It pushed out all the awful things I'd done and filled me up with something.

Hope?

Maybe.

It was more nebulous than that. Fleeting like the flash of silver scales in dark water. Something you longed to catch, devour, or absorb but were woefully lacking in lure and skill to hold.

"Even when you're angry?"

Happy when angry? "Hell yeah. I'm alive and about to beat some dumb motherfucker up. And even if I lose, I'm giving it my all just to fuck their shit up."

She laughed at that. "I worry about you."

"Don't. I got it all under control." As we'd talked, I'd been slowly walking her backward. Her legs hit the bed.

She startled and looked at the mattress behind her. "You certainly seem like you do."

"Trust me."

"Never."

"Smart girl." I kissed her, swallowing any argument before it was formed. In doing so, we made our horizontal nest and slowly lost our senses and our clothes. I laid back, waiting for Kate to shimmy out of her underwear and admiring her freckled skin and the pale flush of pink in its tone.

My hands skimmed her waist, tracing a pattern of silvery lines that started about two inches from her belly button and disappeared into her mound. She caught my hands.

"Stop. Those are stretch marks."

From Zoe.

"Let me see." Now that I knew, I tried to imagine her rounded with child. My breath caught. A wave of sadness threatened to drown me. "I wasn't there." I retraced the marks and counted the largest scars. Eight. There were little ones, almost too faint to see.

"I know."

Was this what guilt felt like?

She nudged me. "Happy."

I could do that. I pulled her close as I sat up to kiss her mouth. She fit on top of me and rocked against my cock.

It only took moments to get hard and wanting. I had to be inside her. I lifted her away and begged. "Line me up, babe."

"Kate," she reminded me.

"Kate." Her name was reverent on my lips. She fit me. Both of us honed in battles neither of us asked for. But we would win. I'd see to that.

She slipped over my dick, and our bodies bonded over and over. But I needed more. I clutched her to me, my dick as far in her as it could go, and I rolled until our positions reversed. Then, as if we hadn't paused, I continued sliding inside and back out, but this time, deeper and harder than before. Her legs wrapped around my waist, and she took me to the hilt.

As the pace quickened, I watched the way her eyes fluttered as she tried to keep them open and locked on me. But we were both losing the battle. Sparks of pleasure started behind my balls and shot up my spine as I fought to stay tight. "Babe?"

"A little more. *Please?*" Her plea strung out.

I slipped my hand between us and pressed on her mound, hoping I'd hit that clit trigger.

She moaned and clamped onto me with her whole body. The twitches of her cunt hit the spasms of my cock and I joined her with a cry that was too loud. In the haze of passion, I had a fleeting thought to buy Zoe noise-cancelling headphones or some shit.

Then my brain filled with all things Kate. Her mussed hair, her rosy skin, the soft smile on her face, and best of all, the sparkle of happiness in her eyes as she opened them to see me.

Me. First and always.

Just like I saw her *first* and *always*.

'Til death do us part. Which was likely tomorrow.

CHAPTER 24

Kate

The cleaning crew was competent. The last of them slipped out the front door, leaving the house looking showroom ready rather than the swath of empty booze bottles and destruction it had been when I woke up.

Alone.

As I checked the house, Bear let me know he'd be downstairs taking a shower. I asked where Jackson was. I got a grunt that sounded like, "Club."

There'd been a time long ago when that word would have meant relief and I'd be celebrating.

But the difference between Shock and Jackson was too clear. I hated that word now.

A few great orgasms, and I was addicted.

Even more addicted when I discovered the refrigerator stocked, the cabinets filled with dinnerware, and, after a small pep talk, I found the pantry packed with more than bikers and blow jobs.

Zoe's Fruit Loops were on the second shelf.

Next to them was a box of healthy stuff. I took that one down and filled a bowl with it.

The spoons were in the wrong drawer.

I pulled out the tray and slid it along the counter to the spot where they made more sense.

In that drawer was a large envelope, some junk mail, and a bundle of real estate flyers and business cards. I sorted through the mess of papers after getting the silverware squared away.

It took a moment to find the trash can, but the circulars and junk mail went into it.

I almost dropped the envelope in it, but stopped when I saw my name scratched onto it.

Bikers. Not one of them had good handwriting.

I opened it, thinking it was something for the house, or maybe Jackson had talked to his lawyer already.

But it was photos.

My first reaction was to run. To deny what I already knew.

I flipped the envelope over and glared at the four letters of my name.

That was Shock's handwriting.

It was the same handwriting that was on my marriage certificate. My father's was in the spots I was supposed to fill out.

He'd found this house. Run!

I stared at the envelope. Then I looked out the windows to the backyard. The post Jackson climbed last night. The slab of concrete where the keg had been. The grass where Sprout landed.

Then my gaze shifted to the pantry door. Hookers. And Fruit Loops.

I had memories here. Barely a dozen hours of living, and there were already roots in the soil.

At that, I got angry. "Let's see what kind of fuckery you've got for me, asshole." I tugged out the stack. It was thick. Photos of all shapes and sizes, both color and black and white, spilled onto the countertop. I spread them out, bracing for images of me at my worst.

Instead, it was Jackson.

And women.

Every single photo held him in various compromising positions. Rarely with the same woman twice.

I flipped through them.

Two on one. Three. *Well.*

Some photos were recent. Some of a much younger Jackson. In those, he was more like the man I remembered than the one now.

Blondes, brunettes, redheads, Caucasian, Black, Hispanic; he certainly didn't have a favorite flavor. I forced myself to look at each one. Shock would want that.

This display, this archive of sin, wasn't about Jackson at all. It illustrated how long Shock suspected I had help. It was intended to split Jackson and me apart.

Funny, if he'd have just let me live in peace, none of the last few days would have happened.

I wouldn't have walked in on Baldy getting a blow job. Zoe would have her summer job. Jackson would still be fucking hookers.

One photo stood out. Whoever captured it caught it right as he orgasmed. The open-mouthed gasp at its apex. But there was something missing. I'd witnessed two of these recently. And in my memories, there were almost a dozen more. Each time, he locked eyes with me.

Even when it was almost impossible to do.

None of these women got that. His gaze was always distant, focused else-where. In some, his face was stuck in that angry but stoic mask he slipped on when he pretended to listen to some fool's problems.

Was it strange that I knew Jackson better than Shock did?

Bear's heavy footfalls tromped up the basement stairs. I shoved the photos back into the envelope. The job was too massive to rush, so Bear caught the end of it.

"What's that?"

Should I lie? I opted for the truth or a facsimile. "A present from Shock."

He rushed to the kitchen island where I stood. Water dripped from his hair. It was usually braided from hairline to neck. The sides were shaved to show off his skull tattoos. But with it down, he almost looked normal…for a six-foot-two-inch biker with too many piercings.

I grabbed a towel and handed it to him so he wouldn't get the photos wet. "They're photos."

"I can see that," he said.

"Of Jackson," I added.

His hands stilled. One photo peeked out, frozen in time. In that one, Jackson glared at the camera.

That must be his "I'm going to kill you face." I didn't like it much.

I tapped that photograph. "He knew this one was taken."

Bear's eyes dipped to it. "Motherfucker. That party was club b…"

I stared at him, daring him to finish.

Instead, he stuffed the photo back in, bending it.

I took the envelope from him and straightened things out so it would close. "Take this, hide it somewhere Zoe will never find it."

His lips whitened. It was the only sign I'd gotten my point across.

Then he nodded.

I handed him the envelope. He went to his coat and fiddled with the lining, making the entire package disappear neatly.

"Do you want some Fruit Loops? They're Zoe's favorite." Jackson was right. I had help. His men were rough, capable, but also competent. Bear being an exemplar in that respect. More importantly, Jackson was smart to begin adhering us to his men. Even if Bear thought I was a bitch, or an ice queen, he'd warm up to Zoe. I'd make certain that happened. Because Shock was too invested in me to let things go easily.

Those photos proved that without any doubt.

"Can we talk about that?"

"Nope."

"Kate—"

"Zoe will be up soon, no." I locked eyes with him. No sooner than I did, the telltale sounds of Zoe sliding her feet down the steps proved me right.

I smiled. She did that in the house in Maine because the stairs were so uneven, it helped to keep her upright. I couldn't begin to count how many times she or I slipped on those damn things.

"Morning, Zoe."

Bear leaned in. "We're going to have to move you."

"After breakfast." I held up the box.

He shook his head. I'm not sure if it was passing on the cereal or at my lame attempt to keep control over a situation that could quite literally blow up in my face.

But Shock wouldn't do something that extreme. He'd proven through his obsessive documentation that he wanted me alive to torture. That meant whoever was near me was safe, at least from explosives, or random splatters of gunfire, or any number of ways someone could die.

"When did you get cereal?" Zoe's mumble made me smile.

"Your father arranged it."

She stared at the bowls, the box, and eventually the clean house. "No shit?"

"Zoe…" Her language was not improving being around all these bikers.

"I mean, *really*?"

There was the sarcastic teenager I loved. "Really," I said.

She curled into a chair and ate a few bites before looking around the house again. "Someone cleaned. I could get used to this."

"Don't." It came out too quickly. I backpedaled. "I mean, I'll still find ways to make you clean up after yourself, so…"

The stabbing urge to run was back. Bear was absolutely right. If Shock found this place, all he needed to do was catch a glimpse of Zoe through the windows and—

My thoughts spiraled into at least a dozen different directions and new fears built up. All of them reminded me of Zoe's vulnerability. I needed to get her somewhere safer. "After you get done eating, we're going to go with Bear."

"Where?"

Bear furiously texted on his phone. He glanced up, acknowledging my hesitation. "Sprout's. He's got a lake house."

"Cool. Lily told me about that place. She and Poppy are building a house next door. It's right on the lake, and it has a boat dock, and a deck that runs the entire back of the house. There's sculpture and art, and it sounds amazing."

I glanced at Bear. The corner of his mouth twisted up. Under his breath, he mumbled, "She ain't building it, Smoke is. That poor dumb bastard." He completely missed my glare. How would Zoe clean up her language around these…

Assholes was the word that floated to the front of the description list, but I decided that word would be relegated to Shock, permanently.

I packed Zoe's bag and my own. Much of what we had fit into two duffles that had somehow gotten lighter since we started running. As I finished, I scanned her showroom-worthy bedroom and noticed some sketches scribbled on the blank backs of real estate flyers. On each was a combo of either Poppy and Zoe, or Lily and Zoe. Whoever did them was amazingly talented. I brought them downstairs to ask Zoe about them. We couldn't afford to leave clues behind like this.

Halfway down the stairs, I paused.

My whole life since leaving Shock centered around leaving no evidence. No trace that I'd lived in a place. Limiting my and Zoe's footprint so it could easily be erased.

The tragedy of it all struck me in the center of the chest.

This wouldn't stand.

I was going to start changing things, starting with trusting my daughter and Jackson. We were going to live in the wide open once things were settled with Shock. I had zero idea how this would work, but we weren't going to live in fear anymore.

But I was still curious about who drew the pictures.

I set them down by Zoe.

She looked up from the last dregs of her bowl and frowned. "Sorry, Mom. I know how you are about leaving stuff like this around." She went to grab them, but I stopped her.

"It's okay."

"Really? You sure?"

"I…" *I wasn't.* But that was *my* problem. "I want you to not worry about stuff like that anymore. I want us to be free. And, I kind of want to know who drew these. They're really good."

Zoe took another sip of milk before answering. "That's Lily's work."

Bear leaned over to look. "She's been doing some flash for the tattoo shop but I didn't know she did portrait work. Damn. I'm going to have to hire her on full-time for this shit. Those are fucking kick ass."

"Language." It came out automatically, and I pretended I hadn't flinched. Bear was a very large man with visible tattoos from knuckle to skull. If you saw him from a distance, you'd think he had hair covering his entire head because the ink pattern fit his natural hairline. Shock had a man like that.

"Whoops, sorry. I'm not used to kids."

"I'm not a kid," Zoe fired back.

Bear checked my expression. I tried not to roll my eyes, giving Zoe the benefit of argument.

"Apologies, again. Young ladies."

"Ugh. That sounds worse." Zoe took her empty bowl to the sink and rinsed it out. "Whoa, this place has a dishwasher? Mom, we can't ever leave here."

Another pang. "Your father is trying to make that happen." Trying too hard if you asked me.

She zipped the drawings up in her bag and set it by the door. "Ready."

Bear looked at the bags, then at us. "Why you bringing that shit?"

Zoe and I shared a sigh. I answered. "Because in the last month we've learned to *always* carry our bug-out bags." For Bear's sake, I tacked on, "We can leave them here."

He shook his head. "Nope, take 'em with. Better to not need them than the other way around. It never hurts to be prepared."

We weren't the only ones with that thought. Gina met us at the lake house.

And it was more of a modern mansion than a house. It sprawled at the end of a long private driveway. Only the top story was in view as we pulled up in front of the massive four-car garage.

Even with that many bays, there were three trucks and an SUV crowding the circle. Bear pointed out one of the vehicles.

"That's Kid's. Looks like we have company."

I didn't know this person. Before he parked, I set a hand on his arm. "This company, are they safe?"

He scanned the cars. "Yup. No van. That means Boots isn't here. That idiot isn't fucking safe at all. Hopefully, Kid brought his wife with. That woman can cook." For a man who didn't smile much, the prospect of food lit him right up. It transformed him into a completely different person.

He grunted as he got out and carried both of our bags into the house. The entrance was designed to awe. No sooner than we cleared the hand-carved double doors, the house split right and left, leaving you staring at a glass-walled sculpture garden. Beyond that was the deck and the lake. It was beautiful. I couldn't imagine walking into a home like this every day.

"Yo, fucker, what the hell took you so long? Jackson's waiting for us. We're getting company, so you gotta get to the club, pronto." Sprout greeted Bear with a slap and grabbed one of the bags. "What's with this?"

"Overnight bags," Bear explained. "You know how these things get."

Sprout groaned. "As long as it's stays small. I want none of those dick-heads from up north or fucking Pittsburgh here." His eyes landed on Zoe and me. "Welcome to the mad house. You're both getting fitted for handguns. Ma wants you on the range."

"Guns?" Zoe sounded too excited.

"No."

Sprout overruled me. "No can do, boss-lady. Jackson gave Ma the green light. So, suck it up."

"Cool!" Zoe cheered, then tore off to find Gina.

No, it wasn't. The swearing was bad enough, but teaching my baby how to kill things? Nothing good would come from that.

"It'll be fun." Sprout extended a hand.

I didn't take it. "Didn't you learn your lesson last night?"

"Hell no."

Great. The madhouse was run by the inmates.

CHAPTER 25

The Clubhouse—Jackson

Bear arrived just in time to be at my side when Shock pulled up. He leaned in with an ominous whisper. "Your woman is pissed." Then he plastered on his work face, leaving me hanging.

That was going to throw me off my game. And I'd need it based on the scowl on Shock's face.

"Gimme one clue, motherfucker," I hissed at Bear.

"Ma."

That was even more cryptic than his prior declaration. I cussed at him, "Asshole."

Speaking of…

"Asshole." I didn't bother holding my hand out to Shock or that shit. The son of a bitch in front of me was going gray. He'd put on at least another thirty pounds since I'd kicked his ass in Sturgis. His dark eyes glittered in the afternoon sun. I read their depths. Yup, he still hated me.

To my surprise, Shock grinned. "I'll remember you said that." He shoved past me like he owned the place. Which wouldn't fly. I slapped my hand on his vest and pushed back.

Did I mention *thirty* additional pounds? Fucker didn't budge. In fact, his momentum dragged me with him.

"This is my house. Let me get the door for you." *And slam your ugly face into it…*

He spread his hand in front of himself like he was a king bidding a subject to wait on him.

Nonno couldn't get his ass here sooner? I squashed that thought down. He'd get here in his own time. Making me wait with Shock would solve all his problems if one of us killed the other. And there was no use in getting my hopes up for an easy solution. *Wish in one hand, shit in the other. See which one fills up first. That's how much good it'd do you.*

Shock stopped in the doorframe, blocking everyone behind him. He casually looked over his shoulder at me. "Your house? Did you get tired of that little white farmhouse you just bought?"

He didn't bother to wait for my answer, because that wasn't the point. He wanted me to sweat.

I shot Bear a squinted message to fill me in on everything *asap*. This was fucked. One of the hookers talked. And did it so well, my home was compromised. The trail of bikers filed inside, leaving me alone with Bear.

"Ma, huh?"

That meant they were at the lake house. Shock hinted that my castle of suburbia wasn't safe. And Bear moved the women to the best place for them. Except, the hookers knew about that place, too. But at least there was a top-notch security system there. Even better than the one that Skinner planned for mine.

Sprout pulled in on his CVO alone. I waited under the eaves for him to dismount.

"How's your house, Sprout?" If Kate was angry and Ma was involved, something had to be destroyed.

"Still standing. Ma's going to show off the new indoor range today. But Kate's the one threatening to cut off my nuts. She doesn't want Zoe anywhere near it." He'd dropped his tone at the mention of my daughter. Smart man.

"Ma's got them on the firing range?" *Holy fuck.* No wonder Kate was pissed.

"I told her you cleared it."

I slapped the back of his head. "Idiot." I didn't hit him hard. He was doing his job. And finally filling me in after the fact so I wouldn't be surprised when Kate bitched me out later.

Sprout grinned. And I silently admitted that he had a point. The more women comfortable with guns, the better. Ma was a crack shot, and Danielle wasn't awful, but also pregnant, therefore still getting her balance right. If Kate and Zoe knew enough to differentiate between the grip end and the boom end, that was a good thing.

"Hagerstown set up shop on the perimeter."

"Who thought that up?"

"I did. Knew you'd be needing a better solution than just bodyguards for a few days."

His normal grin wasn't there.

I nodded at Sprout, giving him credit for having my back. "Your dad would be proud of you."

Sprout grabbed my arm and squeezed it. His eyes were squinted, looking somewhere in the past. Old Jolly wasn't with us long enough. And it was a bitch bringing that up because Sprout missed him the most of all of us.

He changed the subject. "Shock's here. Problems?" He tipped his head at the cluster of bikes.

"I called him an asshole already."

"Dude, I wanna be you when I grow up."

"You're never growing up." I shoved him and laughed. But I'd left Shock hanging long enough to insult. My footing with the club was shaky enough without adding another pile of shit to it. "Take my right, two steps back. Bear?"

"On your left, boss."

Where he should be.

Shock puddled his Jabba-the-Hut ass on a sofa that had been dragged from its spot against the wall to the center of the room. Two of the hookers I'd called in flanked him. Behind him was his new sergeant. Bear's counterpart looked much more competent than the last one.

But I didn't *know* him. And that was a problem because I should know everyone in this club. Especially someone in an officer role.

"Who's the fucking cop?" I pointed out the new guy.

"Shut the fuck up, Jackson. Bandit is legit."

Like hell was I taking Shock's word for it. I slid a finger along my nose to signal Hickey to sniff him out. And with that signal, the men of my club formed ranks. Each man tagging one of Shock's. I had a dozen men. Shock had almost as many. He must have tapped his entire chapter to bring this party to my house. Instead of being honored, I waited to get stabbed in the back. "Whatever."

I pretended it didn't bother me.

Once Nonno got here with his entourage, we'd be outnumbered.

Hagerstown would be a great equalizer, but I needed them watching the lake house more than I needed them here.

Besides, Nonno *owed* me.

Eventually, he'd remember that.

Meanwhile, there was a club to entertain. Maybe two of them. I dragged a bar stool to the center of the room and sat my ass on it, effectively enthroning myself higher than Shock and in a much better position to fight. Besides that, a barstool made an excellent weapon.

We squared off in silence. The usual raucous atmosphere of the room dulled by our icy impasse.

Even the hookers picked up on it. Their nervous glances, the lame attempts at small talk, and repeatedly rebuffed advances made the two parked next to Shock sit straighter than normal. If I wanted to look weak, I'd warn them to get gone. But they were locked in this cage match with us. If shit went down, they were on their own.

Wolf took my lead and dragged another stool next to mine. He sat on it, shifting his weight off his prosthetic foot. His assessment of the situation was much quicker than our other witnesses.

"Jackson filled me in."

I would have elbowed him to shut him up, but he wasn't my VP for nothing. Of all the men in my club, he was one of the most ruthless and smartest. And too goddamn brave for his own good.

Shock shifted his gaze to Wolf. "And?"

"And, what? Everyone knows you aren't serious about Kate. This is just for show."

That elicited a reaction. Shock's skin flushed darker, a sure sign his blood pressure just skyrocketed.

He cooly slid his attention to me. "Do you always let your minions do your dirty work?"

I laughed. If only he knew… "Why else have 'em around?" I hoped like hell that Wolf knew I was bluffing. We'd played enough poker together to read each others' tells. But perhaps I needed to be clearer? "Wolf knows what the hell he's doing. That's why he's where he is."

Shock's gaze drifted down to the state-of-the-art modular foot sticking out of his jeans. "If he were mine, he'd have been replaced. He's a liability."

I fired back, "You know, I'm going to correct my earlier statement. You're not an *asshole*, Shock. You're a goddamned moron. Wolf is five times the man you are. What the fuck? You jealous?"

"Of a cripple? Fuck no."

Ah, I saw the game here. He was trying to get me backed into a corner. Either make my man look weak, or weaken the bonds of brotherhood here by not defending my VP. I shot a look at Wolf along with a heavily arched eyebrow. He dipped his head in that way he does right before quartering off a room and eliminating the greatest threats.

"You do realize all it would take is one accident and you'd be a cripple. Maybe even a vegetable." My comment was delivered with all the charm I could muster for someone I despised as much and for as long as I had.

"Is that a threat?"

"No. It is what I call a *sad* inevitability. You fuck around with *mine*, you'll find out."

Shock reclined against the sofa as if he had no worries at all. In fact, his color had retreated to the normal alcoholic flush he was known for. He spread his arms out, daring me to stab him in the gut, or heart, with how openly he exposed his vital organs. Hell, he even spread his legs further. One good cap in the groin and he'd never fuck around again. *Literally.*

I glanced up. His sergeant watched me carefully. One wrong twitch, and he'd be justified in taking me out. Behind me, I could sense Bear gearing up for action.

Shock grinned. "Jackson, you're a lot of talk."

He had to have heard *some* of my reputation. Anyone who paid attention to rumors knew I was the kind of president who got dirty. I didn't slide pawns around the table to get shit done. I did it myself. Bear's breath on my neck reminded me of the caveat—if my men let me. But sometimes, I did shit whether they let me do it or not.

This time, instead of just a glance, I addressed his bodyguard directly. "Are you ready?"

Bandit's eyes narrowed, but he remained mute. He knew his role. *Damn it.*

"Fuck all this." Shock slapped his hands on his knees. "Bring me my wife. You do that, I'll leave, and you can entertain Nonno all by yourself."

"She ain't your wife."

My declaration was answered by Shock's snap of his fingers. One of his men brought a binder and handed it off. Shock opened it and pulled out a fancy certificate.

"My marriage certificate." He made to hand it to me, but I wasn't going to touch the cursed thing. If I did, I'd rip it up.

Wolf took it and scanned the page. He grunted once and tossed it back at Shock. It fluttered to the floor. No one bothered to pick it up.

Shock filled the silence. "Bring me my wife, and I'll take my hat out of the running for regional president."

My balls tightened. My dream job taunted me. I could run not only a chapter, but twenty of them. With that kind of power, Shock and everyone else would *have* to answer to me. I knew the position was dangling open for the last two years. Ever since Nonno took over, the Eastern leadership slot was empty. No one bitched about it because Nonno managed his region and the national region just fine for Big G's sake. What had changed? I'd missed something that Shock hadn't. I stuck a pin in that to fire a verbal round at my nemesis.

"You say that *now*. What happens when Nonno gets here? I think I'll wait for an official declaration before I make any deals."

He must have expected that reaction. "Have it your way. I'm tacking on another demand because of that." Shock pulled a stapled stack of papers from his binder. "This is a court order to return my daughter."

He knew about Zoe. Ice coated my insides, and the only thoughts in my head were how fast I could kill him. And whether I'd have enough time to take out Bandit before all hell broke loose and the space turned into a big pile of lead and blood. In that space of plotting murder, I projected calm.

This time, I took the paperwork. While I don't speak legalese, it looked legit. I snapped my fingers toward Hickey to have a gander at the bullshit typed in neat lines. There were plenty of signatories on the bottom with one hell of an official seal.

Once my hands were free, the urge to strangle Shock made them twitch. His bodyguard opened his stance, preparing for a fight. I could take down Shock despite his weight advantage. But not his Rottweiler shadow. The odds were all wrong.

Which meant I had to resort to outwitting the son of a bitch who held my balls in a vise.

"Hickey?"

"Legit, as far as I can tell."

Fine. Time to put money on the table and lay down a card. "Zoe's mine."

Shock stood up. He scooped the marriage certificate up from the floor as he did. "Not according to law. I'm legitimately her father because of this." He shook it in my face.

I laid down another ace in my hand. "You'd have to have been living with Kate and having relations with her for one year prior to *and* six months after the birth to have a claim." When Zoe was born, I looked into a lot of law books to make sure shit like this wouldn't happen.

"Page five. Affidavits."

I didn't have to see Hickey fact-checking because I knew they were all lies. "Perjury is a crime. Falsification of witness testimony is another one."

"So is kidnapping. And I'll make sure Kate's charged with it."

All the more reason to keep her away from her dick-husband. "It ain't kidnapping if the child ain't born yet." This was going to get ugly as fuck.

Shock grinned. "So you admit she's mine?"

I leaned forward. I was just inside his reach and invaded deliberately as I raised my voice so others could hear me. "Hell to the fucking no. She's mine. She was conceived in New Hampshire or Maine. I should know, because my dick was there, and *yours* was not." This wouldn't be a surprise to any of my men because they'd all seen Zoe. Not one of them had any doubt she was mine.

Shock pulled out one more page from his binder. It was a photo of me at Nonno's. There was a hooker on my lap. The same one I'd fucked right after leaving Kate. "Where was your dick again?"

That photo could link me to an unfortunate drowning. And with Zoe conceived in Maine mere days before it was taken and a body dead in the time and space between, I was fucked. If I went in for murder one, Kate and Zoe would be on their own against Shock and his shady legal team. But doing that would also expose Nonno as the guy who ordered the hit.

That really wasn't an issue for Shock *if* he was gunning for a spot higher than the regional president.

He leaned in and spoke much more quietly than usual. "Bring them to me."

I stuck out my thumb to begin my count. "One, you gotta burn that photo. Nonno's in it." I added a finger. "Two, do you think you're the *only* one who's been digging up dirt?" I squinted at him to warn him I'd spent sixteen years finding filth on him.

Then I stuck up my middle finger all by its lonesome. "Three, fuck you. No deal."

"You're going to regret that." He stepped back and snapped his fingers to summon his men.

This conversation needed a good course correction. I raised my voice a bit louder. "The only thing I have *ever* regretted was not killing your ass eighteen years ago. One good bullet…" I cocked my fingers and pointed at his head. "Boom."

His mouth twisted into a smirk. "I heard that about you. You're just like your father—killing the competition on your way up."

"It beats blackmailing them," I fired back.

CHAPTER 26

The Lake House—Kate

I found Zoe on the deck. She stood beside Danielle and stared at the lake. "You really live here?" Zoe asked Danielle the question I was too polite to utter.

"Yes. It was my grandfather's house."

Zoe whistled. "I could get used to this."

I had to agree with her; the house was amazing. Jackson's "fishbowl" comment resurfaced, but somehow, this was more an example of letting nature in rather than letting mankind in. The house exuded peace and elegance. I could hardly find fault with it.

Gina heard us and joined our group. "I got your things situated. It's time to take you out on the range for a little target practice."

I shot her a glare over my shoulder. We had not hashed out the details yet.

"It'll be fun," she echoed her son's words.

"This club's idea of fun has people falling from balconies." I paused and addressed Danielle, "Surely you're not okay with this? Sprout could have been seriously hurt. My daughter could get seriously hurt." Guns were much more dangerous than climbing.

"I get to shoot a gun? Fucking cool."

"Zoe, language," I hushed her exuberance.

"I see Sprout is rubbing off on you. That's not a good thing." Danielle's teasing smoothed the conversation into a lighter tone. But I was not on board with this.

"I don't think Zoe's ready for this."

Without hesitation, that set of notes emanated from my daughter. "Ma-ahm!"

Counting to ten wasn't going to work this time because Gina interrupted me. "Firearm training is a must-have in this house. There are too many idiots coming in and out. I *got* her, Mama Bear."

"You do?" As much as I adored Gina for helping me all those years ago, this was crossing a line.

"Certified concealed carry, licensed nurse, part-time paramedic, and I've been shooting since I was six. Please don't do the math."

My mouth opened and shut.

"I bet you've never fired a gun, have you?" Gina asked.

I hadn't. As many times as I fantasized about killing Shock, I never put thought into the actual deed. Maybe that was why he singled me out. I was the proverbial lamb to slaughter. "I haven't."

"Then *you* get schooled first." Gina led us down an exquisitely simple, curved wooden staircase. The expense of this house must have been astronomical.

"What did your grandfather do?" Zoe asked Danielle.

"Dot-com startups before the bust. His was one of the companies that didn't go under, so the stock appreciated in value when everyone else's tanked."

"How much money do you have?"

"Zoe!" I flushed red with embarrassment at my daughter's question.

But Danielle was extremely patient. "On paper? Sprout and I are worth seven hundred million, give or take about four to six hundred thousand in market fluctuations right now. But I can't touch much of that. In reality, there's about a million and a half in liquid assets."

Zoe and I were shocked speechless.

Gina nudged me. "Makes my nursing salary look like shit, doesn't it?"

I nodded.

The ironic part of this conversation was that I knew people richer than Danielle. Two of the vacation houses I cleaned were owned by financiers. Their net worth was much bigger than Danielle's million and a half. I kept that information to myself. Zoe didn't need to know that the teenagers she hung out with on the docks each summer were richer than this. She might get ideas.

Gina led us out of the house to a new outbuilding set on the hill. Inside, there was almost every style of gun imaginable available. From rifles to a tiny .22 caliber pistol that was almost smaller than my hand. "Who uses this?"

Gina looked me up and down. "Someone brand new to guns. That little puppy is only good at close range and fires two shots."

Zoe leaned in to admire it. "Can I get one like that?"

"No," I blurted automatically.

"Sorry, kiddo, you don't carry your own until you've done at least a year on the range. That's the rules." Gina took the tiny gun from me and put it back in the case. She pulled her weapon out of a concealed holster. It wasn't much bigger. "This is what I carry." She explained the name, capacity, and the enhancements in the model to make it easier for people with smaller hands to shoot.

"The very first rule of all firearms is that they are loaded until you confirm they aren't."

"You keep all these loaded?" I took a step away from the gun display.

"Of course not. But you should always treat them as if they were; that's the lesson."

Oh. As lessons go, that was a very good one.

Gina went on to show how to check the gun. More importantly, how to hold the weapon away from anyone as you did. When it was my turn, my hands shook.

I swallowed. This wasn't me. Zoe, however, was practically devouring the lesson. Her empty hands mimicked Gina's motions.

This wasn't right.

"I can't do this."

Gina stopped talking and studied me. "I'm surprised at you."

I glared back. "Why?"

She spoke carefully, "Because I thought you'd do anything to protect your child."

My jaw set. "I am protecting her. What if her grip slips? What if someone takes this thing away from her?" A million other what-ifs ran through my head.

"What if Shock takes *her* and not you?" Gina didn't bother sugarcoating her statement.

That scenario was my worst nightmare.

My grip tightened. I followed Gina's directions and tried to absorb everything. When it came time to fire at the little paper target down range, I pulled the trigger, thinking of his ugly face.

And missed.

There was a lesson there. Life isn't easy. It doesn't go as planned. Actions you take to protect yourself don't always work. I knew that lesson well. I tried again. This time, I took more care in lining up the sights with the target. I hit the paper.

Each time, I got a little closer.

Each time, I learned another lesson. Gina was right there by my side, correcting my mistakes and, more importantly, reminding me what was at stake.

Near the end, I tried picturing Shock's face inside those circles. And missed again. But when it was Jackson's face in them, I hit the big black circle in the center every time. *Go figure.*

Then it was Zoe's turn.

I pinched my lips between my teeth, worried every second of the lesson. Unlike me, Zoe had no ghosts from the past messing with her head. She fired true, even hitting the center of the target once. Gina squashed her celebration by reminding her where she was and what she had in her hand. Then dared her to hit it five more times.

Which didn't happen. Zoe's demeanor turned serious.

Finally, Gina pulled the targets in about fifteen feet and switched Zoe to a lighter gun.

"Her aim is loosening up; that's a sure sign she's tired."

I nodded, not really understanding much more than my daughter was pushing herself too far. "We should stop."

Zoe set the new gun down, defeated. "Just once? Please?"

I'd been expecting a fight, not the plea in her voice. "Once."

The corner of her mouth went up. Gina pointed out the changes in weight, firing mechanism, and loading before Zoe adjusted her ear protection and signaled she was ready.

With the closer target and the lighter gun, she put all ten rounds into the black circle. Four clustered near the center but slightly high and left.

"The gun is so small and light when you pull the trigger; it's kicking the front to the left slightly. And your left hand isn't doing anything because there's no space for it to help stabilize it." Gina checked the gun and then showed Zoe how to stabilize it better. "One more clip so you can feel that pull."

I frowned.

She caught the tail end of my expression before I masked it. "Last one, Mama Bear."

Zoe readied to fire, but one of our bodyguards interrupted. "Gina, get them into the bunker, we got company."

Said bunker was under a false floor in the last shooting bay.

We scrambled to get hidden, but despite the walls and the fake floor rattling as Gina slid it in place, I could make out the distinctive rumble of motorcycles. I prayed it wasn't Shock. I also prayed that our security team kept their cool and their lives. The last thing I wanted was for more people to die because of me.

Zoe rubbed a red mark between her thumb and forefinger.

"Are you okay?"

"It's just a blister, Mom."

From the guns. My right hand was raw in the same spot. "It's a good thing we stopped." I smiled as if to reassure her this was all normal and we were going to be okay.

The bikes sputtered to a halt. There was muffled conversation, just loud enough to indicate someone out there was upset and throwing their weight around, but it didn't match the tone or pitch I dreaded. The footfalls from heavy boots tromped closer.

"Get 'em out."

That was distinct.

I shot an urgent plea to Gina.

She slipped her gun from the holster and pointed it upward.

The floor was lifted from the hole.

Five bikers stared down at us. I didn't recognize a single one, but I recognized the patches and colors of each. They were Destroyers. The oldest's road name patch read, "Nonno."

"What are *you* doing here?" Gina tucked her gun away and held up a hand to be lifted out.

Nonno, the one she addressed, stared down at me and Zoe.

"Seeing what the fuss was about before joining the shit show." He held out his hand. I was loath to take it. "Come on. Let's get a look at you."

I was lifted out. Zoe followed without help, scrambling up the crude ladder fixed to the pit's wall.

Nonno barely gave me a second glance once Zoe stood up. "Well. *Now* I see why that bastard is so pissed."

He reached out to touch Zoe's face. She recoiled and stepped behind me. Instinctively, I blocked Nonno's hand and view of my daughter. "Don't touch her."

That got his attention. "Do you know who you're talking to?"

I didn't care. "Don't touch my daughter." I articulated my words slowly and added every ounce of vitriol I could into the icy tone.

His hand fell.

"She looks like Jackson."

"No shit," I said.

His expression morphed from a scowl to shock. "Got a mouth on you."

I straightened to stand taller.

"And a bitch-ass attitude. No wonder those two are salivating like dogs." He held out his hand. "My name's Nonno. And since you don't know who the fuck I am, I'll tell you. I lead the North American continent's Destroyers. Every chapter in this hemisphere north of the Panama Canal answers to me."

Lovely. I took his hand and shook once, then dropped it fast. "Kate."

His lips curled. "Just Kate, not Kate *Weaver*?"

"Just. Kate."

His eyes dipped to my legs and back, measuring me, assessing my appearance, and performing the action quickly enough that it could be deemed harmless. But it wasn't. The reminder that I was only a woman, no… worse, a woman in their manly world, pissed me off.

"Search her."

When they came up empty, they searched Gina. She relinquished her gun and a knife she had in her boot. Zoe, still huddled behind me, clutched my shirt. "Are they going to…?"

"Absolutely not. If any of you touch my daughter, I swear to God you'll die if it is the last thing I do."

Nonno motioned his men off. "One condition—"

"No," I replied before he could finish.

"Kate, this is for your own good."

I'd heard that line before. Almost without fail, whatever someone else decided turned out terribly for me. "I'll say this even more emphatically, *no*."

"If you insist. We'll take them both." He turned on me. "I was going to suggest your daughter stayed here. But since you wouldn't listen, I changed my mind." He motioned for me to precede him.

Damn it. I sent Zoe a warning with my eyes. But she wasn't looking at me. She was staring at Nonno. Not glaring, like I would have guessed, but studying him ruthlessly. Almost without any outward emotion at all.

"You're my dad's boss."

Nonno stopped in his tracks. He smiled. "That's right."

Her chin lifted slightly. "My dad, Jackson." She pulled her shoulders back and stiffly walked past him, leading the way and forcing me to catch up.

As I slipped past Nonno, he brushed my elbow. "The resemblance in those two is uncanny. Even without looking, I can tell she's related to One-Eyed Jack."

He knew her grandfather. If this were any other time or place, I might have been curious to find out more. But I ignored him. I knew he was taking us for a reason. Probably to maintain control over two volatile men.

Which proved to me that he didn't know Shock or Jackson well at all.

CHAPTER 27

Jackson

The Skilletsville chapter's meeting room was sacred. But that word wasn't in Shock's vocabulary. I tried to pull my men aside for a quick huddle, but he strolled right in, sat his ugly ass in my chair, and surveyed the room like it was his own.

I took one look at him and his men filing in and noped out, grabbing Bear and Wolf on my way out the door to do a circuit around the junkyard. One of Shock's assholes dropped his cigarette and made to follow.

With a quick flag to Smoke, that idea was cut short.

I noted his quick thinking to Wolf. "Fast track him."

"Don't know why you're making him wait."

If Wolf was in my shoes, he'd have done the same thing. Speaking of… "Alright. I ain't strolling around the fucking scrap heap for my health. Wolf, are you ready to step up?"

His jaw worked sideways. "You're borrowing trouble."

Not from my vantage point. "Nonno is on his way here. You know damn well that unplanned visits always signal a regime change."

Wolf stopped in his tracks. "Is that what you're expecting?"

"I can't rule it out. Shock is a little too fucking cocky. He's arranged something. And that can't be good for me."

"None of this is good for you," Wolf stated the obvious.

"Kate's good for me." Of that, I was positive.

Wolf snorted. "You're fucking suicidal."

"Am not. That woman loves me."

I noted Bear didn't laugh. "What?" He knew something.

"Are you sure?" Bear faced the club. I checked over my shoulder to confirm we weren't going to be ambushed.

"Why do you say that?"

"Shock sent a package to Kate."

Ah. "So her mood isn't from Sprout and his Ma riling her up? What was in it?" I scanned the rusting vehicles and the fence that surrounded the entire lot.

"Photos."

Shit. "Of?"

"You. Fucking hookers. About twenty photos." He shifted, almost bracing for a blow. He reached into his coat and pulled out a thick envelope. I took it and handed it to Wolf. I'd lived it, 'didn't need a reminder.

"She knows I'm no saint."

Wolf scrunched up his nose like something smelled bad. He peeked inside, and his expression soured more.

"You got a smart-ass comment for me?"

He shook his head. "I don't think you can count on her support." He peeked at another photo.

That was a given. "I need you to get those to the geek squad. Find out where the cameras were. Check where the security leak happened."

Wolf tucked the flap back inside the package. "Tits has a team on standby to get Kate and Zoe out if needed. They are holed up in a motel along the highway."

"Good. How fast can they get here?"

"Ten minutes," Wolf confirmed.

I triangulated which hotel was within that estimate. "Good. Loop Hickey in on the call; make sure he's monitoring the gates." We had cameras in place, but most of them faced the street, not the cars in the lot. They were there to protect the club, not to prevent theft. No idiot in their right mind stole from us. That was a good way to end up dead.

"Trackers?" I asked Bear.

"Done. Stuck an AirTag under the lining of Zoe's sneakers, and Kate's GPS is in the pocket of the leather coat Poppy picked up for her. She's wearing it."

Good. "Range?"

"About four hundred feet on Zoe's. North America on Kate's."

"Can you get a GPS on Zoe?"

Bear shook his head. "Takes time to program the fucking thing. Skinner's working as fast as he can."

Damn it. I needed them both tagged. I ran through the rest of the shit we needed to worry about. "Shock's hookers are a wild card." Ours were back, minus Tina, of course.

He'd brought a handful. Three brunettes, a redhead, and a bottle blonde. They ranged in age and ethnicity. Too bad he didn't take care of his stable as well as we did. They all looked over-used and scared, except maybe the oldest. She was a Latina woman with some miles below the belt. She wasn't scared at all. If my quick glance was true, she had an agenda. Which was one more thing to worry about. There were too many variables in one place to watch them all. Which meant I was screwed.

My men needed a reminder to stay on their toes. Not only for Kate and Zoe but for their own livelihood as well.

"Wolf? The club's future is at stake. Not just ours. Shock's playing a game with Nonno. I can *feel* it. I think he's blackmailing him for a murder sixteen years ago."

"How would you think that?"

I sent him a look that plainly showed my amusement. "Have you met me?"

He'd not only met me, but helped me with at least two murders. "Oh."

"The funny thing about that is Shock has the wrong leverage." I glanced at Wolf's prosthetic. "Use what you know if they start fucking with us." Wolf had more dirt on Nonno than Shock could dream of. Added to that, his wife probably had enough dirty deeds documented to bury all of us. Wolf was going to be in the right place, with the right arsenal; he just had to use it and damn any sentimentality toward me and the leadership. "Don't fuck up," I reminded him.

"What about you? I think Shock is angling to kick you out."

"That's the least of it. To him, I'm a dead man. Taking my patch is just step one. And that's the only way I see it going down. You need to be ready." If Shock didn't kill me, Nonno might. And if neither of them did, then probably Big G or one of the people I'd worked for somewhere would want me quiet. I'd done too much to live outside the bonds of the club.

Both men were uncomfortable.

I addressed them both. "Look at it this way. All those times I was an asshole to you? I got what was coming."

Bear frowned.

"You got a problem with that?"

He winced. "Yeah. See, the thing is? You're *our* asshole." He kicked the dirt at his feet. "I kind of got used to your bullshit."

The feeling was mutual. But I'd be damned if I wussed out now. "Yeah? You're still ugly. Wolf? Do I need to insult you, too?"

He laughed. "Fuck no. I've seen through you since I was a mere speck."

I dipped my head at him. "That's why you're where you're at. I need both of you ruthless for the next bit. I can't tell you it will be quick. Shock's been trying to get revenge on me for over sixteen years. He's patient."

Except for one thing. Zoe was the age he liked best. I couldn't voice that fear out loud because I knew both Bear and Wolf would have a huge problem with that. I wouldn't like 'em if they didn't have that code of honor running through them. Sure, both were damn dangerous, and both had done more than their share to contribute to the club's illegal activities, but they also were good men. Ones I was proud to call "brother."

I finished my little diatribe. "So when shit blows up, put the club first. Got it? Ruthless."

There was a commotion at the gate. Two blacked-out sedans and a bevy of bikes rolled in. "Nonno's here."

Sprout strolled outside, those long legs eating up the distance between the building and our little group. He had his hand in his pocket as if he hadn't a care in the world, but that speed wasn't his usual saunter.

He noted the entourage arriving and kept walking until he met up with us. "What's wrong?"

He stared at the cars, then turned his back so no one could read his lips except our little circle. "Nonno's got Kate and Zoe. Ma called as soon as she could. He pulled rank on the security team."

Fuck.

I tapped Wolf on the shoulder. "Make that call. Let's go. Party's starting."

I'd never been much of a gambling man. In every deal, every transaction, every plan, I always made sure I stacked the deck.

But for the first time in my life, I wasn't the one holding the cards. And that was dangerous territory. I wanted to pull the plug on this little farce immediately. But first, I needed to see *my* family.

Which meant I beat even Sprout's long-ass strides to get to the cars first.

I stood no more than an arm's-length back from the guy opening the first car. I glanced at the second one. There were four bodies in that one. I'd picked wrong. Nonno climbed out of the first car, and I pretended I'd been rushing to greet him.

As usual, he ignored my hand.

I tipped my head to the second car. "I see you met my family."

Sprout helped Zoe out of the car, keeping a protective arm around her as he hustled her from the vehicle and to our little group. He made a fuss of straightening her hoodie and grinned like an idiot. "Check out that eyebrow, Nonno. Looks just like our man J, doesn't she?"

He was not helping. Nonno didn't like being told the obvious.

Nonno proved me right by ignoring Sprout and focusing on Kate, who was bright red with fury. One of Nonno's guys got handsy as she exited the car, and she spat rapid-fire words at him. "You already searched me once at the lake house. Get your fucking hands off my ass!"

The corner of Nonno's mouth went up.

I jumped into the fray. "That's my woman. Show some respect."

Only then did his minion back off. *Fucker.*

"You finally admit you fucked up," Nonno observed.

I pointed to Zoe tucked in at my side. "That's right, plus evidence. Is that good enough for you?"

He acknowledged Zoe. Then he tossed an accusation at me. "You lied to me."

"When? Name a time and place." I knew he was searching for something to pin me with. But in all my dealings with people, I kept the truth tucked right inside neat little packages of deflections and bluster. "I never outright lied."

His eyes narrowed. "You lied to Shock."

"Again, when?"

"Sturgis." Shock strode up with a big grin on his face. "Nonno, thank you for coming."

"I didn't lie. I said no one stole your wife. Kate? You left all on your own, didn't you? I didn't steal you."

Her glare was not comforting. "To set the record straight, yes. I left that asshole willingly." She pointed at Shock.

His grin dropped, and his color darkened. "I still *own* you." He snapped his fingers and that fucking marriage certificate got shoved back into his mitts. He handed it to Nonno, then requested the other document.

That fucking court order for Zoe.

"I own *her*, too." He flashed the document at Kate but handed it to Nonno.

Nonno glanced at it. He shoved it back into Shock's gut.

"No."

Shock opened his mouth to speak, but Nonno cut him off. "Any idiot can see the resemblance. And all of you idiots have seen Jackson's fucking around. He's made no secret that he's had his dick in almost every woman within a seven-mile radius of this place. I'm surprised he doesn't have a dozen kids."

Nonno paused and motioned Zoe to his side. "You. Come here."

She looked at me for advice. I didn't know what Nonno was playing at, but he'd started well. I sent her a small nod, but I was going to watch this closely. She didn't exactly cuddle up with Nonno, but was within arm's reach.

I didn't like it one bit. Neither did Kate, who pushed herself between Nonno and Zoe. "Look, don't touch."

"Mouthy, aren't you?"

Her jaw stiffened. Wisely, she didn't smart off to the national president.

Nonno stared over their heads at me. "Does she talk to *you* like this?"

I grinned. "All the fucking time. I love it." I meant that. My eyes locked with Kate's. *I meant that.* She wasn't a mind-reader, so I had no clue if she could see the message on my face. But I stuck it there for the whole world. And with that, I went all in and mouthed, "I love you."

She frowned and shook her head.

I glanced around to see who was paying attention.

Nonno wasn't. But Shock was.

A slow grin formed on his face. I didn't like it one bit. It held a promise of pain.

I'd exposed my weakness in front of him.

And you know what? I would not feel bad about that at all. Let the whole fucking world see me being a sap. Loving Kate was the best thing in the world. It was time the world knew. Even if she didn't love me back.

Nonno cleared his throat. "Keep a leash on her, then."

Zoe made a noise of protest.

He quickly added, "*Both* of them."

This time, Kate shushed Zoe with a look, and a single finger held up. She didn't have to say a word, and my daughter obeyed.

I marveled at the way those two could communicate. On the heels of that, I mourned the years I'd missed with them. If I made it out of this shit alive, I'd spend the rest of my life learning their ways. God willing.

Shock mouthed off. "At Sturgis, you made me look like a liar in front of Nonno." He motioned toward our leader.

I noticed he left out Big G. Smart man, but also *really* dumb.

"Shock, have you ever thought about the women you've ruined. Like really thought about them?"

"Jackson," Nonno warned, "Not here. Let's go inside. Officers only. Now."

As I handed Kate and Zoe off to a prospect so he could take them to my office, Shock bumped my shoulder.

Under his breath, he muttered, "You're pussy-whipped."

I fired back, "At least I'm getting some."

No sooner than he was out of earshot, Kate whispered to me, "That was immature."

"You want maturity?" I pointed at Shock's back as he entered my meeting room. "He's at least ten years older than I am."

She narrowed her eyes as I stared her down. But we were interrupted.

"Jackson, get your ass in there. I got these two." Baldy took over for the prospect, motioning Kate and Zoe up the stairs. "You don't want to keep Nonno waiting."

Right.

It was time to face my doom.

CHAPTER 28

Kate

BamBam blocked the top of the stairs. He was one of the older members. I recognized him from Shock's arsenal of torturers. Almost twenty years wasn't enough to erase the fear that paralyzed me.

"Kate." His eyes scanned my body, but quickly flicked past me and locked on Zoe. "I hear she ain't Shock's. Is that right?" He licked his lips as if tasting something savory.

My arm shot out, blocking Zoe and moving her into my shadow. "Move."

He ignored my command. "She's pretty like her mother was when she was younger. If she ain't Shock's, she's fair game."

Like hell she was. I stepped up the last step and kept moving forward. Each inch closer added to my fear, but also to my fury.

"You sick son of a bitch," I started. "Touch one fucking hair on her head, and I will cut you down and then torch the pieces. Move!"

To my surprise, he took a step back. I kept coming until I'd backed him into the lounge at the top of the stairs. Two hookers were on the couch. As I kept detailing what I'd do to that asshole's defiled corpse, one of them stood up.

That caught my attention and broke my train of thought. And *holy shit*, I recognized her, too.

"Cara?"

Her face showed the years between then and now, but she still had those lovely brown eyes and nearly black hair that attracted men. Unfortunately, she attracted the wrong sort, like Shock, and the assholes around him.

BamBam remembered who he was and sneered. "That's right. You might have slipped our trap in New Jersey, but we snagged someone else. Coco here sucks a mean cock, don't cha, babe?"

"Sure do. BamBam, go downstairs. I got this."

His gaze bounced between me and her and back, eventually landing on Zoe. Something unspoken made him hesitate. "I'll be at the bottom of the stairs. When Shock gets out of the meeting, have 'em ready."

What did he mean by that?

Maybe I didn't want to know. I waited until he tromped away before saying anything.

"What are you doing here?" I asked.

"Hell if I know. Been a bit, hasn't it?"

"Cara..." I started, but didn't know what to say or ask first.

"Save it for someone who needs it."

She sounded resigned. And more than a little angry.

"He doesn't own you." It was a long shot, trying to get through to her.

"Do you really think you can stand up to Shock?" Cara asked.

"If it comes to that. But if we can get out of here, then we don't have to find out. Right?"

Cara's eyes narrowed. "Run. You're good at that."

"We both were."

Her eyes shot to mine. In that silence, she shook her head faintly.

The other hooker stood up. "My name is Tina. Hi." She stuck out a hand. I took it and held onto it rather than shaking it.

"I'm pleased to meet you." I meant that sincerely. If there was one thing I knew with my whole heart was that when someone really saw you and appreciated who you were, not what was done to you, it changed you.

The girl smiled. She wasn't much older than Zoe. "Coco, I mean, Cara… and I are stuck up here because Shock doesn't trust us. I'm… well, it doesn't matter what I am, and Cara's used to a different crowd. I'm more than ready to leave when you are. The trick is getting through the gates."

I could tell by the quiver in her tone that she was barely hanging on. "Follow me."

The stairs to the kitchen were in the same spot. I led Zoe, Cara, and Tina down them and tested the door to the outside. Unlike so many years ago, it was unlocked. "Does anyone have keys to a vehicle?"

Cara smirked. She dug inside her bra and pulled out a set of keys with a braided black leather strap attached. "I stole these off BamBam while he was busy."

Tina snorted. In a sotto voce volume, she said, "Busy getting his dick sucked."

It was uncomfortably obvious that my daughter was right next to me, soaking all of this in. I wanted to take time out to explain everything so she wouldn't jump to conclusions, but also not adopt any remnants of the lifestyle Shock helped perpetuate. Hell, he made these women the way they were. I witnessed his methods first hand.

"Right. Here's the plan—I'll talk you through the gates. We drive. As soon as we are safe, you will drop Zoe and I off at a gas station. Then both of you get gone. Go as far as you need. Cara knows the shelter system. She'll tell you what to avoid doing and saying. You can't be totally honest with them, they'll try to help; and that… well, that will get you caught." I stared down at my old friend, daring her to balk.

Her face softened for a moment. There was a small break in her armor. Her mouth opened. Then the hardness of her expression returned. "Sometimes, others pay the price."

My heart bled for her. She'd lived under Shock's thumb for as long as I was free. Longer than Zoe's entire life. I wondered if she hated me for it.

But that would need to wait. What was most important was getting out of this place in one piece. The gate was the least of our problems.

The prospect took one look at me and Zoe in the front seats of the van and waved us through. It was almost as if he'd been ordered to let us go. I wouldn't have put it past Jackson to arrange a miracle for just such a scenario.

Which gave me a lot to think about as I drove away from the junkyard.

Cara pointed to the interstate. "We're going toward Pittsburgh. It will throw Shock off. He'll expect you to stay far away."

With good reason. I had to admit she knew him much better than I did. I followed her orders but tacked on my own demand. "At the first gas station, Zoe and I are out."

We had no phones and no weapons, but I still had my tracker tucked into my coat. No one found it during the pat-down because the brand-new coat was stiff and the tracker was small enough to miss.

Zoe's RFID tag was also in place in her shoe. I had to count on Jackson to care enough to search for us.

Which would take me right back into Shock's hands. I began to rethink the plan. That's why I didn't exit when I saw the first gas station sign. Or the second.

Tina leaned over my seat to check the road. "What are you doing?"

"Getting a bit farther away. He'll have people check the stations. He'll expect us to do the obvious."

Cara overheard. "Good thinking. Let's go right down his throat. What do you say?"

I chanced taking my eyes off the road for a second to read her face. There was a gleam there that was almost maniacal and murderous.

If that intent was aimed at Shock, would I be the terrible person pulling the trigger? The world would be a much better place if he was gone.

Tina retreated to the back and tried to smile as our eyes met in the rearview. Zoe watched the road, sometimes squirming in her seat but remaining eerily quiet and intent on our course without complaint. I worried about her, too. She'd been too quiet through all of this. I'd recently learned her silences were often when I should be most concerned. She had a plan brewing. I could almost feel it; her concentration on the details around us bordered on hyper-vigilance. My trauma and subsequent counseling recognized the signs.

It was one more thing to pile on top of Shock's sins.

For the hundredth time, I wished I had a weapon. I pulled off the interstate about halfway to Pittsburgh. I'd noticed a toll scanner and realized that

Shock would have a method to trace our route. Even if it arrived in the mail a month later, it would give him enough information to search for us.

Cara noticed. "Why did you pull off?"

"I'm finding a superstore."

"For what?" Cara shifted closer, and her nervousness became palpable.

Tina asked where we were. Zoe relayed the information.

"Get back on the freeway," Cara ordered.

"No. We're getting scanned every few miles by the toll system. Shock will have a record of the trip."

The corner of Zoe's mouth quirked up. She knew what I was up to. She popped open the glove box and rummaged through it. "Score." She held up a screwdriver. Trust bikers to keep tools in the most convenient places.

The lot wasn't as full as I preferred. I pulled up to a van near the back and swapped plates quickly.

Cara watched with a raised eyebrow. "*When* did you learn that?"

"It's just something I picked up." *From Zoe's father.* I kept that part to myself. I still hadn't decided if Cara was on my side or not.

With the new plate, we slipped back onto the freeway. I should have taken the opportunity to switch places with Cara and let them disappear without us. But I was too paranoid, thinking that the toll system could be hacked and they'd know exactly where Zoe and I were. I figured I would know Pittsburgh better than any place in the road between, which gave Zoe and me better odds to find somewhere to hide.

Cara pointed to an exit that took us off the toll road. "If those plates are reported stolen, we'll have more to worry about than just Shock. I know a back route." I let her guide us through the winding country highways that led us closer to the place I least wanted to be with each westerly turn.

Tina watched from the back anxiously. Secretly, I was just as scared as she was, but had to hide it for Zoe's sake. I'd done a lot of that lately.

I'd just begun to recognize the surroundings when Cara told me to pull off.

"Why are we stopping now?"

"Just do it." The turnoff she pointed me toward was quickly swallowed by trees. We were deep inside the steep hills and carved valleys where roads followed the rivers rather than any man-made lines. Cara smiled. "Perfect. No one to see us. I need to stretch my legs."

I parked in the lot. It was a trailhead with ample spots for hikers and day vacationers to touch nature. But in the dark that had fallen, it was deserted and ominous. Not a place I wanted to linger at.

"Cool. I need to pee." Tina jumped out of the van and rushed to the squat little building.

"Ten to one, it's locked." Zoe strode off to find a tree to squat behind. We'd learned a lot in our almost two month-long exile.

It was. Tina complained the whole time she searched for a spot like Zoe had found.

I followed Zoe, mostly to get away for a moment or two.

"Why did you do this, Mom?"

I had reasons that I couldn't easily explain to her. The nearest sentiment was, "I've been in their shoes," which I relayed to her. The crunch of Cara's footsteps stopped me from saying more.

Her features were in shadows cast by the lot's lighting. Something about the way she held herself made me push Zoe behind me.

"What is it?" I asked.

She stepped forward, and the moonlight glinted off the object in her hand. In a split second, I knew it was a gun. "I need you both to lose any trackers you got."

I stuck a hand in my pocket, which made her bring the gun higher. "Slow."

My heart picked up pace as I carefully withdrew the GPS unit Bear shoved into the lining this morning. "That's it."

"Nothing on the kid? I doubt it. Zoe, I will shoot your mom if you lie like she just did. I need you to get rid of anything you can be traced by."

Zoe slipped off her shoe and pulled out the little disc that was only good for RFID scanning. She held it out. I took it from her hand and tossed it at Cara's feet.

"Happy?" I put extra grit in my tone. We'd find a way to contact Jackson. Nothing Cara could do would change that.

Except maybe shooting us. But why ditch the trackers?

Tina approached noisily. "That was disgusting. I need a shower, a manicure soak, and probably tetanus shots." She gagged to further illustrate her distaste.

In a move almost too quick to track, Cara turned and shot her at nearly point-blank distance.

The report echoed against the hillside and trees, then returned from the valley as a ghostly distortion of the original sound.

Zoe cried out. I pulled her close. Belatedly, I thought I should have shoved her away and told her to run. But I wasn't thinking right. I couldn't believe what I'd witnessed.

"Why did you do that?"

"She's a traitor. Four years ago, she was planted at Skilletsville to feed Shock information. Yesterday, she came back, ratting you both out." Cara rummaged through Tina's bag and pulled out a tracker. "I *knew* she had one on her. Let's go. Someone probably heard that." The point of gun flicked back to the vehicle.

This time, Cara rode next to me, with the gun pointed at me as she directed us to the suburbs north of Pittsburgh.

"You don't need to hold that on me." I told her.

"Just follow directions. Okay?"

As she dictated each turn, I began to have a horrible suspicion that I could predict her next order as we crossed the Hulton Bridge.

"What did you do to survive all these years?" I kept my tone as neutrally normal as I could.

"I did what I could. It wasn't all bad."

With Shock? *Ick.* I could argue with that, but I needed to keep her talking. "Why didn't you go home?"

She laughed bitterly. "Home? To what? The shelter? Or a man who wanted me dead?"

Death was sometimes better than decades of torment.

"Besides, I couldn't. Shock set me up."

That was easy to believe. He had a knack for blackmail. He enjoyed that more than anything else, even hurting women. "How?"

Cara glanced at the road. "Turn left at that stoplight."

After I did as she asked, she answered my question. "He killed my ex right after he was released from prison. But Shock made it look like I did it."

Oh. "That's terrible."

"I don't know; it was kind of sweet in some ways. I hated that bastard. Turn right."

I'd already flicked the blinker on. It was habit. "Did you spend the entire time with Shock?" I was guessing she hadn't.

Her smile was audible. "No. He set me up with one of his business associates. I had a good life for *years.*" She stressed the last word.

We climbed the slope, and the city dissolved into a mishmash of rural and suburban charm that was either worn or immaculate, depending on which end of the economic spectrum you fell.

"But he died, didn't he? Murdered?" I checked the mirrors. The traffic was almost non-existent.

She stared at me, the gun unwavering from its fixation on my chest. "How do you know that?"

I debated on whether I should be honest with her. But truly? What did I have to lose? "A month ago, Shock sent me clippings of my father's murder. He was gunned down outside his law office. Did you get the house?"

"Fat lot of good it did me. I can't pay the taxes." With her words, the gun lowered to her lap. "I need you to open his safe for me. I never got the combination. With the paperwork in there, I can sell the place and disappear."

"He might have changed the combination." There were two safes. One was the wall safe in his home office where he kept the records he wasn't afraid of losing. The other one was set in the wall of the closet of my bedroom. If Cara knew there were two, it wasn't evident.

"I doubt he did. He never wanted to change anything. Renovating the kitchen was a battle. So, we'll see, won't we?"

I sighed. Being in my hometown and so close to Shock's headquarters put me on the edge of a panic attack, but seeing my home? What would happen then?

Would I finally snap?

Worse? Zoe was with me to witness it.

CHAPTER 29

Skilletsville—Jackson

Nonno only let Wolf and Bear remain with me. Shock had all four of his officers. And Nonno not only had his home chapter's leadership but also two bodyguards to witness. This was going to get ugly fast.

He took a spot at the head of the table, usurping me of my favorite chair without even knowing it. But no one sat.

Without much preamble, he slapped the surface to get everyone's attention. "First. Jackson, give your president patch to Wolf."

I'd expected that. I flicked my knife out and tore the vest off to lay it flat on the table so I wouldn't stab myself while ripping the little rectangle off. I peeled it away from the final threads holding it and pinched it between my fingers as I put my vest back on. Part of me didn't want to let go of the title. But Wolf deserved this flimsy albatross more than I did. I handed it to him, warning him with my eyes that he better remember how to be ruthless. Otherwise, his fate was going to be much worse than mine.

Nonno acknowledged the transfer of power with barely a nod. "Next, regional president. It's long past due. G's been pestering me to get this shit over with. Shock?"

My nemesis's grin turned my stomach. Until Nonno said his name, hope beat in my chest that maybe, just maybe, I was giving up my presidency for something bigger. I swallowed my disappointment and braced for the next insult.

"Thank you," Shock held out his hand to Nonno.

There was a moment of hesitation. I glanced at Nonno's face. If this were a card game, I'd bet all in that he had a shit hand. One of his tells was that he stared too directly, as if he were weighing the odds against his opponent. A player with all the right cards wouldn't need to do that. It told me that this was a farce.

Shock grinned widely as he accepted the small rectangular patch to sew above his president's patch.

I didn't smile. The knife clutched in my hand wasn't nearly deadly enough to kill that motherfucker fast enough. But the tightening of my fist didn't want to listen to common sense.

I forced myself to lower my hand, fold the blade in, and pocket it.

"Are you going to congratulate me?"

I stared at him, mute. I was done pretending. Done lying. That didn't mean I was stupid enough to speak my mind. So my lips pressed together. I didn't frown because I fought to keep the corners from turning south. I finally spoke.

"Are we done?"

"No," Shock said.

Great. I almost rolled my eyes.

His grin turned into a smirk. "First things first. As regional president, I'm ordering Wolf to pull your patch."

That bastard. "On what grounds?" I gritted out.

"Because you are a liar. Now normally, we'd like that in a brother. But not when it is directed at leadership."

My right eyebrow lifted so I could skewer him with the one eye that wasn't twitching from anger. "You weren't my fucking boss."

"Careful. You aren't patched anymore."

I was still wearing my vest. I'd earned my spot. And I'd killed for it. If it took killing that bastard and every son of a bitch between me and the MC I'd lived my entire life in, I'd do it. Brother or not.

Nonno broke our staring contest. "Almost seventeen years ago, you said one of our dealers ran. He didn't. You made it look like he did."

Fuck.

"You lied to Nonno." Shock's smile fell into a grim line. "And, you had one of our feeder chapters lie for you. To me. And, to your former president."

Christ. Walt was going to pay for my sins. That's why Nonno handed that regional patch to Shock. He couldn't count on Walt, although the man deserved a shot at the job more than I did. He'd recruited a new chapter. Preserved our southern border for years. And, most recently, kept a truce between another major East Coast club and our club.

"Do you deny it?"

Nonno was asking me to tie my own noose.

I took off my vest and handed it to Wolf. "Here. Burn it." With that, I took a step toward the door.

"Not so fast."

What now? A beating?

"Blackout your marks."

Nonno's order was benevolent. They were within their rights to burn all the Destroyers tattoos on my body from my skin.

"Anything else?"

Shock stepped forward. "Stay away from my wife."

"Fine," I agreed.

He tacked on, "And my daughter."

"I'll see you in court about that one."

"How are you going to do that?"

"My lawyer, dipshit."

His men visibly fluffed up like a flock of vultures readying for battle over my carcass.

"*Your* lawyer?" Shock asked. He glared at Wolf to speak.

"You can't use the club's assets."

There. That was the ruthlessness I asked for.

Bear outdid him. "Or any of the businesses."

Shock practically gleamed with joy as he tacked on, "Or that fancy little house you bummed off Sprout."

Whatever. I'd made do with much less in my life. I'd squirreled away assets for over twenty years. Shock knew about the house in Maine, but no one knew about some of the other holes in the walls I'd burrowed out. Meeting Kate wasn't the catalyst, but knowing her and Zoe needed places untouched by the Destroyers' network made me get creative.

I pulled my keys out. The SUV was leased to the club. "Here."

"Your bike keys, too."

Wolf was taking his newfound power too far. "Fucker." I threw the second key ring on the table. There was a little Subaru near the back of the yard, tucked behind a false fence every single prospect strolled past nightly. At the base of the twisted metal bars and vines that grew hundreds if not thousands of feet a day was a small, grimy culvert. I'd crawl through it and drive away. I could be five hundred miles from here before any of these assholes figured it out.

Or better, I'd hit one of my rifle stashes and take out every single betraying motherfucker in this room. They wouldn't know what hit them as I hunted them down. They were stupid to let me walk out. And Shock had dug his grave by threatening Zoe. She was mine by blood. No one was going to take her from me again. Not even Kate.

My scowl went deeper. She'd hate me for this. For giving up on her. For playing the games this club had shoved in my face while she hid all those years.

And for what?

Nothing.

Without this club, without my men, without power, I was just another bitter man chewed up and spit out. One step from a lifetime behind bars. And if I was lucky enough to make it that far, I'd be shivved because of the disgrace they laid on me.

If I were a smart man, I'd remake myself working some fucked up polo-wearing backwater job that never got me much more than an obligatory 401k with junk bonds. I'd die poor and unknown after living the rest of my miserable life, swallowing my pride.

That wasn't me.

None of this was me. I'd dug my grave by being a smartass son of a bitch who didn't know how to keep his dick out of someone else's woman. I'd been warned about this very thing all my life.

But I didn't regret a damn thing. Nor would I do anything different.

I turned my back on Shock and Nonno. One final insult as I walked out of my throne room. I barely glanced around the bar as I kept one foot in front of the other. Any second now, the human sharks circling me would smell blood. Once that happened, I would face a gauntlet of at least fifty angry men. I'd betrayed each and every one of them.

For Kate.

For my girl.

For blood.

At the door, I turned back for one last look.

The floor was cleared. Most of the members and visitors opted for the barstools and wooden spools scattered along the rim of the room. I stared at the bare wood where not long ago, Shock had set up his make-shift throne. Where Kate had puked her guts out.

Where, nineteen years ago, I dared to challenge the order of things.

The room was quiet, as if they were waiting for me to say something in a cheap parting shot. Or maybe give an order to test the limits of my fall from grace.

Or perhaps they pitied me.

Whatever.

My palm hit the door as I walked away from it all. My empire, my castle, was a junkyard of broken promises.

I turned as soon as a pile of cars blocked the sight of me from the doors. I knew every inch of scrap in this place. It had been my playground and my life for over two decades. No one knew more about the lay of this land than I did.

The vines covered the culvert nicely but tugged away in a mat that didn't break apart. I slid into the hole, pushing forward. The darkness inside was so complete it felt like a grave. I could die in here, and no one would find the body. Ever.

Fuck that. I shoved at the vines and muck clogging the other end and pulled myself free. The Subaru waited for me. It had been a piece of junk. It was still one, but at least it worked.

And the bag I'd stowed in the wheel well was right where I left it.

I pulled out the burner phone and fired it up as I changed clothes.

It rang twice. The man on the other end answered with a quick, "Yo, who's this?"

"Your worst nightmare. Code black."

In the background noise, I could make out Hickey's fingers hitting a keyboard.

"Where are you?" I asked.

"In the war room. Shock just left."

"Nonno still there?"

"Yup. He's doing shots with Wolf. What happened inside?"

"Fuckers stripped me."

Hickey snorted. "Called it."

"Yeah, you did. Kate and Zoe get out?"

"Yup. Speck says they left about fifteen minutes ago."

Damn, Tits worked fast. "Good. You got a bead on them?"

"They're heading west on the interstate."

West? What the fuck?

"Who let them out the gate?"

"Fucking Hammer."

They'd begun to call the prospect Hammer because he was dumber than a box of them. "Call Tits."

"Dude, Wolf is not going to thank you for that."

"Don't care. I wanna know why they're going the direction they're going." I expected south. Tit's home chapter was that direction. South and east.

"Fucking bullshit," Hickey muttered under his breath.

"You'll be free of it soon."

He didn't bother to reply, opting to concentrate on the other call. There was a brief exchange back and forth, then Hickey swore.

"What?"

He asked, "Are you sure?"

"Am I sure about what?" I asked.

"Not you, Tits. She says her girls haven't moved yet."

"What the fuck are they waiting for?"

And *shit*. If Kate and Zoe had left already, who had them? "Wait a minute, get Hammer on the line. Find out who the fuck was with Kate and Zoe, what they were driving, and—"

"J, on it. Hammer says they were in one of Shock's vans. He figured you planned it that way."

"Dumb ass." I cursed the day we opened the doors to that idiot.

Hickey broke into my diatribe. "I know you're not calling me that, right?"

I tried to keep my shit together. "Hickey, we need a plan B or C right now. Either Kate and Zoe went off on their own, or someone took them. If it is the latter…" I swallowed. My throat closed up on the words I couldn't move from my brain into speech. The next sound out of my mouth was something between a croak and a whimper.

"Hang on, I'm looping in Sprout."

Great, another idiot.

"I need backup and a location. You said the interstate, right?" I got in the car and dug between the seats for the little box with the key. I drove over the weeds and gravel behind the lot and onto a small access road. I was on the interstate and running at five over the speed limit before Hickey got me dialed into a GPS signal heading west. Despite my speed, assholes were still passing me. They didn't have to worry about mismatched plates, fake registration and insurance cards, or cops with long memories and even longer grudges against me.

"Sprout says he slipped Danielle's GPS inside Zoe's hood."

Hell to the yes. "Tell him thanks."

They kept a running tally of locations, and I was closing in on them as they exited the freeway and paused for a grand total of two minutes at a Walmart. I'd barely missed them. But the turn-by-turn directions Hickey gave me were shit. I got fucking turned around twice when he led me under the freeway with no on-ramps. "Dude, look at a fucking map or something."

"I'm trying. But you wanted this kept under the radar. I don't have help here."

The rage threatening to erupt got bit back down. "I know, you're trying."

Sprout got on the call. "Turn right; half a mile, there's a ramp heading east."

"I don't need to go east."

"I know, but if you get on it, then keep right; it circles to the other side of the bridge and then you can go west."

Finally, someone with a plan.

"Ask Hickey if he still has a good signal."

"Affirmative."

Thank God. But my signal wasn't as good. No sooner than I got on the interstate, Kate got off it.

At that point, I lost Hickey's updates in the no-man's-land of steep hills and even deeper valleys. It wasn't until I hit a peak about five minutes later that I found out I didn't go in the same direction they did. Both Hickey and Sprout worked to get me pointed toward them and back on their tail.

I'd make up the lost time and get to them. Then, find out if this was Kate's idea or someone else's.

Which scenario would be better? Kate ditching me because of all the fucking around I did, or someone kidnapping her?

I'd like to think that ditching me was the better choice.

But my dumbass heart didn't.

CHAPTER 30

Kate's Childhood Home, Pittsburgh, Pennsylvania—Kate

"You lived here?" Zoe's voice echoed in the large foyer. Cara insisted my daughter come in with us. I bit my argument back because separating from my daughter also felt wrong.

Cara replied when I stayed silent. "I lived here with your grandfather."

Lovely. That was an image I didn't want in my head. Nor did I want my daughter acknowledging that coked-up pile of human shit was any relation to her.

"It's almost fancier than some of the houses we cleaned." Zoe's comments faded as she wandered into what used to be my music room. "Is that a grand piano?"

I stayed glued to the foyer.

"Zoe, get back here," I called out. The sooner we got out of this nightmare, the better. "Nice marble," I indicated the floor. It used to be tile.

"Thanks, I picked it out." Cara directed me to Dad's study. The same place he'd signed my life away. That room was unchanged except for the bars installed on the windows. Their oddity finally registered. Every window had bars on it, like a prison. I shuddered.

Zoe rejoined us. She stood to the side of the door with her back to the wall.

Cara pointed to the art on the wall. "Have at it."

The painting was new. It used to be a hunting scene with ducks. Now, it was an abstract splash of neutrals with bright red slashing through the plain, as if it were a bucket of blood captured mid-toss in a torture chamber.

I flicked through the numbers. The handle turned easily.

Inside were stacks of leather binders. Most of them were from his firm. I put them on the desk while Cara stood back, gun casually held at her side. A threat, but disguised as an afterthought. It was top of mind as I pulled out the stuffed bank bag under the heavy binders. The lock clanked against the metal rim of the safe.

I almost dropped it. "This is heavy."

It thunked as I placed it on the desk.

I scanned the walls of the now-empty safe, searching for any indication there were hidden panels or a false back. But it was seamless. "That's it."

Cara flicked open a few of the binders, barely glancing at them before flicking another open.

Reading upside-down was never a talent of mine. These were legal documents, therefore they were a lot of words in very little space. Undecipherable at a glance. If she searched for the deed or a Will, they were likely right there. But I couldn't be certain. I shifted my attention to Cara's actions instead. She shuffled through the stacks quickly.

And summarily dismissed each binder. She was after something else.

Cara flipped the last book on the pile shut. "Where's the other safe?"

I wanted to play dumb. But she turned the gun on Zoe. "I know he has a second safe."

Shit. Of course she knew about it. She'd survived at least sixteen years around Shock and my father. That was more than enough time to hear the rumors about Dad's treasure trove. It wasn't gold or money or even property deeds. It was information. That's the main reason he and Shock gravitated toward each other. They were both snakes who'd sell out their own flesh and blood to gain leverage on someone.

"It's upstairs."

Her brow furrowed. "In the bedroom? I've checked everywhere for it."

I shook my head, sick to my stomach. "My bedroom." I'd asked for it when we moved in here. So I could be like dear old Dad.

Her jaw dropped. "No wonder I couldn't find it." She motioned with the end of the gun. "Show me."

I led her up the stairs and to the right. The hall carpet was new.

My room, however, wasn't.

It was still puke pink with scarred patches where the tape from my posters tore the surface color away. The holes revealed the light yellow paint that the wall had been originally. The room was hollow and smelled like old nightmares. My bed and furniture were gone, but the white carpet reminded me of that night. There was a stain just there where I'd scrubbed at my own blood to erase the awful events these walls had witnessed.

Unbidden, memories resurfaced of that night. Not the pain, nor the humiliation, but the aftermath. Shock smiled as he buckled his belt. His club leered at my bare ass and legs.

It was horrific to realize they took as much delight in the sight of blood that trickled down and stained the carpet as my exposed flesh. I ran into my bathroom and grabbed a washcloth. Wetted it with cold water, ran back to the carpet, and scrubbed. Then found another drop, scrubbed there, leaving a trail of smeared, browning pink from the bed to the bathroom and back as it finally sunk in. I should take care of myself before trying to clean the damn carpet. By that point, his men were laughing and joking as they tore down the posters on my wall. They picked up the dresser, clothes and all, knocking my collected nicknacks off and crushing them under their heavy boots.

My bed was dismantled and taken away as I grabbed the first thing I could from my closet to cover my legs. It was a skirt that was a dumb distressed denim I'd been fond of…before. But it was too short.

Shock commented on how it hugged my ass.

Then slapped it.

He uttered four words I learned to hate over the next few months. "That ass is mine." Worse were the nine words that usually followed his declaration, "and I can do whatever I want with it."

I swallowed down the vomit that threatened to stain my carpet.

Not *my* carpet, I reminded myself. My father's. Cara's now. Not mine. Never mine. Not even my ass was mine.

Zoe made a noise. Just a faint questioning note that broke my fugue. She was mine. And, more importantly, she was untainted by all this. And I intended to keep her that way. If it meant handing over the collected refuse Dad dug up on his enemies, so be it. Cara could deal with the filth. I wanted nothing to do with it.

I opened the closet and pulled at the panel in the corner.

Under the fake wall was a metal door, very similar to the one in the study. But the lock was different. I tapped on the numbers in sequence. My birthday, Dad told me. I stored my childhood drawings, my diary, and music sheets in there.

Then one day, Dad asked to store some of his papers there. No, demanded. With that demand, he tacked on another one—that I wasn't to let anyone know the safe or its contents were here. Nor should I peek inside.

But I had. You can't leave something curious in a teenager's bedroom and not expect them to look.

At the time, I learned more than I ever wanted to know about the local judge. It was too early of an age to lose faith in law enforcement, making me ripe pickings for someone like Shock. I burned my diary the same day, along with some of the respect I had for my father. I should have run then.

The door opened easily for something so old.

From the piles of papers in there, Dad used it often after I was gone. I glanced at the carpet stains, wondering if maybe, just maybe, he felt guilt every time he came into this room. I hoped so. He deserved it. I pulled out the first stack. There were photos mixed in with the papers.

My hands shook. "Zoe, please stand by the door." I didn't want her to see any of this.

I handed it to Cara who rifled through the pile and searched for the elusive "house" paperwork she had lied to me about.

The second grab was much more interesting.

I checked to see if Zoe was watching or not. Some of the same photos I'd seen in Shock's package were in this one. Jackson featured prominently in most. There were a few more with Nonno in them. Having just met the man, he'd made an impression. I had a hunch we were getting closer to Cara's goal.

"Here. Anything in there that you need?" My question was pointed, and my words were sharper than intended.

She studied a photo of Jackson, turning it sideways to get a different angle on it. I had the overwhelming urge to scream, "Mine," and rip it from her hands, but one glance at the large, rectangular spot where the carpet was more pristine white than the other sections of the floor made me stuff that desire back down. He wasn't anyone's. Most certainly not mine. And Cara now held the photos to prove it.

Cara pulled out another photo. Nonno. She stuffed it under her shirt.

I tugged out the next stack. The safe was larger than the one in the office, and it was filled to the brim. With each layer, I noticed a pattern. The targets weren't Dad's political or career rivals; they were bikers and dealers. Criminals, politicians, law enforcement, even business leaders. Many of the photos were taken in this house. Probably from parties Dad threw. The ones that weren't bothered me. My father wouldn't be able to get into some of these places. But Shock definitely could.

One particular photo made me pause. It was Dad in his office, shaking hands with a man.

He was wearing the same tie as the one in the crime scene photo.

If he was killed after this photo was taken, why was it here?

I handed that folder off to Cara.

Under it was a crime report for a missing person. Then, a news clipping of a Jane Doe who washed up along the river. Accompanying it was a photo of the same girl with Shock.

A hand-written suicide note… I slapped that file shut and passed it to Cara.

She smiled when she opened it. "Got him."

I dug out the rest of the stacks without looking at any of them. Cara sent Zoe for a suitcase from the main bedroom, describing exactly where it was. Zoe returned and helped load the documents into the bag.

"Are there any other places your dad stored stuff?"

"His office downtown."

Cara shook her head. "They went through that."

"They, *who*?"

She swallowed. "His coworkers. Those blood-sucking, lawyer assholes. Cut me out of the Will. And there's no life insurance policy. Except this." She patted her shirt and smiled.

From what I'd already seen of Nonno, he wasn't a man to be messed with. Worse, now that she had what she wanted, I was deathly afraid she would kill us as easily as she killed Tina.

"I want you to take everything." I indicated the suitcase, now crammed with over sixteen years of blackmail.

Cara's glee evaporated.

"Are you sure?" Her tone was suspicious. "You don't want *anything*?"

I only wanted one thing. "I want to get out of here *with* Zoe. That's all." I looked around the room, at the stains, the dismantled carpet, and everything else. "Take everything. I hate this place, my father, and everything attached to this town. I want none of it."

"Everything?"

"From the basement to the roof. It's all behind me now." That included Cara, but she didn't need to know that part.

"You know your father wasn't a bad man."

My snort of denial stopped cold in my throat. The rumble of motorcycles drifted through the walls. "Do you hear that?"

Cara's eyes went round. "How did someone find us? I got rid of your trackers. I got rid of *Shock's* trackers!"

Zoe's mouth tightened. I knew that look. She had a secret. One I didn't want to know. Because if I did, I'd give her away. "We need to leave." There was a path through the sloping hill behind the house. It was dark and multiple years since I'd used it. There was no guarantee it was even the same. But I'd risk it for Zoe.

"Not without my things." Cara pointed the gun at me. "Zoe, grab that bank bag from the office downstairs. Your mom's going to carry the suitcase. But I'll have my gun on her, so no funny business. Hurry."

Zoe fled down the stairs. I followed at a slightly more sedate pace, hampered by the heavy suitcase, and not wanting to test Cara's aim.

But we were too late.

Shock strode in the front door like he owned the place.

CHAPTER 31

Outside of Pittsburgh—Jackson

"Your GPS is worth shit." My complaint fell on Hickey's deaf ears.

"I'm telling you, the tracker is about three hundred feet from you."

I was in the middle of bumfuck no-fucking-where at some dark park or trailhead of some stupid ass nature walk. A public place with cops and god knows what lurking behind the now gated entrance.

"It's sealed off." Another lit vehicle rolled past. No one was going in any kind of hurry, which… if I thought about it too hard, meant nothing good.

"Kate's tracker is there."

I debated telling him what I was seeing. Squad cars, at least four, an ambulance with its lights shut off.

And… fuck my life, that last vehicle with its little yellow light was a coroner's van.

I'd pulled over as soon as I saw the flashing lights. Then, I crawled past the scene until I found a pull-off to stash the car. I backtracked on foot to see what was going on and tucked behind some trees to stay out of sight. "What about Zoe's? The one that Sprout put on her?"

"Heading west."

"And? Where west?" I needed that information immediately. If Kate was in the park, she wasn't moving. And since no one was in a hurry, I had a guess as to why. But if Zoe was still alive, I might not give in to the urge to say, "Burn it all down," like my gut was screaming to do.

"Zoe's tracker is still on track toward Pittsburgh," Hickey confirmed. "If it stops, I'll send the address in text."

"Tell me you dropped a tracker on one of the bikes," I demanded.

Shock and company skedaddled out of Skilletsville almost minutes behind my inglorious walk of shame out of the club. Nonno was pissed about it.

"They tagged Bandit's bike."

Ha! Served the goddamned bastard right. "Where is he?"

"Almost to Pittsburgh."

Obviously, that's where they all went.

Where everyone went except Kate's tracker.

I tried not to think about the ramifications of that at all. The hi-viz lights on the back of the ambulance flicked on. They were so bright I could make out some details through the trees. About a hundred and fifty feet from the parking lot, the cops and other personnel clustered around a little picnic site. Slapped on top of the white gurney, the black sheen of a body bag took shape. It was almost invisible before but now glistened like snake skin in the flood-lights. I turned my back for a moment, collecting my will.

I'd just hung up on Hickey and turned back to see what the police were doing when I noticed the sheriff's team coordinating a search of the area. A team of two was heading directly for me. I'd stayed too fucking long.

As quickly and quietly as I could, I slipped through the trees and picked my way to the car. I drove away carefully, leaving the scene and my heart behind. At least a piece of it.

One body bag. Not another one in sight.

That meant Zoe was out there… somewhere. Or her tracker was. I needed to find that. If she was still alive, I'd make it work. Didn't know how, or what kind of man I'd be, but I'd do my damndest to fix what broke tonight.

And that was a vow.

Hickey's promise to get me a location hit right before his cell signal faded again. I kept going on the most direct route I knew toward Pittsburgh, hoping and praying this wasn't another wrong turn. By the time I hit the city, I was ready to jump out of my seat.

Practically everything was across a river, over a mountain, or no fucking kidding, through a damn tunnel. Claustrophobic wasn't nearly a strong enough word for this wretched place. Knowing that Shock lived here and actually enjoyed this dirty, cramped-as-fuck town with hills so high, it felt like they were going to fall on you any minute; made me hate the place even more.

I know I wasn't being fair to the folks who loved their city, but I only saw the cracks. The places to exploit, the poverty. The run-down factories, the too slick "old-town" charm that some politician used as a vanity project to get re-elected. I hated every damn thing I saw. I picked up his call while I crossed a bridge that headed toward the northern section of Pittsburgh.

"Has Zoe's tracker moved?"

"Nope. They've been there at least thirty minutes.

Good? Or bad. A hell of a lot could happen in that span.

My mind turned to dark places. How a half second of inattention could earn you a pipe in the back of the head. How fast I could empty a full clip, reload, and empty a second. How similar cutting a throat was to gutting a fish. The same thrust, drag, catch on viscera, and the squelching noise as flesh split open.

I cleared my throat. Hickey tapped away at his keyboard. That meant he had something going on to keep him busy. I needed a distraction. "Whatcha working on?"

"Tracking Nonno."

Color me surprised. "The fuck you say?"

"Don't worry, he authorized it."

I almost missed the turn, trying to figure out what the fuck was going on. "Authorized what?"

"Well, once you and Shock lit out, he got suspicious. Then he was pissed off. Even more so when Tits showed up with a bunch of those bitches she hangs around with, and Kate wasn't there to pick up. He said he's going after Shock."

"Really now?"

That was *all* I fucking needed. The national mother-fucking president crawling down my ass. "I suppose you sent him Shock's signal?"

There was too long of a pause on the other end.

"Hickey? Did I lose you?"

"Sorry, J. Yeah, he wanted Shock's location." He trailed off, almost constipated in his strangled tones. If I didn't know him as well as I did, I might not have pushed for more, but I knew him. Trained him, raised him from a puppy-ass rice-rocket rider to full grown Destroyer.

"What the fuck is going on?"

"Shock's signal is with Zoe's."

The hell it was.

I ended the call. For good measure, I turned off the goddamn phone. I was less than a mile from the address and despite it being a residential neighborhood, disregarded all sorts of traffic laws as I double-timed it to the address.

I'd beat Nonno there; that was certain, even with my little side trip. Most importantly, I needed to be there, where Zoe was, over an hour before Shock found her.

All of those dark thoughts turned really fucking dark.

"If he harms one hair on her head, I'll…" I spoke aloud in the car as I drove.

It wasn't an empty threat, just open-ended. I'd start by getting my baby girl safe. Then shoot the motherfucker in the balls. First aid enough to keep him alive so I could tear his skin off. Then I'd cut him up and feed him his own parts.

Damn.

I sounded just like my old road brother, Pinner. I finally understood his motivation to serve life in prison for killing the man who hurt his little girl, Lily. I could learn a thing or two from his fuckups, though. He went to prison. I wouldn't. Whatever end Shock deserved, it would fly under the radar of law enforcement.

I backed off the accelerator. It wouldn't do any good if I was caught. I had to go in knowing the scene would be right out of Hell. I also needed to deal with one fucking problem at a time and not get myself caught doing it. Usually, I was better at that shit.

The problem was, I hadn't planned this heist. I altered my plan, driving past the house at Hickey's address. I parked farther down the road where the road dead-ended and quickly wiped down the car. As I crept downhill toward the house carrying my gear, I tried to figure out what I'd do if Shock or the police trapped me in this god-forsaken suburb.

If I had to use the car for a getaway, it was a bad idea to leave it where it was. I should have turned around and parked it closer to the mouth of the cul de sac. *Fuck wasting time to move it.* I'd do whatever was necessary to get Zoe out—even hot-wire a car. Once I got the situation controlled, I'd head north. News of my demise couldn't have traveled fast enough to reach everyone in the Destroyers' network. There was a smuggler on the border by Detroit who'd get me into Canada.

Me and Zoe.

Plan set, I stuck to the shadows of the overgrown trees and landscaping that surrounded the McMansions and stately ranch homes that somehow still looked good despite being almost a quarter century old. When Hickey told me the address, it pinged in my memories. I'd looked up her father's house once as I plotted his demise. Too bad the asshole got himself shot before I could get around to finally doing it.

Kate's former house was one of the newer ones, built in the eighties. It was a mishmash of all the outward trappings the houses of that time featured. A big ass arched window over the front door, colonial decor, but mansion-style scale and amenities that didn't quite create symmetry in the exterior design. From my perch on the stone fence, I studied the exterior to picture the layout on the inside. On the main floor, there were two windows to the left of the door, another doubled window off to the right. I scanned the roof line. There was a chimney on the left, which was likely attached to the great room. No chimney on the right meant either office space or other whatnot, maybe ending with a formal dining room in the back or maybe a second family room where the kids watched movies and shit.

The farthest room to the right on the main floor was lit up.

The upstairs bedroom above it was lit up as well. The other side had more room for a main bedroom, but the lack of light coming from any of the windows over there told me a lot. Shock would want to see what he did.

I'd slip in through the back. Come up the middle or hopefully find a back staircase off a kitchen and get upstairs without being spotted. Then, down the hall to the lit bank of windows on the end. Gun ready, knife in the other hand.

Hopefully, Zoe wouldn't try to hug me. That would be a fucking mistake.

There was a van in the driveway. Flanking it were two motorcycles. At least one of them was Bandit's because of the tracker. I guessed the other would be Shock's. *Fucking morons.* Taking their bikes here? Dumb mistake. Noise like that was noticed. The denizens of residential neighborhoods loved to peek out windows whenever they heard loud pipes. In a way, that was a good thing. Maybe I could pin Shock and Bandit with this whole thing and keep the cops from crawling up my ass later. That meant killing them both. But how?

One problem at a time, dummy. My dad's voice was pretty loud tonight. I didn't need it distracting me. Then again, the old bastard got away with a lot before it finally caught up with him. I might want to listen.

I tucked my bag under a bush and slipped around to the back of the house.

There was a balcony over the deck that wrapped across the main floor. Both jutted off into darkness.

Fuck a staircase.

This balcony was much easier to climb onto than Sprout's greased pole. I managed it in about a third of the time it took me to breach my home's security.

I hung from the railing, listening for problems. There were none that I could tell. I sensed movement in the house, but nothing indicating they'd heard me. In a moment of stupid imagining, I remembered Kate's kiss. The longing for another was like a dagger in my heart.

There wouldn't be one of those waiting for me here.

The French doors at the top were easy as fuck to pry open. My anger made me quick, brutal, and mostly silent. The thick carpet didn't make any sound when I padded to the open door to the hall.

I hoped like hell I wasn't too late.

CHAPTER 32

Kate

Behind Shock was another man, one of his lackeys who'd accompanied him to Skilletsville. What was his name? Did it matter? I froze on the stairs. The tableau of my doom waiting for me at the bottom.

Cara, however, didn't freeze. She opened fire.

I dove to my knees on the stairs, letting the suitcase slide down the carpeted steps where it crashed into the wall as the staircase turned ninety degrees.

The case broke open, and papers and photos spilled out.

More gunfire erupted, and Cara made a strange noise. I glanced up just in time to see her face. Her mouth was open. A bloom of red expanded across her shirt. She staggered, leaning on the railing for support, and the gun in her hand slipped from her fingers. It landed on the carpet with a dull sound. Or was that imagined? Another blast of noise, this one bringing down paint and debris from the ceiling. Cara tried to bend over to pick up the gun, but her balance was all wrong. Instead, she fell against the banister. Her momentum dragged her down. In a last effort to control the slide, she sat down, her shoulder against the railing, mouth open, eyes dead.

The lackey slipped on the piles of papers and then raced past me to shoot Cara point-blank in the head. Her body pitched backward to the carpet. "All clear." His voice sounded muffled to me.

Bandit was his name. What a dumb time to remember useless trivia. I cursed silently.

I slid down a couple more stairs, my feet landing on the folders and the carpeted steps strewn with photos. Faces, names, events, blackmail. One in particular stared at me. A woman… the Jane Doe who'd washed up along the river.

That would be Cara's fate. Mine, too, if I didn't act.

I scrambled to stand, but the pile under my feet was slippery.

Bandit beat me to the turn. He grabbed my arm and pulled me with him as he side-stepped the debris littering the staircase. Something caught his eye, though. He halted abruptly and picked up a photo from the pile. His face darkened with anger.

"What the fuck is this?" He held the photo up so Shock could see it.

"None of your business. Bring Kate here." Shock scanned the scene. "Where's the kid?"

My lips tightened, and I fought Bandit's grip, going onto my ass so he'd be fighting my entire weight. But gravity and the slippery contents of the suitcase were my enemies. He dragged me down, rumpling papers and making the mess expand.

Meanwhile, Shock turned in a circle. "Zoe? Come out. We have your mom." His tone turned into a sing-song. "Come out and play, Zoe."

It shifted to his normal, more menacing one as he addressed us.

"Move your asses." Shock pulled out his gun and pointed it at Bandit.

But Bandit was distracted by the photo in his hand. "Are you blackmailing Big G?"

Like a snake, Shock's focus fixed on his henchman. I'd witnessed that glare before. It promised pain. I shrunk lower so I wouldn't be caught in that tsunami of destruction.

"Bring Kate here."

"That's how you got Nonno to agree to make you regional president, isn't it? You forced his hand."

The casual way Shock took aim at his own man chilled my bones. "I'm giving you one chance because you're a brother. Bring. Kate. Here."

Bandit's nostrils flared. I cowered at his feet, covering my ears because I knew what was going to happen next. He'd hesitated. Bandit's final act was defiance. And Shock hated defiance. So much so he'd kill a member of his own club.

Bandit's body slammed against the wall. He crumpled at my feet. I cried out, not screaming but whimpering like some wounded animal. I scrambled for the door. It was the only thing I saw in my tunnel vision of fear. Not Shock standing there with a smoking gun, nor the new marble Cara installed on the floor that was slippery as heck, nor the papers and photos clinging to me like dark shadowy demons.

But one thing stopped me short.

Zoe.

She stood in the doorway of the office.

Run!

I willed it but did not speak it. I froze at the door, climbing to my feet to save my daughter. "Fuck you, Shock."

I didn't stop there. I spewed out a tirade of all the injustices he'd ever had a hand in. From the vile way he raped me to the crimes I'd witnessed in my short time with him. Even spitting on the floor and blaming him for Cara's death. "It's all because of you. All this death. All of this torture and loss are because you are the most vile man I've ever met."

The bastard smiled. "You finally noticed?"

"I noticed."

If anything, his grin got wider and more macabre. "Then you won't be surprised by this." He lifted his gun and aimed it at me.

Adrenaline dumped into my system. But I had to distract him from my daughter. "Surprised? No. I'm only surprised it took you so long to kill me. Why?" Keep him talking. Feign interest into his twisted mind, cater to his fucked up ego. I'd learned all of that from him. Now, I used that knowledge to buy time.

"You always were my favorite."

Oh, spare me. "I'm sure that's not …completely accurate." I'd almost called him a liar. Survival instincts screamed at me to change my phrasing at the last second.

"I suppose not. Girls are a dime a dozen. But you were... how to say it?" He stared off into space for a theatrical moment, searching for the right words to cut me. "Defiant? No. More like patient. You knew when to back down. But you were always searching for a way out. I never knew when you'd run. You were only biding your time. That's because, deep down, you're truly like your father. He was a patient man, too. Waiting for his time to strike. Eating my shit for years."

Shock paused to rid himself of a bad memory that flashed on his face like he'd tasted something bitter.

"He went to the Feds. Right behind my back." Shock lifted his head to the upstairs railing. "Thank God Cara warned me. That's why he died. She did it."

"She didn't pull the trigger." That was all his doing; I had no doubts about that.

That ugly smile came back. "She might as well have."

Zoe tried to slip from the office to the kitchen hallway. It caught Shock's attention. "There you are."

"Shock." I tried to get his attention, but he was having none of it. And I was too far away to throw myself on him so Zoe could get away.

"She's pretty like you. I wonder if she blushes?"

"Leave her alone." My voice didn't sound like mine.

He noticed that. "Your mom was always such a shy, quiet creature. But I knew she had a backbone. I loved beating that fight out of her."

Zoe's eyes darted to mine for answers. I shook my head.

No, he didn't beat it out of me. I would fight to the very last breath. But I'd do it my way. Patiently. Like water eroding stone.

"Do you take after your mother?"

"Don't answer him," I interjected.

"Aw, you can talk to me, sweetheart." He turned on the charm.

"I repeat, leave her alone." I stepped forward, hoping to draw his attention.

It worked. He refocused his aim on me. "Or what?"

"Or nothing. You don't talk to her; you don't touch her."

"How are you going to make that happen?"

His leer sent a chord of terror through me. But I kept my face calm. "Whatever it takes." I took another step forward. I was almost within touching distance of the gun.

"Try again. You're old. Bred. Used. Using your body won't work on me, Kate; you're useless. I'm thinking I need something newer. Fresher. More… virginal." His head tilted toward Zoe. She edged away from him, moving back toward the office. Her shoulders were hunched, and her hands tucked tightly in the front pocket of her hoodie. I wanted to scream at her. Not that way. Don't walk like prey. Don't come closer to me so he can shoot both of us. *Please.* She took another shuffled step toward me.

Damn it. I spoke with my "mom" voice, "Zoe? I'll do whatever it takes, but that's *my* sacrifice, not yours." I meant it.

Her eyes locked on Shock. Her eyebrow, the crooked one, lifted. It was so similar to Jackson's that my heart hurt. Whatever she was planning, it wasn't good.

"Zoe, please," I begged her to listen to me.

Shock laughed. "Teenagers, huh? They never listen."

Zoe straightened, her hands sliding out of the pocket of the hoodie. They met in front of her. In them, she had Gina's tiny gun. The one I'd thought she'd set on the ledge by the gun range hours ago when Nonno interrupted us. Zoe must have grabbed it when we scrambled into hiding.

Shock's laughter died. "What are you going to do with that thing? Shoot m—"

Bang!

He stepped back, reeling from the impact of the bullet.

Bang. She fired again. Then she emptied the clip into his chest, not stopping until she stood over him, and the trigger clicked over and over again as she tried to pump more bullets into his corpse.

I approached her to take the gun from her hand, but she flinched and nearly pointed the gun at me, still pulling that damn trigger.

I held my hands up. "Zoe, it's me. Mom."

Her eyes were empty.

I tried again and put a little more force into my words. "Your *mom*. You know, the woman who almost had you in the back of a squad car because you decided to be born in the middle of an ice storm?"

She blinked.

Her hand shook.

I took that as a sign to take the gun out of her hand. "It's okay."

She hit my chest like a freight train, hugging me so hard I had trouble breathing.

The weapon in my hand was hot. I shifted it away from her so she wouldn't get hurt. Then I wrapped my free arm around her so she'd be safe. So she'd know she was loved, no matter what. I whispered it into her hair. "I love you."

"Mom."

The word caught in her throat. I tucked the useless gun into my pants pocket to hold my baby. Damn, all the safety tips Gina had drilled into my head. Hugging Zoe mattered most right now. I figured the gun had been dry-fired enough times to prove it was harmless.

Seconds later, I wished I hadn't tucked it away.

Bandit groaned.

I spun, pushing Zoe behind me, and dug for the useless gun. Maybe he'd been out cold long enough that he didn't know it was empty. Or maybe I could bluff my way through this bullshit.

He was slow in sitting up, making all sorts of noises a healthy young man shouldn't make.

He rubbed at his chest. "Fucking bullshit cheap-ass vest..." he spat out as he struggled to catch his breath.

I kept the gun trained on him. He finally noticed.

"Don't shoot."

"Then don't move." I sounded calm on the outside, but inside I was wondering what the fuck would happen next. This night rivaled some of my worst nightmares.

"Don't plan on it." He leaned heavily on his arm. As he did, he stared at the flotsam of blackmail surrounding him. He shifted a page to see what was underneath. "We need to pick this up."

He was on his own with that. "I don't think *we* need to do anything. You can." I lifted the gun a bit higher.

He squinted at me. "Woman, I heard at least seven shots. That gun's empty." He shifted and displayed his weapon. "And this one ain't."

"Zoe, this time, *listen* to me. I want you to run. I don't care where, and I certainly don't want your opinion on it. Just do it."

Bandit set the gun on the floor. "Damn it. I'm not going to shoot you. I just… need some help."

"No."

"Please?"

"I didn't stutter. Zoe?"

She glanced up. "Cara had the keys to the van. He could catch up to us on foot."

My daughter had a point. "I don't suppose that boyfriend of yours taught you how to hot-wire and drive his motorcycle?"

"I wish. If Dad were here…"

See which one fills up faster… "He isn't."

"Then maybe one of us should help him and the other one get the keys?"

That was a dilemma. Send Zoe upstairs to deal with a dead body? Or let her be close to an asshole biker with a gun? I'll add, a place where she could be used as leverage? I opted for neither.

"Not until he's tied up. Go in the office, see if there is any packing tape, cord, you name it, something."

Zoe followed orders and came back out with a roll of clear packing tape. Probably not the best tool, but not completely worthless.

I approached Bandit cautiously. He might be faking. "Toss your gun into the foyer."

His incredulous look was not comforting. "I'll slide it, okay? After it's unloaded." He took his time, first ejecting the clip, then clearing the chamber. He tossed the clip to the floor by Zoe's feet. It landed with a clatter, and one bullet inside popped out and rolled to a stop against Shock's body. Bandit then held the empty gun out to me, handle first. "We're cool, okay?" He held out his hands to be taped.

No, we weren't. I passed the gun to Zoe, who picked up the clip and reloaded it. That single lesson with Gina was coming in handy for her. I grudgingly admitted she paid attention. If only that also applied to her schoolwork.

Which would not happen unless we got out of here and somehow magically made it home. And then, somehow magically stopped a bunch of bikers from tracking us down again. Maybe Cara had a good idea?

"Pass me that suitcase." He'd landed within arm's reach of it.

With a little more complaining and a very delicate hand off, I had the suitcase. I flipped it on its back and began stuffing papers at random into it. We were almost done when a noise above us made me freeze.

"Cara's dead, isn't she?" Zoe asked.

I sighed. "I fucking hope so."

"Yay, Mom, way to get ruthless."

I side-eyed my daughter. We waited—Bandit, Zoe, and myself for the next shoe to drop.

CHAPTER 33

Jackson

The first thing I saw when I peeked over the railing was Kate. The second? Zoe. Seeing both of them whole? Well, it fucked me up. I forgot to check the rest of the scene. The dead woman at the top of the stairs wasn't moving, but a goddamn biker at the bottom sure was.

"Freeze, motherfucker."

All three living people stopped mid-movement to stare up at me.

"Hi, Dad."

I acknowledged Zoe with a dip of my head. "Kate?"

"About time you showed up. You're late."

Bandit had his hands taped but still tried to hold them in the air. He was the only one of them with any sense.

"Sorry about that. I'd have been here earlier if you'd kept your damn tracker on you."

Kate sucked in a breath and turned red.

Zoe asked, "Did you find Tina?"

"Who?"

Zoe looked at her mom to answer. But I knew, almost before Kate replied.

Kate's eyes squeezed shut, then she dug deep for a brave face. "One of Shock's hookers. She came with us. Cara killed her." A nod toward the top of the stairs at the dead woman's body gave me a name to put to the corpse.

"Who killed Cara?"

"Shock. Or him." Kate indicated Bandit.

"Well?" I asked.

"I'm pretty sure it was me." Bandit didn't look pleased about his confession.

I scrutinized Shock's bullet-riddled corpse in the middle of the foyer. There was more blood on the marble than in his body. "Who did that?"

Kate turned redder. Zoe blanched.

With a grab and tug, Kate pulled Zoe close. "I did," Kate said.

"Mom." Zoe's face betrayed the truth.

Meanwhile, Bandit tried to stuff papers into a suitcase with his bound hands.

I stood on the final step and put the gun in my hand against his head. "What the fuck are you doing?"

Bandit froze. "Picking up the pieces."

"You can stop that for a bit. Keep those hands in the air."

If no police had arrived through this entire bloodbath, I highly doubted any would.

No sooner than I thought that, headlights flared through the windows as a vehicle turned from the road. I peeked out the huge-ass window but couldn't tell whether it was a cop or not. "Zoe, Kate, get the fuck out, now."

Neither listened. Zoe peered out one of the door's side windows, keeping her body out of sight. I couldn't have done it better myself. "It's an SUV."

"Is it the cops?" I asked.

"No, I think it's Nonno."

Kate threw her hands up in the air in disgust. "Fucking great. Another biker. Someone just shoot me now? Please?"

"Babe? You might not want to say shit like that," I spit out. I was happy as fuck she was still alive, but now was not the time.

She had the nerve to glare at me. "If you knew half of what happened to us tonight, you'd mind your words, mister."

Bandit snickered. Then he tacked on a hasty, "sorry," and tried to hold his hands up.

"Well? Someone fill me in."

Preferably somewhere other than here. "On second thought… Kate, Zoe, let's get the fuck out of here."

The door swung open wide. Nonno and five of his fucking bodyguards strode in and stopped dead in their tracks as soon as they saw Shock's body. Nonno caught my declaration. "You're not going anywhere, asshole."

"And you're not my boss anymore, so fuck off." I turned to put him in my sights and get closer to my family. As I stepped past Bandit, I made sure to stay out of tripping distance. Kate gathered Zoe to her side and guided her until we finally were together. I pulled Zoe in for a one-armed hug. Then, I told her, "Stay behind me."

Nonno stared at Shock's body. "Did you do this?"

He directed the question at me.

"Fuck no. I'm not messy." I nudged Zoe to stop peeking around me and get her ass fully behind my body as a shield. Kate stood at my side.

"I did it."

This time, my woman lied convincingly.

Nonno frowned. He turned to the one person who wouldn't, couldn't, lie to him. "Bandit?"

He sent me an apologetic glance. "Zoe killed him."

Nonno's eyebrows lifted. "Really?" He tried to see around me to get a gander at my baby girl, but I puffed up larger to block his line of sight.

His eyes fixed on me. "A chip off the old block, huh?" He huffed out a humorless laugh. "Just like One-Eyed Jack." His head shook in disbelief. His motion finally stilled when he fixated on Shock's body. "How am I going to explain this?"

"Blackmail?" Bandit offered. He pulled a photo from the suitcase he'd been stuffing. Most of the photos were crumpled. A few were blood-stained. That would be a problem if anyone else showed up, mainly the police, but the item in Bandit's hand was incriminating as hell. Because I recognized the face in it.

One "Tercel Timmy" stared at me from his watery grave.

Nonno took it from Bandit. He studied the photo and the notes written on the back. "Huh."

That could mean any number of things. And since I was no longer a Destroyer, none of those interpretations meant shit to me. "We're leaving."

Nonno had questions. "Jackson?"

We'd made it two steps. "What?"

Nonno hadn't taken his eyes off the photo. He started slowly. "I fucked up tonight."

No shit? But again, not my fucking problem. I tugged Kate's hand, indicating the gauntlet of bikers at the door.

Had to give her credit, she held her head high and took a step in that direction.

Nonno had to ruin our escape. "I promoted the wrong man because of shit like this haunting me." He finally lifted his gaze to skewer me with his stare. "And I think you already knew that."

I did, but there were more important things in my life than fixing Nonno's shit. But maybe I could use it to my advantage? Zoe's fingers hooked onto my belt loop. *She's more important.* "So? That's a *you* problem." I wrapped my arm over Zoe's shoulder and kept her there all the way out the door and down the street. Both Kate and Zoe remained quiet as I bundled them inside the ugly Subaru.

Meanwhile, Nonno stood in the driveway, monitoring my every move. But he didn't stop me from driving away.

I headed north, then east, practically retracing the route I'd taken out of Pittsburgh with Kate the very first time. She noticed and reached for my hand as we put miles between us and anything biker-related. A long-ass drive later, we were in Maine. I followed them inside the little house I technically did and didn't own.

"Wow, this doesn't look like the same place." It utterly didn't.

"I had a landlord who didn't give a shit what I did with the place."

Kate was funny.

"Thank God for that."

Zoe stumbled past us. Even though she slept most of the ride, she still was in that zombie state of exhaustion, and she hadn't eaten a single thing the whole trip. "I'm going to bed."

That sounded like a great idea. Except, I didn't have one here… unless… I tracked her ascent to the split attic above. Then, quietly asked Kate, "One of those rooms is yours right?"

Her shoulders jiggled with silent laughter. Her slow steps toward the stairs invited me forward. "I guess it's ours now?"

Maybe. If nothing followed me here. "That would be nice."

She stopped to stare at me. "What are we going to do?"

I'd thought about it most of the night, the following day, and all of this night. Long drives in the dark were great for making plans. But shit for executing them. "I think I'll run for mayor."

Her face stretched into amused disbelief. "No way. You?"

"What? It's not a hard job. Sit on your ass by the ice cream shop and wave. When they don't wave back, whip a middle finger at their back, and put 'em on John's shit list."

Kate snorted. But she thought about it. "I hate to admit it, but you'd be good at that."

No shit. I was born to run things.

The closest I ever got was president of some backwater biker gang that was nothing but trouble. And was the best damn family a man could ask for. "I gotta call Hickey. Apologize."

Kate's expression fell. She reached out and tugged me close. "After. Right now, we're going to go upstairs. Sleep, maybe more. But mostly? Pretend. Okay?" Her eyes filled with moisture.

"Baby, don't cry."

She swallowed. "You're going to leave me again."

Never.

Even thinking about it, I wondered if that was a lie. "I don't want to."

"You never did. But you had to."

"I'm out. The only thing that I have to do now is be a good man for you."

I didn't mean it as a joke.

Kate sure thought it was funny, though. She wiped her eyes and couldn't hold in her amusement. "You? Good? *Please*."

Put that way, she had a point. "I can be bad." I pointed my eyes to the ceiling and wiggled my eyebrow.

She scrunched up her face. "Can you be bad… and quiet?"

"Let's find out."

I let her lead me up the narrow steps, taking time to admire her ass. I was so focused on that I hit my head when I reached the top.

"Fuck. You never fixed this?"

"The roof? Yeah, on the outside. You just need to be shorter."

"Funny. Don't quit your day job." I glanced at the door to my right. At some point in the past, Zoe plastered a poster on the outside surface, warning anyone who could read that there was hazardous waste inside. "Do you think she's going to be okay?"

"I was going to ask you that," Kate whispered.

That deserved an honest answer. "If she's got my instinct and your resilience? Yeah. But we'll be there for her." If we could. It wasn't easy for a biker with my reputation to survive on the outside. Someone would eventually decide I shouldn't breathe. When that happened…

Fuck it. I'd kill them. I'd kill all of them. This life already had its hooks in me. I'd brave anything the Destroyers threw at me if I could just have my girls.

"I love you for that." Kate kissed my cheek. It took me a bit to realize she wasn't talking about my vow to kill my former club members, but because I'd offered to be there for Zoe.

I backed her into the room on the left, this time minding the rafters that threatened to take a piece of my skull. We'd done this dance before. Almost seventeen years ago. "I love you, too. Not just 'cause of Zoe. You, Kate. I love you." It felt so damn good to admit it finally. "I have loved you for…" *Nineteen years*, my inner voice said. Ever since I got snared by her clear, green eyes.

"Shh." She put a finger over my mouth. Then replaced it with her lips. They tasted sweet. I'd never desired anything more than the sensation of Kate being the beautiful woman she was. From her bravery to her kindness, her dedication, and the compassion she displayed even in horrible moments.

"Whose idea was it to leave the compound?" I had to know.

She leaned back. "Mine."

I wasn't going to tell her that was stupid. I'd been planning a similar escape route for her. But she didn't know that. So, I had to ask, "Why?"

After a moment of contemplation, she answered. "A long time ago you talked about your mother. How she had no choice but to go back to prostitution after your father was locked up. I wondered if she, or Cara, or … poor Tina… if they had a choice, would they take it?"

Shit, I didn't know Cara like Kate had, but I'd have done the very same for Tina. She wasn't a bad person, just someone caught up in Shock's issues.

"It was dangerous."

Kate nodded. "And if Cara hadn't betrayed us, or if Tina hadn't lied, then what? I'd have helped two women get out of a situation they didn't want to be in."

"It's still dangerous."

The look she sent me was designed to put me in my place.

I tried to reframe things so we wouldn't argue anymore. "Next time, ask for help."

"Next time?" she prompted.

It took decades to figure out why my father did what he did for Mom. But I finally understood why. "Hopefully, there won't be a next time, but I know you have a good heart. A wonderful, caring one. And you'll need help. Please ask."

Her expression softened. "You will always be my partner in crime."

"Partner, huh?"

"Always."

Damn. That sounded like… forever. "I'm going to be a terrible mayor. You know that, right?"

Kate opted to give her answer as a kiss. One that led me to her bed. It lingered and extended into more kisses, and clothing discarded to the floor. I climbed into her tiny bed and held her in my arms. We kept kissing, until I slid inside her, and our sharp inhales of wonder freeze-framed the moment and I had to tell her again how much she meant to me.

"I love you, Kate. With all that I am."

She repeated my words back at me, adding my name… my real name—the whole damn thing.

"Hold up. When did I tell you that?" For the life of me, I hadn't.

"Crystal Ann told me. And Zoe found you online. You made the papers."

I grimaced and tried not to go soft while seated inside her. "Good or bad?"

"Something about a river walk being built in Skilletsville."

Ah. The good shit. "That's all Sprout's fault." I pumped out, then back in, enjoying the feel of her on my dick.

"I think it was you. Trying to be mayor."

"Don't make me laugh, woman. I'm inside you." I pumped again, setting a slow pace guaranteed to drive her over the brink of ecstasy.

Her eyes glimmered with amusement, and her fingertips squeezed my biceps. "Laugh, Jackson. Life's too short not to."

I thrust three times before answering her. "Nope, we're going to live a long time. You're going to get sick of me." I dug in a little harder and gave her all of me.

A small moan escaped her. She tacked on a breathless, "Not if you keep doing, that. More?"

"You gotta be quiet, too," I whispered in her ear and pulled to the edge of our connection to watch her face as I slid back in. She was so beautiful.

Her eyes met mine as she clamped her mouth shut. She put her hand on my mouth as I picked up speed. I nipped at her fingertips, but she moved in for the kill, trapping my neck and wrapping her legs around my ass. "Kate…" I warned.

"Shh. Bad. Very bad. And very quiet," she whispered in my ear.

This woman was going to kill me.

Her teeth caught my earlobe, and I lost my mind as I rocked harder and faster into her cunt. My brain teetered in that state of nothing and hyper-awareness as her vaginal walls pulsed against my cock.

Quiet? *Fuck.* I held my breath and let go of as much control as I could as I orgasmed inside her. My soul was pouring into her, and she wanted quiet? Why? It screamed.

A groan escaped. Kate's fingernails dug into my skin as my dick's pulses roared inside her while I admired how damn gorgeous she was with her clear green eyes and her skin all flushed and—"Fuuuck."

"Zoe," she reminded me.

Right. Less than a scant hallway and two thin walls away. I breathed through my mouth for control.

Kate smiled at me. "If this were a competition…"

"You'd win every time." My head fell to that little nest between her shoulder and neck where I could smell her shampoo and skin. "Every time," I vowed.

"I think we both deserve an award for quietest sex."

"Gold medal."

"At least." She breathed out a satisfied sigh. "We probably should put our clothes back on."

That would be a good idea. But I didn't want to move. "Give me a minute."

Hours later, the sound of Zoe's door opening had us scrambling for clothes. Kate set a land speed record, snagging her shirt off the floor and tugging it over her head. Too bad it was inside out and backward. Meanwhile, I'd gotten my pants over my ass and dick tucked in when the door to Kate's room opened.

"Mom?"

"Here, honey." Kate shot me a look of panic. I flicked my fingers at my bare chest, right about the spot where her shirt tag stuck out. She looked down, and her eyes got bigger. Her face turned red.

"I'm here, too, Zoe."

My baby ran into my arms, and she hit me like a train. I didn't flinch this time.

CHAPTER 34

Maine—Kate

Zoe sobbed in Jackson's arms while I righted my shirt and found my pants. I handed off his shirt and took my turn to hold her.

Jackson slipped the t-shirt over his head and then took her back.

"Bad dream?"

Zoe shook her head and wiped her runny nose on his shirt. He looked at me in panic.

Get used to it. I thought, with only a hint of malice. "What was it?"

"I didn't dream, but when I woke up, I thought you were gone. I got scared."

I rubbed her back. She still had a death grip on her father. She was still, in small ways, our little girl. And after the horrible ordeal we'd had, she deserved as much comfort as we could give. Even if I wondered why she wasn't in my arms instead of his.

Jackson dipped his head. "We'll never leave you." He grimaced at his words.

A shot of remorse passed through me. He'd left us before. While I could vow I'd never leave her, he might have to. Although I knew he didn't speak the lie lightly.

"Nothing would make us leave you." I tried to bolster my own doubts.

"I'm a murderer." Her confession was punctuated with a sob.

Jackson frowned. His searching gaze locked with mine. He was looking straight at me when he spoke. "So am I. I killed my first man when I was fifteen."

Jackson certainly wasn't the best role model.

But Zoe didn't need a virtuous man; she needed someone who understood.

He continued. "I wanted to kill Shock. You only beat me to it."

Zoe's snort was short. "Do you feel remorse, Dad?" She looked up at him.

"Hell no. And you shouldn't either. That son of a bitch deserved it. Shock was an asshole."

They were bonding. I could practically see the threads knitting them together. "Who's thirsty?"

"Beer?"

I checked the clock by the bed. "It's eight in the morning. Water. Tap water. I'm sure we've got an empty fridge downstairs." Crystal Ann had been taking care of the place, but there were no plans to return. She'd do what we did for every rental. Clean it out, turn off the fridge, and keep the property in stasis until the family returned.

"Water's good. Ice cream would be better. What do you say, Zoe? Do you think that shop is open?"

"Not until noon. And if I show up there, they're going to yell at me for quitting without notice. So, no ice cream."

"Damn. I had a hankering for some Rocky Road."

"I'll give you Rocky Road." I shook my fist at him in jest.

A knock on the door made us freeze.

Jackson slid out of Zoe's arms and found his gun. He moved with quiet stealth as he snuck down the stairs. I followed, grabbing the closest thing I could, which was an old bottle decorated with seashells.

The knock sounded again, followed by a female voice. "Hello?"

"That's Crystal Ann." Zoe shoved past me and her father and ripped open the door. She greeted her with a hug that latched on.

"Zoe." Her eyes searched for and landed on me. "Kate, you're home." Then she saw Jackson. Her mouth fell open. "What the fuck are you doing here?" Crystal Ann looked like she'd seen a ghost.

"I'm home."

"The hell you are."

Jackson rushed to Zoe and covered her ears. "Language."

Crystal Ann squared off with him, hip cocked, one hand fisted against it. "That's a load of bullshit from the biggest bullshitter I've ever met."

Instead of getting angry, Jackson laughed. "Goddammit, Crystal Ann, you haven't changed a bit."

"Why should I? I'm perfect just as I am. Have you called your mother lately?"

He avoided the question by putting a hand on Zoe's shoulder. "We were going to go for ice cream. But then Zoe reminded me she's not welcome there. You've lived here a bit; where do you recommend?"

Crystal Ann's eyes narrowed. "You're so full of it." Her gaze drifted across Zoe and me. "But I'm beyond happy that these two are safe. John's been worried sick, and that ain't helping his recovery."

"John's okay?" Zoe and I said it at the same time.

"Not a hundred percent yet, but he's home. I was fixing him breakfast and saw the strange car out the kitchen window. Came over to make sure no one was messing with your shit."

"Can we visit?" Zoe looked to me and Crystal for approval. Crystal nodded.

Zoe hesitated. Then she looked at Jackson.

He stepped forward and held out a hand to guide her outside. "Absolutely. Let's see if he remembers me."

Jackson and Zoe left.

Crystal watched their progress until they entered the house next door before turning to ask me. "Who'd he kill?"

It wasn't like that. "No one."

She shook her head. "Someone has to be dead. You're here, and he's here."

A few people were dead. But none of them were his fault. I opted for the diplomatic response. "It's handled."

"I'm sure it was. But…"

The very last thing I wanted was for her to pry into Shock's demise. So, I deflected the conversation. "Do you have a problem with Jackson?"

She shook her head slowly. "It's just… if he's here, who's going to be coming after him? Or, when is he leaving you?" She stared me down and tacked on, "Again."

I didn't have answers for that. "Can you just be happy for me? For us?"

Her long glance out the window didn't bode well. "He's trouble."

"The best kind."

Crystal Ann's eyes widened in surprise. "Who *are* you?"

"Kate."

"No. The Kate I know is quiet. She's a planner. She likes long walks, small towns, and wants nothing to do with trouble. What did you do with that woman?"

"I guess I confronted my ghosts?"

There was worry on my friend's face. "And those ghosts? Are they truly gone?"

"As much as they can be." There was a lot to be done before we'd be safe. Things we left behind in Skilletsville, lives affected by the sudden changes. Not just ours.

Zoe's wasn't the only job lost, or employer left in the lurch. "Did you replace me yet?"

"I got a bead on a couple of college students looking for income and a place to stay while they do marine study."

Damn. Someone needed to cover the rent money she'd lose if we stayed. The winters here were brutal. Even more so when you couldn't afford the nicer things, like propane for the water heater. I began revising the work we'd need to do, including chopping wood and heating bathwater on the stove. I'd done it before Zoe was born. With three of us, we could manage.

"There she is. That's the Kate I know. Good to have you back. Even if it is only temporary."

"What do you mean?"

She shook her head. "Jackson isn't going to stay here. You know that, right?"

Deep in my heart, I did. And if he left, at what point would I go after him?

"You have loved that man since at least a week or three before we met. That ain't going to change any time soon. I just hope that this time it works out for you." She glanced outside. "And for Zoe. She's got him wrapped around her little finger, doesn't she?"

"Absolutely."

We joined them over at John's. Every once in a while, my neighbor's calculating gaze would drift to me. There was a question there. One we would never tell a person who was in the position John was in.

"And Hank's retiring," John said, as he caught us up on the happenings since we left.

Jackson reached over and tapped my arm. "Hear that? The mayor is retiring."

I shook my head. Only he and I knew his hair-brained plans.

John went on, "They asked me if I wanted to run."

"You didn't tell me that," Crystal Ann said.

"Well, I didn't know whether you'd get mad at me or not." His eyes dipped to his lap and the chair encompassing him. "I know you've been trying to get me on my feet again. And taking that job is kind of like giving up."

His jaw worked in silent shame.

Crystal reached for his hand. "I want you happy." She squeezed.

Jackson frowned. "Do they need a new constable here?"

Oh, dear God. "Like you'd qualify?" I joked.

He shrugged. "Cops, criminals, they think alike."

John's knowing gaze shot between Jackson and I. "Speaking of criminals. The scuttle is, there's a certain biker missing. You wouldn't know anything about that, would you?" He pointed the question at Jackson.

"I'm here. Hiding in plain sight."

John's eyes crinkled at the corners. "I was talking about a different biker."

Jackson shrugged. "Don't have a clue, they kicked me out."

"Dad?" The concern in her voice was clear.

"It's okay, Zoe. I'm a big boy, I can handle a little rejection." His mood sobered, and he was distracted for the rest of the conversation while Zoe, Crystal Ann, John, and I caught up.

Zoe's appetite returned, which gave us an excuse to leave.

That evening I sat on the old picnic table in our backyard, watching the sky darken with Jackson. "You're quiet."

"I gotta make a call."

One that would tear us apart, I was certain of it. "The last time we were in this situation, you stayed a few days." I reached for his hand and squeezed it so he'd know I wasn't angry with him.

"I'd stay forever if it was safe. But the longer I put off this call, the less chance there is of that happening. I'm sorry."

I shook my head. "Don't be. I like safety. Sometimes that's more important." Especially with Zoe.

He frowned. "No, it isn't. What we have, and what Zoe needs—isn't that important? Maybe even more important than some fucked up biker rules?" He rubbed his beard and the unshaven stubble around it. "Canada."

He offered it like a statement, but it really was a question.

"What's in Canada?"

"More bullshit, less safety net, and maybe some anonymity? I don't know. But I do know, I don't want to leave you. I know I *can't* leave Zoe. I just can't." His inhale and exhale were heavy with frustration. "Tell me what to do."

"Make the call. Find out where you stand. We'll figure everything else out after that."

His throat worked as he swallowed. He pulled out his phone and powered it on.

As it came to life, the notification chimes started. And didn't let up for a full twenty dings.

He stopped looking at the screen after the fifth bell rang. Instead, he stared at the sky.

I pulled it out of his hand. "Twenty-three messages."

I swiped to open the list and read off names. "Hickey, Sprout, Wolf, Walt—"

"Jesus. They got Hagerstown calling. I'm fucked."

The rest of the names didn't mean much to me except one. "Nonno."

That deserved a grimace. But Jackson motioned for the phone. "I'm not ready for this. Just so you know."

"I'm not either. But ready is a relative term. We got this, one way or another. What are they going to do? Come after us? Try to kill us? Been there. Got the gun to prove it. I'm going have to step up my game to match you and Zoe."

I wasn't trying to make Jackson smile, but he found humor in them. "You are the most amazing woman I have ever met."

"That sentiment? Right back at you."

His grin didn't fade, at least not until he dialed. Then it did. The night was so quiet, I could hear the whole conversation, not just Jackson's half.

"Yo, Wolf, what's up?"

"Big G is here. He flew in. And he's asking for you."

Jackson hung his head. I moved closer to rub away the tension building in his shoulders. I whispered very quietly. "We. Together."

He nodded in agreement with me. "What's your bead on it? More importantly, what is your wife's opinion?"

That was answered with a tirade. I smiled, hearing the tone. Wolf wanted to be a bad ass, but even in the short time I knew the couple, I could pin down who really drove that dynamic, and it wasn't him.

"And she thinks you should listen." His words trailed off into a resigned silence.

"Tits would make a damn good VP."

"Fuck you." Wolf's response fired back with the ease of habit. But he tacked on, "If she could be. Hate to say this, brother, but you need to come back. I know we had to let you walk out, but man, this place… it fucking needs you."

"No, it doesn't. You and Bear need to keep your heads on. I told you that."

"I'm not a mind-reader, but there is a rumor going around about Shock."

Jackson met my stare of fear. I couldn't read his face at all.

Slowly, he asked Wolf, "What is it?"

"Can't say much over the phone, but it sounds like he betrayed the club."

Silence. Jackson could tell his man those rumors were true, and he chose to keep silent. I knew part of that was because he was out. Once out, you didn't talk about the club, ever. Nor did you speak with the members. They turned their backs, ignored your entire existence. This conversation was significant in its unusual breach of protocol.

I added a quiet kiss to Jackson's neck. Lending my support and letting him know we were a team.

"Jackson?"

"Can you buy me a day and a half?"

"I don't think so. Do you need cash for a flight?"

Oh, dear. I was losing him. I shook my head, not ready for this to be over. Not willing to part with him again. I mouthed, "Zoe," at him, infusing that one word with as much demand as I dared.

The muscles around the edges of his face tensed. He opened and shut his mouth, seeking a response.

"Sprout's right here; he says he'll charter a flight. Just give us a location. You *have* to come back. It's Big G."

Jackson took time to answer. When he did, it was short. "Bangor, Maine. Tell Sprout I need a jet waiting at the airport there in two hours."

"Maine?" Wolf's question had nuance.

"That's right. I'm in Maine. With my *family*." Jackson stressed the last word and hung up on his former VP.

"We're going with," I spoke my decree to the twilight.

"The hell you are. You and Zoe need to take the car to the border. I don't know how you'll get across without IDs, but I need you to do it. Get the hell away." He dug into his jeans for his wallet. He pulled out a stack of money and tried to hand it over. I pushed it back at him.

"I'm not leaving you. And you're not leaving Zoe. She needs you. Now more than ever."

Yes, I was playing dirty, but this was my family... *our* family at stake.

He pleaded with me, "I can't protect you if I'm dead."

"Then don't die."

He laughed abruptly. His brows twisted with anguish. "Yeah? You don't either. And keep Zoe close. And no saving any hookers this time. Got it?"

"Got it." The implications of this sunk in. "We're doing this."

"Yeah. I guess *we're* doing this."

CHAPTER 35

Skilletsville—Jackson

When and why did I pick a junkyard to call home?

Sprout's chartered flight offer also included a blacked-out SUV waiting for us at the local airport. Kate, Zoe, and I had no luggage. Not even a change of clothes since we fled Pittsburgh. I'd been too preoccupied to stop and see to their needs. *Some father I was.*

Kate's jeans had little flecks of blood on them. I scratched at one. She glanced down, saw what I was picking at, and slapped her hand over mine.

"Cara's." She glanced to the front, where Zoe sat opposite the nameless guy doing his job.

"I should be in front," I muttered for the fifth time. But Kate was determined in her quest to keep us together. I worried she was wrong. I worried about the meeting and the people involved. Big G was the one guy I did fear—for good reason. His word was law.

Kate squeezed my hand. "I love you."

Zoe heard that. She turned to look over the seat. "I love you, too, Dad."

My throat was too tight. The words came out hoarse. "I'll love both of you with my dying breath." *And beyond.*

"Shh. No dying talk." Kate's rebuke made Zoe smile.

"That's right, Dad. We'll kick their ass."

These two. "I don't deserve you two." I truly didn't.

"We know." Kate's quiet confidence was everything I'd ever wished for. I soaked it in by staring at Kate as the car came to a halt.

"You'd have been a great biker wife. You know that?"

"I hated being a biker wife." Her eyes fixed forward, locked on the group of men who emerged from the building to usher us in.

"Marry me," I uttered the words before I could think about them. But as I did, I knew they felt right. "Kate please marry me. Me, James. That's all I am. Son of One-Eyed Jack and a prostitute. Marry *me*."

The door on my side opened. Sprout's grinning mug filled the gap.

"Welcome back, boss."

I locked eyes with Kate.

"Yes."

Like a key fitting into a lock, my life was complete. I winked at her, then turned on Sprout. "What's this 'boss' shit?" I shoved out of the car and caught his attention. In the small space of time before the rest of the rabble closed in, I hurried to ask a favor from Sprout, "I don't have any right to ask you for this, but make sure Zoe and Kate are safe, got it?"

"Got it." He looked past me to the car. "Ladies. Welcome back."

Kate's glare matched my own. She joined me, fidgeting.

I nudged her. "This was your idea."

"I can change my mind, can't I?"

"Might be a little late for that," I replied.

She huffed. "Sorry."

I wrapped my arm around her. "Don't be. I get to walk in with the two most beautiful women in the world." Zoe climbed out and took my free side, wrapping an arm around my waist. We stayed like that until the door forced us to walk in single file. I went first, hoping I wasn't going to get shot crossing the threshold.

The crowd inside was larger than usual. My crew, *former* crew that was, Hagerstown's lot, at least four of the rednecks from West Virginia who were struggling to lay the foundation of a chapter in that state, a few guys down from Dad's old chapter in Wilkes-Barre, Nonno's entourage, and even Bandit and a couple of Pittsburgh's crew were present. Not all of them, though.

Kate caught up to me and wrapped her arm around my waist. Zoe was on our six, quiet, and I'm certain she was deciding who to shoot first.

Yes, she had my gun. And yes, I gave it to her despite Kate's protests. I scanned the crowd to judge what we could expect.

Noticeable was the lack of certain attendees. Not a single hanger or hooker was in sight. Big G had been seated at the bar when we walked in. But he headed in our direction.

Nonno followed him—a dog for the master.

I kissed Kate's cheek, hoping it wouldn't be the last time for it, and not taking my eyes off the men who held this room and the army of men outside it in their greedy fists.

Big G noticed that kiss. "Introduce me."

I swallowed. "This is Kate."

His eyes scanned her. "Just Kate?"

"Just Kate," she confirmed.

He tipped his head toward Zoe. "And this one?"

"That's Zoe, my daughter."

The small twitch of G's mouth made me nervous. He scanned her, too. "She looks like you. She even looks a little like old Jack."

That she did.

"But Jack wasn't nearly as charming. I'm glad she got some of her and your mother's looks."

Kate stiffened beside me. Her sharp inhale and the set of her jaw spelled trouble.

Big G smiled. "I meant that in a good way. I have a daughter, too; they don't always listen." His tone changed. "Jackson, I have to ask this in front of all of these men. Did you kill Shock?"

I would not look at Zoe. "Nonno knows who did." And Bandit. I glared at him.

Big G's gaze shifted to Zoe. "Yes, he told me the events. But I need you to speak the truth to all of these men."

That was an order. "Truth? The truth is, I don't have to say anything. Nonno kicked me out." I stepped forward, pulling on Kate to slide her behind me.

We were dead. I'd just killed my family with my defiance. But I'd be damned if I tossed Zoe to these wolves. Shock deserved to die. But saying that would get us killed faster.

"Nonno? Is that true?"

"It was temporary."

Fuck me. I glared at Nonno.

"For good reason, right, Bandit?" Nonno motioned Shock's enforcer forward. "For the record, what did you see that night?"

Bandit glanced at Zoe. I stepped sideways so he'd see me instead. He locked eyes with me. "Shock collected blackmail on the club, on the members, the presidents, even the national leadership."

A rumble of male whispers swept around the room from one wall to the other. With each whisper, the sound grew.

Nonno held up a hand. "Quiet!"

Big G studied me like a bug. "I heard a rumor that he planned to leak it to the Feds."

Kate shifted beside me. She curled her fingers through the crook of my elbow. Big G's eyes locked on her. "You did me a favor, killing him. Thank you."

The room sucked in a breath. I felt Zoe's palm on my back.

Kate smiled. "He wasn't killed to protect you."

Big G's expression hardened. "No?"

"Shock wanted my daughter. I'd kill anyone because of that."

There were no lies there despite how it sounded. I liked this ruthless version of Kate. "Ditto to what she said. But someone beat me to it." Let them think Kate did it. She had more than enough reason. All my men knew about that. Walt's crew likely knew her story, too. But Bandit could bring us all down. I still hadn't lied…only omitted some facts.

"Understandable." Big G scanned the crowd of Destroyers. "You said temporary, Nonno?"

"That's right."

Big G stared at my chest. "Where's his vest?"

Wolf motioned to Smoke, who stepped into our meeting room and returned with my cut. He handed it off to my former VP, who then handed it to Big G. As he turned away, he winked at me.

That damn son of a bitch. He had to have known. I wondered how much he stuck his neck out for me, looping Big G into this fiasco.

"Here." Big G handed me the leather vest. I noticed the hole where my president's patch should have been. I slipped it on anyway. If I wore it, I could protect Kate better. Especially in this crowd, with her false confession lingering in their memories.

"That's better. Nonno? There's a gap in your leadership. You've been without a regional president too long. I think there is a man ready for that job."

Big G reached out and put his finger on the spot where my officer patch had been. "This chapter has leaders in place that he groomed. He's proven loyal not only to the club, but in his defense of the club." There was a bite to his tone. He aimed his next words directly at Nonno. "I think Jackson is your *best* choice."

A couple of men near the back spoke out of turn, but no one within the circle around us. Bandit even dipped his head at me, then Kate.

My men cheered. *Assholes.*

In the commotion, I quietly asked Kate if she was okay with the offer. "I can turn it down," I whispered against her hair. But if I did, she and Zoe were in danger. She must have read that on my face, because she shook her head. Then she mouthed, "We." There was a fierceness embedded in her silent guidance.

Nonno tried to quiet the room again, with marginal success. I held up a hand. My crew quieted immediately. Big G raised a finger and his men glared at anyone still making a sound.

"One condition."

Big G straightened, not accepting my request, nor denying it.

"I asked Kate to marry me, and she said yes."

"Fuck yeah, called it!" Sprout's voice carried around the room. Bear shoved him into silence.

Nonno studied Kate. "Is that your condition?"

"No. My condition is that, we stay here in Skilletsville as a family. I'll go wherever you want, but my base is here."

"Not Maine?" Nonno's question caught me off guard.

Someone muttered, "What the fuck is in Maine?" He was quickly silenced.

"Maybe in the summer. It gets fucking cold up there in the winter."

Zoe couldn't catch the laugh before it burst out of her.

Under her breath, Kate whispered, "Crystal Ann is going to need a raise."

Big G tapped Nonno's shoulder. "Give him whatever he wants, as long as he stays *out* of Chicago. Too many people die around him."

Nonno smiled, knowing exactly how those rumors were true. "He's better on our side than not."

Big G didn't blink. "I believe that. Good luck with him."

He didn't stay to party with the clubs. Apparently, being the power behind the throne got you perks like that. Zoe and Kate retreated to Wolf's office with the key he gave them. Smoke stood outside the door as a guard. I stayed downstairs to take the backslaps and lies like a true lackey should.

"You're going to get old and fat in this job," Griz joked.

"Me? Fat? Never."

"Two years, you'll be looking like Walt." Sprout was not funny. I shook my head.

"I ain't fat." Walt pulled up a barstool and ordered two whiskeys. He slid one under my nose, the other he lifted in toast. "You know, I wanted the regional spot. But I think I don't now."

The small glass dangled from his fingers like his words.

"Why is that?" I asked.

He smiled, almost in depreciation. "Sounds like a lot of work. And fuck working."

Liar. He worked ten times harder than I ever did. But a toast was a toast.

"Fuck working." I lifted the cup and waited to see if he'd drink to my sentiment.

He didn't. Instead, he mused. "Politics means a whole lot of folks lying to you so they can get what they want."

"I'll fit right in."

He blinked. "No, you won't. And that's why you're the best man for it. You lie about two things, women and fish. Anyone who doesn't know that about you, doesn't know you at all." He grinned. "To women and fish."

He had me pegged. "To women and fish." I drank with him.

Once the whiskey hit bottom, he leaned in. "She was worth the trouble. I see that. Congrats."

Had I properly thanked him yet? *Probably not.* "Kate's prettier than Mary, isn't she?"

Walt's expression shifted. "No one's prettier than my wife."

I expected that statement.

I also expected the quick succession of Sprout and Wolf putting their wives into the contest. Walt's own men began listing their women, including their newest victim, I mean "ol' lady."

Speaking of, Kate was upstairs. I wanted her in my arms. I wanted to go to our borrowed showroom home and wake up with her. But there was one thing I needed to do before that happened. I found Bear in a circle of my men. They'd always be mine. I trusted them like no others. It helped that I had a hand in picking all of them. I sat down and leaned in to make a request.

"Bear? Do me a favor."

"Anything, boss."

Hell, that felt good. *Boss.* "Run razor wire under my balcony. Make sure it is sharp enough to cut a man's hand off."

"You're not messing around, are you?"

Nope, I was dead serious. "Either that or tear the fucking thing off. I want it gone or protected before I take Kate and Zoe home."

"I'll do you one better."

I was listening.

Bear explained. "Sprout set me up in the house next door. And Wolf said, now that you're regional president, I'm officially on your detail."

That was comforting, but also a concern. I motioned to my VP... my former VP. "Wolf?"

"Yeah, boss?"

"Bear still gets a cut here, right?"

Wolf nodded.

I exhaled in relief. I wanted no bad blood soaking the ground where my family would live. "Who's taking Bear's place?"

"We moved Griz to Sergeant, and Smoke's an enforcer as of tomorrow's vote."

Those were good moves. I let him know that. "I knew you'd make a good president."

Wolf opened and shut his mouth. Finally, he simply said, "Thanks. I learned from the best." He used my shoulder as a crutch to stand, keeping the weight off his bum leg.

He was letting me see his weakness. "You good?"

"Will be when I get home." His voice rumbled, laced with a quiet yearning.

I understood that.

He studied me.

"What?" I asked.

"Kate's going to make one hell of an ol' lady. I can tell. She's got that… I don't know." He moved his hand in front of his face and chest.

"The word is command or compassion. Both are great qualities in a wife." I kept my words quiet, hoping he'd understand I meant his wife no disrespect. Tits had command in spades. Compassion? Only if you were a blade, or shot bullets, or were Wolf. Everyone else could fuck right off. I respected that sentiment immensely.

Bear ruined the moment. "The only quality I want in a wife is sucking a mean dick."

"Oh, you just cursed yourself, dude." Sprout leaned on him, obviously drunk. Or faking it well enough that even I couldn't tell.

Griz and Hollywood joined Team Bear. They rambled on about who gave the best blow jobs and what that entailed. Notably, Sketch was quiet. "You got insight, crazy man?"

His eyes, usually sharp and scary, weren't. "Blow jobs aren't everything." He stood up to leave. I caught his arm.

"Is your ex still giving you shit?"

He slumped. "She wants to move to fucking Delaware."

He had a kid he barely got to see even though he lived in same town as his ex did. Delaware? *Shit.* "Come talk to me tomorrow. I'll get a lawyer on it." Being regional president had to count for something, right?

Sketch smiled. "Thanks, boss." The slump didn't quite leave his shoulders as he quietly exited. I felt every step of that weight on him. I was once that man. Living without my family. Not knowing or being there for the milestones and the little moments.

But that was going to change. Starting immediately.

CHAPTER 36

Septemver 13—Kate

Sprout swore he'd never dreamed that his lake house wasn't big enough for a party. Against my wishes, Jackson pulled out all the stops and invited every chapter in the region to our wedding. He conned Sprout into erecting a series of tents on the outdoor gun range to handle the overflow. The largest of them was where Jackson held court.

And in doing so, placed me at his side to meet every member from every club, their ol' lady—if they had one, and the children.

Numerous children.

At a biker party.

They ranged in age from a few months to almost adult.

I glanced at Zoe. She looked beautiful today in her tea-length, plum-colored bridesmaid dress. A few roses in my bouquet matched that deep shade of purple. Zoe's idea. The black ones were Jackson's. Since we didn't know if he was joking or not, we ran with the concept.

The rest of the wedding was a group effort. The Hagerstown chapter had talented event organizers and chefs in their arsenal of wives, and that complimented Danielle's vision for my wedding. And a post-wedding party befitting the new regional president.

Of course, the guest list was all Jackson's fault. I couldn't argue with him inviting the Destroyers, now could I? I put my foot down about one thing—the ring.

He wanted a gaudy diamond-encrusted tribute to the skulled Destroyers patch. I said no, remembering the fake diamond Shock stuck on my hand. Simple was my directive. Nothing flashy, nothing gaudy. Real was the only other stipulation.

Jackson complied with the engagement ring, up to a point. The three-carat diamond caught on everything. I almost made him return it. He argued he couldn't, as Nonno gifted it to him in apology for what he did.

I had it appraised just to see what an apology from the head of the Destroyers Club was worth. Apparently, at least thirty grand. In retrospect, I should have carried on believing it was a fake. But I'd worn it every day since, except for today. Jackson took it back to have it set inside a ring guard I hadn't seen yet. I fiddled with my bare finger while I waited for the cheers to die down so I could hear my music cue signaling me to walk the gauntlet of black leather coats, beards, and scattered dress clothes. But the noise wasn't stopping.

Gina motioned for me to start despite the ruckus. She stood by Zoe, the only other person I wanted at my side, as I said my vows. Without her, neither Zoe nor I would be here.

Sprout stood to Jackson's left, being his mother's escort for the day. Beside him, Bear looked completely out of place in his designer suit, braided mohawk, piercings, and tattoos. I didn't ask them to wear suits; they did that on their own. The three men matched with soft gray linen summer dress wear and pristine white shirts. Not one of them wore a tie. Apparently, ties were against some biker code.

Jackson tipped his head with a lifted eyebrow as if to say, "Getting cold feet, lady?"

I sent him one right back, which made him smile.

Resolute, I took that first step forward.

The whole way down the aisle, Jackson's men pumped the crowd to holler, cheer, whistle, or make noise. It was daunting, to say the least.

I finally got to my place at Jackson's side. That was when the crowd finally quieted.

Jackson leaned in. "Zoe told Sprout you hate music. But Danielle had already hired the string quartet."

Oh. That explained it. I leaned in, gently tapping my soon-to-be-husband's beard with my nose. "You should have warned me."

"Surprise?" he whispered.

"I expect every day will be a surprise with you." I didn't say it loudly, but the people seated in the front rows heard it and snickered.

From the back someone yelled, "Hurry up, the beer's getting warm!"

Jackson shot a glare at the audience. "You should have brought a flask, dipshit."

"I did, it's empty."

"That sounds like a *you* problem," Jackson fired back, which got the crowd riled up again.

Amidst the laughter, jests, and insanity, we were married. The announcement of husband and wife was punctuated by over twenty motorcycles roaring to life.

Since the party was already going and promising to be one big chaotic debacle, I tossed the bouquet over my shoulder at the groomsmen and crowd of Jackson's men who flanked the path to the quadrant of tents where the cake, beer, and a whole smorgasbord of food waited.

I glanced back to see what Jackson was laughing at.

Both Sketch and Bear ended up with parts of the arrangement. In the scuffle to grab the flowers, it had separated into at least two main clumps. Bear held a cluster of roses, while Sketch had the main section of the bouquet. Both looked dumbstruck.

Zoe laughed at the two men's consternation. "It worked!"

"What worked?" I asked.

"The breakaway Lily designed. It was supposed to do that. Couldn't have only one person getting hitched next."

Jackson was still laughing.

"That's funny to you, isn't it?" I said.

"I'd have guessed Hollywood or Hickey to be next. Not those two."

We'd have to see. Aside from Wolf and Sprout, nearly all of his men balked at settling down. Which worked for some of them. Others needed a keeper—as in a *zoo keeper*. Hell, most of them required one.

We posed for photos quickly. The men of his club were getting antsy because the smoky smell of pit beef wafted through the meadow. The grass was wet from a sudden shower that passed almost as quickly as it began, and the day grew warmer.

Jackson and I posed on his bike. I'd draped over the gas tank in a very uncomfortable backward lean that threatened to spill my tits out. Jackson braced above me, barely inches from devouring me. The world narrowed down as I held perfectly still, my ring hand against his cheek so the light would catch the diamonds just right. His breath brushed my face, and his erection grew hard against my leg.

"I wish we could do this in private."

I agreed. "With fewer clothes."

"Oh fuck, yeah." His grin broke my pose. I laughed right along with him. Of all the shots, that one was my favorite.

We'd just gotten the bulk of the photos done, and the photographer was trying to get the groomsmen to pose with Jackson and I.

Boom! I flinched as the loud noise was followed by a series of fireworks. "Let me guess, Hagerstown?"

My husband grimaced. "I knew I shouldn't have let Walt talk me into that."

"They're keeping it over the lake, right?"

"I fucking hope so."

There were no guarantees with this crowd. "Firearms?"

"Checked at the gate," Sprout confirmed.

"Thank God." With this many bikers in one spot, there was going to be an accident or twenty tonight. We had two paramedics on call, just in case.

The photographer snapped a photo. Sprout clapped his hands. "That's it. It's time to get fucking drunk!"

Coop stepped away, hooking an arm under Jackson's. "Come on Boss. Someone grab Kate! You guys gotta do the first dance. It's tradition."

No. I backed away from the trio of Destroyers stalking me. And landed right into Bear's arms. He hoisted me up, and with some quick finagling of my train, Zoe and Gina followed us while slowly hooking the loops and buttons so I wouldn't drag it on the ground.

"Traitors!" I yelled over the noise.

The DJ waited until both Jackson and I were stranded in the middle of the dance floor. Obviously my husband was in on this. He had that look. One of mixed guilt, a smattering of "don't hurt me" and "trust me" written all over it.

The song started slowly. Just a small sustained chord and the clear tenor of a talented singer joined in. I braced myself for memories to flood back, but I didn't know this song at all. Jackson held out his arms. I stepped into them so he could lead me through a shuffled waltz.

As we danced, he began singing along. Surprisingly, he had a decent voice. I paid attention to the words. Who would have guessed this man to be such a romantic? I forgot all about the pain of the past and lost myself in his eyes, arms, and softly sung melody. He promised love, a future, and more tenderly, telling me how perfect I was for him. And how our family was every-thing he asked for, and more.

I couldn't help it. Tears began to leak out of my eyes. He stopped mid-shuffle to whisper in my ear.

"Sorry, baby."

I shook my head. My bottom lip quivered. He was apologizing for nothing. What he'd done was a miracle. I fought to speak so he'd know he hadn't fucked up at all. "You're giving me music back."

More tears streamed down my cheeks, but I smiled despite the pain releasing from my soul.

He hugged me tight, sang softly, and swayed with me until the song ended. No sooner than it did, another song followed on its heels. This one was even more poignant. He motioned for Zoe to join us, and in our little trio, we celebrated being a family.

Of course, it was too good to last. The next song was a typical biker song. The floor filled up. A few of the men without ol' ladies invited strippers or cam girls as their plus-one. And some of the ol' ladies were strippers at one point. That meant there was no end to the talented antics on the dance floor.

I tried to keep up for at least three songs but was so out of practice that I tripped over my own feet. Luckily, Jackson caught me before I went down. I couldn't stop laughing and smiling.

We retired to the table for food, drinks, and the obligatory make-out sessions each time someone clinked their silverware on anything that would make noise. The whirlwind of the day wound down, and the cake was distributed without tipping it over or getting a piece mashed in my face.

Everywhere I looked, the men wore black vests. Women did, too. Jackson had ditched his suit jacket during the photos, opting to cover his dress shirt with his vest. I marveled at how good it looked on him. He looked whole in it. Happy.

"What?"

"You are one handsome man," I replied.

"Babe." His grin grooved deep.

My finger traced the indent there. "I love you."

The smile lines at the edges of his eyes deepened. "Really now?"

"Yes."

He inhaled and looked at the crowd. The smile faded to something I couldn't read.

"Jackson?"

He took my hand and helped me stand up. As he did, he motioned to Wolf, who brought up a wrapped box. Sprout whistled loudly. "Cut the music! This is fucking important."

While the noise didn't cease immediately, we had their attention.

Jackson handed me the box. "I was going to spring this on you after I got your permission, but…" He bit his lip nervously.

I had an inkling of what was inside, because not a single woman in my circle kept secrets well. Gina flat-out asked me to try on leather vests two weeks ago. And Betty Jo, the woman who embellished most of the custom leather coats for the club women, asked me my favorites for almost everything from food, plants, colors, the whole works. I think after all that, she knew me better than Jackson did.

The wrapping paper ripped easily, and I shook the box to loosen the bottom from the lid. It was heavy.

The vest and coat inside matched Jackson's with a few differences. The name patch on each read, "Boss Lady." I flipped the vest over to see the back, just to be sure it didn't say what my former one said.

"Property of Jackson!" I yelled with a grin on my face. Not Property of Destroyers, but one man, alone. Yes, he was a Destroyer, but there would be *no* sharing.

With that, I held it up and showed it off to his men. All of them. The ones from the home club and all the others he supposedly ruled. But he didn't treat them like subjects. He knew every name. Who was married, who had children, the names of their loved ones, what they drank, and what they did for the club. He was more than their leader and would never ask for more than they could give.

Just like he'd never ask me for more than I could give. But what he didn't know was that I'd give him everything. Including loyalty to the club's traditions. The good ones, and even some of the antiquated ones like wearing a garment declaring me his property.

I handed the vest to Jackson with a request to help me put it on.

He whispered in my ear as he did. "I love you, too, Kate." Then he looped an arm over my shoulder and presented me to the crowd. "See this woman?"

Cheers and a few wolf-whistles followed.

He waited until they quieted.

"She's *mine*. Only mine!"

Then he swept me up and carried me out of the tent. I was afraid he'd insist on carrying me all the way to the house, but he set me on my feet. "We better run; they're going to try kidnapping you."

So we did. All the way into the house, locking the door to the private bedroom Sprout loaned us for the night. We barely beat the fastest of them to it, but he'd positioned two prospects on the door to run interference for us. I fell to the bed in a flounce of chiffon and silk. Jackson double-checked the lock and then stalked forward to stand between my feet. "Wife."

"Husband," was my reply.

He worked the layers of fluffy cream fabric up to expose my legs. "Dress on, or off? Your choice."

"Off."

He slipped some layers free. His fingers lingered on my vest.

"We're leaving the vest on," he declared.

Heck yeah. It took some doing, but he managed to unlace the bodice of the dress and remove everything but the black garment. As the night darkened and the party continued, I pondered his phrasing. "We're." We are.

We.

No longer just Kate or just Jackson. We were a unit. A family. After everything it took to get *us* to this point. We were no longer apart.

We. Us. Family.

The best words in the world.

About the Author:

Calia Wilde believes the hero isn't always the good guy. She believes some heroes and heroines cannot play by the rules to get their happily ever after.

She is a writer of misfits, anti-heroes, villains, underdogs, fringe elements, and other tropes that will likely get her barred from polite society.

As a feral Gen-Xer, she spent numerous hours roaming the woods in search of elves, fairies, dragons, or anything that would take her away from the dreaded curse of doing dishes. She once fell off a wardrobe, but instead of landing in Narnia, a very emphatic order of *"Don't tell Mom,"* was decreed. In case you are wondering, yes, she did land on her head.

Rainy days and dark nights landed the author in other worlds between written pages or immersing in her favorite space and time travel TV shows. Whether it was exploring the final frontier or simply disappearing down rabbit holes with shapeshifting aliens, the escape was the same, only the moonscape differed.

One time in Sturgis, she was offered twenty bucks to climb a ladder. She declined as there was some fine print regarding the quest that went beyond conquering a fear of heights and some activities which were definitely illegal for someone her age. But it was there... in that magical realm of bikers, booze, and foul language, that she came into the possession of her very first item of armor... aka, black clothing. The forbidden was in her grasp and became an life-long obsession to avoid anything pastel.

As she searched for a career that would indulge this penchant for wearing black, she stumbled upon the world of special effects and excitedly pursued the art of sleeping in strange hotels, working ungodly hours, and handling anything that could, and would, burn, blind, explode, freeze, or otherwise entertain wildlings like herself.

Her current fictional worlds are forged in a hippie world where music and nature peacefully co-exist away from modern conveniences, like bathtubs. Okay, there's a shower, but she has to share it with spiders. Yuck. Which is why she looks forward to going on the road once more where the hotel may have a real tub. Or a hot tub... maybe a heated pool... please?

So, she BEGS you to leave a review and do a good deed by encouraging others to read her books. With enough fans scattered across the globe, she'll have to travel, right? Then she'll have an excuse to leave the farm.